£1.50

20

Life in th............................Scotland brought .... date —in the fictional village of Achanult.

Funny, easy reading, yet sharply observed, George MacLennan fills the gap in humorous Scottish writing.

Highly entertaining, wry, comical and compelling, *Achanult* hits the mark.

Brilliant!

**EVERYTHING ABOUT *ACHANULT* RINGS TRUE.
THESE CHARACTERS SEEM LIKE REAL PEOPLE
AND THEY ARE STILL LARGER THAN LIFE. . .**

PETER McQUEEN has lived in Achanult all his
life, now retired, traditional, slow, steady,
deliberate in his doings—shares his house by the
sea with his wife JEAN. Their expectations of life
are modest.

MAGGIE STEWART is a passionate energetic
woman who lives in a loveless marriage. Her
unhappiness seeps out sometimes
uncontrollably—she seems interfering and
dominant. She is widely dismissed as a busybody.

JIM STEWART, her husband, feels life is passing
him by. He is out of a job and has little interest in
anything including his wife.

MARJORY SHUTTLEWORTH is an English
"incomer". She lives alone, loves the scenery but is
less than enthusiastic about some of the locals
who never seem to want to get anything done.

JENNIFER McLACHAN is a long-time friend of Miss Shuttleworth from England. A visitor seeking the rural idyll and possible future Achanult resident.

DONALD MORRISON is the nextdoor neighbour of the McQueens'—a fiercely independent Highlander who does not suffer fools gladly.

ALEC CAMERON has a slightly incoherent way— he talks always with pipe in mouth—that confuses the "incomers". He is the self-styled local historian who bores visitors in the bar of the local hotel –the locals know him better.

REV DAVID NICHOLSON recently moved from a busy city charge in Edinburgh to become the church minister. He is looking for a quiet life but the demands of his flock in Achanult still seem to impinge on his obsession with crosswords.

ANNA NICHOLSON is his long-suffering, hard-working wife who originally hails from Uist. Among her many other chores, she teaches a local Gaelic class.

ACHANULT

George MacLennan

ACHANULT

George MacLennan

© George MacLennan 1993

First published in 1993 by
Argyll Publishing
Glendaruel
Argyll PA22 3AE

British Library Cataloguing-in-Publication Data.
**A catalogue record for this book is available from the
British Library.**

ISBN 1 874640 20 3

The publisher acknowledges subsidy from the Scottish Arts
Council towards the publication of this volume.

Cover painting and design by Marcia Clark
Typeset and origination by
Cordfall Ltd, Civic Street, Glasgow
Printed and bound in Great Britain by
Harper Collins, Glasgow

do Christine Marion Fraser,
a sheall dhomb an t-slighe.

Contents

Prologue

THERE was a definite highland feeling to Achanult. It was something in the air, almost tangible, something that told you that the Lowlands had been left behind. There was a cleanness to the air that seemed to enhance the surroundings—the smell of the sea, yet of coal fires which never seemed to go out. And the wind.

The wind was never far away, blowing from the west usually, persistent, bringing the smell of the islands with it.

Behind the village the hills began—a backdrop of changing scenery, dark and rocky, with fir trees on the lower slopes, occasionally covered in white in the winter. The snow seldom spread its icy fingers over the village and when it did, it soon began its retreat. No road went through these hills—just a few forestry tracks segmenting the landscape. The wind blew fiercely up there but the village below paid little heed. There too were the deer, up in the summer to escape the midges. In the winter hunger brought them down at night. Starvation would see them in the village during the day.

The sea also changed. Sometimes when the ground froze in the hills, it would protect the village with its warmer currents. Sometimes, when it repeatedly tried to breach the wall that ran along the road by the shore, it would threaten. From time to time it succeeded if the tide was high and the wind was strong. Yet it withdrew almost immediately, as if unsure like the snow, of how far it could go.

The hills behind said little. The sea told you all. White horses on the water and you could see the cold of the wind. You could feel it from the warm shelter of your window. And the gulls would flee screaming towards the hills, but not too far. The same gulls would flap out to sea with a deceptive lethargy in the calmer days of summer, the long light days, as if looking for another land in the hazy distance. At such times they vanished and you almost missed their raucous noise.

The village faced the sea for the sea had been its means of existence for generations. Most of that had now gone, though a few hardy souls still went out occasionally in small boats, and returning, cursed the trawlers that fished all day, all year. The pier stood crumbling, a reminder of the old ways when you could travel everywhere by boat. But that was long ago before the road was taken seriously.

There had always been some kind of a road, most of it single track, which didn't matter when nobody had a car. Now a fine wide road followed the coastline, forever disappearing round the next bend. Here and there you could still see the old road, overgrown with grass and sometimes the eloquent walls of an old cottage beside it. Those were the roads of the old faded photographs, where the charabancs posed and the cyclists meandered along three abreast.

Now the luxury coaches sped along, pausing in the village long enough to mention the old church—"a fine example of Highland architecture"—and the churchyard with the grave of Donald Ross, author of *An Cladach garbh*. For this was the land of the Gael, a land apart, remote.

The water ran down from the hills in burns which never dried up, except maybe in June when there had been no rain for a few weeks. This was the best time of year but the tourists who passed through did so in July and August and some vowed never to return. It mattered little. Achanult was an experience of years, not hours or even days. Its events unfolded slowly beneath the surface, beyond the vision of the casual visitor.

The village straggled on for about a mile along the coastline. The oldest houses had been near the water—solid stone buildings at the end of driveways dripping with sodden rhododendrons. Later the town encroached a bit on the hills behind but their steepness defended them. Their height also held back the early morning sun, so that Achanult lay cold and damp in the early Spring and Autumn until the sun rose over the peaks. Often you could see the sunshine out to sea and the village still in shade. But the evenings could be glorious and the summer days lengthened their magic.

Visitors always remarked on the beauty of the area. Those who had been born and brought up there, while gratified by such comments, often wondered what all the fuss was about. They had become so accustomed to the scenery that they thought little of it and simply took its presence for granted. Some of them would even have preferred to live in a place where there were more shops and better facilities. The scenery was a bonus but not essential. Not that many would have openly admitted this.

When questioned they invariably asserted that Achanult was one of the finest spots in the whole country and they wouldn't want to live anywhere else. In the same way they would not tolerate criticism from visitors. There was nothing wrong with their weather, their shop, their roads. Privately they admitted otherwise.

Tourists had been coming to the village in gradually increasing numbers over the years. Few of them stayed long and until recently, little effort had been made to cater for them.

People had mixed feelings about tourists, with their loud voices and clicking cameras. The village wasn't built to take their big coaches, polluting the air they had come to breathe. But that was in the summer when the population increased as holiday homes were occupied and caravans filled.

In the autumn they all went away.

1 Maybe

PETER McQueen stood by the window and looked out at the rain. You could tell it was a Tuesday just by the weather—at least Peter could. He'd had this theory about Tuesdays for a long time now. Jean had said it was just silly Highland superstition but Peter had no shortage of evidence. Look at the time *Te Bheag* was smashed up and sank in that storm a few years ago. He'd forgotten now which year it was but it was certainly a Tuesday. Aye, that was a disaster, particularly since it hadn't been insured. And just last Tuesday he'd dropped that big piece of driftwood on to his foot as he was carrying it up to the house. His toe was still bruised, so the gardening had come to a halt. Still, he might do some digging tomorrow if the rain stopped. No point in even thinking about it today.

He gazed, hypnotised, as the rain slowly filled up little trenches where his potatoes had been. Aye, he'd even heard that the First World War had started on a Tuesday—or was it the Boer War? When he'd mentioned this to his neighbour Donald Morrison, Donald had said that he remembered his grandfather saying that it had started on a Thursday. Peter knew that had to be wrong and suggested to Donald that since his grandfather had been a Gaelic speaker who was never completely at home in English, he might have confused Tuesday and Thursday.

Donald hadn't spoken to him for weeks after that which just showed you how unreasonable some people could be.

Peter turned slowly away from the window and went through to the kitchen. Jean was setting the kettle on the range and spoke over her shoulder.

"Well, what are you thinking of doing today? You won't get anything done in the garden anyway. Why don't you go to that class this afternoon?"

Peter sighed quietly. Ever since he'd retired she'd been on at him to take up something new and not just sit around all day.

"Oh well, maybe."

She'd even brought a leaflet in from the library—full of afternoon and evening classes it was. He'd had a look. Basket-weaving, politics, local history, wine-making—now if it had been whisky-making . . . Peter didn't like wine. Not that he'd ever had any but you had to be careful with foreign stuff sometimes . . .

"Well, I think you should go. Maggie Stewart was there last week and she said it was very good."

. . . He'd had some rice a few years ago at that posh restaurant in Glasgow. Aye, and the meat had been cooked in wine, somebody said. Good job Betty's father was paying.

"You could try it. It's for beginners you know—that's what it says in the leaflet. Although what Maggie Stewart's doing there I don't know."

"Maggie? Does she go?"

"I just told you. She was there last week. She was telling me about it on Sunday. I thought she had plenty of Gaelic anyway."

"She doesn't know anything about it. A few words maybe."

"Oh well, I don't know. I thought she'd learnt it from her granny when she went to Barra in the school holidays."

"Och, I think she's just having you on. D'you remember that time the new schoolteacher was looking for somebody who knew Gaelic? He ended up at Maggie's but she couldn't translate that piece from the paper he had and she couldn't understand the tape he had either."

"Oh, aye, I remember that. She said it was a different dialect from what she was used to."

Peter laughed. Maggie Stewart was well known as a great source of uninformed opinion, and the local authority on Gaelic— at least until the incident with the teacher. She often used to greet you in Gaelic—what was it now?—*madainn mhath*—aye, that was it. She said it meant "Good-day" or something. He hadn't heard her saying that for a while now.

On the following Friday Peter was standing in his garden in front of the house. He'd maybe do a bit of digging later. As he turned towards the tool shed he noticed a figure coming along the road. Peter recognised the diminutive features of Miss Shuttleworth. His first instinct was to nip round the side of the house, but it was too late. She'd spotted him and given a wave with her stick. Waving back he waited resignedly.

"Good morning, Mr McQueen," boomed Miss Shuttleworth still twenty yards from his gate. Peter looked at her without much interest. She'd maybe want to see Jean. He couldn't think what else she'd be doing at this end of the village. Although she did wander about a lot. A funny wee woman, really. English of course, but still . . . Jean had said she'd been a matron of some hospital in England before she retired. He sometimes wondered why she'd come to live in Achanult— she probably couldn't even pronounce it.

"Yellow hillock," Miss Shuttleworth beamed.

"Um . . . pardon?"

Miss Shuttleworth tapped the name plate on the gate with her stick.

"Yellow hillock. That's what it means, you know."

"Oh, aye. I believe so."

"And how would you pronounce it?"

"*Tom buidhe*? Well just like that . At least, that's how I've always heard it." Miss Shuttleworth made a gallant attempt at the name.

"You're probably wondering how I know. Well I've been to that Gaelic class on Tuesday afternoon. Very good, it is. You should be there."

"Well, aye . . . I've other things . . . the garden . . . "

"Nonsense, man. It's part of your heritage, I'll tell Mrs Nicholson that you're interested. There's quite a good turn out, you know. Your neighbour was there too."

So that's where Donald had been on Tuesday! Peter had seen his car coming back about 4.30. Funny that he'd never said anything. Of course, he wasn't speaking at the moment after that business with the sheep.

Och well . . . Peter decided to take him a bag of seaweed tomorrow. That would break the ice.

"And his is the house by the shore." He knew that actually. "It's really 'house of the shore'—the genitive, you know—but I don't think he quite understood that."

"Aye, well, of course . . . Mind you, his grandfather was from Uist originally."

"Yes, but they don't really *understand* these things, you see," intoned Miss Shuttleworth, with a look of earnest resignation. "The name's misspelt. There are at least two mistakes in it, I told him. I've offered to write it out correctly. Not that I'm an expert, of course, though I'm not unfamiliar with other languages. It's really just a matter of checking these things in a dictionary or grammar book. I did mention it to Mrs Nicholson."

Peter moved towards his spade.

"Well, I'll let you get on. I hope we'll see you there next Tuesday."

After a few minutes Peter put his spade down again. There were an awful lot of English in the village these days, buying houses. Even the hotel. They were supposed to be retired, most of them, but they rushed around doing things all the time. That was the trouble with them really. He'd nothing against most of them personally. It was just that they never seemed to be satisfied with things the way they were.

Take that business of the bus. Mitchells had wanted to stop the weekday service and just run one bus to Oban and back on a Saturday. You could see why, of course, since there weren't a lot of passengers on weekdays. Still, it was a handy service for the older folk—most of them didn't have cars. Peter looked over at his Mini and wondered if that tyre would get through the M.O.T. He'd have a word with Archie first. So the incomers had got up a petition—mind you, it was mostly incomers who'd signed it. Peter had signed it, a bit reluctantly. He would rather have kept out of the way. Donald next door had flatly refused, like a lot of others. Well, you could understand. Charlie Mitchell had given good service with his buses over the years. Everyone knew the family and quite a few were related to them in one way or another. So nobody would want to upset things. Anyway, the incomers formed a committee, so he'd heard—not that most folk would have anything to do with it—and had got some grant from the region to keep the buses running. So that was all right, in the end. Funny thing though, all the incomers had cars—some even had two.

Peter wheeled the bag of seaweed up Donald's driveway. It had been a bit of a job to find a bagful at this time of year and he was half-minded to keep it for himself. Donald saw him coming and came out in his wellingtons. He wouldn't be inviting him in, then. Donald was funny like that. Sometimes he invited you in but more often he kept you standing outside, especially the last year or two, whatever the weather. Jean said it was because he was an old bachelor. A woman would have made the house a bit more welcoming.

"Aye," said Donald with a vague look in the direction of the seaweed. He always began a conversation like that.

"I thought maybe you could use a bit."

"Aye."

"Oh, while I mind, I was hearing you were at the Gaelic class. Jean's been on at me to go."

"Och well, I just looked in to see what it was like."

Peter waited.

"It maybe wasn't for the likes of me."

"It would be right up your street," replied Peter encouragingly.

"Well, you might think so but it wasn't Gaelic as I'd understood it to be. Och, they were even using books."

Peter looked suitably surprised.

"I told the minister's wife—she's taking the class—that my grandfather had never read a Gaelic book in his life and he spoke Gaelic as good as anybody. He never needed to learn to read it. So she said, what about the Gaelic bible?—her being the minister's wife, of course—so I said, true, he did have a Gaelic bible, now that she mentioned it, but he never read it."

Peter remembered that tact had never been one of Donald's attributes. After a while he said,

"Maybe you'll enjoy it better when you get further on."

"Och no. I don't think I'll be going back next week. It's not really for the likes of me. There was Mrs Nicholson talking about nouns and verbs. I told her my grandfather wouldn't have recognised a verb in all his ninety years. And spelling—

that was another thing. There was no call for any of that in the old days, I told her. My grandfather couldn't spell but he could speak fine Gaelic. And that was all I wanted to do."

Donald could be a bit difficult at times, Peter thought to himself. Miss Shuttleworth had probably put his back up a bit as well. As he wheeled the barrow back up his own driveway, Peter wondered what this Gaelic class was really like. Maybe he'd have to go and find out after all.

2 Unspoilt

ACHANULT wasn't really all that far from civilisation these days—maybe a couple of hours by car—but it had long had the reputation of an unspoilt, remote, highland village. Which was why the film crew had been there.

The national press had articles from time to time comparing shop prices in various parts of the country and of course, the highland village was always the most expensive. Peter wondered if they ever used Achanult in their comparisons—the prices in the village shop certainly were ridiculous. Maggie Stewart said that the papers just phoned the nearest corner shop. Donald next door said they just made up the prices. There certainly wouldn't have been much point in phoning Willie down the road. He hardly knew the price of anything but then everybody knew that he'd never really recovered from decimalisation. He was getting on a bit of course. His daughter Jeannie, who married in her late thirties much to everyone's surprise, knew most of the prices, as did most of the customers. Which was just as well, since Jeannie couldn't manage in all that often now that she had the bed and breakfast business. Willie however, could safely be left there to serve tourists, when he tended to round prices up, just to be on the safe side. Peter had watched him doing it time and time again.

The film crew had been a bit vague. It was all rather confidential. And they just wanted to get an impression of the area. They stayed for five days, on four of which it rained for most of the day. Several of the film crew, Glaswegians all, sought refuge in the bar of the local hotel. They seemed to be a bit upset by the weather.

"See that rain!" began one of them, shaking his head.

The locals in the bar turned to the window.

"Have yous all got webbed feet up here then?" asked another, a young man with a beard from which he wiped a few drops of rain.

On cue, Alec Cameron sprang to the defence of Achanult.

"You've come at the wrong time of shycar."

Alec was the self-styled local historian and usually managed to put in an appearance whenever a group of tourists turned up. He was particularly successful with Americans, which was a bit surprising since they couldn't understand him too well. Many of the locals had difficulties as well, now that his teeth no longer fitted him as they used to. His reluctance to take his pipe from his mouth when talking didn't help either.

"When should we have come then?"

"Well, the shpring, early shummer."

"Slackens off a bit then does it?"

"No mishes."

"Eh?"

"There's no mishes then." After a pause Alec decided these townsfolk didn't know what midges were and so he gave a few quick swats to his face and neck by way of illustration. If they'd been Americans he would have told them about the year of the midge, 1921, when the whole village was confined indoors for weeks by the vast swarms of midges. A child had been bitten almost to death and dozens of sheep had jumped into the loch to escape them and had drowned. But these Glaswegians knew about midges, so Alec restrained himself.

"So what happens up here then, when it's not raining?"

"Och, it's an intereshting wee place. Shome funny things have happened here."

At this point, Peter decided to leave, in spite of the rain. He'd heard Alec's nonsense too often for comfort. In fact he was getting worse. He was nearly unstoppable since he'd been on the BBC —in that Highways and Byways programme, or whatever it was called. Peter remembered listening to the programme.

"It doesn't sound quite like Alec," he'd thought aloud.

"They'll have got him to take his pipe out of his mouth," said Jean. "Is that true what he said about seaweed covering the house roofs after that great storm?"

"Och, I doubt it."

But later on Maggie Stewart had said that she'd heard that they'd got some actor to impersonate Alec and that was why everybody understood him for once.

The rain hadn't kept all the locals indoors. The chance of appearing in a film even as a brief figure in the background, proved a great attraction. No one would admit it, of course. So dogs were walked, letters posted, errands undertaken and visits made, all beyond the call of duty. Old Mrs MacPhail, normally a bit on the grumpy side, made a point of standing at her open door every time the crew were in the vicinity, giving a cheery wave with her stick. She even exchanged a few words with Miss Shuttleworth, who just happened to be passing as the film van drove by. This caused some surprise in the village since old Mrs MacPhail seldom had much to say to anybody and certainly not to incomers such as Miss Shuttleworth.

Like some of the other older residents Mrs MacPhail could remember a golden age when there were no foreigners in Achanult—apart from the minister—no English vowels, no tourists either. In those days you could still hear Gaelic occasionally. Not that she understood it herself, but she liked the songs, provided they didn't go on too long. Then the doctor had come and that had been the start—or the end, as Mrs MacPhail saw it. From up Aberdeenshire way he was, apparently—spoke a bit funny. Not that she'd ever spoken to him . . . If she was ill, she might rest for a while or, if she really felt unwell, she might get her neighbour's daughter to have a word with the chemist in Oban.

At the end of the week the film crew packed up and left. Life in Achanult returned to its leisurely pace. There was some discussion about whether the film would be in colour or black and white. Maggie Stewart said it would definitely be in colour because nobody had made a black and white film for years now. Alec Cameron greeted this news with some relief, since it justified his decision to repaint his front door. He'd originally hoped that they might come to interview him, maybe outside, or even inside his house, and he was still a bit huffed that they hadn't. After him shaving every day too!

Peter also reverted to type.

"You're not back to wearing that old thing?" sighed Jean.

"Why not?"

"I've told you before why not."

"Well, I've been wearing it for years and you've never complained."

"I've been complaining for years, for goodness sake. You looked so smart all week in your new jacket."

Peter occasionally envied his neighbour Donald. He'd told Jean often enough that he was more comfortable in his older clothes and tweed was supposed to last for years. And anyway he didn't go to church in it. He decided to take the initiative.

"But you've had all week to mend it."

"It's past mending," replied Jean wearily.

"Well if I wore my good jacket all the time, I wouldn't have a good one."

"You could buy another one."

Peter looked out the window at the rain. He knew he would lose this battle, so it was really only a question of playing for time, delaying the inevitable.

"Well, if there was a sale . . . "

"We could look next time we're in Glasgow."

"Glasgow?" queried Peter with unconvincing amazement. Since they'd got their bus passes, Jean had gone herself a few times. He'd been with her once, though it seemed a bit daft not taking the car.

"We'll be going next month anyway, so we could have a look round then."

Maybe he'd think of something before then.

3 Silence

MRS NICHOLSON stood by the desk with a slight frown. She had a habit of looking worried even when there was nothing to worry about. This was partly due to her belief that a minister's wife should not display undue levity and partly to an innate sense of uncertainty and insecurity. She had always felt that people didn't show the same respect these days. David's church in Edinburgh had been a struggle really, especially in the last few years—falling numbers, vandalism, public indifference. Of course it told on him. After his spell in hospital he could have retired, but they'd decided to move to a less demanding situation.

She looked up from her notes. In the front row Miss Shuttleworth beamed at her.

"Nothing ever starts on time here," she boomed.

Mrs Nicholson smiled weakly and looked at the others. Eight of them. There should really be ten. Oh God! There's that awful man at the back . . . what's his name . . . Muir? . . . Mrs Nicholson looked down at her register. Morrison, that's it. Donald Morrison. Terrible. Didn't want to use a book. She'd hoped he wouldn't be back. She'd mentioned him to David when she got home after last week's class. "Well at least they're interested," he'd said, "It's better to have argument than apathy."

Mrs Nicholson sighed and turned to the door as another body entered smoking a pipe. Her heart sank. She'd known Alec Cameron for some weeks and like everybody else thought that he would be better to make himself understood in English first. But he'd duly enrolled last week. The pipe however, was going to be a problem. At the end of last week's class Miss

Shuttleworth had waited until the rest had gone then said,

"We can't have that man smoking in here."

"Well I . . . of course I agree . . . but . . . "

"I'll make sure he's made aware of our feelings," Miss Shuttleworth had promised as she strode out.

Mrs Nicholson looked around and counted again. Nine. She closed the door and turned to the class.

"Well, if we're all here . . . "

"There may be one or two later," interrupted Miss Shuttleworth. "They never come on time, you know. One gets used to it, of course. Ah, Mr Morrison, did you persuade your neighbour to come? Pity. I had a word with him myself. We discussed house names and I told him he should come. I'm surprised he's not here."

As Miss Shuttleworth turned to face the front again Mrs Nicholson began afresh.

"We really should have ten . . . "

"Don't worry about the numbers," said Miss Shuttleworth briskly. "I'm quite prepared to pay for an extra place."

"Well, that's very kind but we shouldn't really . . . "

"Nonsense! I'm sure we'd all be prepared to give a little extra to keep things ticking over properly."

In the ensuing silence Mrs Nicholson tried again.

"Well, good afternoon, ladies . . . "

"Before we begin—and I'm sorry to interrupt," said Miss Shuttleworth, chastened slightly by the lack of support on the previous point, "but most of us would prefer a no-smoking environment."

Mrs Nicholson, looking more worried than usual, turned to Alec Cameron.

"Ah . . . Mr Cameron . . . " she faltered, "I wonder if we could perhaps come to some, um, arrangement about smoking

31

during the class?"

"I'm not shmoking."

"Sorry?"

"It'sh not lit."

"Ah. Well, if you're not going to light it . . . , and that's very kind of you, and if no-one . . . "

"I don't mind," broke in Mrs McKenzie, who hadn't said a word last week. "I quite like the smell of a pipe, really."

Mrs Nicholson avoided looking at Miss Shuttleworth and turned to her book. Not the best of starts, which was a pity since Mrs Nicholson always liked to get things off to a good start. To this end she'd rehearsed her opening remarks countless times during the previous days. Clearing her throat she began,

"Now, as I think I said last week, I'm assuming—well, we're all assuming—that none of you has much knowledge of Gaelic—although of course, some of you may know more than others . . . "

This was intended for Maggie Stewart who had let Mrs Nicholson know last week that she had a good acquaintance with the language. She'd understood it fine as a child but of course, not using it or hearing it nowadays, she'd forgotten some of it. After saying a few words to her Mrs Nicholson was surprised to find out that Maggie seemed to have forgotten all of it. She'd mentioned this curious fact to David, who'd said,

"She probably never knew any in the first place."

"So it seems. But why pretend she does, or rather did?"

"Probably because it's fashionable nowadays."

"Yes, I suppose it is a bit."

Mrs Nicholson remembered an elderly aunt who was a native Gaelic speaker, but pretended otherwise. She could still hear her saying—especially if there were what she considered genteel company present—"Of course we always spoke English at home." A downright lie, according to her aunt's sister. Neither of them could speak a word of English before they went to school.

"So," resumed Mrs Nicholson, tugging at her pearl necklace, "I think it's best for us all to start at the beginning. I thought it might be useful to build on some of the words we mentioned last week, words which most of you were familiar with from place names, for instance. We must remember . . . "—at this point Mrs Nicholson herself remembered that she'd rehearsed a short historical synopsis of Achanult—"that not so long ago this was a Gaelic speaking area. But today of course, any Gaelic speakers are incomers. I suppose I'm a good example." She laughed nervously.

"Where are you from?" asked Miss Shuttleworth.

"From North Uist."

Miss Shuttleworth nodded sagely to conceal her uncertainty. At this point Mrs MacKenzie obviously emboldened by her successful defence of Alec Cameron's pipe, ventured,

"I've an uncle in North Uist. We go there for holidays sometimes. It's a lovely island . . . " She tailed off, reddening.

"Quite," retorted Miss Shuttleworth, who had no intention of allowing anyone else to assume undue prominence. "One wonders why people ever leave it to live elsewhere." She looked questioningly at Mrs Nicholson.

"Well yes, you're right. In my case I had to leave to finish my schooling. Then there was training college . . . "

"And you never went back?"

"Well, for visits, of course." Feeling rather guilty, she added defensively, "It was the same for everyone. The bright ones all had to leave and only those who left school at fourteen stayed on the island. It was the same on the other islands too."

Mrs Nicholson felt she'd said enough. Just as she stopped

there was a shuffle at the back. The tall elderly gentleman with the white hair whose name she'd forgotten stood up and walked past her. He was obviously slightly confused since he opened a door which revealed, to everyone's surprised gaze, a collection of pails, mops and brushes. Recovering himself, he successfully found the door to the corridor, opened it and departed without a word.

The lengthy silence was broken by Miss Shuttleworth.

"How strange!" Then, *sotto voce*, "Most peculiar man."

Mrs Nicholson floundered, "Well perhaps we . . . does anyone know? . . . I hope he isn't . . . "

"I think Mr Grant may have taken offence," said Mrs McKenzie.

"Can't see why," snorted Miss Shuttleworth.

"Well he was telling me last week that he was born in Harris but left it when he was four, which is why he hasn't any Gaelic now. He maybe thought that you were saying that all the bright ones leave the islands, so those who are left are . . . " She paused, clearly reluctant to go on any further.

"Oh no, goodness! I didn't mean anything like that," whispered Mrs Nicholson turning white. "Oh dear."

"He left the islands early enough anyway," said Miss Shuttleworth dismissively.

4 View from the bridge

PETER walked past the end of the village, out towards the bridge. Since he retired he'd got into the habit of walking quite a lot, sometimes by himself, sometimes with one or two of his cronies. Funny how you got used to it, he thought. He'd been at a loose end the first three days of the week when he couldn't get out because of the rain. He liked to stand on the bridge and look at the water. There might be a bit of a spate today after all that rain.

He looked up at the bridge as he drew near. To his surprise there was something written on it. In large, red letters someone had painted the word, CEARTAS. Peter wondered what it meant. He'd ask Jean. It couldn't be anything official since it wasn't very well painted. Kids probably. He'd better write the word down in case he forgot it.

From the bridge Peter looked back at the village. It had changed a lot over the years. All these new bungalows. Incomers mostly. Strange how a lot of the new bungalows didn't have chimneys. Daft, really, with all that driftwood on the shore. Still, if everybody collected it there wouldn't be enough for him.

After about twenty minutes, his usual time at the bridge, Peter began to walk slowly back into the village. As he passed the new bungalows it occurred to him, as it always did when he came this way, that he didn't know any of the people who lived in them. They seemed to be all incomers and kept themselves to themselves. He could still remember what the place was like before the bungalows went up—an open field, a few small trees and shrubs. He'd heard that there was a collection of old photographs of the village in the local library.

Very interesting, apparently—now who'd told him that? He couldn't remember. Peter wasn't in the library too often but Jean was a great reader. Mind you, he'd nothing against the library. It was a fine warm place if you could get a seat. But there wasn't much room and Jean complained that they hadn't had any new books for years. Peter couldn't really see that was too important. She couldn't have read *all* the old ones, surely— there were hundreds of them, maybe even thousands. He'd once thought of taking a book out himself, one he'd noticed while he was waiting for Jean. She always took quite a while and although he'd wait outside in summer, it was nice to get in out of the rain in winter.

While he was waiting for her one afternoon he'd noticed a book on display which was all about his old regiment and full of photographs. He'd had plenty of time to look through it and decided he'd like to take it home. Jean had disappeared into the room marked, FICTION. She went in there quite a lot—it had something to do with science, he thought. So he'd gone over to the counter.

"Good afternoon, Mr McQueen. Waiting for Mrs McQueen?"

"Aye. Um . . . this book, can I take it home?"

"Certainly. Can I have your card?"

"Card?"

"Haven't you got it with you?"

"No. I don't think I have one."

"But haven't you taken out books before?"

"No."

"Oh. Well, I'll give you a form. Just fill it in and that's all we need," said the assistant as she turned to deal with a lady who'd just come in with a sleeping infant in a pushchair.

Peter smiled to himself as he remembered the expression on the face of the sleeping child. He still had the form, a bit crumpled after being in his pocket for over a year now. He'd never mentioned it to Jean. Pity about the book though. After a few months it had occurred to him that Jean must have a card. But her card might not be valid for books about the war and the army. She never came home with any like that. He'd need to ask her some day.

Once he was past the bungalows Peter looked back and tried again to remember the place as it had been before the buildings went up. He was beginning to forget the detail—there was a lot of gorse, he remembered, and bracken. How it had all changed! On the spur of the moment he decided to go to the library and ask about these old photographs of Achanult. Might be quite interesting. At the same time he could look up that word written on the bridge, if they had a dictionary.

Achanult public library was a fairly recent creation. Peter could remember when a van came from the Oban library once a week—Tuesdays, in the afternoon. Jean used to be waiting for it. It always stopped five doors down at Mrs McKay's, who found walking difficult and always took a few minutes to get down onto the road. That house had been empty since she died—must be about a year and a half now. You'd have thought that some of these incomers would have bought it, a fine big house instead of these daft wee bungalows. Maggie Stewart had told Jean that it wasn't the price that was the problem but rather the dry rot. It looked all right from the outside,though something would have to be done about that hedge. Mrs McKay, a widow, had a daughter who was married and lived in England. Peter remembered her as a child, skipping on the pavement, chalking mysterious boxes on the tarmac. When she came to the funeral, she had a child of her own whose features took Peter back thirty years. Jean had gone to the funeral service although she hadn't known Mrs

McKay all that well. She liked funerals, Jean. Always turned to the deaths column in the local paper before anything else. Quite a number of people had come to look at the house. They were just nosey, Jean said.

The library was situated on the upper floor of a large detached house which stood in extensive grounds about a quarter of a mile from the pier. It had belonged to a wealthy Glaswegian businessman who used to come up with his family during the summer and sometimes at the Christmas and New Year holiday period. After the war it had somehow passed into the hands of the County Council but it was only recently that they'd turned the top floor into a library.

Peter climbed the stairs and pushed open the door. That funny smell again. Must be the books. He always felt a little uneasy in here by himself. It always seemed to be full of women, though Donald used to come in to read the local paper. Apparently he would get annoyed if someone else was reading it and would sit pointedly waiting till he, or more usually she, had finished. He never read any of the other papers, though there were quite a few in the library, even English ones. Donald never took any books out though. Maybe he didn't have a card. Peter suddenly realised that he might need a card to see that collection of old photographs. He'd better not mention them. Feeling a bit awkward, he was just wondering how to extricate himself, when a young lady said eagerly,

"Can I help you?"

"Aye . . . um . . . I was looking for a dictionary. Just to look a word up."

He waited to be asked for his card. It seemed very hot in here, he thought.

"Reference is over there." She pointed to the wall behind

Peter. "An English dictionary is it?"

"Yes."

The young lady came out from behind the counter. With a smile she ran her fingers over the backs of several volumes.

"Take your pick."

Peter thanked her and took a large blue book down and walked over to a table. Fishing in his pocket for the piece of paper, he pulled out the crumpled library membership form. Hoping that no-one had noticed he covered it with his other hand and continued searching in his pocket. Eventually he found the scrap of paper. CEARTAS. Opening the dictionary he eventually made his way to the required page. He noticed words beginning with CE . . . but no sign of CEARTAS. He looked at the page again, marking the words with his finger: cease . . . ceaseless . . . ceaselessly . . . ceasing. That was it. Nothing else. Maybe it was just a meaningless word. Some kids' nonsense. Peter closed the dictionary and took it back over to the shelf, passing the same young lady on the way.

"Find what you were looking for?"

"Yes. Thank you."

When Peter came out of the library it had started to rain again. Quickening his pace, it wasn't long before he was approaching his house. While he was still a few houses away he could smell the coal burning. It gave him a curious feeling of satisfaction and warmth. Some of his neighbours had oil and gas central heating. Peter thought that was a waste of money, especially the way the price had gone up. Look at the cost of petrol now! Anyway, it had an awful smell. Jean had fancied some peat. You could buy it now from the coalman. Peter had nearly bought a bag once but had baulked at the price. It was cheaper than coal of course, but still . . . the idea of having to pay for something you could go and dig yourself for nothing. Not that anybody in Achanult did nowadays. Peter couldn't even remember if there was any left in the area.

Passing Mrs McKay's house he noticed that a light was on downstairs. That would be someone looking over the house again. Quite a big car. One of those funny French things— Citroen was it? Peter didn't really like foreign cars. He was quite happy with his Mini. This was the second one he'd had and they were fine cars. Everything you needed. Jean complained about the size of the boot but—give her her due— she'd be the first to admit she didn't know anything about cars. Anyway, you could always put stuff on the back seat. Peter recalled a programme on television about the Mini—some anniversary or something. He'd got a bit annoyed when they said it was too slow and noisy. It didn't seem noisy to him and some of the roads round Achanult didn't let you get into top gear all that often anyhow.

5 Visitor

MISS SHUTTLEWORTH looked closely at the first sentence again. She always liked to make an impressive start. After some thought she scored out "delightful" and wrote "nice" above it. She had always written letters this way—one or two rough drafts then a final polished version. Miss Shuttleworth prided herself on her letter writing. She read it through again.

Dear Jennifer,
How nice to hear from you. I knew you were soon to retire of course, so welcome to the club. Your visit would give me

much pleasure. The locals can be a bit trying sometimes, so a bit of southern comfort would be most welcome. I have bags of spare room here, so just let me know when you'd like to come.

Best regards,
Marjory.

Miss Shuttleworth looked again at the phrase "a bit of southern comfort." She hoped Jennifer would appreciate her witticism, even though an occasional sherry—medium dry—was all Jennifer aspired to, as far as she could remember. Still, Jennifer might have changed. She herself hadn't known much about whisky before she came up here. She then considered writing "a little" in place of "a bit of" but on reflection she left it unchanged. Jennifer was rather tall for a woman.

After a few days Miss Shuttleworth received a reply.

Dear Marjory,
Thanks for you letter, just received. I'm hopping to travel north on the Friday of next week, the 17th. Perhaps I could stay the weekend if it isn't too much trouble. If I take the overnight sleeper I can arrive in Oban at 12.50pm. Perhaps I could ring you from there? Do let me know if this is convenient.

Kindest regards
Jennifer

After reading the letter Miss Shuttleworth took her pen and scored out the second p in "hopping". The idea of her friend making kangaroo like progress up the motorway was really too ridiculous. Anyway, she was coming by train. Miss McLachlan's letters were never very elegant but at least she always used a fountain pen. Miss Shuttleworth also used a fountain pen although she now kept one of those biros in her car since the time when her fountain pen had leaked wildly all over her gloves and hymn book in the glove compartment. She'd been driving to church at the time, really most unfortunate. You could still see the stain if you looked. You had to bend your head at an awkward angle to see it properly but Miss Shuttleworth was quite concerned about it. Several times she'd tried to clean it but it remained—slightly less conspicuous perhaps. She'd tried to line the glove compartment with paper, but discovered when she'd eventually found a pattern that she felt was suitable that it wouldn't stay in place properly. Miss Shuttleworth knew that there was no point in taking it to a garage. Men just didn't understand these things, especially here. And their hands! Filthy. They'd only make things worse.

As she put down her friend's letter, she supposed it would be all right for Jennifer to telephone from Oban. Miss Shuttleworth had an ambivalent attitude to the telephone. Very useful of course, at certain times. Yet somehow it invaded one's privacy. All sorts of people calling her! She'd thought of going ex-directory of course. But there wasn't much point here. Maggie Stewart would take pride in letting the whole village know—even if she got the number wrong, as she probably would—"just in case". She rose slowly from her writing table. Jennifer obviously thought that Oban was just five minutes away. She'd better meet her with the car.

Miss Shuttleworth took her foot off the accelerator as she descended the hill into Oban. At least it wasn't making that banging noise now. Embarrassing, really. Every time she got above a certain speed the car spluttered and banged.

She waddled into the station to find that the train had

arrived a few minutes ago and the few passengers that there were had departed. So she had no difficulty in finding Miss McLachlan who was standing outside a telephone kiosk wearing a brown coat and hat, looking rather like a benign teddy bear.

"Ah, Jennifer, there you are. Sorry I'm a bit late."

"Hello, Marjory. I've just telephoned you—no reply, of course." She laughed awkwardly. As they walked over to the car Miss Shuttleworth said primly,

"I'm a bit late because of the car. There's something wrong with it."

"Looks all right to me."

"Quite. I think it may be something to do with the engine." Miss Shuttleworth gestured vaguely towards the front.

"It's certainly looking very smart."

"Well yes, I do try to look after it," replied Miss Shuttleworth hoping that Jennifer wouldn't want to use the glove compartment. "These muddy splashes on the wheels will soon disappear in this rain."

"Does it rain all the time here? That's what we hear down south."

"More or less."

"I say, how can you stand it?"

"It stops from time to time. The locals say that it's warmer in the summer."

"Of course."

"The rain, I mean."

"Oh!"

On the drive back to Achanult conversation was inhibited by the banging and spluttering of the engine. Miss Shuttleworth sat grimly hunched over the steering wheel.

"It's not too far now, is it?"

"About half an hour. It would be half that if the car would run properly."

"There certainly don't seem to be many garages around here," volunteered Miss McLachlan whose only previous visit to Scotland had been to attend a conference of midwives in Glasgow some years ago.

"I'll get someone to look at it when I get home. Trouble is, you never feel you can trust people. Not completely anyway. Some of them are all right of course, but you'll find there's a bit of an anti-English feeling here and there."

"Well, I needn't worry. I'm of Scottish ancestry, you know."

"Really Jennifer, you surprise me!"

"Well, surely my name says it all?"

"Of course. I hadn't thought of that. But you're no more Scottish than I am, are you?" asked Miss Shuttleworth with some concern.

"Of course not."

They both laughed. The car spluttered and banged as they crawled to the top of a rise. "These roads!" muttered Miss Shuttleworth.

After a few minutes' silence she added,

"So do you have a clan chief and a tartan and all that sort of thing?"

"I haven't a clue. I suppose we do."

"Some of the locals take all that stuff quite seriously, apparently. Perhaps when they discover you're one of them they'll give you a real highland welcome. Expect you to drink a pint of whisky out of a haggis's caber."

"Oh, I couldn't possibly have anything to do with that kind of nonsense."

"Don't worry, Jennifer. I'll keep your ancestry a secret. Where are the McLachlans from anyway?"

"All I know about them is hearing my father once saying that they were from a place called Cowal." She pronounced it with the stress on the second syllable.

"Where's that?"

"Well, I don't really know. Somewhere in Scotland. In the north, I think. I did look it up once in an atlas, but I couldn't find it."

"Never heard of it."

"Perhaps I've got it wrong. I never could understand these Scottish names."

Miss McLachlan appeared to be enjoying her drive in spite of the antics of the car. At one point she peered forward and said with a shriek,

"Look. Quickly. Is that a sheep?"

"Yes."

"But it's on the road. Goodness there's another one, no . . . two. Have they escaped from somewhere?"

"No, they're just local beasts. They wander about where they like."

At this point one of the sheep which had been sitting at the edge of the road got up—possibly alarmed by the noises coming from the car—and began to walk across the road. Miss Shuttleworth braked quickly and the car stopped with a heavy clunking noise. They looked at each other.

"I don't suppose you'd care to get out and see what that noise was?" asked Miss Shuttleworth rhetorically.

Miss McLachlan looked at a sheep staring at her from the road side.

"I don't think that would do much good," she replied. "I know absolutely nothing about cars."

Further on, just as they were approaching a bridge which crossed a stream at right angles to the road, Miss McLachlan noticed something written in large letters on the side of the bridge. CEARTAS, it appeared to say. She was about to ask Miss Shuttleworth—who was making her customary hash of the sharp turn to the bridge—what on earth it meant when it occurred to her that it might be something unpleasant, some rude Scottish word.

"Well, here we are," boomed Miss Shuttleworth above the noise of the car. "This is my home nowadays."

Miss McLachlan peered through the rain and hoped that she looked impressed. After a few moments' thought, she said,

"It's very peaceful."

6 Decisions

THAT weekend a handwritten notice appeared in the window of Willie McLeod's shop:

ACHANULT COMMUNITY ASSOCIATION
Inaugural Meeting of Winter Session
Mon. 20th Oct. at 7.30 prompt.
M Stewart (Secretary)

Maggie Stewart's notice was the same every year. She'd been secretary for about five years now and had found the post very enjoyable. You did get a bit of trouble from the incomers from time to time but Maggie felt equal to that. They had to be discouraged of course, which was why she no longer wrote "everyone welcome" on her notice.

The first meeting of the session was always important,

since that was the occasion when the winter's activities were decided. This was done in a more or less democratic way. So it was important for Maggie to get her troops out. Until recently, a committee had decided the programme. The committee consisted of Maggie, Jeannie who did the bed and breakfast, two other friends of Maggie, Alice and May and from last year, Mr Nicholson the minister. It was a source of regret to the Rev Nicholson that more men did not take part in these village activities. The situation in his church was similar.

Of the women, Alice had proved to be somewhat unreliable after the incident over the royal wedding. Maggie had wanted to put out flags and some bunting on the village hall on the great day but Alice, who was a staunch nationalist, objected. Maggie, who always voted Tory but never said too much about it, said that politics should not come into the issue. In any case, she'd already been in touch with a photographer from the local paper to record the scene as she raised the flag.

"I take an independent view of politics," declared Maggie with an injured air. "Everybody knows that most of our local government isn't tied to any particular party."

"And everybody knows that all the Tories here have to stand as independents. That's the only way they'll get anybody to vote for them," replied Alice.

A spirited discussion had followed. Maggie duly won the day and the flags went up. Alice bided her time.

Now however, the committee no longer existed, officially at least. This was felt to be largely the fault of the incomers who had questioned its legitimacy. They were right, of course. The committee had in fact, set itself up some years ago to resolve the issue of how to spend a small grant which had unexpectedly arrived from the regional council. Notwithstanding its *ad hoc* nature (or *ab hoc*, as Maggie called it) the committee then continued year after year. Maggie had some vague idea that the committee's importance was enhanced by its Latin title and she made constant reference to the *ab hoc* committee, until one of the insufferable incomers corrected her and pointed out that the committee had served its purpose some time ago and was, *ipso facto*, no longer valid!

Maggie, who always smoked more than usual on these occasions, had put three ash trays on the platform table. There were three chairs on the platform—one for herself as secretary, one for Mrs Baines the treasurer and one for the Rev Nicholson. Maggie felt that his presence would lend a certain legitimacy to the platform. The minister had wondered why he was to sit there.

"I thought it might be nice if you could say a few words," replied Maggie who'd suspected that he might demur. "Maybe a prayer to start things off—or at the end, if you like. Ministers have a lot of respect."

Mr Nicholson wondered.

"Well, I can see your point, of course, but . . . um . . . "

Mr Nicholson could always see everyone's point of view and was generally most reluctant to be seen taking sides in any conflict of interest. " . . . Perhaps this is not quite an appropriate occasion. I don't think we've done it before."

This he felt, was a clinching argument. But Maggie merely said,

"Well, just say a few words of welcome then. Whatever you like."

The Rev Nicholson had an uneasy feeling that he was being used although he wasn't quite certain how. He had really come to Achanult for a quiet life although he had not yet thought of a way to get this across to his parishioners.

Mrs Baines peered anxiously at her balance sheet. Unlike

Maggie, she had no aspirations to office and had only been made treasurer on the grounds that her daughter had worked in a bank in England before her marriage. She had spent an anxious week checking and rechecking the figures. The total amount spent during the previous year had been £79.14. Their income had been £112, raised mainly from a sale of work in the spring and a coffee morning in the week before Christmas. Mrs Baines checked the figures again, a familiar feeling of panic sweeping over her. They really needed to raise more money in order to put on a more attractive programme. Something new.

Mrs Montgomery's slides of the Holy Land for instance, were all right in their way but they'd already seen them twice. Some people had in fact, seen them a lot more than twice since Mrs Montgomery was eager to inflict them on friends and visitors. She gave her services free, it was true. And she did try. Last time, in an attempt to add a certain novelty, she had also shown some slides which she'd borrowed from the library. These consisted of early views of the Clyde resorts in black and white. She had arranged the slides in order in her projector as usual. As she was being driven by a friend to the hall, the car was forced to brake violently to avoid a cat which had suddenly darted across the road. As a result most of the slides had fallen out of the machine and lay scattered on the floor of the car. Mrs Montgomery, whose eyesight had been deteriorating for years now, had hastily put them back in some sort of order. However the ensuing blend, which featured the Mount of Olives followed by the Jeanie Deans at Dunoon, was not thought to have been a success.

The hall was rather slow to fill up. Maggie Stewart noted with satisfaction that most of her friends and allies were there and that few of the incomers had arrived yet. So that might put a stop to those silly suggestions about hall improvements, such as putting in another toilet so that the ladies could have one all to themselves. That would have been a waste of funds, Maggie thought. Anyway, they couldn't afford it and they'd managed for years without a toilet at all. Someone had even wanted hot water to be laid on!

Maggie looked down at the sheet of paper on the table. She'd written a few subject headings, the first of which was "Funds—suggestions". Raising funds had been the first topic to be discussed for several years now but it was always so difficult to reach agreement. The incomers—where were they tonight?—were full of suggestions of course but there was always a body of objections. The idea of a sponsored slim for instance, had been taken as an affront by several of the ladies. A sponsored swim had also failed to get off the ground. The Rev Nicholson had pointed out that in his previous charge, sponsorship had been a very good way of raising money but of course, he could see their point and perhaps something else might be more appropriate here. In the end they decided on a sale of work and a coffee morning.

"Welcome, ladies and gentlemen, to our first meeting of the new session. Before we get down to business, I think Mr Nicholson would like to say a few words." Maggie sat down again and the minister rose reluctantly to his feet. As he began, Maggie was about to lift her cigarette from the edge of the ash tray but decided that this might be seen as disrespectful just at this moment. She looked round the hall and waited for him to finish. Not many incomers. Not much of a turn out at all really.

" . . . and so we hope that our modest efforts will be blessed with fruition during the coming months."

After the applause the meeting continued along its usual

lines. Suggestions were made and there was some discussion but in the end it was agreed that a programme roughly similar to last year's would be a suitable compromise and that consequently next month's meeting would be a beetle drive.

"Well," said Maggie, winding up, "if there are no more suggestions . . . "—she paused ritually.

"I would like to make a small suggestion."

All eyes turned towards Alice who, feeling herself reddening, continued,

"Well, since it was national no-smoking day recently, I was wondering if we could set a good example at our meetings."

There were one or two cries of "good idea!" and "hear hear!"

"What! All the time, you mean?" asked Maggie defensively.

"Well, why not?"

"But I'm sure no-one objects. I've never been one to tell others what to do."

"We could at least have a vote on it," insisted Alice.

"But people come here to enjoy themselves, Alice. We can't stop them, can we? I'm sure we don't want rules and regulations all over the place. Don't you agree, Mr Nicholson?"

"Well of course, I can see your point. But on the other hand there is a body of feeling nowadays . . . um . . . I wonder if anyone else has any views on the matter?"

He looked at Mrs Baines who was sitting next to him.

"Oh . . . um . . . I wouldn't mind really," stammered the treasurer.

"Is that a *for* or an *against?*" asked Maggie.

"For—no, against. I mean, it gets in my hair and . . . of course I don't smoke myself. But I don't mind, really," she finished and retreated back into her shell.

"I'm sure I've heard it said that more people would turn out to our meetings but the smoky atmosphere gives them a headache," said Alice.

Liar, thought Maggie. She was about to add that she knew some people who wouldn't come if they weren't allowed to smoke. But she thought better of it.

"Could we not open some of the windows?" asked the Rev Nicholson.

"It's far too cold for that—or else our heating bills would go up."

The minister looked at the clock at the back of the hall. He'd been looking at it on and off for most of the evening. It now showed the time to be 9.40. After a pause he said,

"I think a show of hands would give us some guidance. I think it is only right that I myself should abstain."

There was quite a large majority in favour of a ban.

"Oh well," said Maggie "I suppose if it's a democratic opinion . . . The only thing, and I'm just trying to be fair, is that we don't really know in what way many of those not here tonight might have voted."

"Mind you, if they can't be bothered to come . . . " began Alice.

"It's not that. Some of them may be ill or have had something else on."

"Well, the vote seemed fairly clear cut to me."

"But it's not very . . . um . . . democratic, if people aren't given the chance to vote."

There was a pause. Maggie looked at the Rev Nicholson who was beginning to stir uneasily. Clearing his throat he said,

"We seem to have reached an impasse. I suggest that we arrange some sort of ballot of all the members, so . . . um . . . if we fix a date for that . . . we can always find out the opinions of those who can't come. Achanult isn't such a big place, is it?"

7 Wait and see

PETER wandered out the back to see how much coal was left. It didn't seem to last very long these days. That was Jean's fault. He seemed to be lighting the fire earlier and earlier. A few years ago he never lit it in the morning but Jean wanted it lit by mid morning sometimes, even though the range in the kitchen was always warm. Of course, if she went out for a walk like he did, she'd feel warmer. Mind you, it was fine to come into a warm fire.

The coal came once a fortnight. Until recently it had been once a week but Alec had said that it wasn't worth his while now—too many folk using gas. That was the bottled gas of course—no mains supply in this part of the country. Jean had a bit of a notion for it, he recalled.

"I see the Wilsons have got one of these gas tanks in their garden," she'd said. "We'll soon be the only people left who don't."

"Ach, it's too dangerous," replied Peter, who'd recently found out the cost of it.

"Nobody else seems to think that."

"Look at all these explosions they keep having in England—and in Glasgow as well!"

That was a good line. Jean had been horrified by the television pictures. They'd left it at that.

Once the fire was going, Peter settled down with the local paper. It only took him a few minutes to read it. Jean, on the other hand, spent ages studying details of prize winners at the flower show, at the school sports and so on. She would study photographs and announce, with obvious satisfaction, that Mrs So and So wasn't getting any thinner.

If there was ever any real news in the paper—and there occasionally was—it was on the front page. This week's headline was all about the threat to the village school—SCHOOL TO CLOSE AT SUMMER HOLIDAYS? Peter seemed to have heard something about it before.

"This school thing isn't new, is it?"

"What thing?" Jean hadn't had a chance to look at the paper yet.

"They're thinking of closing it."

Jean paused from her darning. She'd heard that you couldn't darn these new socks—no wool in them. He'd never know the difference.

"I remember Maggie Stewart saying something about it a few weeks ago."

"Looks like she was right for once."

"Oh well. By the way, I asked her last night about that word painted on the bridge. She says it's the name of some Irish band, pop singers or something. She's seen them on television. They're quite famous, she says."

Peter knew nothing about pop music. But it seemed reasonable enough and that would be why they weren't in the dictionary.

"So why is it they want to close the school?"

"To save money apparently."

"So when will this be?"

Peter scrutinised the paper and after a pause said,

"It doesn't seem to mention that. There's a lot of stuff about the village organising a protest."

"What's the good of that? They'll shut it anyway. I don't want to get involved in a lot of fuss. D'you remember all that fuss about Charlie Mitchell's bus—and that petition. I refused to have anything to do with it. Didn't you sign it though?"

Peter admitted it.

"Well, I didn't see what harm it would do," he added.

"Maybe not, but I don't see any good reason in getting involved in these things. Anyway, this school business has got nothing to do with us."

Peter and Jean had no children. This was a source of great regret to Peter but Jean had never really bothered too much. As he grew older Peter had become accustomed to the situation. In the early years he had often wondered what was wrong but Jean didn't really like to talk about it. In fact she didn't like to mention anything like that at all. Nowadays of course, the papers were full of tests that could be done and clinics to visit—everything. Maybe he should have put his foot down . . . Och no, it wasn't really the sort of thing you could discuss with Jean. Aye, a pity though . . .

"I said if you've finished with the paper . . . "

Peter handed it to her. Och well, they got on fine together. So that was what CEARTAS was. Terrible things, these pop groups. Always drunk—or worse. Irish, didn't she say? Aye.

"So how did you get on last night?" asked Peter. He'd been asleep in the chair when she came in. She must have been a bit late.

"I told you last night." Jean was still studying the paper, looking closely at a photograph of Mrs Keller holding a bouquet of flowers.

"Oh aye, that's right," said Peter hesitatingly. Jean had always been like that. When you asked her about something, she was too busy to tell you properly. But when you didn't really want to know, she would tell you everything and repeat it later for good measure. Peter wasn't really interested in the community association, though he'd been along once or twice just to keep Jean happy. The place was full of women which didn't help. Still, Jean was keen on it, always had been.

Peter wandered through to the kitchen to make a pot of tea. He seemed to drink a lot more tea in the winter when the range was lit and the kettle was always on the boil. Recently he'd read something in the paper about too much tea being bad for you—or was it the water? What next! Aye, that was it, the water. Something to do with lead pipes. A lot of nonsense. There had been a bit of a stir about it here a few years ago. A lot of the older houses in the village had lead water pipes and you were supposed to get them replaced. A woman from the council had come round.

Funny the way women were doing these things now. Look what happened when Sandy was on holiday last year. Peter found his mail delivered by a wee girl—couldn't have been much more than twenty. He didn't get a lot of post certainly, but still . . . maybe somebody had said something because when Sandy was on holiday this year, they'd got a proper postman in his place. He'd sounded English though, Peter recalled. You wouldn't think there'd be much need for that here. Aye, Achanult was changing, maybe not for the better.

So there had been this woman from the council office talking to Peter about his lead pipes:

"I assume you *have* lead piping, Mr McQueen?"

"Oh well, I might." Peter wasn't really bothered. His father hadn't had water in his house at all until after he was married.

"I think you'll find you do. Now, with a 90% grant you shouldn't have to pay more than £20 to £25. We can arrange it all for you if you prefer."

"I'll need to see."

"Of course, it's your decision. There's an explanatory leaflet here—or did you get one before?"

"Um . . . aye . . . och, I'll just take one anyway," said Peter, hoping to hasten her departure.

"And there's a form here to fill in if you do decide to go ahead. I'd certainly advise you to."

"Well, I'll think about it."

"Most people are doing it." She'd found this important reassurance essential.

He'd discussed it with Jean who, he knew, would like things to be left as they were. Jean was worried about the mess, people coming into the house with dirty boots, dust flying everywhere. So that was that. In retrospect they'd probably done the right thing. Look what happened to Miss Graham. All that noise from digging up the road. Then they'd put a drill through her sewage pipe. They'd fixed it quickly enough but seemingly Miss Graham hadn't liked to use the toilet for a few days after that. Or so Jean said. Some of these old folk were a bit odd of course.

Jean put her cup back in the saucer.

"Well, I don't know what's going to happen. I mean, there wasn't that much of a turn out. A lot of the incomers hadn't bothered themselves. It's much better when there's a good crowd. And this smoking ban will drive people away as well."

Peter recalled her saying something last night about a smoking ban. Jean had never smoked.

"It does make me cough sometimes right enough but I'm not particularly bothered one way or the other."

"Did you vote against smoking then?"

"Well no. I just waited to see what everybody else was doing. Most of them were against it."

"Ach well," said Peter, who'd lost interest.

"But seemingly," continued Jean, "they'll have to have another vote with so many folk not being there. So I'll just wait and see what happens."

8 Initiative

OVER at the manse the Rev Nicholson had finished the crossword with the exception of one word which he wanted to check in his dictionary. Unfortunately his dictionary was in the dining room as they called it, although they never dined in it. When they were first shown round the manse by Mr Gillespie the beadle, he had referred to it as the dining room and so it remained. To visitors, Mr Nicholson referred to it as his study although he had little intention of putting it to such serious use. This afternoon his wife had a visitor in the dining room, a young man of about 19 or 20 who'd come to see her on some matter relating to the national Mod.

In due course the dining room door opened and Mrs Nicholson emerged with the young man. Mr Nicholson waited out of sight until he heard his wife coming back alone up the driveway.

"Who was that then?"

"A Mr Alan Smith—the son of Mrs Smith, the one who does the bed and breakfast."

The Rev Nicholson looked vague.

"The grandson of Willie who has the shop."

"Ah yes, I see. What did he want?"

"He's going to be singing in the Mod, so he just wanted a bit of help from me."

"Goodness me Anna, I didn't realise you were quite so musical!"

"Oh no, not the music, the Gaelic."

"What do you mean?"

"He wants me to help him with pronunciation, tell him what the song means and so on."

"You mean he doesn't know these things?"

"Not much, as far as I could make out."

Mr Nicholson paused, curious.

"So that's why you were talking to him in English?"

"Oh yes. He hasn't a word of Gaelic really"

"How strange. Isn't it a bit absurd? I know it's nothing to do with me—your field entirely—but, well, I could enter too!"

"You can't sing!"

"Ah! So there are some criteria."

"Of course. Anyway, the language has got to be encouraged and the more people we have to take an interest in it the better."

"Oh well, none of my business really. But you've just reminded me of something. Do you remember Miss Williams and her friend Mrs Keith in the choir at St. Columba's?"

"Yes I do. I didn't know them well though. They didn't come very often did they?"

"I think they came the year before we left Edinburgh."

"Mmm."

"Well, they told me once that they sang in a Gaelic choir in Edinburgh. Didn't I tell you? Oh well. Anyway, I assumed that they spoke the language but from what you've just told me, I wonder."

"Well, of course I don't know in their case. I think you're being a bit negative, David. You shouldn't say that sort of thing too openly here."

"Oh no of course not. I wouldn't like to tread on any toes . . . just creates trouble."

"Yes, you have to be careful. Actually, I'm told that there used to be an Achanult Gaelic choir until quite recently."

"Really? That's interesting. Mind you, I wouldn't have thought it. This isn't a Gaelic speaking area, is it? But that doesn't matter apparently."

"Now David, that's not funny you know. If people are interested they should be encouraged."

"Still seems odd to me. So what happened to the choir?"

"I don't really know. Maybe they all got too old. I'll ask someone anyway."

"You've become much more interested in your background since we came here, haven't you?"

"A bit, maybe. It's a lot nearer home. Edinburgh wasn't quite the same."

"Oh I don't know. From what you tell me, there's probably a Gaelic choir somewhere in Central Africa. Yes that's it—the Timbuktu Gaelic Choir."

"Don't be silly, David. Timbuktu's in North Africa. Anyway, why shouldn't I spread the gospel just like you do?"

The Reverend Nicholson was quite pleased that his wife had regained an interest in her Celtic heritage. It gave her a sense of purpose outwith her traditional role as a minister's wife. He hoped that he would also derive some benefit from this. Up until recently his wife had busied herself with church matters—women's guild, the young wives' group, bible readings in the evening, things like that. Mr Nicholson had in fact never been too keen on this, finding his house full every other evening and during the occasional afternoon with earnest groups of ladies eager to tiptoe down the Christian path. Harmless of course, but . . .

Yet he could hardly be seen to be discouraging such endeavours. Matters had turned out quite well all in all, since they came to Achanult. Things were far less organised on the pastoral front and his wife seemed to have enough on her plate with the language class. Mr Nicholson had already decided that she should be given every encouragement to pursue this and any other safe occupation.

In the dining room the Rev Nicholson was pleased to see that "adipose" was correct. His skill at solving crosswords had improved since they had come to Achanult. Putting the dictionary back on the shelf he settled in an armchair to read the local paper. After noticing the headline about the threatened closure of the village school, he turned to the churches page, or rather half-page as it now was. When he first arrived in the village, the Rev Nicholson had discovered with some misgivings, that he was expected to contribute a weekly paragraph on a religious theme as his predecessor had been doing for years. Mr Nicholson had persuaded the newspaper owners to reduce this paragraph to a single quotation from the bible on the grounds that God's word was more important than man's word. The paper had been quite happy to agree to this since it was widely felt that few people actually read the church page and so more space could now be devoted to popular items such as the domino and darts results.

Mr Nicholson found his wife in the lounge with a book open on her knee and another, which he recognised as a Gaelic dictionary, on the arm of the chair. He remembered the dictionary from the time of John MacDougall's retiral as an elder. Searching around for something out of the ordinary to say at the retiral presentation, he had discovered that the motto of the MacDougalls was *buaidh no bàs*. Slightly uneasy at his total inability to distinguish between different translations—"victory or death" or "conquer or die" he had bought a Gaelic dictionary on the spur of the moment. Anna, whose education had been solely through the medium of English, was somewhat uncomfortable with written Gaelic but had coached him in the pronunciation, which he'd practiced assiduously. The Rev Nicholson fleetingly wondered exactly why he'd introduced the motto at the retiral presentation. He couldn't remember.

Holding the paper towards his wife he asked, "Have you seen this about the school?"

"Yes, I noticed it. It seems a shame."

"I can see their point of view, of course. There's something about a petition of protest."

"Oh yes, there's always one of these, isn't there?"

"Don't you think we should do something about it?"

"Us?" queried Mrs Nicholson, slightly taken aback by her husband's unexpected show of initiative.

"Well, I'm sure you could—both of us really. Just to help out, that's all."

"I don't know. We haven't been here very long. It's really a matter for the local people. They're the ones it affects directly."

"Now Anna, you know perfectly well that the locals will do little or nothing—nothing effective, anyway. Besides, folk always look to ministers and other professional people to take a lead in such matters. I think you should give it some thought."

"Well, of course. I'm always willing to help."

"Good, good. Splendid."

Mrs Nicholson looked doubtful. After a few seconds she asked,

"What sort of thing do you think we could do?"

"Oh . . . whatever seems effective. You could write a few letters—to the local MP, newspapers and so on."

"Well, maybe. I'd better see what anyone else is doing. Have you heard anything?"

"Not as such. In any case, I've never felt that the church should rush to take sides in such secular matters. And of course I do have one or two other things to deal with just at the moment."

One of these things was the rewiring of the manse. When the Nicholsons moved in they noticed that there was a scarcity of power points and those that existed were of a rather old-fashioned design and could not be used with the plugs which the Nicholsons had. The minister was not too surprised by this since he had always had a suspicion that Achanult was a bit backward. This he felt was one of its charms. When he had tried to buy other plugs, one thing had led to another and in the end he was told that the house should have been rewired years ago. The wiring was apparently in a dangerous condition. Mr Nicholson had, of course, met his predecessor, the Rev Arthur Neil a few times before he had gone off to live in retirement in Ayrshire.

He had learnt much more however, about the Rev Neil since coming to live in Achanult. He had apparently been very straightlaced—dour, some people said—and strict. He also had an innate suspicion of any innovation. He would not have a television in the manse, nor of course a record player nor cassette player, of which he had probably never heard. People said that he did have a radio but rarely used it. Consequently, electricity was not much in demand in the manse apart from lighting.

The electrician who had come to examine the wiring had said when he was finished, that there seemed to be a lot of dry rot about. So that was another thing. A survey had been done and Mr Nicholson was asked to give a date on which it would be convenient for work to start. No date was convenient for him but after some thought he remembered that he and Anna were hoping to visit her sister for a few days next month. So it would be done then.

The garden was going to be another problem. Mr Nicholson was still surprised at how large it was. It was very neat, with a vegetable patch at the back and a small lawn with rockery behind it. At the front of the house was a larger lawn bordered by flower beds. The Rev Neil had been a keen gardener as Mr Gillespie, the beadle, had emphasised when first showing the Nicholsons round.

"Of course, Mr Neil did much of the work himself—the digging and so on. Mrs Neil looked after the flower beds"

The Rev Nicholson was not a keen gardener.

"I'm afraid I don't have much expertise in that direction."

"Och, there's nothing to it. I'll be happy to give you any advice you need."

"Um . . . yes. I don't know if I'll have much time this year. Lots of things needing done here, as you know."

"Oh, don't worry. The garden doesn't need much done to it at this time of year. Just dig the seaweed in."

"Seaweed?"

"Aye. Mr Neil always had a cartload of seaweed spread on the vegetable plot at the end of the autumn. It's getting a bit late but you still might be able to get some. Or there's always manure—but it's a bit dearer, mind. Mr Neil didn't like any of these fertilisers—chemicals, he used to call them. Of course they're a lot easier."

"Ah, well. We'll have to think about all this."

"Mr Neil was very keen on his garden. The soil round here is very poor of course, as you'll have noticed. I think that's one of the reasons he retired to Ayrshire. You'll have had quite good soil over Edinburgh way."

"I didn't have much of a garden there, to tell the truth."

"No? This'll be a welcome change for you then."

"Well . . . yes . . . um."

The Rev Nicholson paused. This was proving to be rather difficult. It would be much simpler to turn everything over to grass if he could get someone to cut it. Or maybe he could let someone else make use of the vegetable plot. Yes, that would be better. A touch of altruism wouldn't go amiss.

" . . . and first prize again last year."

"Oh. He was obviously gifted, then." First prize for what wondered Mr Nicholson?

"Not really. A bit of effort, that's all. You'll soon pick it up."

"Well, we'll have to see about this. Ah, there's my wife. I think she wanted to have a word with you about flowers for Sundays."

9 Letters

MAGGIE Stewart received two letters on the Saturday morning. One was from her brother in London. She laid it on the table unopened. The other letter was also from London and had "House of Commons" printed on the front of the envelope. Maggie opened it eagerly and read.

> Sir William Kiels-Mather, M.P.
> House of Commons
> London SW1A 0AA

Dear Mrs Stewart,

Thankyou for your letter of 17th November. As you know, I have always been particularly concerned with the educational opportunities available in my constituency and I can assure you that I share your concern on this issue. Closure of schools, you will understand, is a matter for the Education Department and you may therefore care to get in touch with the Director of Education.

Yours sincerely
p.p. Sir William Kiels-Mather

Mrs M Stewart,
3, Clachan Cottages,
Achanult, Argyll

Maggie re-read the letter with an increasing feeling of importance and authority. A letter from Sir William from the House of Commons! No-one else in the village would have had one. She immediately decided to read it out at the next meeting of the community association, since it was in her capacity as secretary that she had written, entirely on her own initiative. Secretly, she had wondered if she would get a reply but here it was.

Sir William Kiels-Mather had been the Conservative Member of Parliament for the area for many many years. He was rarely seen in the constituency, hinting that travelling to and from London was becoming a strain at his age. That no-one should doubt his commitment to the constituency however, he had purchased a large mansion house some years ago on the shores of Loch Briagha and was said to spend a week there each summer.

After reading the letter once again she decided to show it to Jim. Even he would surely be impressed. Maggie walked through to the bedroom and said in what she hoped was a casual tone,

"That's the post. There's a letter from Sir William Kiels-Mather."

"Who?" Jim was always a bit slow first thing in the day.

"Sir William Kiels-Mather."

"Who's he?"

"Our MP, for goodness sake. You know fine who he is."

"How should I? I never voted for him."

"You've never voted for anybody."

Jim turned round in the bed.

"Is that all you woke me up for?"

Maggie was becoming a little annoyed. It was hopeless trying to get Jim interested in things these days. Most men were just like that of course, which was why the community association had been such a struggle. She'd been wondering if the Rev Nicholson could persuade a few more men to participate—not that they wanted too many of course.

"So what does he want?"

"Oh, just a reply to my letter."

After a pause, a hand emerged from under the blanket. Maggie handed over the letter. Lying on his side Jim read it slowly.

"Doesn't say much, does he?"

"What d'you mean? It's perfectly clear that he agrees with what I wrote."

"What were you writing to him for?"

"About the school closure, of course. Can't you read?"

"But why write to him?"

"He's our MP. He should be able to do something."

"Judging by his letter, he couldn't give a damn. He hasn't even signed it."

Maggie took the letter back quickly.

"It *is* signed. Look."

"That's not him. That's why it's got *pp* in front of it."

Maggie looked again. Somewhat deflated, she said,

"He's very busy, of course."

"Busy? He's probably been dead for twenty years. Just gets elected anyway."

"Don't be daft."

"Well, when did you last see him?"

Maggie thought for a moment as Jim slid back under the blanket.

"I can't remember exactly but there was the election three—no, four—years back, when he was re-elected again."

"I don't remember him being here."

"No, but he sent out leaflets. Remember?"

"I never read any of that rubbish. What's for breakfast?"

Maggie shrugged and wandered through to the kitchen. It had been quite an effort for her to write to Sir William and at the time she was quite embarrassed by her boldness. The proposed closure of the school was not really of much concern to her but she had always felt that she liked to be involved in issues and not let others in the village have everything their own way. There was also the fact that the mere mention of her correspondence with the MP should raise her standing. Now that office bearers in the community association were to seek re-election every two years, this would clearly tell in her favour.

It had occurred to Maggie that Sir William might have been told of her activities at the time of the last election and therefore might not have answered her letter. She had given some small assistance to the cause of the Liberal candidate, distributing leaflets and putting up one or two posters. She hadn't done this from any firm conviction, of course. Her neighbour Mrs Gray, who was on some committee or other to do with the Liberals, had asked if she wanted to help. Maggie had been watching what seemed to be half the village rushing around involved in the election campaign and decided that she had better get involved too. Purely from a social point of view she'd felt that it would have been better to have been associated with the local Conservative group but they seemed rather impenetrable. There was the Labour Party of course but it seemed a bit, well, common, she thought, although her parents had been Labour voters all their lives.

Rather to her surprise Maggie found that her brother's letter contained an item of interest. Although the main part of it was concerned with travelling arrangements for Christmas and the New Year, at the end he referred to something on television. He thought he'd recognised parts of Achanult in an advertisement and wondered if Maggie agreed.

A bit puzzled, she mentioned this to Jim over breakfast.

"It'll be that film crew that were here a couple of months ago," he said, sounding still half asleep.

"Oh—but they were supposed to be making a film."

"How many film stars did you see then?"

"Well, I don't know much about these things of course but I thought it was some sort of film. They were here long enough."

"It was raining all the time, mind."

"I know, but still . . . He's maybe just seen a wee advert for the film. That's what it'll be. They do that a lot nowadays."

"What advert was it?"

"He doesn't actually say what it is."

"Typical!"

"No, that's what I mean. Maybe it's not an advert at all."

"Well, I haven't seen anything."

"Neither have I. Of course I don't watch a lot of STV."

This was a lie. Maggie watched STV because she liked the programmes and because she also liked the adverts. She had heard however, that the BBC was considered to be more "up market", although she couldn't really see why, especially since she rarely watched it.

To Maggie's satisfaction it seemed that no-one else in the village knew anything about the advert. With practiced ease she was on the point of letting it be known that *she* had seen it, when it occurred to her that she'd better find out if it really was an advert or not. After staying up past midnight for three nights in a row, she was becoming a little fed-up with the whole business, especially after sitting through a programme in Gaelic, of which she followed next to nothing and a snooker programme which she likewise failed to understand. Although the thought of an eventual triumph drove her on, she decided as she crawled half asleep into bed early on Tuesday morning, that she would write to her brother for some details. She didn't correspond with him very often but this was clearly a matter of some urgency.

Staying up to the early hours was having its effect and Maggie considered having a rest in the afternoon, which would have meant missing the Gaelic class. There might be some mention of the advert there though, or something about the school, so she certainly had to go. Nodding off to sleep she had a vision of Sir William Kiels-Mather standing in the House of Commons with her letter in his hand, asking a question about school closures and demanding an assurance on the matter for his constituent, Mrs Stewart.

In the morning Maggie regarded her dream as a good omen and confirmation from the highest quarters, of her importance to the village. She had once read a book about dreams and horoscopes, and knew that there was definitely something in it. Jim just laughed of course but she'd noticed on other occasions that men didn't really understand these things. Mind you, there wasn't very much that Jim*did* understand.

10 A look at the village

MISS SHUTTLEWORTH'S bungalow had three bedrooms which was rather more than she had originally wanted but she had found it difficult to find anything smaller. One of her reasons for retiring to Achanult had been that you could get a reasonable sized house in the area for very little money. Another reason was that she had been impressed in her earlier years by a film called "Brigadoon", as she had told Miss McLachlan last night. In spite of sitting up late chatting Miss Shuttleworth was up at an early hour and prepared breakfast while she waited for her friend to appear. Eventually a bedroom door opened and Miss McLachlan emerged, covered decorously by a heavy duty dressing gown.

"Good morning, Marjory. Is that kippers I smell?"

"Good morning, Jennifer. Yes, kippers. They're a local product. I can make some porridge too, if you like."

"Porridge? How Scottish! I say, Marjory, you haven't gone native, have you?"

"Hardly."

"Well, I might try some. It's bound to be authentic, anyway. Is it a local product as well?"

"Doubt it. I get it in the supermarket in Oban."

Miss Shuttleworth reached down the packet and scrutinised the small print.

"It's from Kirriemuir."

"Where?"

"Kirriemuir."

"Where's that?"

"I've no idea. I think I've heard of it but I can't remember in what connection."

"Oh well, it sounds Scottish enough, so it should be all right. I'll just try a little, thank you."

Miss McLachlan ate her kipper with enthusiasm but was rather more dubious about the porridge. After politely sampling a small amount she rearranged the remainder in the bowl. Miss Shuttleworth munched stoically on. Hoping to divert attention, Miss McLachlan said as she pushed her bowl aside,

"I must say, your house is bigger than I thought, Marjory."

"Yes, it's a bit too big for me really but it's difficult to get anything smaller up here."

"Hmm. A lot of the older houses seem huge as well."

"That's right. They were all built last century as country houses or holiday homes for the rich."

"Who lives in them now?"

"The locals mostly. They're divided into flats now, many of them. Most of the incomers live in bungalows."

"I see. Quite right. One must have a certain amount of privacy. Shall I top up the teapot?"

"If you like. I only have one cup in the morning. Any more is liable to make me feel queasy. What would you like to do today?"

"Well, I thought I'd like to have a look at the town first, the shops and so on."

"That shouldn't take long. There's only one proper shop and it's pretty awful. There's a so-called craft shop and tea room which is only open in the summer."

"That sounds a bit grim. How do people manage?"

"Oh, well, the locals are used to it of course. But I don't know what I'd do without the car. Which reminds me, I'd better see someone about it this morning. It probably won't start so we'll just have to walk round the village. Give you an idea of the place."

"Righto. I'll just get dressed. Will it be very cold? I've brought a lot of really warm things. I expect you've got used to it by now.",

"Used to what?"

"The cold. It's pretty bleak up here, isn't it?"

"Nonsense. I don't think think you'll find it too bad.".

While Miss McLachlan bounced off to dress for a highland winter, Miss Shuttleworth began to make a list of things to do that day. First the petrol station, though there wasn't any point in going there too early. She looked at her watch: 9.20. There ought to be someone there by ten. The village usually came to life on a Saturday morning at about quarter to ten, when the first bus left for Oban.

Miss Shuttleworth had never been on the bus but regularly saw it as it passed slowly on its way. But now that her car was somewhat out of order it occurred to her that she might need to make use of the bus. Not a pleasant prospect—all these people smoking in it. That would have to be sorted out. To conform with regional regulations, Mitchells had designated a section of the bus a no-smoking area, with appropriate notices stuck on the windows. No-one paid any attention to them. Not only that, there were sometimes sounds of pop music pounding from the bus as it passed, on the occasions when it was being driven by that young man, just a boy really, who'd recently joined the company. Miss Shuttleworth shuddered. Something should be done, of course. The fact that she herself never used the service was not the point, she felt. It was once again a matter of principle and were it not for the fact that she had recently been involved in a lengthy battle to get a reasonable service maintained, she would have dealt with the matter by now. It was really appalling how one's privacy was constantly being invaded these days!

Miss McLachlan re-emerged from her bedroom looking even more like a large teddy bear, wearing a brown woolly hat which covered her ears and a pair of light brown knee-length boots. A beige tweed coat and a scarf and gloves completed her defences.

"I'm ready," she announced somewhat superfluously. Miss Shuttleworth restrained herself.

"Right, Jennifer, I'll just get my jacket."

"You said you wanted to go to a garage first, didn't you?" ventured Miss McLachlan. She had been looking forward to a tour of the local scenery and was wondering if it might be possible to hire a car for a day.

"Yes, I'd better do that first."

As they walked from the house to the main street, Miss Shuttleworth pointed out some of the local landmarks to her friend. They passed several people on the way, some of whom exchanged a brief "good morning" with Miss Shuttleworth and looked enquiringly at Miss McLachlan. Passing the village shop they stopped to look in the window, which was covered in notices advertising venison, logs and eggs for sale. Pinned on the door was a handwritten notice which read NO DOG'S, NO PRAM'S. Underneath was written, in a different hand, NO APOSTROPHES.

Miss Shuttleworth ushered her friend inside while she picked up her copy of the Daily Telegraph. She originally had the paper delivered every day but problems arose on the occasions when no copy of the Telegraph reached Achanult. No-one ever seemed to know why the paper sometimes failed to arrive and eventually, in her frustration, Miss Shuttleworth had written to the editor of the newspaper, wondering if he was aware of the situation in Achanult. In due course she received a reply mentioning temporary distribution problems and transport difficulties and enclosing a by then three days old copy of the paper, which she had already seen.

There was no doubt of course, that Willie and his daughter Jeannie did their best. When a copy of the Telegraph was not available, Willie would ensure that some other paper, usually a tabloid, was delivered to Miss Shuttleworth. He even succeeded once in sending a copy of The Guardian to her. Shortly after this Miss Shuttleworth called in to say that she would pick up the paper herself each morning. The exercise would do her good. And if her own paper hadn't come that day she might, or might not, select another one.

As it happened, none of the papers had yet arrived that morning, so Miss Shuttleworth left empty handed. On their way to the petrol station Miss McLachlan asked,

"When will they arrive, then?"

"Oh, later on this morning. They're always a bit late on Saturdays."

"Oh well. D'you know, Marjory, that while you were talking to that old man, I had a look at some of the stuff on the shelves and—did you know?—quite a lot of the things were past their sell-by date."

"I'm not surprised."

"Yes but . . . doesn't it bother you?"

"Not really. I never buy anything much there."

"No, of course not. Still, perhaps we should have told the shopkeeper. Or do you think he knows?"

"I imagine he does."

"Hmm. I must say, Marjory, you cope with life very well here. You just take things in your stride. I'm not sure that I could manage. Oh! Is this the garage?"

"Yes. It's just a petrol station really but I'm told they can fix cars."

"Oh good. Let's see what they say—if we can find someone. It seems very quiet. Oh, look! It's closed."

Miss McLachlan pointed to a rusty notice standing beside the petrol pump.

"Oh. It always says that. I'll just go into the office."

But the door to the office was locked. As they looked at each other in silence, Miss Shuttleworth shrugged and they both turned back to continue their tour of Achanult.

11 Downmarket

ACROSS in the manse the Rev Nicholson was talking to his wife over breakfast.

"The paper seems very late this morning."

"Yes. It's sometimes late on a Saturday though, isn't it? I've forgotten why. Mr McLeod did tell me once."

"I don't suppose he's any idea himself."

"Anyway while we're waiting, David, I wonder what you think of this arts society business—if you've had time to think about it."

Mr Nicholson had forgotten about it. His wife had been talking on the phone last night to Mrs Maxwell and one of the points they'd discussed had been the proposed creation of an arts society. He'd been watching television at the time and hadn't paid too much attention to what she'd said.

"Umm . . . well . . . I don't see any problem."

"She was wondering if they could count on your support."

"I don't see why not. What exactly did you say it was again?"

"An arts society is what she said."

"Sounds very enterprising. Of course, I may not have too much time at the moment. Um . . . but . . . by all means."

"Mrs Maxwell wondered if you might see a conflict with the community association."

"Ah! Well, no. Um, could there be?"

"Maybe. She thinks, and so do some of the others apparently, that the community association has become too parochial—too downmarket was the phrase she used—and they really want something a bit more stimulating. I agree with her in a way. I mean, all this stuff about whist drives and so on. It's the same every year apparently. So a lot of them didn't go to the opening of the session. They had a little discussion among themselves instead. That's what she was telling me about last night."

"I see. Well, I'm sure there's no problem."

"I certainly wouldn't mind something new like that starting. Mrs Maxwell feels that Maggie Stewart and her cronies run the community association for their own benefit and prestige and it's really all a bit limited."

"Well yes, of course. I can see her point."

"The thing is, David, you're on the committee of the community association, aren't you?"

"True but, um, that's only a temporary measure, I believe. Why do you ask? Is there a conflict of interest?"

"Well, it's all a bit complicated. I suspect that Mrs Stewart and her friends will see anything else—such as an arts society—as a challenge to them, a slap in the face, you might say."

"But that's all getting rather personal, isn't it? The community association is for all of us. Mrs Stewart doesn't run it on her own."

"No? She does have a tendency to take things over, so I'm

told. In fact, between ourselves, Mrs Maxwell was hoping that she could somehow keep Mrs Stewart and her friends out of things."

"That doesn't sound very nice, Anna. I'm sure there is no need to go these lengths. How would she manage to do that anyway?"

"She thinks that if an arts society could put on a programme of a sufficiently high standard, Mrs Stewart and her friends wouldn't want to come anyway."

"Beethoven sonatas instead of beetle drives, you mean?"

"Something like that."

"Well, I'm sure there's room for something along these lines. Of course, it wouldn't be right for someone in my position to be seen taking sides, as it were. So I think I'd better stay in the background. Has the paper come yet?"

Mrs Nicholson trotted off to the front of the house and returned with the paper. As her husband sat reading it, she reflected on the curious way in which Achanult ran its social life. Before moving there she had assumed that peace and harmony would reign and that everyone would see eye to eye on most issues. That had certainly been the way of things in Uist in her young days. But that had been a tight-knit community with next to no incomers. A bit suffocating in a way, she'd had to admit to herself later, but predictable and with a comforting unanimity of outlook. Here, however, she often found herself being expected to side with one body of opinion, only to find herself being lobbied a few days later by a rival group. She supposed it was because she was the minister's wife. David maybe got the same treatment although he probably didn't notice. She would have to talk to him about it one day. In the meantime she just had to be careful not to offend anyone, but it was a bit difficult sometimes. She'd been chatting to Mrs

McKenzie last week when the sound of a car horn made both of them turn to see Mr Powis beckoning to a friend on the other side of the street.

"Huh," said Mrs McKenzie. "Think they own the place, these incomers. There was none of this when I was young, you know. Look at it now. They come in here, take half the houses, take the best jobs. Why is it that they get all the best jobs and *we've* got to do what *they* tell us?"

"Well," Mrs Nicholson had replied hesitantly, "they are, um, well qualified, of course . . . "

"Huh. That's just bits of paper."

"Well, yes . . . but . . . I think it's probably just that the cost of moving and the general upheaval mean that it's got to be a reasonably well paid job to make it worthwhile coming here."

Mrs Nicholson wondered if she'd said too much. After Mr Grant's dramatic walkout from the Gaelic class after that misunderstanding, she'd resolved not to say anything that might possibly be misconstrued.

"Huh. They come in here and tell us what to do. All the lowest paid jobs are done by people like us—have you noticed?"

Mrs Nicholson tried to remember what job Mrs McKenzie had. Wasn't she a cleaner somewhere? Or was that somebody else? Playing safe, she said,

"But these jobs are just as important in their way, you know."

"Of course they are. But look at the money we get. Peanuts compared to them. Now there's talk of closing the school and that'll be my job gone. But I bet the teachers don't lose *their* jobs—oh no—they'll find somewhere else for *them*. They probably won't even lose a day's pay. I don't know why they get all that pay anyway. Teaching qualifications? Huh, all they do is read them stories. I've always had a good idea what went on but now that Donna—that's my neighbour's daughter—has started school, I've been hearing all about it. Aye, they just read them stories and give them toys to play with. Well, I could do that. I like children. In fact they don't even have to read to them now. They just all watch the television. And yet they give you all this stuff about college and teaching certificates. I think they just think these things up to stop people like us from getting these jobs. We could do them just as well, you know. I don't know what they need all these incomers for. We're not stupid, you know. I was quite clever at school. Sometimes I think they think we're here for them but they wouldn't be here without us either."

While Mrs McKenzie paused, seemingly confused by this non-sequitur, Mrs Nicholson wondered how to terminate the conversation without seeming too abrupt. Mrs McKenzie was, after all, a valuable member of the Gaelic class, where numbers were paramount, especially since Mr Grant had not reappeared. Deciding to change the subject, she asked brightly,

"And how is your husband . . . and family?"

"Oh, Bob's just the same as usual. Ronald's doing really well, though."

"You must be really proud of him."

"Well, he's fairly getting on."

"Where is he now?"

"In Slough. That's in the south of England. Did I tell you he'd recently got a job as a lecturer in the Polytechnic there? No? Well, it's a good promotion of course and it's not far from the school he worked in before, so he hasn't had to move home, which is handy. Oh no, he was quite happy teaching. He was the head of the department, you know. But when this job came up he applied for it and got it. And there were dozens of people applied for it seemingly.

"Ronald said he didn't think he'd get it because he hadn't been in the area too long—well, it's four years now—but I wasn't surprised. We Scots have always had the ability to go and become a success in other places. Just look at what we've done in Canada and America, Australia, England as well. Of course, Ronald's got the qualifications and I often think our qualifications are better than theirs. He'd recently got a Diploma in Education—I think that's what he called it—from the Open University—that's on top of his university degree—and he thinks that's what made the difference. Maybe it was. You're just as well to get all the qualifications you can these days with all this competition for jobs.

"So he's doing really well and of course, gets paid even more now, though he was saying that his new job is actually easier for him. Well, I said to him, it can't be all that easy if they're paying you as much as that. And he's got a lovely house. I must show you a photo of it. It's far too big for him but I think he'll be getting married soon. That's the thinking behind it. Anyway, I'd better rush. I'll see you at the class on Tuesday. *Slan leibh*. Is that right?"

"Yes, that's good. You're coming on. *Slan leibh*."

12 Aspiration

MRS NICHOLSON set out for the class immediately after dinner. She had a dread of forgetting something important so she liked to be there as early as possible. She could switch on the electric heaters and still have time to go back home again to collect anything she'd forgotten. The class was held in a part of the school no longer used for teaching purposes.

Although the school building was only about twenty years old, part of it had been built with a flat roof. After a few years rain water had started coming through and the room in question soon became unpleasant to work in. The dampness and mould caused the children to be moved into a temporary classroom which had arrived on the back of a lorry and had been deposited in the playground. The education committee had every intention of doing something about the flat-roofed section of the building but in the meantime Mrs Nicholson and her class were permitted to meet there once a week as a temporary measure.

As she walked through the playground Mrs Nicholson noticed Alec Cameron sheltering in the porch, a cloud of smoke around him and that smell which she found rather pleasant. After Miss Shuttleworth's remarks about smoking however, she had no intention of broaching the subject.

"*Feasgar math*," said Mrs Nicholson brightly as she passed through the porch into the room.

Mr Cameron nodded to her, his pipe still in his mouth but said nothing. Not wishing to seem rude, she left the door ajar but he did not follow her in. After she had placed her bag on the desk, she noticed that he'd closed the door behind her. What a strange man, she thought. She wondered if he'd not returned her greeting because he hadn't understood what she'd said. Or maybe he hadn't heard her clearly. That was a problem with some of these older folk, of course. Yet he would insist on sitting at the back of the room. On reflection Mrs Nicholson remembered that on the few occasions when she'd met him in the village and had addressed him in English, he'd reacted in the same silent manner. Yet she'd heard him described by a number of people as a long-winded bore.

One by one the class straggled in. Mrs Nicholson waited a few minutes while they settled down and exchanged a few words with each other. At length she asked no-one in particular,

"Does anyone know if Mr Cameron is coming? I believe I saw him outside a few minutes ago."

"He'll just be finishing his pipe," replied Mrs McKenzie.

"That could take all afternoon," said Miss Shuttleworth briskly. "I suggest we start."

"Maybe I'd better tell him . . . " began Mrs Nicholson but her dithering was interrupted by Alec Cameron's entrance, his pipe dormant. Nodding to her as he passed, he took his seat at the back of the room. Mrs Nicholson looked up at the class. Today she was going to tell them about aspiration. She'd meant to do that last week. In fact she'd intended to start off with it on the opening afternoon but somehow she hadn't got round to it yet. They had discussed many things, certainly, but had not really begun looking at the language yet beyond a few simple words and phrases. Most of the class didn't seem to mind. She'd mentioned this to David.

"I wouldn't worry about it," he'd said. "I expect they see it as a get-together—a nice cup of tea and a chat. It'll make a change from sitting at home—somewhere warm for them too."

"You've become very cynical since we moved here, David. The room certainly isn't warm—it's very damp actually—and there's no cup of tea."

"Isn't there? Well, you should organise one. That'll bring them in in droves."

"But it's supposed to be a language class."

"Oh, there's always room for a bit of that as well. What are they like, anyway?"

"A mixed bunch, really. Some claim to know a bit but I can't say I've seen much evidence yet. Anyway, I've decided we've got to get on with the language this week—whether they like it or not."

They'd both laughed at this.

Mrs Nicholson gathered up the rules of aspiration which she'd written on a sheet of paper and, ever optimistic, had made a dozen photocopies. As she was about to hand them out, Miss Shuttleworth intervened,

"I wonder, just before we start, if you can tell us what that word on the bridge is all about. I'm not sure if I can say it properly but it's spelt, C-E-A-R-T-A-S. I expect you've seen it. Now I've looked it up in my dictionary . . . "—she waved a volume in her left hand—"and it says something about "justice" or "equity". Is that right and if so, what's the point of it?"

Somewhat taken aback Mrs Nicholson set down her sheaf of papers and tried to make the best of this digression.

"Does anyone know? It's not a terribly common word, although you'll meet the adjective quite a lot."

She wrote the word carefully on the board.

"I've heard that it's got something to so with an Irish band," said Maggie Stewart smugly.

"An Irish what?"

"Band. A pop group or something like that."

"Oh. I wondered if you'd said an Irish*word*—a lot of our words are from Irish Gaelic, you know. I think I mentioned that last week. But I don't think it has anything to do with a band. As Miss Shuttleworth says, it simply means*justice*."

"Thank you," said Miss Shuttleworth with an air of earnest triumph. "But what exactly is the point of it?"

"I think it's intended to be some kind of political message, to do with the Scottish National Party, I believe."

Miss Shuttleworth snorted,

"I'm sorry I mentioned it. I thought it might have been something important."

"Well, I think you'll find that's all there is to it," said Mrs Nicholson, glancing at Maggie Stewart as she spoke.

"But there's no reason why it couldn't be the name of a pop group, is there?" insisted Maggie, digging an even deeper hole. "Some of them have such funny names nowadays."

"Umm, well. I don't really know anything about these things . . . "

"What'sh the point of an Irish band here?"

Mrs Nicholson paused, then said,

"I think Mr Cameron has summed it up. There isn't really much point in writing the name of an Irish band on a bridge in Achanult, especially if no-one had heard of them."

"It could be some sort of advertising," said Maggie, reluctant to concede defeat, especially to Miss Shuttleworth.

"Well, maybe. But anyway, looking at it from a purely linguistic point of view, *ceartas* means justice. Now, I'd like to give you all a copy of these notes I've made. All about aspiration."

"Breathing!" boomed Miss Shuttleworth.

"Pardon?"

"Breathing. Isn't that what aspiration means?"

"Oh! Yes, you're probably quite right. What it really boils down to—to keep things as simple as possible—is the use of the letter H. Now you'll find that this is probably the commonest letter in Gaelic since it can feature in almost every word".

"Shnot in that shustice word."

"Which word, Mr Cameron?"

Alec Cameron pointed to the board.

"Oh, not in this instance, it's true. But it could be."

Maggie Stewart nodded vigorously to let everyone think that she was well aware of this.

"Could you explain that, please?" asked Mrs McKenzie, looking a bit sheepish as usual.

"Well, if you all just have a look at this sheet of paper I've given you, we'll start from there."

As everyone turned their attention to the sheet of paper, Mrs Nicholson began to unravel the mysteries of aspiration.

13 Stuck

JEAN answered the door and found their neighbour Donald standing there. She automatically invited him in but as usual, he declined and after exchanging a word or two she shouted to Peter.

"Aye. I just came to see if you were using the ladder," said Donald as Peter came to the door.

"No." Peter couldn't remember when he'd last used it. Probably when some slates were blown off in that storm last spring.

"Ah, well. I thought I might give the chimney a sweep."

Peter's heart sank. And it was a Tuesday as well.

Old Crawford, or Dallan as he was universally known—though nobody could remember why—had swept the chimneys in Achanult since the end of the war. A few years ago he'd decided that he was really too old to be climbing around on roofs and had finally retired. Now a firm from Craigmore came and vacuum swept the Achanult chimneys but Donald wasn't having any of that. So he'd gone off to Oban and bought himself a brush and a set of rods from an ironmonger there, reckoning it would save a lot of time and bother if he did it himself.

He had got the brush up the chimney fine but when he came to pull it down he found that the rods were coming down a lot easier than they had gone up. As he pulled out the last rod he discovered that the brush was missing—it had become unscrewed and was lodged somewhere in the chimney. Donald, who had not foreseen this, pushed the rods up again to see if he could somehow dislodge the brush. When this failed, he'd gone to have a word with Peter, who'd suggested that they have a word with that firm in Craigmore. It appeared however, that the Craigmore people only dealt with unblocked chimneys. So, after some thought, Peter had suggested that Donald try dropping another brush or something from the top to push the first one down.

Next day Donald went off to Oban again and returned with a brush which had a metal ball dangling from it, the whole lot attached to a length of rope. Taking the ladder Donald climbed on to the roof and vigorously dropped the new brush and ball down. When it stopped, although he continued to drop it with considerable force, the new brush refused to go any further. It was only when Peter, who'd been keeping an eye on things from the fireplace end, came out and asked Donald when he was going to start, that they both realised that Donald was dropping his brush and ball down the wrong chimney and the ball was probably sitting in the fireplace of one of the upstairs rooms, which he hadn't used for years.

Once he'd got the correct chimney Donald began again and soon found where the first brush was stuck. By now it had started to rain quite heavily but he continued dropping the brush and ball repeatedly as he gradually pushed down the first brush. It took nearly an hour before Peter was finally able to come out of the house with the first brush in his hand, by which time Donald was soaked.

On his way down off the roof Donald dislodged a couple of slates which slid down and settled in the guttering. This was quite fortunate since they might otherwise have landed on the head of Peter who was watching with interest below. Finding that Donald was not in the best of tempers Peter handed him the first brush and went back to his own house to wash the soot from his hands. Jean, who'd been watching events before the rain started, met him at the door.

"He's too old to be up on roofs, especially in this weather. I'm glad I talked you out of that. Why doesn't he get the vacuum sweep from Craigmore?"

"Well, maybe he will next time. He thinks they wouldn't get all the soot down. He told me he'd be much better doing it himself."

"They got plenty of soot out of ours. Just as much as Dallan used to. What was that rumbling noise I heard?"

"He knocked one or two slates off on the way down."

"What a performance!"

"Och, it's easy done. A lot of the nails are rusty and a wee bit of pressure snaps them. Our roof'll be the same."

The next day it had rained most of the time. So it wasn't until the following day that Donald had managed to get up on the roof again to repair the slates. Peter heard him banging and decided to keep clear.

Peter gave Donald a hand round with the ladder. It was the only thing they shared between them. Although Peter had said often enough in the past that Donald was welcome to use the wheelbarrow or the lawnmower at any time, Donald preferred to have his own.

"You haven't got it stuck again?" asked Peter as they walked up Donald's driveway.

"No, no I just thought I'd do it from the top this year. It's a lot easier really once you're up there."

"I suppose it might be. I was thinking that if you used the rods from the bottom again you could tie a rope to the brush and then pull it down if it came loose from the rods."

This was an idea he'd got from Dallan when he'd mentioned Donald's escapade. Donald himself would never have admitted that anything had gone wrong.

"Och aye, I could have done that but I didn't have a long enough bit of rope."

This was Donald trying to pretend that he'd thought of that himself. For some reason he didn't like Dallan very much and would obviously be reluctant to accept any suggestions of his. He'd probably guessed where Peter had got the idea from.

"You could always tie some short bits together."

"Aye maybe. Knots are apt to loosen though."

Peter gave up. He knew that next year Donald would have got himself a rope and would be sweeping the chimney from the bottom up. From experience he knew already how the conversation would run, more or less. He would say to Donald,

"I see you're sweeping the chimney from the bottom up this year."

"Och yes, it's a lot handier. Saves me having to climb on to the roof. And it doesn't matter what the weather's like either, if you're inside. I've got a fine long bit of rope tied to the brush, so if it comes off, I'll just pull it down."

14 Video

MAGGIE Stewart had made some progress regarding the film or advert for a film, which her brother had mentioned in his letter. She had now discovered from him that the item was shown on Channel 4. This was a blow since Achanult could not yet receive this channel. But Maggie persevered.

Making discreet inquiries, she discovered that the nearest area to receive Channel 4 was Glasgow. She knew one or two people there, of course. And then there were Jim's relatives but they didn't see much of them and Maggie was quite happy to keep things that way. Still, if she could just see the film—or whatever it was—once, she could write a prestigious letter to the local paper making sure that everyone in the village was informed of her scoop.

She toyed with the idea of pretending to have seen it and proceeding from there. This was a tactic which she thought had served her well in the past. But there was a danger. Her brother had mentioned that the item would not necessarily be shown in all regions of the U.K. and that this might be why she hadn't seen it. He obviously didn't know that Channel 4 hadn't yet reached Achanult. Maggie had decided she'd better write to him again.

This was a time of great anxiety for her, temporarily eclipsing her plans for the community association and her promising correspondence with Sir William Kiels-Mather. Unfortunately, she could not really discuss the problem with anyone, since if she did, there was a good chance that the news would be round the whole village in about half an hour. There was Jim, of course, but there was little point in discussing anything with him.

Within a matter of days, Maggie received a reply from her brother.

Dear Margaret,
I think I can solve your problem. I can easily record the advert on a video cassette and send it to you. Tell me the type you want. Mine is VHS but I can arrange something else if it suits you better. I suppose there will be a few video recorders in Achanult now. Everybody's got one here. You'll have to pay me if you want to keep the cassette, if you think it's worth it. If not, just send me it back when you've finished.
Yours again,
Hugh

Maggie put the letter back in its envelope. She wasn't very sure what exactly a video recorder was. But whatever it was, she didn't have one. Still, she could buy one. They must be quite good if everybody in London had one. In any case, someone in her position in the village really ought to have one. She decided to drive to Oban that very afternoon. It wouldn't take long.

Maggie entered the premises of a large television and radio shop which she'd used a few years ago to buy a small transistor radio.

"Good afternoon, madam."

"Good afternoon. I'd like to see a . . . " Here Maggie paused, forgetting the name of the item in question. "Just a minute," she added, pulling Hugh's letter from her pocket while the assistant hovered bemused. ". . . a video recorder. How much is it?"

"Video recorders? They start at £249.95 and go. . ."

"What?"

"£249.95 with a year's guarantee is our cheapest model. Very popular. We've sold a lot of them. Would you like to see it?"

"It's a little bit more than I thought. Can you hire them?"

"Certainly. A lot of our customers prefer to do that."

"So how much would that be?"

"Our rentals start at £15 per month."

"Oh! I wouldn't need it for more than a day or two."

"The minimum rental period is one year, madam."

"A year? What's the point of that? I only want to see one thing."

"I'm sorry. That's how the scheme works. I think you'll find other retailers are roughly similar."

"Well I'll have to think about it. What do they look like anyway?" She'd be better to see what this piece of machinery they were talking about looked like.

On the way back to Achanult, Maggie considered her next move. Buying a video recorder was clearly out of the question. And Jim would have a fit at the price. Look at the struggle she'd had to get him to agree to buying a proper radio, one with VHF. He couldn't see the need for it and claimed to be quite happy with that huge old thing with its limited choice and even worse reception. He still insisted on playing it of course, from time to time—just out of spite.

He was coming round though. At first he would have nothing to do with the new transistor. Then he would play it when she was out. Maggie knew this because when she came to put it on herself, she found he'd switched it off at the wall. When she asked him about this he claimed he was just trying to save electricity. That was a favourite line of his of course. He knew nothing whatsoever about electricity and was convinced that power was being used up whenever a switch was on at the wall even if the apparatus itself was switched off. He'd even gone through a stage of switching off the fridge from time to time when they'd first got it.

By the time she reached Achanult, Maggie had decided that she would have to find someone who had a video recorder. It would have to be the right sort of person of course. It was bad enough having to share her triumph. She would make discreet inquiries. She already had a good idea of the sort of person who might have one—the Miss Shuttleworths of this world.

Any of the incomers really. Maggie didn't fancy cooperating with them. That Miss Shuttleworth was far too bossy for a start. They were all like that, the incomers. Most of them anyway. Mind you, she'd never actually heard any of them mention a video recorder. That was another funny thing about them. She'd never seen one in Achanult either. Not that she was one to pry into other people's affairs. Mind you, now that she knew what these video recorders were, she would know what she was looking for this time. And you really had to look. When she'd got *her* new transistor, she'd automatically put it on the window ledge.

Maggie didn't consider her afternoon by any means wasted. There were always annoying little obstacles to be surmounted. But she generally succeeded in the end. Had the video recorders not been quite so big she might have asked Hugh to bring his up from London. In any case, the New Year was a few weeks off yet. Still, she might mention it to him. She had a feeling though, that her brother wouldn't really appreciate the importance of the matter.

15 Progress

AS USUAL, Mrs Nicholson arrived before everyone else and switched on the lights. She thought she would ask the class today how they thought things were proceeding. Get them involved, David had said. Keeps them interested.

She wondered. Although she hadn't said too much to David, she was a bit disappointed with the way things had gone so far. Most of the class seemed to want to sit and chat about the Highlands and ask her to tell them about Uist, all in English of course. Well, they obviously wouldn't have learnt enough Gaelic yet but at the rate they were going they would never learn very much. It was becoming a bit disappointing. Still, if they were happy . . .

One by one they came in. Miss Shuttleworth had now acquired several books in addition to the small booklet which Mrs Nicholson had suggested the class might use—*Gaelic for Beginners*. She had chosen this particular booklet because she knew it was available in Oban and because it cost only £2. But they hadn't really been able to work from it since not all of them had a copy. Donald Morrison for example, had pointed out that he was reluctant to commit himself to any purchases until he found out how things were going, as he put it. Mrs Nicholson coughed nervously.

"Well, I think we're all here. Now, before we start today, I'd just like you to give me a brief idea of how you feel things are going."

After a pause Miss Shuttleworth said,

"I think we're all quite happy." She turned and looked at the rest of the class. "I'm certainly enjoying myself."

Mrs Nicholson nodded. No-one else spoke.

"Has anyone any suggestions—any ideas we might use?"

Silence. Then Maggie Stewart's voice.

"I think you're doing a wonderful job, Mrs Nicholson. It's important for us with our highland blood to be reminded about our music and literature and . . . um . . . our . . . what's the word? . . . "

"Our culture?" suggested Miss Shuttleworth.

"It's hardly yours."

"No. Quite. I was merely thinking of the word you were looking for."

"Thank you. I don't think we give enough attention to our background these days. Of course, we get all this foreign music on the television now,—English pop music, for instance."

"I suspect that most of it is American," retorted Miss Shuttleworth.

"Just as bad. It's high time we stood up for our own."

Mrs Nicholson decided to intervene.

"Um . . . I wonder if any of the gentlemen have any views?"

Again there was a pause, then . . .

"I've no time for thish pop mushic."

"Ah. Yes. I really meant any views on how the class was progressing."

"Shuits me fine."

"Good. How about you, Mr Morrison?"

Donald frowned, as he always did when anyone asked him a question.

"Well, I would like it if you could give us a few more words and phrases. I'm not so good on the grammar myself but my grandfather and grandmother used to say a few things to me now and again when I was a wee boy. I just can't remember them exactly."

The rest of the class were slightly stunned by Donald's

remarks. Normally you could hardly get a word or two out of him all afternoon.

"Well, you're better off than me," confided Mrs McKenzie. "I can't remember my grandparents at all. Of course my grandfather . . . "

"No," interrupted Donald, frowning again, "the words they used to say. That's what I can't remember."

Mrs McKenzie subsided into embarrassed silence.

"You're like me, Donald," said Maggie. "In fact, most of us have a Gaelic background."

Miss Shuttleworth staightened her back.

"I may not have your background and culture but I'm more than willing to learn about it. That's why I'm here. I think the world would be a better place if we all learnt a little about each other's background."

"Oh, don't get me wrong," said Maggie, bristling. "We're quite willing to learn about the English. In fact, we don't normally have much choice. But this is Argyll we're in now."

"I don't think you've quite grasped my point."

Mrs Nicholson stood up from her chair.

"If I could just interrupt you both there. I think Mr Morrison has raised an interesting point." She turned to Donald. "Have any of the words or phrases you've heard on the wireless for instance, brought back any memories for you?"

Donald frowned.

"I haven't really had time to listen to it very much."

He hadn't in fact listened to any programmes since he could never remember when or where they were on.

"I've tried listening," said Miss Shuttleworth. "I'm afraid it's all Greek to me still. There's an occasional television programme on too. That's a bit better because the pictures give you some idea of what they're talking about. They're on a bit late. That's the only snag."

"Yes they are," agreed Mrs Nicholson. "I've got into the habit of recording them and watching them the next day."

Maggie tried to keep calm. So Mrs Nicholson had a video recorder! This would have to be investigated. But it certainly looked promising. You could say what you liked about Mrs Nicholson, mused Maggie—and many people did—but at least she wasn't a blatant incomer like some of the others. Not a local, of course, but not English either.

Meanwhile, the class continued on its customary course. The mention of television moved someone to ask Mrs Nicholson if she could recall when TV first arrived in Uist. Most of them remembered its arrival in Achanult and a pleasant half hour or so was passed as various members of the class contributed an anecdote or two. They all agreed that Mrs Briggs, a wealthy Englishwoman who had retired to Achanult, had possessed the village's first set. Maggie Stewart claimed to be among the first to have been invited to watch it, which was probably a lie since Mrs Briggs did not mix socially with the locals. But Maggie had told the story so often over the years that she now believed it herself and Mrs Briggs was no longer around to contradict her.

All of this was of great interest to Alec Cameron in his self-appointed role of local historian and he was just warming to a saga about the entertainments in Achanult before the arrival of radio and television when the others suddenly remembered the purpose of their meeting and hastily asked Mrs Nicholson if she could remember the first arrival of radio in Uist.

While the reminiscences continued, Maggie was working out a method of asking Mrs Nicholson about the possible use of her video recorder without having to reveal her purpose in detail. As the class ended, she delayed until the others had finally gone then approached Mrs Nicholson.

"I was very interested to hear abut your video recorder."

"Oh. I haven't had it very long but it's proved quite handy already. Have you got one?"

"Oh no. I don't know that I'd get the use of it."

"Well, you're quite welcome to come and look at any of these Gaelic programmes I record."

"That's very kind of you. What I was really wondering was—well, my brother—he lives in London—wrote to me recently—he's got a video recorder himself, you see and he said there was a short programme I ought to see—I don't know why really, he was a bit vague. Apparently they have programmes down there that we don't get here. So what I was wondering—I don't want him to think I'm not interested—he might be a bit disappointed—but, um . . . of course I don't want to trouble you either . . . if he just sent something up once, do you think I might see it on your video recorder? I'm sure it wouldn't be more than ten minutes or so."

"Certainly. That's no trouble. Ten minutes seems a bit unlikely though. The tapes run for two hours."

"Oh! Maybe I've misunderstood him. Anyway, I'll write to him today about it."

"My machine is a VHS. That's important. Other kinds of tapes won't work—so I'm told. I don't know anything about these things."

"I'll mention that. It's very kind of you," said Maggie, holding the door open for Mrs Nicholson.

As soon as she got home, Maggie wrote a brief note to her brother.

Dear Hugh,

I've now discovered someone here who has a video

recorder. They're not as common up here as you think. So if you send me the cassette, I'll send it back when I've finished. The lady says hers is an NHS model, which she seemed to think was important. I expect you'll understand all about that.

Yours
Margaret.

On her way to post the letter Maggie felt a heightening sense of excitement now that her importance to the village was about to be demonstrated yet again.

16 Minority interest

MRS MAXWELL welcomed Miss Shuttleworth with a nervous laugh and brought her through into the lounge. There were already seven others seated there, sipping the sherry which Mr Maxwell had just dispensed. The only abstainers were the Hastings, who were well known to be teetotal almost to the point of obsession.

After giving Miss Shuttleworth and his wife a sherry, Mr Maxwell poured himself a glass of whisky, aware that the Hastings were watching him, and sat down near the door. Taking a seat by herself in the corner, Mrs Maxwell began.

"We all know each other, of course, don't we?" she enquired brightly.

"I think so," said Mr Hastings solemnly. He was a rather tall, cadaverous figure whom no-one had ever seen smile. Mrs Hastings was a rather prim person, wearing her hat as usual. She was rumoured to wear it in bed but that was just malicious gossip. Mrs Maxwell had thought long and hard about inviting them but as her husband had pointed out, they could hardly invite the minister and his wife without inviting the organist, especially as they were to discuss an arts society and Mr Hastings was quite a talented musician. And of course, they could hardly invite him by himself. Still, with a bit of luck they might all drink too much and the Hastings would leave.

"Right. Well, the reason we've invited you all here, as you already know, of course, is to consider the formation of an arts society. That maybe sounds rather grand. We don't have to call it that but something along these lines, anyway. If we do decide to go ahead, then we would have to do things properly I suppose—a committee, a secretary, treasurer and so on. But first we really ought to see what we all think about it."

Mrs Maxwell paused and looked at the others. Realising that she was still holding her glass of sherry she took a discreet sip and set the glass on the floor at her feet. After a few seconds of silence she added,

"So what does anyone think?"

No-one appeared to think very much so the Rev Nicholson felt it incumbent upon himself to make an effort.

"Um . . . quite. I can see your point, of course. There's certainly room for something along the lines you suggest."

"But what exactly would we do?" asked Miss Shuttleworth, practical as ever.

"Well, our programme, if you want to call it that, can be decided once we've agreed to go ahead," said Mr Maxwell, eager to smooth the discussion along. "I take it we're all in favour of going ahead, then?"

"I feel things are a little vague," said Mrs Hastings, who had never been known for her enthusiasm.

"Yes, quite true," added her husband. "After all, there are

only seven of us which doesn't seem a great deal to go on."

"Eight actually," said Mr Maxwell. "There should have been nine but Mr Winters couldn't manage tonight."

"Why ever not?" asked Miss Shuttleworth. "He never does anything much in the evenings, does he?" She looked at Mrs Maxwell.

"Well, I don't really know," replied Mrs Maxwell uncertainly. "He simply said he couldn't manage tonight."

Shuffling her feet in her confusion Mrs Maxwell kicked over her glass of sherry. She hoped no-one had noticed.

"I think you've spilt the contents of your glass," said Mrs Hastings, who seldom missed anything.

"Oh dear, so I have." Now Mrs Hastings would be convinced she was drunk.

"He did say he was interested though," interjected Mr Maxwell, coming to his wife's rescue.

There was a lull in the conversation. Mr Maxwell took a sip of his whisky.

"Let me refill your glass," he said, aware that the Hastings were making a mental note of the proceedings. While he took his wife's glass into the kitchen, Miss Shuttleworth leaned forward and said authoritatively to Mrs Maxwell,

"Methylated spirits is what you need."

"Pardon?"

"Methylated spirits. Very good for removing wine stains."

"Oh, I see."

"Isn't that so, Mrs Hastings—or have I confused it with something else?"

"I really wouldn't know."

"Well, I've always found it very useful."

"Indeed?"

Mr Maxwell returned with his wife's glass and another

bottle of sherry.

"I've brought another bottle in case anyone else kicks their glass over," he said with a smile. The Hastings looked at each other. Mr Maxwell refilled a couple of glasses and sat down.

"So where were we?"

"Mr Hastings was saying we were rather few in numbers," replied Mrs Maxwell, "which is quite true of course."

Mr Hastings nodded sagely.

"I can see his point of course," began the Rev Nicholson. "I wonder how many others in the village will care to join us?"

"We don't want too many anyway," retorted Miss Shuttleworth.

"Yes I think there's something in that," said Mr Maxwell quickly, relieved that someone had raised this rather delicate point. "I think we've got to be realistic and realise that the arts are a minority interest."

"And the majority have always got the community association to cater for their tastes," added Miss Shuttleworth.

At this point Mrs Nicholson thought that she had better intervene.

"I don't think we should see ourselves as being in competition with the community association. We may not agree with everything they do but in their own way, they make a valid contribution to the village."

"Yes, I think Anna has a point there," said the Rev Nicholson. "I see no reason why there has to be a conflict of interest."

"So you think an arts society would get sufficient support?" asked Miss Shuttleworth.

"Well, we'll have to see. Obviously this is just an exploratory meeting among friends," replied Mr Maxwell. "I suggest that we call a general meeting of all who are interested once we've got some programme of activities in our minds."

"So what ideas have you got?" demanded Miss Shuttleworth.

Mr Maxwell produced a sheet of paper from his jacket pocket.

"I've just jotted down one or two things here which you might like to consider—and of course we can add any other points you all care to mention. I think the first point to make is that if we have a group of a reasonable size we can then get reductions on tickets—for concerts in Glasgow, or whatever. The second point is that it might be possible to get some sort of grant from the region if we can be seen to be contributing to the welfare of the village. I may say that these grants appear to be quite generous—up to £1500."

Murmurs of surprise filled the room.

"But why on earth should the region want to give us a grant?" enquired Mrs Hastings.

"The idea seems to be to help voluntary groups in the area to get underway, especially if they provide services and so on which are otherwise lacking. We can always claim to be interested in Scottish fiddle music or folk songs or something like that, to stress our relevance to the locality."

"If there's going to be anything like that you won't see me there," said Miss Shuttleworth firmly.

"Oh that would only be for the sake of appearances. They're not going to send someone down to check on us are they? Anyway, that's only a suggestion. I don't think we should worry too much about a grant, then it won't matter if we don't get one. Right! Now the other points that I've jotted down.

"Firstly, I think we should make use of our own talents. Now from what my wife tells me—and she knows more about this than me, I must admit—some of you are quite accomplished musicians. So there's no reason why we couldn't contribute something, either individually or as a group. Organise a little musical workshop of our own. And I believe that Mr Hastings is quite an authority on Bach's organ music—so perhaps you could give us a talk on some occasion, with your own musical illustrations."

Mr Hastings looked non-committal.

"Would that be in the church then?" enquired Miss Shuttleworth. "I only ask because I've heard it's rather cold there in the winter."

"And in the summer," added Mrs Hastings with a laugh that quickly faded as no-one else joined in.

"How does the church come into it?" asked Mrs Bates who hadn't said a word all evening. As usual, she had been trying to think of something apt to say as the discussion progressed but her courage always failed her at the last minute. Now on her second glass of sherry, she had finally broken through.

"I think if Mr Hastings is going to illustrate Bach's organ music, he will need an organ," replied Miss Shuttleworth witheringly.

"Of course, there's a piano in the village hall," said Mrs Nicholson.

"Perhaps that's not quite suitable for Mr Hastings' purpose," mused her husband. He looked across at Mr Hastings.

"There are of course, certain technical differences," intoned Mr Hastings. "And everyone knows that Bach did not write for the modern piano. Still . . . "

"Ah, but did he write for the modern organ?" interrupted Miss Shuttleworth.

"Um . . . not as such . . . although . . . um . . . "

"I think," said Mr Maxwell hastily, "that all of this would make a very interesting topic for Mr Hastings to talk to us about, once we get established."

Mr Hastings nodded gravely.

"I'm beginning to see the possibilities of all this," said Mrs Bates, encouraged by the upheaval her question had caused.

"That's good," said Mr Maxwell, circulating with the sherry bottle. "And of course, music is only one part of it. No doubt some others who're not here tonight will have some ideas of their own too."

"That could be a problem," said Miss Shuttleworth.

"Well, we don't want to prejudge issues. Let's just wait and see."

It was agreed to hold an introductory general meeting in a fortnight's time. That settled, the Hastings departed as they always did, before any of the others. There was a general feeling that it had been a profitable meeting and the Rev Nicholson agreed with his wife as they walked home that there need not necessarily be a conflict with the community association. To be on the safe side however, it might be better if he withdrew from the community association committee, whilst continuing to support it from the sidelines, in the interests of impartiality. For similar reasons he felt he should not be seen to be too involved with this new arts society if and when office bearers were required.

17 Vanity

MR NICHOLSON handed the letter to his wife with a sigh and poured himself another cup of tea. She read quickly through it.

"Didn't they have something like this in Edinburgh?" she asked.

"I seem to recall something like that but I don't think I was ever much involved in it."

"As I remember, there was quite a lot of fuss about it."

"Possibly, possibly. There would certainly have been no shortage of volunteers. It'll be different here. Churches are a bit thin on the ground."

"Oh well, I suppose it will make a change."

"Hmm . . . "

"Or have you something against the whole idea of an ecumenical service, David?"

"Oh no. Not at all. I'm all in favour, naturally. I've always said as much."

"Yes. I suppose if we can't be seen to show tolerance and mutual understanding, then how can we expect others to?"

"Exactly. Mind you, these things can't be rushed here. There's not the same atmosphere as in Edinburgh. I should think you'd have to proceed far more carefully here. We'll have to see what some of the others think."

"I imagine they'll feel much the same as you do, David."

"Yes, I suppose so. I expect I'll be hearing from some of them. Of course, there may still be some hostility to the idea. After all, there has been a history of hostility—or indifference, at best—in the Highlands as a whole. So I don't think we can just rush straight in."

"But surely that's all in the past?"

"I wonder. I suspect that some of our colleagues in the Free Church may not take kindly to the idea of being preached at by say, a Roman Catholic priest—or vice-versa."

"Oh, does it involve them too?"

The Rev Nicholson had another look at the letter.

"It doesn't actually name names. Just general remarks about ecumenicism and unity. Actually, the more I think about it, the more I have my doubts."

He put the letter down. It was all a bit unnecessary really. Things were going along quite quietly—no great difficulties of any sort—so why create potential problems? The Rev Nicholson had always felt that too much enthusiasm was a bad thing and here was yet another example. Most people were surely happy with things the way they were, so why not just keep it that way?

"Well, I must admit I can't see anything wrong with it," said Mrs Nicholson.

"Oh, there's nothing wrong with it in principle, I'm just being a bit cautious."

"But I still don't see what harm it would do. Surely you wouldn't mind preaching in, say, an Episcopalian church, just on the one occasion would you? It is only a one-off, isn't it?"

"So they say in the letter but you never know what this sort of thing might lead to."

"Christian unity?"

"Exactly! Um, not that I've anything against that. Of course not. It's a fine idea but we have to be realistic."

"So what are you going to do then?"

"I think I'll wait and see what happens. We don't really want to rush into anything as I've learnt in the past."

Mrs Nicholson, who could not recall the last time her husband had rushed into anything, wondered briefly about asking him what event he had in mind. Instead, she said,

"You could write a few words about it in the local paper."

"Ye-es, possibly. The only snag with that might be that some people could think that I was trying to get my side of the story, or my point of view, if you prefer, across first. In any case, the local paper as good as told me that they didn't really want items of a religious nature."

There was a grain of truth in this, although it would have been fairer to say that the editor, with the wisdom of years behind him, had realised that the Rev Nicholson was not excited at the thought of contributing a weekly article, so had been quite prepared to do without it for the time being. Both men were well aware that few things are more permanent than temporary arrangements and there the matter had rested.

In any case, the minister found that he had less and less time available because of his increasing interest in crossword puzzles. Since moving to Achanult this had become a major preoccupation. Indeed, there were times when he had to admit to himself that it was almost an obsession. As a result, he was becoming quite good at them and was considering taking an extra daily paper to cater to his increasing appetite. His wife, who had never done crosswords, viewed all this as a harmless eccentricity and indeed welcomed it as solving the annual present problem. She occasionally thought that her husband perhaps spent a little too much time at it, particularly on a Sunday, but provided he was discreet she supposed it was all right. Mr Nicholson was more than usually obsessed with crosswords at the moment because he had qualified to take part in a crossword competition organised by one of the national newspapers.

The next step was to take part in a regional final for which he was due to go to Glasgow in a fortnight's time. Consequently he felt that he ought to be practising more than ever and as a result, viewed distractions—such as this latest letter about ecumenicism—with some alarm. Normally he would ask his wife to look into such things since he was a great believer in the equality of women and prided himself on encouraging them to take part in running church matters whenever possible. But this was something he would have to deal with himself. Later.

Removing the middle pages of the newspaper, he handed them to his wife and turned his attention to the back page, which contained the crossword. Looking at his watch he wrote the time on the page. He had never completed the crossword in less than half an hour which, according to the paper, a good percentage of readers could. But he was improving. In his study was a sheet of paper detailing the times taken to complete the crossword over the last two months. Sometimes of course, he was unable to solve all the clues. But the gradual reduction in time encouraged him greatly. He turned to one across:

"We eased out fertiliser"

The Rev Nicholson paused for a moment, then wrote "seaweed". That was easy! If only they were all as simple as that he would finish in five minutes. Then he remembered.

"Oh, by the way, Anna, there was a chap telephoned yesterday when you were out asking if we wanted some seaweed delivered."

"Seaweed?"

"Something to do with the garden apparently."

"Oh yes, of course."

"Anyway, I don't think I'll have time to do anything with the garden so I had to decline his offer. I told him you weren't too happy about the smell and the general mess."

"What? David, it's lovely stuff."

"In the sea, yes."

"We used it all the time in Uist—still do. I wish you hadn't mentioned me. He'll think I've grown posh or something. Who was it anyway?"

"I can't actually remember."

"Well, I hope it's nobody we know, although there's little

chance of that here. Really! Everybody knows that seaweed is good for the garden. Miss Shuttleworth puts it on her roses."

"She would."

"What do you mean? Why shouldn't she?"

"Simply that when people such as Miss Shuttleworth decide to go native they're liable to become more highland than the Highlanders, if you see what I mean."

"Not really."

"Well, all this nonsense about seaweed. And then she's learning Gaelic too, isn't she? She's probably got a whisky still in her garden shed as well. Anyway I didn't realise you felt so strongly about seaweed. I suppose we can think about it next year if you want. I don't really think it's something I want to get too involved in. I don't see me having a lot of time for such a big garden."

"We can always get somebody to dig it."

"Possibly. But then there's the grass. Of course, we can get a gardener but that costs money."

"We really need to discuss the garden, you know. After all the work Mr Neil put into it, we can't just let it go wild."

"I can see your point but it's a question of priorities. Ministers are expected to have other things on their minds. But we can discuss it later."

The Rev Nicholson returned to his crossword, looked at his watch and wrote a new time on the page.

His wife, recognising that the conversation was at an end, got up from the table and took the breakfast dishes through to the kitchen. The kitchen was at the back of the house and looked out on to the garden. Mrs Nicholson gazed out of the window as the drizzle gently fell. The grass looked sodden and the soil was probably too wet to dig at the moment. She would discuss it with David later and plan a labour-saving garden. It was quite a challenge really but she'd always wanted a big garden and now here it was! She wished David would show a little more enthusiasm sometimes. He would probably just leave it up to her, as usual. Of course, being a minister was a full-time job and David spent hours in his study each day.

18 Company

AFTER a few uncharacteristic moments of doubt, Miss Shuttleworth was sure that she had done the right thing. It was very difficult of course, but she had finally made up her mind and had written to Jennifer last week inviting her to spend Christmas with her in Achanult. At the time of her visit a few weeks ago, Miss McLachlan had been dropping broad hints about how undesirable it was to spend Christmas alone and how pleasant it was to see an old friend again.

Miss Shuttleworth ignored this. After all, although Miss McLachlan was about to retire shortly and would have to move out of her hospital accommodation, there was no reason, Miss Shuttleworth presumed, why she should not do as she herself had done and find a nice little bungalow somewhere peaceful.

After her friend's departure however, she began to consider the matter seriously and even entertained the possibility of inviting Miss McLachlan to move in with her so that the two of them could live in retirement together. There were many reasons that had led her to consider this somewhat drastic step and while she had not yet made up her mind, she was gradually tending to the view that it might be a good idea. With her usual methodical efficiency she had adopted her normal device for dealing with a difficult decision. Taking a sheet of paper, she had drawn a line down the middle of it. At the top of the page on the left hand side, she had written the word PROS, and on the right hand side CONS. The first item in the left hand column was "money". There was no doubt that an extra source of income would be welcome. She didn't know Jennifer's financial position of course, but no doubt it was rather similar to her own, in which case that would solve several small problems.

Miss Shuttleworth had always intended to travel a bit when she retired and rather fancied a few holidays in exotic locations. And now her attendance at the Gaelic class had inspired her with an interest to visit the Western Isles. But even this, she soon discovered, did not come cheap for all its proximity. Another point was that Miss Shuttleworth had a dislike of the sea based on her single experience of it—a rather rough crossing of the English Channel in a ferry that seemed to be full of drunken football fans. Constant references at the Gaelic class to the "experience" of crossing the Minch only reinforced her doubts. She had also been surprised to find that she could fly more cheaply to several European destinations than to the Outer Hebrides. Miss Shuttleworth had a reasonable income, naturally, one which many of the locals would have thought quite lavish had they known. But none did, not even Maggie Stewart, who nevertheless had announced that Miss Shuttleworth had retired on a pension of £8000 per annum.

The cost of living in Achanult had proved greater than Miss Shuttleworth had anticipated. Houses of course, were very cheap which had inevitably led her to buy one that was really too big for her and of course the garden was quite large too. It was the other expenses that she resented. The need to travel everywhere for any decent kind of shopping or other services and entertainment meant that she had to do far more driving than she had expected. Petrol prices were an outrage of course. And the roads—the last bill for her car had been a bit of a shock! There was a bus service certainly, as Miss Shuttleworth well knew since she had been a leading figure in the campaign to retain it. She herself however, had no intention of using a bus.

So that was the financial situation. Underneath "money" she had written, after much hesitation, "company". There was no doubt that there were times when she would welcome the company of a friend of similar background and education. Life could be quite isolated at times in Achanult from an intellectual point of view and of course, she had little in common with most of the inhabitants.

Other more mundane points had to be considered. If she should fall ill for instance it would be useful to have someone at hand. She eventually excluded that from her reckoning however, since she had no intention of becoming ill.

On the social front, Achanult was hopeless really even although Miss Shuttleworth felt she had made a great effort. She continued to attend Mrs Nicholson's Gaelic class although mastering a new language was only one of the problems there. The presence of some other members of the class was not really conducive to learning since they seemed to make little effort. Although she naturally would not have expected to have anything much in common with most of them, she was nonetheless disappointed at their general attitude.

Last week's brief discussion of house names was typical. When Maggie Stewart—that awful woman—had had an argument with someone else—Mrs McKenzie wasn't it? strange woman—about the spelling of a house name at the south end of the village, Mrs Nicholson had pointed out that most Gaelic house names in the village were wrongly spelt. Miss Shuttleworth already knew this of course, but the rest of the class didn't seem to think it was of any importance one way or the other. Although this indifference to literacy astonished and annoyed Miss Shuttleworth, she had maintained an uncharacteristic silence during the discussion, slightly embarrassed by the recent history of her own bungalow.

When she had first arrived in Achanult and bought the bungalow, it was called Chirnanogg, a name that the previous owners—an elderly couple who were moving to somewhere nearer their daughter in Edinburgh—had retained when they had bought it. They'd been told it was Gaelic for "Land of the Young" or "Land of Eternal Youth" or something like that. Miss Shuttleworth had no time for any of this nonsense and promptly changed its name to Fairview. This was an eminently reasonable thing to do she felt, since not only did it have the advantage of being in English, it also made sense. A large wooden sign with the name Fairview duly went up on the gate. From time to time however, she noticed that the locals still referred to the house by its previous name which infuriated her. She was quite sure that they did it on purpose and so she ignored them.

Since her recent interest in Gaelic however, Miss Shuttleworth rather regretted her haste and once she had discovered how to spell *Tir nan Og*, she was tempted to change the name back again in spite of the upheaval this would cause. There was a magic quality, she had to admit, to the name and to the imagery which lay behind it. Fairview now seemed rather flat and unimaginative. It was really her embarrassment which held her back, since all her life she had seen herself as someone who took decisions, difficult and unpleasant though they might be, and stuck to them.

Realising that putting the original name back, properly spelt of course, would give the village—especially that awful Maggie Stewart—something to laugh at, she eventually decided that her friend Miss McLachlan might be used to provide a suitable pretext. If Jennifer were, after all, to come and live with her, Miss Shuttleworth could claim that the name Fairview had unpleasant associations for her friend. There would be no need to go into details particularly since most of the village would be itching to know what exactly these unpleasant memories were. Jennifer would naturally have to be made aware of the Machiavellian minds at work in Achanult and the need to remain one step ahead all the time. But this could easily be done and would give the pair of them considerable satisfaction. So Miss Shuttleworth had written "house name" in the PROS column.

There was only one entry in the CONS column—the word "peace", after which she had written *sith* in brackets, in an attempt to extend her Gaelic vocabulary. This was a habit she had lately adopted to replace her earlier system which had consisted of pieces of paper pinned to objects in the room with the name of the object written in Gaelic. Soon the house was festooned with bits of paper pinned to doors, locks, keys, walls, windows, lights, chairs, tables, pictures, beds and so on. As a result Miss Shuttleworth soon recognised these words when she met them in print, even if she did remain uncertain how to pronounce them.

The impending arrival of Miss McLachlan a few weeks earlier had brought this system to a sudden end, for not only was Miss Shuttleworth uncertain as to her friend's reaction to her interest in Gaelic, she also had no wish to appear unduly eccentric. She had not replaced the pieces of paper but wrote down words here and there from time to time as something caught her interest.

What she had meant by "peace" was the lack of it. Looking back, there were undoubtedly occasions when Jennifer had disturbed, even irritated her. Her insistence on the severity of the weather in Achanult was a case in point. Miss Shuttleworth found the climate bracing and expected everyone else to do likewise. Still, Jennifer would soon find out about the weather for herself. Miss Shuttleworth wasn't too sure about some of her friend's other faults, such as her habit of talking rather a lot. She did not like people who talked too much—such as that awful Maggie Stewart—but at least Jennifer's accent was reasonably acceptable. There were of course, other drawbacks to Miss McLachlan, such as her appalling dress sense but Miss Shuttleworth was content to leave that till later.

So for the moment the PROS outweighed the CONS although she would be sure to think of something else. It was better to keep the entries on the sheet as vague as possible in case Miss McLachlan came across them. What was really worrying however, was how to get rid of Jennifer if the experiment proved to be unsuccessful. But Miss Shuttleworth instinctively knew that she would be quite capable of handling such a situation.

19 Deaf as a post

EVENTS had moved at their customary speed in Achanult and at last, a meeting was being held in the village hall to discuss the proposed school closure. There was a very small attendance since, curiously enough, none of the parents who had children at the school turned up. The old familiar faces however, trooped into the hall where Mrs Nicholson was waiting nervously.

Her husband had been asked to chair the meeting but had found his time occupied with ecumenical matters. There was to be an exploratory meeting of the clergy tomorrow—which Mr Nicholson had completely forgotten about, his mind being on other things—so he'd decided that he'd better spend the evening at home considering his response to the question. He had already decided that he was broadly in favour although, of course, the present system was reasonably satisfactory and they should not rush into any precipitate decisions.

A large number of chairs had been set out but only the front two rows had any occupants.

"I wonder," began Mrs Nicholson, fumbling with a sheaf of papers, "if we should begin. Or is anyone else coming, do you think?"

Various people in the room looked at each other. Maggie Stewart, who was keen to get things started so that she could produce her letter from the House of Commons and hint at a productive correspondence with Sir William Kiels-Mather, said, hoping to appear nonchalant,

"We could maybe just wait for a minute or two."

"Oh, let's get on with it." said Miss Shuttleworth. "I can't afford to stay too long. I realise you probably think I shouldn't be here anyway since the closure of the school is hardly likely to affect me but I thought you might like to hear what Sir William, our M.P., has been saying to me about it."

Maggie hoped that no-one noticed her sudden flush of annoyance. So Miss Shuttleworth had been in touch with Sir William! Who did she think she was? It had nothing to do with her. Maggie felt herself going redder by the second.

"I hope," began Mrs Baines, who saw herself as a friend to Maggie. "I hope," she repeated, "that some of us are here from a sense of duty and whether we are personally affected by the issue doesn't matter. We're here for the general good of the village. It's just a pity some others can't be bothered to take an interest."

This remark was greeted by a feeble sprinkling of applause from three or four people which quickly tailed off. Mrs Nicholson thought she'd better say something.

"I'm sure that's right. It *is* a pity that none of the parents of the schoolchildren seem to be here. Maybe they felt that there was nothing that they could do at this stage. I was also hoping to have one of the Education Officers here tonight to discuss things and answer any questions. Unfortunately, no-one was able to manage . . . "

"Why not?" interrupted Miss Shuttleworth.

"Umm . . . I think it was rather short notice and they . . . um . . . may have had other commitments."

Miss Shuttleworth snorted.

"However," continued Mrs Nicholson who had always felt that anything to do with education should be treated with the greatest of respect, "I, or rather my husband actually, have—or should that be has?—received a letter from the education department stating the main arguments for their case."

"We all know what their arguments are already," said Maggie, whose colour had more or less returned to normal.

"I think you might as well read the letter to us," ordered Miss Shuttleworth.

"Yes, I'll do that now," said Mrs Nicholson, taking the top sheet of paper up in her hand. After glancing at it she said,

"Oh dear. This isn't it. It was on top a minute ago."

She searched frantically through her sheaf of papers.

"I'm sure it's here somewhere." One or two papers fell to the floor. "I know I haven't left it at home." Eventually she found the letter at the bottom of the pile. Her embarrassment slowly subsided and with a little cough, she began to read.

When she had finished, Miss Shuttleworth said,

"Well, that's a lot of help!"

Mrs Nicholson smiled weakly.

"Why don't we send them a letter?" ventured Mrs Baines. "That was really very one-sided."

"Ye-es. I thought we might perhaps let them know of our views. That's really why we're here tonight, of course. If we could make a list of our objections to the points raised in the letter . . . "

"Well, for a start, that's a lot of nonsense about Dalmory being a better environment for the children—whatever that means," asserted Maggie. "They're much better off here where it's quieter. The traffic in Dalmory is terrible and the school's not far from the main Glasgow road."

"Well, um, yes. Of course they'll say that the children will be supervised all the time."

"Well," continued Maggie, "I was in Dalmory just a couple of weeks ago and the traffic was awful. These heavy lorries! One of them screeched to a halt just beside me with that awful noise from the brakes. I can tell you I was literally petrified."

"Really?" queried Miss Shuttleworth. "That must have been an interesting experience. Quite painful, I imagine."

"Exactly. And just imagine how much worse it would be for young children. So that's *one* point we should emphasise."

Various other points were raised and discussed during the next half hour and were duly noted by Mrs Nicholson. As they began going over the same ground yet once more, she said as she tidied her bundle of papers,

"I think I've got all the points that we want to make. I'll get my husband to send off a letter as soon as possible. So, unless anyone has something else to add, I think we could leave things like that for the moment."

"Hasn't Miss Shuttleworth got something to tell us from our MP?" asked Alice who enjoyed meetings of any kind and went to as many as she could.

Everyone except Maggie had forgotten about this. Mrs Nicholson looked queryingly over the top of her bundle of papers.

"Ah yes," began Miss Shuttleworth. "I'd almost forgotten. That's really why I came tonight. I've been discussing one or two things with Sir William recently and I just happened to mention the proposed school closure."

She delved into her handbag.

"Now which is the letter that mentions the school? Yes, it's this one, the most recent one."

She ran her eyes down the page, then on to the second sheet.

"Here it is. I don't know whether he would want to be quoted but the gist of his remarks is that the education authority are not necessarily serious about closing this school. If they want to close, say, two schools in the region, they'll mention that they're considering closing six and allow four to be 'saved' by parental pressure or whatever."

"What on earth is the point of that?" asked Maggie rapidly losing her regard for Sir William.

"Well, I think it's obvious. People imagine they've achieved a great victory saving a majority of the threatened schools. The authority gives the impression of bowing to local democracy and finds it much easier to close two schools which is all it really wanted to do in the first place."

"You don't expect us to believe that, do you?" asked Maggie with a somewhat artificial laugh.

"It does seem a bit, um, cynical," said Mrs Nicholson. "I suppose Sir William does know what he's talking about." she added doubtfully. "Of course, I haven't met him. We've only been here just over a year now."

There was a pause in the conversation. Miss Shuttleworth had put her letter back in her handbag and seemed to be ready to leave when Alice said,

"But what happens if we're one of the two schools?"

"Exactly!" added Maggie emphatically, wishing she had thought of that. Alice could be quite useful sometimes. She must try to mend a few fences.

"You mean what if we're one of the schools they *really* intend to close?" asked Mrs Nicholson, resuming her worried look.

"I don't think you have to worry about that," said Miss Shuttleworth dismissively. "Sir William obviously doesn't think we are. He feels we shouldn't have anything to worry about."

"Well, that's nice of him," retorted Maggie hotly. "I suppose we're just wasting our time, in that case."

"I didn't say that. I think you're quite right to protest as loudly as possible, just in case."

"Just in case what? Sir William might be wrong—is that what you mean?"

"What I mean is that Sir William has given us some advice but the education authorities are a law to themselves."

"And they know more about it than he does. He's never here. I don't suppose he's ever been near the school—probably doesn't even know where it is. So how can he know anything?"

"Decisions of this nature are not made in Achanult and even Glasgow may be influenced by the government's guidelines, you know. I expect Sir William has heard something somewhere."

"Huh. He's as deaf as a post, or so I've been told."

Miss Shuttleworth ignored this last remark, leaving Mrs Nicholson to say,

"Well, perhaps we should leave it at that for the moment."

When she got home Maggie's first reaction was to throw Sir William's letter on the fire but she thought better of it and put it at the back of a drawer. In spite of herself she couldn't help wondering what Miss Shuttleworth had been discussing with Sir William. Much as she tried, she couldn't convince herself that it was all lies. She would have to find out.

20 Don't blink!

WHEN Maggie returned from the shop a small parcel was lying on the kitchen table. Jim must have put it there. So he was up now, or had been.

As soon as she recognised the writing Maggie knew that the long-awaited video had arrived. Not knowing quite what to expect she opened the parcel gingerly and eventually found a rectangular plastic box. With it was a note from Hugh.

Video of Achanult enclosed. If you blink you'll miss it. I'm not sure now whether I'll manage up at the New Year but if not, you can send me it back. But keep it in the meantime.
Hugh.

In the afternoon Maggie set off for the manse. The door was

opened by the Rev Nicholson.

"Ah, good afternoon, Mr Nicholson. Is Mrs Nicholson in?"

"Yes, I think so. I believe she's with someone at the moment."

"Oh. Maybe I should come back later?"

"No, no. It's nothing important. Something about Gaelic, I think."

"Oh?"

"Yes, a young man who's going to sing at the Mod. Some advice on pronunciation apparently. All above my head, I'm afraid."

The Rev Nicholson smiled vaguely, then remembered that his wife had mentioned Maggie's presence at her afternoon class.

"Of course, you'll understand all about these things, Mrs Stewart."

Maggie gave him a patronising smile.

"Well, I suppose you could say that. I used to understand it fine when I was a child but I seem to have forgotten a bit of it now. I'm sure Mrs Nicholson must have said as much to you."

"I can't . . . I don't think so," said the minister warily, suddenly remembering his wife's remark that Maggie knew next to nothing. "I'll just see if she's nearly finished."

He retreated into the house. After waiting a few seconds Maggie began to examine the fur collar of a coat hanging in the hallway. She hadn't seen Mrs Nicholson wearing that before. It was real fur too. Of course she wouldn't really have expected otherwise. A bit old-fashioned, maybe. Some of these photographs looked quite interesting too. Just as she was peering at the small print in the bottom corner of one of the photographs—a group of young men—Mr Nicholson returned.

"Ah! You're admiring my photographs. That's one from my

college days."

"I assumed that's what it was," lied Maggie, somewhat flustered. "I was just wondering if I could spot you."

The Rev Nicholson placed his finger on the glass.

"A long time ago of course. I looked quite different then."

"Well, we're none of us getting any younger," laughed Maggie.

"Quite true, quite true. My wife will be with you in a minute."

"Oh, there's no hurry."

"Well, do come into the kitchen. It's warmer there."

"I hope I'm not disturbing you. I know how busy you are," added Maggie as an afterthought.

"No, no. I wasn't doing anything terribly urgent."

In fact the Rev Nicholson had been doing a crossword puzzle to which he was anxious to return. He had timed his start as usual which was slightly irrelevant now. But his train of thought had gone too. Although he'd been thinking about one of the clues while Maggie had been talking. This was a habit he'd recently acquired and one of its unfortunate consequences was that often his mind was not concentrated on whatever was being said to him. As a result, he frequently had to ask people to repeat things and there was now a belief in the village that he was growing deaf.

Just then there was the sound of voices in the hall as Mrs Nicholson escorted young Mr Smith to the front door. Returning, she found Maggie alone in the kitchen.

"I'm sorry to keep you waiting, Mrs Stewart."

"Not at all. It's very good of you to see me. I know how busy you are."

"Not really. I was just helping Mr Smith for the Mod."

"Yes, Mr Nicholson told me. How's he getting on?"

"We-ell . . . He has a very good voice, of course. It's really the pronunciation we're working on. He's not finding it too easy but he tries very hard. Have *you* ever competed at the Mod, Mrs Stewart?"

"No. Singing was never one of my better accomplishments. Although, having said that, we were always singing Gaelic songs when I was young—ceilidhs and that sort of thing, you know."

"You must know quite a lot of the songs, then."

"Yes, I suppose I did at that time. I've forgotten most of them now."

"Maybe we should look at one or two songs at the class?"

"Yes, that would be a good idea."

"Well, I'll see what the others think. Now . . . um . . . "

"I've come with the tape."

Maggie produced it from the depths of her shopping bag which formed the first line of defence against the prying eyes of Achanult. Mrs Nicholson looked blank.

"Don't you remember? I mentioned it at the class a couple of weeks ago."

"Oh. Yes, that's right. Well, we'd better go through to the sitting room."

"Hughie—that's my brother who sent it—says it's to do with Achanult. But he says it's very short."

"Well, let's see then."

Mrs Nicholson put the cassette into the machine, switched on the television and pressed another button. In due course a picture appeared—a car with an oriental driver patting the bonnet and then the name of a car dealer in London.

"It's been recorded a little too early," smiled Mrs Nicholson. "These are just the adverts."

Then the picture changed again to a wet street with damp

looking pedestrians scurrying along it. A voice made some remark to the effect that what kept them going was the thought of a bowl of hot highland soup. The scene changed to a view of the sea with a close-up of raindrops falling on the waves. Then there was a picture of a family sitting round a table, with a warm fire in the background, contentedly supping soup while the same voice announced the makers. Then a young lady appeared and began to read a list of programmes which were to come later that evening. Halfway through her second sentence she was cut short and the screen went a fuzzy white.

They both watched the fuzz for nearly a minute before Mrs Nicholson said,

"Maybe it's further on in the tape. I'll just fast-forward it."

After a couple of minutes she stopped.

"No sign of it yet. Should I just fast-forward it right to the end?"

"Well, if you want," replied Maggie, who was unfamiliar with the term "fast-forward".

"Maybe," she added, "It's on the other side."

"Pardon?"

"The other side of the tape—like a cassette—or a record."

"Video cassettes only have one side, I'm afraid. Is it possible that your brother might have sent the wrong one?"

Maggie thought that was quite possible.

"Surely he wouldn't have been so silly," she said with a little laugh.

"Well, I'll just fast-forward it to the end to make sure."

They sat and gazed at the machine in silence. Eventually there was a click from the machine and Mrs Nicholson said,

"That's the end of the tape now. I don't know what's happened."

Maggie knew. While the tape was being fast-forwarded she

had had to come to a quick decision. She could agree with Mrs Nicholson that this must be the wrong tape and disappear with it as quickly as possible. This course would deprive her of the glory of being the person responsible for bringing a glimpse of Achanult to its inhabitants.

So without too much hesitation, Maggie adopted the alternative decision. The village would be greatly disappointed of course, to put it mildly. The worst of it was that all of her friends would feel let down, since they'd been the ones who'd paid all the attention at the time. The incomers had given the impression of not being particularly concerned, though Maggie knew that it was only a bit of snobbery on their part. Old Mrs MacPhail , who waved cheerfully every time any of the film crew or their van passed her door —which was several times a day—would no doubt be furious. But Maggie didn't care about her.

What she would do then, would be to make the best of a bad situation and present the video to her friends as an example of the sort of insult to be expected from people who didn't know Achanult and who came here and tried to make fools of us. Then she would write a strong letter to the local paper about it—in her capacity as secretary of the community association—and maybe a letter to the Glasgow Herald as well, though they hadn't printed the last—and only—letter she'd sent them.

That was the time when that French family, who were spending a few days in Achanult, had parked their funny looking car illegally, partly on the road and partly on the pavement about half a mile from Maggie's house. When they did it again the next day, Maggie sprang into action, happy to fight an issue which would allow her to be seen as a defender of the rights of Achanult against incomers, especially English and other foreigners. The Glasgow Herald had thanked her for her letter but regretted that they did not feel that it was of sufficient interest to their readers nationwide. And by way of insult they'd had the cheek to add that foreigners sometimes did things differently and that tolerance and , more importantly, tourism were to be encouraged. The local paper, however, had printed her letter.

"I think," said Maggie, "we'd better look at that bit at the beginning of the tape again."

21 Christmas tea

IT HAD been a long standing custom that the community association should provide a Christmas tea for the old folk in the village. This took place in the village hall, generally on a Wednesday afternoon. It was a very informal occasion, just tea and home baking provided by members of the association.

The affair was slightly overshadowed this year by transport difficulties. Bringing some of the older people to the hall required the co-operation and the cars of members of the association and the committee were expected to see to the arrangements which usually meant doing the driving themselves. This year however, Alice's little Fiat and Mr Hastings' Rover were both unavailable due to the fact that they had collided with each other the previous Saturday and were a bit damaged, although neither of the drivers was hurt. The accident had caused quite a stir in the village and quite a number of people had their own views on what had happened and who was to blame. This lent the incident a certain amount of colour which was much needed, since no-one apart from the drivers had actually witnessed the crash. So as usual, there would be three sides to the issue—Alice's, Mr Hastings' and the truth, which was that both drivers had been going a little too fast as they approached each other at a bend in the single track road which wound round the back of the village. It had been raining quite heavily, otherwise they might have been able to stop in time.

For many years Mr Hastings had been complaining about local motorists who drove around as if they owned the place and the accident merely strengthened his view. He had become more lugubrious than ever in the few days since the accident.

Alice also had little to say, which was quite surprising to those who knew her. Normally she would have ensured that her version of events was widely circulated in Achanult. This time she invoked a clause in her insurance policy which indicated that she should not admit anything. Alice took this to mean that she should make no comment. No-one was fooled by this of course and there was much speculation over Alice's reticence. Various views were put forward, including Maggie's opinion that Alice was suffering from delayed shock. No-one except Maggie and Alice knew the truth, which was that Alice had been on her way home from Maggie's house when the accident happened. While chatting with Maggie earlier she had drunk a glass of sherry—since it was the festive season—and although this was unlikely to have made any difference to her driving, Alice was nevertheless a bit worried. As it happened, it was not felt necessary to call the police since the damage was solely to the cars—more spectacular than serious, both sets of headlights smashed,—and especially since the nearest policeman lived about fifteen miles away and neither Mr Hastings nor Alice—particularly Alice—felt like hanging around till he arrived.

On the day after the accident Alice paid another visit to Maggie, this time on foot, on the pretext of clarifying arrangements for the community association's Christmas tea. As they both well knew however, she was also there to suggest to Maggie that it might be wiser if no mention was made of her glass of sherry the previous afternoon. Maggie protested that she would never dream of mentioning it to a living soul— which they both knew was a lie—but it was clear to Alice that she had better keep on the right side of Maggie for the next few weeks at least.

The Christmas tea went quite well although there was inevitably a slight hiccup over the transport. Alice helped with the tea as usual. As she refilled Mr Gray's cup, he asked quietly,

"Are we allowed to smoke in here?"

"Of course. Why shouldn't you?"

"Oh. I thought it wasn't allowed."

"Of course it is."

"Nobody else seems to be."

Alice looked around the hall.

"Well, it's maybe a bit early yet. Oh look, there's Maggie with her cigarette as usual."

"It's different for her, though."

"How?"

"She runs this do, doesn't she? I mean, she's in charge."

Alice swallowed her pride.

"In a way . . . I suppose so."

"So she can do what she likes. Anyway, if you say it's OK . . . It's just that I'd heard that they were going to ban smoking in here."

"Oh, well, there was some suggestion like that I believe, but I always say you've got to respect the rights of the individual."

Mr Gray nodded and held the packet towards Alice.

"No thanks."

Towards the end of the proceedings a photographer from the local paper paid his annual visit. Maggie made sure she was in a prominent position in every shot. The photographer, a young local lad whose mother was from time to time a friend of Maggie's, took about a dozen photos, although the paper would only print one, or at the most two. Maggie had removed her cigarette from view while the photographs were being taken because she had a strong suspicion that most of the village regarded smoking as slightly common, though most of them smoked themselves.

There was also the editor of the paper to consider. He disapproved of cigarettes and alcohol and refused to allow his staff to smoke during working hours. On the other hand, if he were to come across a shot of Maggie with a cigarette which he thought made her look cheap and ridiculous, he was liable to publish it. He was well known for this and frequently selected the most unsuitable photograph to publish of anyone he didn't like, which meant that about three quarters of the village were eligible. Events of which he did not approve, which included anything where alcohol was in evidence, were subtly photographed to show them in the worst possible light. Of course, he could have omitted them altogether which had in fact been his policy for a few weeks when he succeeded his father as editor but the decline in sales had prompted him to reconsider. In any case, as he frequently remarked, a man in his position had to show fairness and impartiality. So, in spite of its imperfections—or maybe, as many suspected because of them—the local paper continued to flourish.

Mr and Mrs Hastings did not attend the Christmas tea. In

fact, most of the incomers regarded it as something put on for the benefit of the locals and had no desire to take part. On this occasion the Rev Nicholson and his wife were the only incomers present. They had been invited by Maggie because she thought their presence raised the tone of the proceedings a little. In order to prevent Mr Nicholson from disappearing early as he had done last year, she had asked him to propose the vote of thanks. He had agreed without realising what he had let himself in for but compensated by sending his wife on ahead and turning up midway through.

He didn't really enjoy this sort of thing. Many of the old people were deaf, wholly or partly, which made conversation trying. Last year he'd been trying to have a chat with Mrs Willis, who was really quite deaf but refused to acknowledge the fact. They'd been discussing her great-granddaughter. Mr Nicholson had discovered that this was a fertile topic.

"I saw your great-granddaughter last week. Isn't she getting big?" he said with an effort at enthusiasm. Mrs Willis' brow furrowed again which indicated that she hadn't heard him clearly. Being reluctant to admit her deafness she seldom asked for anything to be repeated and conversations with her often went off at an unexpected tangent.

"Your great-granddaughter. She's big."

"A pig?"

"No, no. Huge. She's huge."

Mr Nicholson had raised his voice further. Various heads turned in his direction. Mrs Willis nodded. She'd got it at last, thank God. Mr Nicholson had smiled benignly and passed on. This year he'd decided to let*them* do the talking and this had proved surprisingly successful, even if they all had more or less the same to say. His wife, he reflected, was really much better at this sort of thing. He would have to think of a way of getting her more involved. She even seemed to enjoy these occasions, so she probably wouldn't mind taking on a little extra responsibility.

22 Another visit

MISS SHUTTLEWORTH was stirred by the noise of her letterbox. She looked at her watch. A bit early for Sandy—as he was known in the village—although Miss Shuttleworth eschewed such familiarities and simply referred to him as the postman—so maybe it was someone else. The only time the post had been regularly early was when they'd had that young woman but she didn't stay very long.

Of course, there was no reason why Sandy couldn't deliver his round more quickly but this would mean foregoing his lengthy chats with the locals and cups of tea—or so she'd been told. This was apparently considered quite acceptable here in Achanult, to Miss Shuttleworth's initial surprise. She had even come across him parked in a lay-by at the edge of the village, reading a newspaper when he should have been getting on with his round. Miss Shuttleworth felt quite strongly about this sort of attitude and had made a complaint at the main post office in Oban. She was told that they would look into it. That was over two years ago—nearly two and a half—and she hadn't noticed any change. But it didn't bother her so much now. Either she'd got used to it or was subconsciously lowering her own standards. Possibly both. In fact, she'd been quite amused at Jennifer's reactions to the local way of life when she was here on her last visit.

She thought of getting out of bed. In the winter she tended to lie in a bit later, since the prospect facing her out of the window, once she was up, was usually pretty discouraging. Curiosity however, eventually got the better of her and she waddled through to the front door. She recognised Jennifer's handwriting and returned to bed.

The gist of the letter was that Miss McLachlan would be very happy to accept Miss Shuttleworth's invitation to spend a few days over Christmas in Achanult and hoped that Miss Shuttleworth could pick her up in Oban as before. She indicated that she would be arriving by the late afternoon train on Wednesday. Unfortunately, Miss Shuttleworth had intended to combine a shopping trip with her visit to the station but Wednesday was half day there.

Lying back in bed she wondered if she should write to Jennifer asking her to come on another day but in the end she decided against it. Her letter might not arrive in time due to these inevitable delays in the post at this time of year.

Miss Shuttleworth arrived a few minutes before the 4.10 train which arrived twenty minutes late. Miss McLachlan was among the first to get out looking rather like Charlie's aunt with a quite unsuitable hat and rather old-fashioned gloves. Watching her friend struggling with her luggage, Miss Shuttleworth's spirits sagged slightly. She would really have to have a word with her this time. As Miss McLachlan began to show signs of heading off in the wrong direction, Miss Shuttleworth hailed her loudly.

"Jennifer! Over here!" She waved her arm vigorously.

"Ah. There you are Marjory."

"Hello. You've arrived safely then."

"Yes. I think we're perhaps a bit late. Have you been

waiting long?"

"Oh, about half an hour. I like to be in good time just in case the train arrives early."

"Does it ever?"

"No. Are you managing that luggage?"

"Well, they're a bit . . ."

"Good. My car's just over here."

As they turned the corner a gust of wind blew off Miss McLachlan's hat and it came to rest a few yards away in a puddle.

"Oh dear. It's so windy up here. I remember that from last time."

"Don't worry, I'll get it," said Miss Shuttleworth, putting her foot on it as the wind threatened to blow it further away. "You still want it, I presume?"

"Oh yes. It was my mother's, you see."

"Really?"

Miss Shuttleworth placed the hat on the back seat of her car. She pulled the choke to make sure that the car would start easily and would drive off smoothly. Trying as she always did to show herself efficient and capable, she felt that she had been let down rather by the car's behaviour on Jennifer's last trip. Of course she understood nothing about cars but it was nevertheless important for her to appear to be in control of a situation. Still, Jennifer knew even less about cars and had probably forgotten all about it.

"Your car's running much better this time, Marjory."

"Yes."

"No wonder you were early for the train."

"The train was late."

"Yes, it was. I think we were on time till we got to Glasgow. Of course, everything's a bit slower up here, isn't it?"

"Some things travel fast enough."

"You surprise me, Marjory. What sort of things?"

"Oh, gossip, for instance."

Miss McLachlan laughed and leant back in her seat.

"You wouldn't have thought there was much to gossip about up here."

"Oh, that doesn't deter them. They just make it up."

"Oh dear. How amusing."

"Yes, it is in a way."

"Still, I don't suppose anybody pays much attention."

"Some people do nothing else."

"How odd! By the way, did you ever discover what was wrong with your car last time?"

"Something to do with the points, apparently—whatever *they* are."

"Hmm. Where have all the sheep gone this time?"

"Oh, they're still here."

"I don't see any."

Miss Shuttleworth gestured to the hillside on the left.

"Those off-white woolly things over there."

"Don't be silly, Marjory. I mean I don't see any on the road."

"No. They usually keep more of an eye on them in the winter."

"Oh, what a pity. It was quite exciting meeting them on the road, wasn't it?"

"Oh, you get used to it."

"I suppose you do. I was quite taken with it, I must say. I told everyone at home that there are more sheep than cars on the roads up here."

"Did you really?"

"They couldn't believe it, of course. Well it does seem a bit, um, uncivilised. So this time I've brought my camera. Perhaps we'll see one later. You know, I must tell you, when I saw those sheep last time I remembered I'd read somewhere that everybody up here kept a few sheep around the house—only it wasn't called a house; something else, some Scotch word; I can't remember. Anyway, I was beginning to wonder if *you* would have a few sheep in your garden."

"I'm sorry to have disappointed you, Jennifer."

"Well, I didn't *really* think you would. By the way, how safe are they? I don't like the look of those horns they have. Scotch people stick them on walls, don't they?"

"I can't say I've noticed any."

"Haven't you? You see photographs of them in castles and hotels—these sort of places."

"Ah! I think you're thinking of deer."

"Am I?"

"Antlers. *Cabar feidh*."

"What's that?"

"You do find stags' heads mounted on walls, certainly."

"Yes. That's what I must have seen. What a quaint idea."

"It might even be your crest."

"My what?"

"Crest. You know. All the clans have some sort of crest—a haggis rampant, or a rowan tree, or something."

"Do they? Why?"

"I haven't the slightest idea. You're the one who should know."

"Really, Marjory. You can't expect me to take all this seriously. Mind you, I wonder what the McLachlan—what did you say it was called? . . . "

"Crest."

" . . . crest is. Have you got a book about these things?"

"No. I don't think so. You could try the library."

"Is there a library here?"

"Don't you remember? I pointed it out to you."

"I . . . umm . . . "

"I'll show you it again. We'll be passing it in due course."

"Oh good. Let's go in and see."

"I'm afraid it'll be closed."

"What? Already?"

"I think so."

"Isn't that a bit early?"

"Not for Achanult."

Miss McLachlan glanced at her watch.

"I can't see in this light."

Miss Shuttleworth pointed to the dashboard.

"Will it open later in the evening?"

"Goodness, Jennifer. I didn't realise that you were so eager to become a fully paid-up member of Clan McLachlan."

"Of course I'm not. I just wondered what the hours were."

"It'll be open tomorrow."

They drove on in silence. Miss Shuttleworth wondered if she herself had seemed as odd to the locals when she first arrived. She hoped not. In fact, she knew that she had never been quite so gullible as her friend but of course, the locals tended to regard all incomers in the same light—without any justification. Just ignorance really. She'd been amused to discover that Miss McLachlan on her first visit had been regarded by some as her sister—or was it her sister-in-law? No doubt that awful Maggie Stewart had been responsible for that particular piece of nonsense. It was best just to ignore them all.

23 Ceilidh

AT THE Gaelic class there had been a suggestion that the final afternoon of the term should take the form of a ceilidh. This idea had been received with enthusiasm until Mrs Nicholson started to go into details. It then became apparent that for most of the class a ceilidh was an event where you listened to other people without doing anything yourself. So Mrs Nicholson was then asked about ceilidhs in Uist She then described what she could remember of the informal ceilidhs which took place in her childhood and which were coming to an end about that time. These reminiscences had occupied most of the afternoon which had not been Mrs Nicholson's original intention. But the class seemed to enjoy it and Mrs Nicholson had to admit that she had found it surprisingly interesting.

The class ceilidh however, was another matter. Maggie Stewart was determined that they should have one but regretted that she herself had no talent to contribute. Miss Shuttleworth was astounded by the suggestion that she might like to sing something. Donald Morrison, who rarely said anything, had surprised the class by offering to read a poem since Mrs Nicholson had mentioned that she could remember bards reciting their own verses at ceilidhs. What Donald had in mind, however, was "Tam o' Shanter", or rather, since he'd forgotten most of it, just part of it. The rest of the class didn't think much of this idea until Mrs Nicholson remembered that she had a Gaelic translation of "Tam o' Shanter" at home and asked them if they would like to hear part of it. They were all very keen except Miss Shuttleworth, who raised her pen in the air.

"What," she asked, "is Tam o' Shanter?"

139

"Ish a hat," growled Alec Cameron at the back, to the general mirth of the others.

"A what?"

"Mr Cameron's just joking," said Mrs Nicholson quickly. "Of course, it is also a hat but it's really the name of a well-known poem."

"By Robert Burns," added Maggie. "Our national bard. He's famous all over the world, you know."

"Yes, yes. I've heard of *him*. I just didn't know about the poem."

"It's very famous as well," continued Maggie.

"I see. What's it about?"

"Umm . . . of course it's a while since . . . well, it's about Tam o' Shanter."

"Get away! Really?"

Mrs Nicholson, who'd been fidgeting with her necklace again while this exchange was going on, interrupted,

"Why don't we discuss the poem next week when we have the ceilidh? Then it will be fresh in your minds and maybe make it easier for you to get the gist of the Gaelic version."

This was agreed and the discussion of the format of the ceilidh resumed. Some of the class recalled that Mrs McKenzie could play the piano but she denied this. She had to admit however, that she had played the national anthem at some function or other many years ago. But as she herself said, she'd had to practise for weeks beforehand and even then had made a bit of a hash of it. Under pressure however, she agreed to think about maybe accompanying someone if he or she didn't mind her wrong notes.

Mrs Nicholson was relieved that at last somebody was going to do something, until Miss Shuttleworth said,

"There isn't a piano."

Maggie saw her chance. A neighbour of hers had recently bought one of those small electric keyboards for her daughter and Maggie had been invited along last week to hear the child playing it. She hadn't been very impressed with the instrument which seemed very limited.

"I might be able to do something there," said Maggie, adopting her business-like pose. "I can probably get you one of these electric keyboards. You just have to plug it in."

"You mean it plays itself?" asked Mrs McKenzie who, like most of the others, was quite unfamiliar with electric keyboards.

"No, no, you still have to play them."

Mrs McKenzie nodded vaguely.

"Aren't they just toys?" asked Miss Shuttleworth.

"Of course not," bristled Maggie.

"The ones I've seen don't look up to much."

"Well, I think they're very impressive," lied Maggie. "I was amazed at what they can do."

Miss Shuttleworth said nothing, leaving the way open for Mrs Nicholson.

"There must be many different types of course and obviously some will be, um, better than others," she said soothingly. "I'm sure we'll all be delighted to hear it."

Maggie nodded with a faint smile on her lips.

"You *do* get pianos that play by themselves," whispered Mrs McKenzie to Donald sitting in front of her but neither he nor anyone else wanted to pursue the subject.

Another suggestion made that same afternoon was that people who weren't members of the class should be invited to the ceilidh on the final afternoon. Mrs Nicholson was a bit unsure of this but was eventually persuaded that it might be a good idea. Various points were raised and discussed. Firstly there was the question of whether non-members of the class should be charged for admission to the ceilidh and if so, how much? After a lengthy discussion Miss Shuttleworth finally pointed out that since they themselves were quite unsure about the format of the ceilidh, they shouldn't really be charging anyone anything.

Then there was the question of who to invite. Mrs McKenzie suggested one or two acquaintances of hers who were in her opinion, quite talented musicians. But it was agreed that they could hardly invite people and expect them to perform as well. Maggie, who did not like the way Mrs McKenzie was asserting herself, pointed out that they would have quite a job *stopping* some people she could think of from performing.

Mrs McKenzie relapsed into silence for a few minutes but eventually came up with the suggestion that they should invite those people who'd been thinking of coming to the class but, for one reason or another, hadn't yet got round to it. This would give them an idea of what the class was like and might persuade them to come next year. Everyone thought this was a very good idea except Maggie, who was by now automatically opposed to any suggestion from Mrs McKenzie. So it was left to individual members of the class to invite whoever they wished. Maggie however, was determined to impose her presence.

"I still don't think that's a very good idea. Not if you think about it properly." No-one said anything. "If we get some new people in the class, they'll be beginners, won't they?"

"Well, I . . . "

"That's right. So where does that leave the present members of the class?" persisted Maggie, trying to involve the others on her side. "We'll be further on than the beginners. How would they fit into the class?"

"I'm sure a little revision wouldn't do some of us any harm," said Miss Shuttleworth dismissively. There were murmurs of assent to this.

"Well of course, if that's what everybody wants," said Maggie stiffly. "I just thought I'd point out some of the problems."

"Of course. Thank you," said Mrs Nicholson, looking surreptitiously at her watch.

"We haven't done all that much this term anyway," volunteered Mrs McKenzie. "I mean," she added, reddening, "we wouldn't be that far ahead of any beginners."

"I wonder what any of the gentlemen think?" said Mrs Nicholson brightly.

Neither of them seemed to think anything. Mrs Nicholson persisted,

"How about your neighbour, Mr Morrison? Did someone not say he might be interested?"

"Oh, well, I don't really know," replied Donald, who wasn't sure if he'd be back himself next year.

"I'll have a word with Peter," said Maggie quickly. "But I don't really know if he'd be interested."

"I think he'd enjoy it," retorted Mrs McKenzie. "It would get him out of the house if nothing else."

So it was agreed to leave it at that and whoever wanted to bring any music could do so.

Later that evening Mrs Nicholson had confided to her husband,

"I think our meeting next week is going to be a bit of a fiasco."

"Again?"

"Really David. You might be a bit more helpful. After all, I did wait until you'd finished before I mentioned it."

"Right. What's the problem this time, then?" said the Rev

Nicholson, his mind still on 27 across which had so far defeated him. DEAR FRUIT (10). He didn't like these brief clues. Could be anything! _L_M_N_ _N_. Oh well, he'd find out tomorrow. Annoying, though. Nothing to do with lemons? No, he'd already tried that.

" . . . so do you think I should?"

"Umm, well, I . . . It's difficult. I'm sure you'll do the right thing, Anna."

"I suppose we'll just have to wait and see what happens."

"Very wise."

Mrs Nicholson sighed. David was becoming very withdrawn these days. He had a lot on his mind of course, particularly with this recent ecumenical business where he'd been asked to make a contribution to a joint service to be held at Christmas. The Rev Nicholson had been quite happy to go long with this and had intended to resurrect one of his old Nativity sermons for the occasion. But at a preliminary meeting it had been agreed that they would all stress the message of unity as seen from their own particular standpoint. So that meant extra work for Mr Nicholson at what was one of his busiest times of the year. Still, if the service was not well attended it would maybe not be repeated next year. He hadn't said anything official about it to his congregation but had put up one of the posters he'd received on the notice board in the church hall. The hall was out of use at the moment due to problems with the heating. The boiler had broken down again and it was thought that repairs might be rather expensive this time. Mrs Nicholson had suggested that her husband might be a bit more positive.

"You could mention it from the pulpit."

"But they all know about it already. It's the same every winter anyway."

Mrs Nicholson sighed again.

"I meant the ecumenical service."

"Oh, that! Well, ye-es. On the other hand, some people might take offence."

"I don't see why."

"Of course not. Neither do I. But there are a lot of closed minds here still. We have to tread warily. In any case, as relative newcomers, we shouldn't appear too . . . what's the word?"

"Innovative?"

"That's it. Exactly. We don't want to seem too pushy either. Humility is a great virtue, after all."

Mrs Nicholson wondered if there was anything interesting on television.

24 Invitation

JEAN had come back from her shopping rather wet in spite of wearing her heavy boots, oilskin hat and other defences. It had been one of those mornings again, when the rain was almost horizontal. As she hung her dripping hat over the rack beside the range in the kitchen, Peter shook his head in disbelief.

"I don't know why you had to go out in that."

"It's Thursday. There's the shopping to do. Anyway, it's stopped now and it's supposed to be sunny later."

"Surely it could have waited?"

"Och well, I usually go out on a Thursday morning. It's fine to meet other folk then."

Peter could never see the point of it.

"So what did you get?"

"Oh, nothing much. Some eggs,—oh and some fruit."

"Oh?"

"Well, I'll need to bake something for the New Year and we need some apples and oranges in case we've any visitors."

"Visitors?"

"We might be having a visit from Donald, you know."

"Oh aye. Not till the New Year though."

"Well, I don't know. I was talking to Jean McKenzie just now—you know—she goes to that afternoon Gaelic class."

Jean paused while she struggled with her coat. Eventually she emerged from it, placed it on the rack beside her hat and turned to her boots. This was a major task but working methodically, she at last got them off and stood in her wet stocking soles.

"I thought these boots were supposed to be waterproof. They were dear enough, anyway," said Peter, who'd forgotten now exactly how much they'd cost but still remembered the shock.

"Oh they are! The rain's just been running down into them. They'll soon dry out."

"So what's all this about a visit from Donald?"

"Oh yes. Jean McKenzie was saying that we'd been invited to a ceilidh at the Gaelic class."

"I've never heard anything about this."

"No. Well, neither had I till this morning. It'll make a fine change."

"So why did *she* invite us?"

"Well, she actually thought we'd already been invited by Donald. He'd apparently said at the class that he'd mention it to us."

"Well, I was talking to him yesterday and he didn't say a

word about it."

Jean wasn't surprised. If he was going to mention it at all, which was by no means certain, he would wait till the last minute when he was on his way to the ceilidh himself. And then he would only have invited Peter. In fact, he wouldn't have invited him as such but would have made a passing reference, in the middle of a tirade about his tobacco, to the fact that there was a ceilidh that afternoon, if Peter wanted to go along. That was just Donald's way of doing things.

"When were you talking to him yesterday?"

"Och, in the morning. He was complaining about his tobacco again."

For years Donald had smoked "Rob Roy's Mixture", a black concoction of formidable strength. This blend had never been widely sold but Donald had always been able to get it in Achanult. Recently however, it had become unavailable. Donald blamed Willie of course, but the manufacturers had apparently stopped making it. Donald was reluctant to believe this and even waylaid the travelling salesman on his last visit, without success. Not one to give up easily, Donald had then driven to Oban and returned with five packets of "Rob Roy's Ready Rubbed", which was the best he could get. Since that finished he had been experimenting with various other tobaccos but had yet to find anything acceptable.

"Why," asked Jean, when Peter mentioned this to her, "doesn't he just stop?"

"Oh, I don't know. Why should he?"

"Well, a pipe looks so silly. and it annoys other people. I was hearing about the rumpus at the Gaelic class. Did I tell you?"

"Oh aye. Donald's pipe was annoying them."

"Not Donald's. Alec Cameron's. You know how he's never seen without it. Well, apparently Maggie Stewart had to tell him in no uncertain terms to stop smoking in class."

"Is that so?"

"So she told me. Nobody else liked to say anything seemingly, but she wasn't standing for any nonsense from Alec."

Peter wondered what on earth Alec Cameron was doing at the Gaelic class. He'd known him since he was a boy in the village and they'd been at school together. Alec wasn't very bright in those days and as far as Peter could see, he hadn't improved much. Now that he thought about it, Alec's granny had had the Gaelic—that would be why he was at the class. Aye, and that would be where he got all his stories about the old days—if he got them from anywhere. Peter was inclined to think he just made most of them up. Well, if Alec was at the class, it couldn't be too difficult. That was really why he himself hadn't gone—one of the reasons, anyway. If there was going to be any of this grammar stuff, he'd better keep clear.

But there was Alec at the class. Who else went? Maggie Stewart, that's right. She was no great brain either, though she would disagree with you on that. Maggie liked to let on that she'd been really bright at school but you couldn't help wondering why she'd done nothing with it.

"You'll be able to ask Donald about it soon, if you like. That's the sun out now. He'll be sitting in his car again."

Donald had recently taken to sitting in his car on sunny days, reading his paper. They'd wondered why but hadn't liked to ask him.

"I think I've an idea why he does that ," said Peter.

"Oh? What?"

"It's warmer there. When I went into our car the other

148

day—the last time we had a sunny day—you'd be surprised how hot it was. It's all that glass—a bit like a greenhouse."

"But why doesn't he just sit by the fire?"

"He'll be wanting to save coal."

"Goodness, what next? He's not short of money is he?"

"Not that I know of. He's not too keen on parting with it though."

"You could be right about the warmth. I noticed once that when the sun went off his car in the afternoon—it had gone behind his house—he got out and pushed the car back into the sun again."

They both laughed. Mind you, Donald had always been a bit strange. He'd be better off selling his car and saving money that way. He didn't need such a big car either. Peter couldn't remember when he'd last seen him giving anybody a lift.

"I think I'll wait and see if he mentions it to us," said Peter as an afterthought.

"To you, you mean."

"Probably. Of course, he might not be going himself. I wouldn't have thought he was all that sociable."

"Well, it's in a good cause."

Peter considered this last remark.

"D'you mean we have to pay to go?"

"Mrs McKenzie didn't say. But there's usually some sort of charge for these things, isn't there?"

"I suppose there is. Mind you, if it's for a good cause, I'm surprised that Donald has anything to do with it. Remember that time the school children did that sponsored walk."

"Och, that wasn't the first time. I think he thinks these things are dear. I don't know why. It hardly costs anything."

"How much did we give them?"

"50p, wasn't it? 5p per mile. That's what nearly everybody

else was giving, except for Mrs Muir. She only gave 2p per mile."

"How do *you* know?"

"You have to write it on their sheet of paper. Some people just give donations. Miss Shuttleworth gave a pound. Maggie Stewart says she just does that to look superior."

"Maggie doesn't like her, does she?"

"Not much. I find her OK though. Not that I ever see much of her. In fact it's Maggie I could do with a bit less of at times."

Peter nodded in agreement. Although he tried to avoid Miss Shuttleworth if possible, he really had nothing against her. In fact, he knew very little about her, and was quite happy to leave things like that.

"How much did Maggie give then?"

Jean thought for a moment.

"I don't remember seeing her name. That's right, they'd be doing her part of the village after us."

"Maybe she wouldn't give anything."

"Oh no, she's not like that."

25 Festivities

PETER didn't really enjoy Christmas. For a start he could never think of anything to get Jean. He didn't bother with anyone else but realised that he ought to give his wife some sort of present, mainly because she always gave him something. He had suggested more than once that there was no real need to exchange presents at their age but he always got the same answer. Jean didn't at all mind not having money spent on her but she would like to get him something anyway. And she always did, which made him feel even more guilty.

So he did his best. But in the last few years he had been reduced to accompanying her on a shopping expedition and paying for whatever she chose. That was if he remembered to take his wallet, something which he'd forgotten to do two years ago. So Jean had bought her own present. She never seemed to mind his lack of enthusiasm.

So here was another Christmas approaching and Peter had spent days worrying about a present for Jean. The main problem was that she already had everything she needed as far as he could make out. She *had* mentioned a few days ago that she would like a pair of gloves. But since she already had three or four pairs Peter couldn't see the point of that. She didn't wear them all that often anyway. Sometimes he wished he could think of something really original, like that composer he'd heard about on the radio a while back who'd composed a tune for his wife's birthday. Not that he himself could ever do that but he appreciated the unusualness of the present. And it wouldn't have cost anything either.

Jean enjoyed Christmas. She rushed around buying cards and presents for all their relatives. Not that there were all that many, as far as Peter was aware, but then there were their children apparently. He was a bit vague about this. The neighbours too, had to get something, so it was all quite hectic.

Peter kept well clear. It had become obvious to him over the years that women enjoyed these things and there was very little that could be done about it, except to lie low until it all blew over. He'd always felt that she spent rather a lot on such occasions, although he'd never really liked to say so. Jean however, must have sensed this, for she rarely discussed the price of anything with him. It wasn't that Peter was mean. It was simply that he was reluctant to spend money on anything which wouldn't be useful. Women, he had come to realise, had a much more frivolous attitude. Nevertheless, he was happy to leave it all to her.

Christmas hadn't been anything like that when Peter was young, as he frequently reminded Jean. She was equally aware of the changes that had occurred but, unlike Peter, could see nothing wrong with them. He put it all down to the incomers. It must have been about twenty years ago that he'd first seen a Christmas tree in Achanult, with those funny lights on it. He'd got quite used to the sight after a few years though.

It was the Brownleys who'd started the trend, he recalled. He'd come from somewhere in England to live in Achanult and be a writer—well, he was a writer already apparently, though Peter had never heard of him, not being much of a reader himself. So they'd settled down in Achanult, him and his wife, who was supposed to be a painter and their two children—or was it three? They didn't stay long, two or three years, then they went back to England. They couldn't stand the rain apparently.

Quite a lot of the incomers were like that, arriving with a passionate enthusiasm for the great outdoors which soon evaporated in the face of the relentless highland drizzle. No doubt they were fine enough people but Peter reckoned Achanult was better off without them, with their daft ideas about lighted Christmas trees. And carol singing—that was another thing. They seemed to have a restless urge, always wanting to do things. The trouble was as soon as one lot went, another lot arrived in their place.

But Jean thought that times had changed and it was nothing to do with the incomers. You would have to shut yourself off completely from television, radio, and newspapers in December—and even before—if you wanted things to be the way they had been. She didn't mind the changes. In fact, she thought they were an improvement, although she wouldn't exactly say as much, especially if Peter was around. The place was somehow brighter these days and she often found herself wishing that things had been as they were now when she was a child.

Then there was the New Year. But that had changed as well. Peter was glad really, although he probably would have denied it. In his young days Hogmanay and the New Year had been a great occasion and he'd played his part with the rest of them. As the years advanced however, his enthusiasm had waned and now he was rather glad when the whole thing was past. Not that there was a great deal happening nowadays anyway. Gatherings in the village square were a thing of the past and first footing seemed to have gone out of fashion as well. Peter didn't really mind. Donald next door said it was the incomers who'd changed things and maybe he was right. But then Donald had never really taken to any of the incomers and didn't have much to do with many of the locals either. Peter and Jean often agreed that the old ways were passing but they were never quite sure who to blame—or who to thank.

On New Year's day they always went to visit Donald usually around noon. He didn't really like to see anybody before then and it gave them the excuse to leave in an hour or so for their dinner.

This arrangement obviously suited Donald who was far from gregarious. Some years he gave Peter's glass a refill. Jean always had a sherry, just one, and it was always a bit too dry for her—although when Donald asked her how it was, she always said, "lovely, thank you". Well, you wouldn't want to hurt the man's feelings. After an hour of swapping platitudes, they left and that was that for another year.

On the way out they always followed the same pattern. Donald was invited to have something to eat with them but declined, claiming to have something of his own waiting. So he was then invited to look in after his meal and he agreed to try to do so at some time in the afternoon. He always turned up about four o' clock, which gave him about an hour before he could safely leave for his tea and the ritual was finally over.

Sometimes Peter wondered why they bothered. He and Jean still stayed up on Hogmanay to see the New Year in although Peter had been known to fall asleep by the fire beforehand. Sometimes they watched the television but Jean didn't really enjoy it. It was all a bit artificial she thought. Peter had just accepted it as part of the gradual change in the way of things. Plenty of tartan, fine singers and a determined gaiety, everyone speaking in the accents of the south—Glasgow mainly. That was where the programmes came from of course, so maybe it wasn't surprising that there was none of the old highland Hogmanay that Peter remembered.

Jean preferred to put the television off and sit and talk. She liked to analyse the past year with Peter, remembering the good things that had happened and the not so good. As a rule, nothing much had happened so any minor illness or some win in a raffle achieved undue prominence. They were both glad really when it was time to go to bed.

Donald felt that he and Peter would happily ignore the New Year ritual if left to themselves. But Jean didn't feel that would be right somehow. Donald found her a bit irritating at times. She was keen to please but often only succeeded in annoying him. She would always agree with everything you said and although she would occasionally argue with Peter, nobody took that very seriously. Donald always felt slightly uneasy about her. It was different with Peter. Donald didn't mind being rude to him if he thought the situation demanded it. Most of the village found Donald a bit difficult.

Last New Year's day after Donald had left about five as usual, Jean had said, "I feel a bit sorry for Donald. We should really invite him in more often."

"He wouldn't like that."

"Why not?"

"Och, I think he likes his own company."

"Maybe I'm in the way," wondered Jean. "He'd probably rather just talk to you."

"I doubt it."

"But he talks to you a lot."

"Only when he feels like it. Anyway that suits me fine."

"You're as bad as he is."

Peter couldn't see the point of this conversation. They had it every year.

Jean wasn't quite so concerned now since that business with the meals-on-wheels but she still tended to take her role as neighbour a bit too seriously. Donald had flatly refused a year or two ago to have anything to do with people cooking meals for him and had been a bit rude in his refusal. Nobody minded. That was just the way he was—as Peter could have told them if he'd been asked. It was mainly the incomers who ran the meals-on-wheels service so that was maybe another reason for Donald having nothing to do with it. Jean hadn't felt quite so bad about Donald after that and as Peter remarked every New Year, it was quite an achievement to get him across their threshold even once a year.

26 Dispute

IT WAS extremely rare to find an industrial dispute having an effect on Achanult, so the current situation caused a great deal of interest. Many of the villagers were reminded of the merchant seamen's dispute of many years ago. At that time Achanult, in common with most other coastal villages in Argyll, had refused to have anything to do with the national dispute.

The present action had begun in Glasgow and concerned the non-teaching staff in schools. The union to which these members belonged had, after a ballot of all members, declared an indefinite strike throughout the schools of the region.

Peter had noticed a reference to it on the front page of the local paper as he and Jean sat by the fire after tea.

"There's something here about a strike at the school."

"I saw that," replied Jean. "A bit daft with the holidays just coming up."

"You never used to hear of teachers going on strike when we were at school. It would've been a fine thing if they had, though."

"It's not the teachers. It's the other folk."

Peter had another look at the paper.

"Oh aye. Well it won't make much difference then."

"Maybe not. Mind you, janitors keep the schools running just as much as teachers do."

"Oh! Willie's involved, is he?"

"Not according to the paper. Why don't you read it properly?"

Peter settled back and read the article. As Jean had indicated, Willie was quoted as saying that he wasn't going on strike although he admitted that he was a member of the union and that the membership had reached a democratic decision.

"I see what you mean about Willie," said Peter.

"He's about due to retire anyway, isn't he? So I don't suppose he cares one way or the other. Mind you, he's always been like that—a great one for the majority decision as long as the majority agree with him. Remember that business about the bowling club?"

Peter remembered. He wasn't much interested in bowls and in fact there wasn't a bowling club any longer in Achanult but he'd been quite amused at the time. The bowling club had an annual outing and Willie, who was a committee member, had wanted a trip to Inverness, which he hadn't visited before. It was rumoured that Willie's real aim was to see if he could catch a glimpse of that monster. There had been a lot in the papers about it and he'd been talking about it for weeks afterwards. He categorically denied that it had anything to do with that, which made everyone even more convinced. Most of the other bowling club members wanted a day in Edinburgh, particularly the women for whom the shops were a great attraction. So as usual a vote was taken and Edinburgh was a convincing winner.

Willie promptly resigned from the club and took to playing golf, something which he'd last done about thirty years previously. He claimed of course that this was what he'd been meaning to do for years and that it would get him out and about more.

Since the nearest golf course was about twenty miles away, there was some truth in this latter point. Willie would go with some of the other men in the village who were keen golfers, each using his car in turn. But this arrangement hadn't lasted too long and Willie was soon going by himself. Maggie Stewart said he'd fallen out with the others over whose turn it was to take the car. Everybody else thought it was Willie's turn.

"So there's just four involved then," said Peter when he'd finished reading the article. "And only one of them on strike."

"Mrs Thorne. I'm not surprised," said Jean with a shake of her head. "Though you might have thought she'd been here long enough to know better. I knew Bella wouldn't go on strike though."

"Och, she knows the kids would just take their own food if she did."

"Well, that's what we had to do. No such thing as school dinners in my day."

"Anyway Bella likes the children. She fair enjoys her job. That's really what I don't understand," continued Peter. "Willie's the same. He's told me more than once what a fine job it is—and a free uniform as well. What would they want to be going on strike for? He even gets a free meal from Bella though he's not supposed to. And Mrs McKenzie's not going on strike either I see. She says there's nothing wrong with the pay."

As Jean got up and went through to the dishes, Peter gave the fire a few prods with the poker, placed a couple of pieces of wood on it and settled back to read the rest of the paper. On the letters page the words, MESSAGE FROM MP in large type drew his attention.

Beneath them he read:

Sir,

My attention has been drawn to a strike by some part-time school auxiliary employees in my constituency. There is no doubt that this action, emanating, I am told, from Glasgow, is part of a socialist conspiracy to undermine our traditional standards of education and community service. I am confident however, that the good sense of my constituents will prevail and they will have no part in this subversive agitation.

Yours etc

Sir William Kiels-Mather

Peter read the letter again.

"Have you seen this letter from our MP?" he asked Jean when she returned.

"I don't think so." Jean hadn't read beyond the front page and the births, marriages and deaths. "What does he say?"

Peter read her the letter.

"Does that mean he doesn't approve of the strike?" asked Jean after a pause.

"I think so. He seems to be taking it awfully seriously anyway."

"Och, I don't know. Now that I think of it he wrote just the same sort of thing last year about that petition the churches had got up."

"I don't remember that."

"You do. It was something to do with nuclear weapons. The minister was quite offended, I remember."

"Who? Mr Nicholson?"

"No, Mr Neil. It was just before he left. I think he would have made an issue of it if he'd still been here. He was quite right too. As he said, *we* have to live here beside these things all the time but Sir William never comes near the place. But he left soon after and this new minister—Mr Nicholson—hasn't done anything so far about it, or about anything, or so I hear."

"Och, that's just gossip. He'll take a while to settle in."

"His wife seems quite keen to get involved though. She seems very nice from what I've heard. There's her Gaelic class as well."

"Aye, trying to teach the likes of Donald a bit of Gaelic can't

159

be all that easy. I suppose you'd need a lot of patience."

"Not just Donald. Alec Cameron's there as well. You wonder why she does it."

"Does she get paid?"

"I don't know. I think she must get something. I seem to remember there was something about class fees in that leaflet— the one I showed you. Why? It wasn't the cost that put you off going, was it?"

"Och no. Well, not just that," said Peter, a little uneasy about the direction the conversation had taken. "I'll maybe think about it again next year."

Jean left it at that. It wasn't that Peter had no interest in Gaelic. In fact he enjoyed the songs and the lilt of the language, even if he couldn't understand a word. He'd recently discovered quite by chance, that there were programmes in Gaelic for very young children on television on weekday mornings. He'd taken to watching them since he was otherwise at a loose end on these dreich winter days. Yet he was continually frustrated by his inability to understand anything, feeling that if young children could understand the programmes he should be able to. Jean had stopped trying to reason with him.

Peter kept the sports pages of the paper and passed the rest to Jean. He particularly enjoyed looking at the domino results and league table, finding out who had beaten who. He'd played a lot of dominoes when he was younger but hadn't bothered for a few years now although he was always being told it was a fine game for older folk. Willie was always on at him to play again, telling him they needed him in the team. Looking at the league table he could see what they meant. He'd been a very good player but now . . . he just didn't seem to be able to summon up the enthusiasm.

27 Broaching the subject

THE rain beat steadily down on Achanult as Miss Shuttleworth and Miss McLachlan sat in the lounge after their tea.

"So what happens on a Wednesday evening in Achanult?" asked Miss McLachlan with the enthusiasm of a recent arrival.

"Oh there'll be something on somewhere. There usually is. Scottish dancing or some such nonsense."

"Oh! That sounds quite interesting, Marjory. Do you go?"

"Certainly not! But you can if you like that sort of thing."

"Oh no. I'll be quite happy to sit and chat or read or whatever. I see you've got the local paper." Miss McLachlan gestured to the arm of the sofa.

"That," pronounced Miss Shuttleworth, "is the *Glasgow Herald*. It's a national paper."

"Well, I've never heard of it."

"The local paper," continued Miss Shuttleworth, "is on top of the television set."

"Oh well. I'll have a quick look at that first. Must keep up with local affairs. What's it called?"

Miss McLachlan walked over to the television and lifted the paper.

"Oh is that all? How disappointing."

"Why? What were you expecting?"

"Well, I thought it might have an interesting name—like *The Highlanders' Umbrella* or something."

"The *what?*"

"*Highlanders' Umbrella*. I seem to remember my father telling me that there was a local paper in Glasgow with that title."

"Seems a bit unlikely, Jennifer," said Miss Shuttleworth

drily. "Hardly the name for a newspaper."

"Maybe they put it over their heads when it was raining."

"Maybe," agreed Miss Shuttleworth, turning to the *Glasgow Herald*.

Miss McLachlan went off to her bedroom to find her spectacles and returned after a few minutes wearing a large pair of woolly slippers, each knitted to resemble a cat. She settled down to the local paper. After a few seconds of silence she gave a little gasp and said,

"Goodness! Do you have strikes up here? I thought they only happened in the large towns."

"That's usually where they start anyway," replied Miss Shuttleworth, putting down her paper. Jennifer *did* have this tendency to chat to you as you tried to read something—a bit annoying sometimes. But as she remembered from the last time, Jennifer talked virtually non-stop for the first day or two of her visit, then abruptly returned to a more normal pattern. Just as well really, for Miss Shuttleworth was not accustomed to being outvoiced.

"I don't think you'll find it has much effect here," she added then wished she hadn't. Jennifer's impression of Achanult as a rural backwater just short of the Arctic Circle in which nothing ever happened needed no reinforcing from her.

"No, I don't suppose so," agreed Miss McLachlan. "This paper certainly doesn't have much to say about it. Of course, I don't know who the people are. Who's Mrs Thorne? Doesn't sound very Scottish to me."

"We're not all Scottish here, you know, Jennifer. She came here with her husband from Birmingham a few years ago. I think he'd taken early retirement. His health's not too good."

"So she works as a taxi driver. Is that right?"

"She's employed by the education authority to drive some

of the outlying children to school. It's just part-time."

Miss McLachlan read on for another minute. Then she said, "I must admit they don't seem to get paid very much."

"Oh? I haven't looked at the details," said Miss Shuttleworth who had little interest in the matter, regarding strikes as beneath her dignity. Miss McLachlan gave her the details and Miss Shuttleworth, somewhat to her own surprise, admitted that the rates of pay were very low.

"And now they want to pay them even less!" exclaimed Miss McLachlan. "It hardly seems possible."

"You're beginning to sound dangerously left-wingish, Jennifer."

"Of course I'm not. It's just . . . well . . . anyway . . . "

"I expect the region wants to save money."

"Yes. I suppose so. So Mrs Thorne is wasting her time then?"

"Well, yes and no. She won't have much of an effect here. The locals will be queuing up to do her job."

"Really? Even if the pay is cut?"

"Even if the pay is nothing. They'll do it out of spite."

"Goodness! What a strange place."

Miss Shuttleworth turned a page of her newspaper and Miss McLachlan lapsed into silence for a few moments. Until, looking puzzled, she asked,

"What's the NO?"

Miss Shuttleworth peered quizically over the top of her paper.

"When I said Mrs What's-her-name was wasting her time, you said Yes and No, didn't you?"

"Oh, I see. I just meant that she won't really lose out because the whole region is involved. The other areas— Glasgow for instance—will all be on strike along with her.

They're the important places. Nobody really bothers about what happens here."

"I see. It's not as straightforward as it seems, is it?"

"There's more about it in this paper, Jennifer, if you're really interested," said Miss Shuttleworth turning another page. Silence reigned again.

When she had finished reading, Miss Shuttleworth wondered whether she might broach the subject of Jennifer taking up residence in Achanult. On the whole, she thought it might work out to the advantage of them both, in spite of occasional doubts. Jennifer did have these irritating little habits. For instance, the length of time she spent in the shower.

Miss Shuttleworth had had an electric shower unit installed last year—the kind which heated the cold water as you used it. Knowing nothing about electricity, she was convinced that the element would burn out if used for too long—especially since the accompanying leaflet kept referring to a "quick" shower. So she never took more than five minutes herself and was very surprised when Miss McLachlan spent what seemed like a very long time on her first use of the shower.

So Miss Shuttleworth had timed her on the second occasion and was shocked to discover that she took eleven minutes and forty seconds. She would clearly have to have a word with Jennifer, particularly since the guarantee period of one year had now elapsed. She seemed to want a shower every morning too. But Miss Shuttleworth had not yet thought of a suitable way of voicing an objection to that. And this morning she had taken over twelve minutes!

On the other hand, as she frequently reminded herself, if she and Jennifer were to pool their resources, then she could afford not to worry about such things. In fact life would be a lot easier in many ways and on balance it seemed the sensible thing to do. She decided to break the news to Miss McLachlan.

"Umm Jennifer, what are you going to do when you retire?"

"Oh, I've no great plans—a bit of travel perhaps."

"What I meant was, where are you going to live? You can't stay on in the hospital, can you?"

"No, I've got to find somewhere else. But they say I've got plenty of time. They're not rushing to kick me out as soon as I retire."

"Have you anywhere particular in mind?"

"Well no, I haven't. I suppose I really ought to start thinking about it. Perhaps you can help me there."

"As it happens, I probably can."

"I mean, you'll know about house buying, moving and so on. You certainly moved far enough."

"True. Umm, what I was wondering was . . . what do you think of it up here?"

"Here? It's a bit, well, wet . . . and remote."

"Remoteness has its advantages you know. What I mean is that if you're going to be at a bit of a loss, or you feel you would need some sort of guidance, you could move in with me."

"Oh, I couldn't possibly do that!" said Miss McLachlan firmly.

Miss Shuttleworth had not been prepared for this possibility.

"Oh well. I was only trying to be helpful."

"I quite understand, Marjory. There's no need to be angry."

"I am not angry," intoned Miss Shuttleworth, raising her voice further. "I merely suggested it as a solution, however temporary, to your problem."

"Well, yes. Thank you. It's just that you've rather sprung it on me."

Miss Shuttleworth was about to say that she had been considering it for weeks but instead, after a pause said,

"Perhaps you'd like to think about it. I wouldn't like to see you stuck."

"Yes, I'll certainly think about it. I haven't really considered the problem properly at all. What made you come up here?"

"Peace and quiet, I suppose. Houses are cheap too. Marvellous scenery."

"And do you ever regret it?"

"On the whole, no. Wherever you decide is bound to have some drawbacks."

"I suppose so. I really must think seriously about all this. I presume it's better here in the summer."

"Oh yes. The place is full of English tourists, Jennifer. You'd feel quite at home."

28 Guests

MRS NICHOLSON had suggested to her husband that he might like to come to the ceilidh on the final Tuesday of the Gaelic class but he had declined. On the previous Saturday he had travelled to Glasgow for the regional crossword competition and had returned bemused by the experience. He had done as well as he'd expected. Slightly better even— and he managed to finish a crossword in the allotted time. Unfortunately most of the other competitors had done better still, some of them even completing three crosswords.

Disappointment however, had now given way to determination and the Rev Nicholson had decided that he needed to practise a lot more. He had brought back several crossword books from Glasgow and so he would just have to find more time from somewhere.

So Mrs Nicholson had gone herself and for once she was not the first to arrive. As she entered the room she saw Maggie Stewart bringing out extra chairs from the cupboard in the corner. Once she had arranged the chairs to her satisfaction Maggie took up a position near the door with the intention of welcoming any new arrivals.

"I'll just stand at the door for a minute," she said. "I think there might be one or two guests coming and they probably won't know their way around here."

"Thank you," said Mrs Nicholson, feeling at a bit of a loss and still rather worried about what precisely they were supposed to be doing that afternoon.

"Some of the new people might not know you," added Maggie, stepping out into the playground.

Mrs Nicholson retreated into the classroom and watched from the window as the familiar faces duly appeared. There were at least three however that she couldn't put a name to but Maggie, who had welcomed them effusively, introduced them to her. Mrs Nicholson, as was usual with her, immediately forgot their names but it didn't really matter, she decided.

When she thought that everyone had arrived Maggie closed the door and said in an undertone to Mrs Nicholson,

"I don't want to interfere in your plans for the afternoon but if you get stuck I've got a few tapes here and I've brought a radio to play them on—if you think that's a good idea."

"Well . . . that's very kind of you. I haven't really decided on anything in particular. I just thought we'd see how things developed."

Maggie nodded and went to her seat only to find it occupied by Jean who was whispering something to Peter. Maggie's decision not to make an issue of this was prompted by the sudden realisation that the only power socket in the room, as far as she could see, was on the opposite wall. Lifting her bag with the radio and tapes, she moved to the other side of the room.

"Ah, you're coming to join us," said Miss Shuttleworth with patently false hilarity. She and Miss McLachlan were sitting together at the front. Maggie, who'd been desperate to find out about Miss McLachlan, had been taken aback when the pair of them had swept past her at the door with merely a nod from Miss Shuttleworth. She decided to try again.

"Are you enjoying your visit, Miss . . . umm . . . ?"

"It's been *most* interesting," replied Miss McLachlan, who'd been forewarned by her friend.

"Good. Of course, you're maybe used to it a bit warmer," probed Maggie.

"I haven't found it *too* cold."

Maggie decided to play her ace.

"I'm Maggie Stewart, by the way."

"I think," interrupted Miss Shuttleworth, "that Mrs Nicholson is waiting to start." Raising her voice she said to Mrs Nicholson,

"I'm sure we're all here now. We might as well begin."

The chatter in the room subsided and Mrs Nicholson began her words of welcome.

On the whole the afternoon went well after a slight hitch at the start. Mrs Nicholson had begun by inviting someone—anyone at all—to start the proceedings with a song or a story or whatever they liked. In the ensuing silence it soon became apparent that everyone had come to listen, not to perform. Maggie, who had anticipated this, broke the embarrassing hush.

"If you like , just to get us started, I've got one or two tapes here . . . " She looked at Mrs Nicholson.

"Well, yes, maybe we could do that."

"Right. Well, is there anything you would particularly like? They're all Gaelic or Scottish, of course."

"Just you choose, Mrs Stewart. Just something to get us started."

"Well, here's quite a good one. This is a band—four or five, I think. A lot of their songs are in Gaelic."

"Ish it that one she shaw on the bridge?" Various heads turned towards Alec Cameron.

"What was that, Mr Cameron?" asked Mrs Nicholson.

"Shon the bridge!"

"Of course!" cried Miss Shuttleworth with a beam of triumph. "Mr Cameron is quite rightly reminding us of that word written on the bridge. I've forgotten at the moment what it was," she added to conceal the fact that she was uncertain how to pronounce it.

"Oh yes, *Ceartas*." said Mrs Nicholson tactfully. "But, umm . . . , I thought we agreed that it wasn't the name of a band."

"*We* did," concurred Miss Shuttleworth, "but perhaps Mrs Stewart is going to prove us wrong by letting us hear them on her tape."

Maggie formed her features into a thin smile.

"This is a Scottish band," she said, naming a group which none of those present had heard of. "I'll just play one side to see what you think of it."

After a few minutes it became clear that most of the audience were not too enthusiastic about the music. To Maggie's obvious irritation they began chattering among themselves, discreetly at first, then with increasing disregard for the sounds coming from her radio. She turned the volume up a little but the audience only chatted a little more loudly to compensate. The sudden end of the tape however, brought a general silence.

"Well," said Mrs Nicholson, "that was quite interesting. Who did you say it was?"

Maggie told her again.

"Ah yes. They're new to me, but of course . . . I wonder what anyone else thought of them." Mrs Nicholson looked hopefully round the room.

"I thought they were a bit noisy," volunteered Miss Shuttleworth and a few heads nodded agreement.

"Well of course, they are very modern," replied Maggie, a bit annoyed to find some of the others siding with Miss Shuttleworth. She decided to try to isolate her.

"Of course you may not be used to our traditional rhythms."

"Didn't sound very traditional to me," retorted Miss Shuttleworth. "Just a lot of bang bang mostly. What do you think?" she asked, turning to Mrs Nicholson.

"Well, umm, I have to admit I didn't recognise any of the songs," replied Mrs Nicholson coming off the fence. "But I feel we should always be prepared to give a hearing to any new Scottish music," she added, climbing back on to it.

So the ceilidh got underway. Mrs Nicholson told a few traditional stories from the Outer Hebrides which she'd rehearsed during the week. These went down very well and led, as she'd hoped, to a general discussion in which most of the audience became involved. After that they decided to have some music again. This time Maggie thought it wiser to play safe and allow her audience to decide for themselves what they wanted. As she read out the titles of her tapes it soon became clear that there was to be no unanimity of choice. As various views were expressed, Mrs Nicholson tried to restore some order.

"I think it would be nice," she suggested, "if some of our guests made a choice." No-one could find anything wrong with this, so she looked expectantly at the new faces, none of which volunteered an opinion. After a period of silence she turned with incipient desperation to Peter who was the only new face to which she could put a name.

"What do *you* think, Mr McQueen? What would you like?"

"Oh . . . anything. I don't mind at all. Just whatever you like."

Mrs Nicholson sighed quietly to herself. Jean, however, sensing that her husband had not helped matters along, intervened with some reluctance on his behalf. "We both like dance music."

29 Maggie

MAGGIE yawned and stared at the dying fire. She might as well let it go out now. Jim had gone to bed over an hour ago, only just managing to make it to midnight. It was all that drinking at dinner time, of course—well all afternoon, to be truthful. An awful waste of money. Jim seemed to think that now she'd got this job they'd have plenty of money. She'd told him that it was an important position but the salary had still to be decided. There was possibly some truth in this latter point but Jim wasn't particularly interested in the details. The question of the salary had in fact, been a prominent part of the interview.

"I'm afraid we can't offer more than the basic salary," said Mr Dorward, who'd come down from Oban to conduct the interview. Maggie wondered what would be a suitable reply to this.

"Is that acceptable to you, Mrs. Stewart?'

"Um . . . "

"It's all we're allowed to give under the circumstances as was indicated in the advertisement. We'd like to offer more, but . . . "

"I understand. How much, in fact, umm . . . "

"Well, as you know, the basic salary was given in the advert. There is a series of annual increments, of course, rising to . . . I forget exactly."

The lady sitting beside Mr Dorward drew his attention to the details. Maggie had forgotten her name.

"But you would have to start at the bottom. It's regional policy, I'm afraid. This may be why you're the only applicant for the post."

This was news to Maggie. So she would definitely get the job then. She beamed at Mr. Dorward and the other lady.

"Well of course, money isn't everything," began Maggie. Mr Dorward looked relieved.

"I quite agree. It's simply that we have found it advisable from experience, as Miss Mathers will confirm, to make sure that the question of salary is fully understood before any decision is arrived at."

"What it will mean, of course," said Miss Mathers leaning forward, "is that you will be paid less than the previous holder of the post, at least for the first few years."

Maggie struggled to control her annoyance. That silly wee girl paid more than she would get? She'd never really liked Janice and had refused to make a contribution to her wedding present on the grounds that she and Jim hardly used the library.

"That may seem unfair," continued Miss Mathers, "especially

since you're a good deal older, but . . . " She paused with a shrug. Maggie wondered how old Miss Mathers was.

"So is there anything else you'd like to ask us?" enquired Mr Dorward, eager to get back to Oban. About fifty-ish, Maggie thought, as she searched for a suitable question.

"You'll be quite familiar with the library, of course," added Miss Mathers as an afterthought.

"Oh yes. My husband and I are both regular users."

So she'd got the job all right, to start after the holiday period. Maggie decided once again that she might as well go to bed. It didn't look like they'd have any visitors. Not surprising really. It was a few years now since they'd had a first foot—a proper one, that is. Some friend of Jim's it was, who'd known him from his Glasgow days and who happened to be visiting friends in the area. He wasn't much of a first foot. Far too drunk for one thing. He hardly knew where he was. After an hour or so of incoherent ramblings Maggie had had enough but they didn't get rid of him till after three. He was sick all over the hall table on the way out and finally left threatening to return next Hogmanay. All that the rest of the village had heard from her had been what great company he'd been and what a great night they'd all had.

She shut the living room door behind her as she went through to the bedroom. That would cut down some of the noise from next door. How did they expect other people to get to sleep? They'd be going on for hours yet if last year was anything to go by. That couple from England were up staying with them again. Well, they wouldn't be all that comfortable, that was one thing. Their house was no bigger than Maggie's. Just the same, in fact. Room for two people and that was about it. Still, Maggie's garden was about a foot and a half longer, where the road took a slight curve. She was quite pleased about this but Jim said it was just more grass to cut. Not that he cut it all that often. She'd even had to do it herself once.

She'd have to shut the bedroom door as well. That silly laugh of May's! You could hear her a mile away. She'd obviously had too much again, same as last year. Thank goodness they wouldn't be coming round till the evening—if at all. May might have quietened down a bit by then. Maggie had thought of popping through for a quick visit just after midnight but Jim wouldn't and she could hardly go herself. She wondered whether to leave some lights on so that folk would think they were still up, entering into the spirit of things. There was that laugh of May's again. Much more of this and she'd have to bang on the wall. Maggie was all for people enjoying themselves, especially at the New Year when she herself invariably had a GREAT TIME. But some folk didn't know when to stop.

She was up quite early the next morning. It looked like being a dry but cold day so she'd better get the fire going. She liked to feel that her house was warm and welcoming and created a good impression—particularly at this time of year. There was always somebody turning up unexpectedly like Mrs Hendry last year. She and Maggie were far from being friends, especially since that debacle over the raffle tickets. That was a good few years ago now but the coolness remained and would continue, as far as Maggie was concerned, until Mrs Hendry felt like making some kind of apology. Jim had said that he'd heard some people saying that it was Maggie's fault. But then , there had always been folk like that in Achanult who resented Maggie's prominent position in the community and thought that they should be running things just because they lived in big houses.

So Mrs Hendry had turned up last year with Alice of all

174

people. As far as Maggie knew, Alice was no great friend of Mrs Hendry either but she did have this unfortunate habit of trying to keep in with the likes of Mrs Hendry just because they had a bit of money and a big house. Maggie had welcomed Mrs Hendry with a smile which fooled neither of them and had chatted to Alice while watching Mrs Hendry cast her critical gaze over the room. Maggie felt like asking her if she would like a guided tour of the rest of the house but there was just a slight danger that Mrs Hendry would accept the offer. Sheer noseyness of course. So as usual Maggie made her ritual apology.

"You'll have to excuse the state of the house," she said, having spent hours the previous evening making sure that nothing was out of place. "Oh, don't worry about that," replied Mrs Hendry, "I don't know how *we* would manage without Mrs McGrotty."

Maggie had forgotten about that. Sheer snobbery, of course. She would need to ask Mrs McGrotty what Mrs Hendry's house was like inside.

"Of course, you're lucky here, in a way," continued Mrs Hendry. "Such a compact house. It must be a lot easier to keep clean—when you can find the time."

Maggie thought she'd better change the subject.

"And how is Mr Hendry?" she'd asked.

Alice and Mrs Hendry hadn't stayed long. When they'd gone, Maggie sat down on the sofa with the cigarette she'd needed about an hour ago. She'd never seen Mrs Hendry smoking. Maybe she smoked at home, out of sight. Something else to ask Mrs McGrotty.

Maggie wondered what sort of impression Mrs Hendry had taken away with her. Of course the house *was* small. So much so that Maggie was occasionally rather embarrassed about it—

she would never have invited Mrs Hendry to visit her—and she was quite envious of those who lived in the larger houses in the village. Still, maybe Mrs Hendry hadn't noticed too much. What was it she'd said? Compact, that was it. Maggie quite liked the sound of that.

She looked out of the window to see if anyone else was up and about. Not much evidence of anyone. It would be a bit early for some of them of course, after last night. Maggie didn't have much of a view from her house. Clachan cottages were set in a hollow at the back of the village and were almost the only houses in Achanult not to overlook the sea. Maggie didn't mind this, because who wanted to stare at a lot of water all the time? They got enough of it falling on top of them all year without having to look at it stretching in front. And the rubbish you got on the shore—driftwood, seaweed—that could smell a bit in summer. Maggie was glad she couldn't see any of that.

She'd noticed that a lot of the incomers put seaweed on their gardens but that was just them trying to pretend that they belonged here. Which they didn't. Very few of the locals used seaweed, preferring to buy fertilisers in bags from Oban. You got some good stuff there—peat, lime, even dried seaweed. A bit dear, mind you, but she'd used some herself. Not that her garden really needed anything. There was nothing wrong with the vegetables *she* grew.

The incomers complained about the soil in Achanult but then they would. They complained about the weather too. In fact they spent so much of their time complaining about things that you wondered why they bothered to stay. After studying the incomers over a period of years, Maggie had been surprised to learn that they liked to play down their wealth. This seemed very odd but the more she considered the matter the more certain she was that they tried to give that impression. That would be why they put seaweed on their gardens. Quite open about it, they were. Miss Shuttleworth had even recommended it to Maggie. (The cheek of the woman!) After exchanging a few remarks about the weather one day she'd said, "Well at least there's one good thing about these gales. They bring up lots of seaweed. I must get some more for my garden. Do you use it a lot?"

"No we don't. It's regarded as a bit old-fashioned round here."

"Really?"

"Yes, the sort of thing the older generation used to do. But we've moved on a bit since then," said Maggie who liked to inform anyone who would listen how go-ahead Achanult was.

"Oh well, I'm quite happy to use it anyway." It was on such occasions that Maggie suspected many of the incomers were quite unconcerned about her opinion of them. Which only made her all the more annoyed.

With no sign of life out the front window, Maggie walked through to the kitchen to see if she could spot any deer at the back of the house. They could be a real pest at this time of year, lurking in the dense woods. She wished that they could get rid of some of the trees and leave a bit of open ground at the end of their garden. That way she might get a bit more of the sun for the tall pines shaded the garden. They might have a lot less of the midges too. Maggie knew that they were rife in among the trees. Jim used to be always complaining about them when he worked for the Forestry. They were so bad that Maggie couldn't sit in her back garden in the summer evenings unless there was a strong wind. Things weren't much better in the front garden. As she filled the kettle Maggie reflected that winter in Achanult had its good points. You didn't get the midges, for one thing.

30 Cards

PETER came through into the living room with the letter in his hand.

"It's from Perth. Who do we know in Perth?"

Jean paused from her knitting and thought for a moment.

"Oh, it'll be the Fishers sending us a New Year card. We didn't get a Christmas card from them."

"Didn't we?" Peter wasn't interested in Christmas cards and left the whole business to Jean.

Jean opened the envelope, extracted a card with flowers all over it and the words "Best wishes for the New Year". Inside she read:

"*To all our friends both far and near,*
 We wish every happiness in the coming year."

Underneath, Mrs Fisher had written "Sorry about the delay. Away over the holidays."

"Nice words, aren't they?" said Jean, trying to remember what was written in the card she had sent them. Something about absent friends, she recalled. Jean put a lot of thought into choosing Christmas cards and liked to pick ones with nice words in them. You got all sorts of cards nowadays and a lot of them didn't seem to have much to do with Christmas. Not that Jean was narrow minded. She wasn't one of those people who insisted on holy cards, as she called them, with angels, wise men, a few camels and all the rest of it. She had to send one of those to the minister of course, and to one or two other people. But mostly she was quite happy with robins, snow and a few stagecoaches—a proper Christmas card. Well, that was what most people liked.

She and Peter had got a funny one last year from the

Maxwells with a map of Argyll on the front. You'd hardly have known it was a Christmas card at all. It wasn't even a very good map. Quite old, by the look of it, with few of the places that she knew on it but quite a number that she'd never heard of. Peter had had a look at it.

"It's not very good, is it? A lot of the names aren't spelt properly."

"Maybe that's the Gaelic spelling," suggested Jean.

"Oh aye. Maybe."

"And what's this here?" She pointed to the words *Mare Vergivium.*"

Peter shook his head. "That'll probably be another bit of Gaelic. Better ask Donald." This was a wee joke of theirs, now that Donald had started going to the Gaelic class.

"Oh , Donald wouldn't know that. He's only been going for a few weeks."

"Ask Maggie Stewart then."

"She probably wouldn't know either."

"Aye, but that wouldn't stop her telling you all about it."

"Och, it doesn't really matter. It's a daft card anyway."

So Jean had stuck the card on the kitchen mantlepiece, where not too many people would see it. Not that they had a great many visitors, but Jean liked to chat to them in the living room, where the nicer cards were prominently displayed on the mantlepiece and surrounding area.

"So why are the Fishers sending us this card?" asked Peter.

"Because we sent them one."

"Did we? Och well." Jean sent a lot more Christmas cards than Peter thought necessary or even knew about. He'd no great objection but the amount of stamps she got through was a bit worrying.

"Maybe we don't need to send them a card anymore. It

179

must be—what—fifteen years since they left. We never knew them all that well anyway," suggested Peter.

"Och, it's nice to get a card."

Peter knew there was no point in pursuing this line. Jean always sent a card to anyone who sent her one the year before and since most of her acquaintances operated on the same principle, the cycle continued remorselessly. She used to try to get Peter to take part, asking him to pick out cards with nice words which might be suitable for various people but she'd eventually realised that he wasn't really interested. You could tell he didn't think it was important. Look at the time she'd asked him to pick a nice card for the Vetuccis.

"The who?" he'd asked.

"The Vetuccis. Mind? Willie's brother who was here on holiday last summer with his wife. Well, that's their daughter."

"Who?"

"Mrs Vetucci."

"Funny sort of name for Willie's daughter."

"Willie's brother's daughter."

"Oh."

"It's one of these foreign names, Willie was telling me. French or something."

"Oh well."

"So I thought we could send them a card. It'll be a nice surprise for them."

"Aye, so it will."

So Jean did all the Christmas cards by herself now.

"It's a bit late to be sending a card," mused Peter, picking up the envelope to look at the date.

"Well, if they were away somewhere . . . "

"Aye, I suppose so. Where were they?"

"I don't know. Visiting relatives, maybe."

"It'll just be an excuse for being late with the card."

"Och, I don't think so," said Jean who took a charitable view of human nature.

"Anyway, they've been late for the last two or three years and had to send a New Year card. I suppose if we didn't send them one they might forget altogether."

"Aye, it's worth a try, I suppose."

"Well I always think it's nice to get a card. Mind you, this one won't be up for very long. I was going to take them all down tomorrow."

Jean always took her Christmas cards down at the end of the New Year holiday. Before putting them away she checked them against her list. She'd had this list for years now with various names crossed out and a lot more added. There were none to add this year. Peter was always amazed at the length of the list.

"I don't know who half these people are. Seems an awful lot."

"Not really. Some people get far more cards than we do."

"Oh?"

"Well, Maggie Stewart told me last year that she'd got so many cards she didn't know where to put them all."

"Hmmm."

"I haven't seen her yet this year."

"She'll have got even more cards."

"I expect she'll let us know," agreed Jean. "I wonder how many Donald gets?" she added as the sound of Donald's car starting up reached them.

"I'd be surprised if he got any. Where's he off to now?"

"Well he certainly got one from us."

"Did he?" Peter looked doubtful.

"Of course he did. We always send him one."

"Did we get one from him?"

"No. He hasn't sent us one for years."

Peter wasn't surprised. A few of the older folk in the village would have nothing to do with Christmas cards on the dubious grounds that they were vaguely popish. Donald though, probably just thought that they were vaguely expensive. Well, so they were. Peter remembered seeing the prices pencilled on the back of them from time to time. He'd wondered why Jean didn't buy cheaper ones. Something to do with unsuitable or non-existent words, apparently. Well, he didn't want to get involved in that, which was probably why she'd said it. Jean had a mind of her own sometimes he had to admit. He'd also tried to get her to save on the postage. Half the cards were for Achanult anyway and he wouldn't have minded the walk. But she didn't like to. It wasn't the proper way to do it seemingly. Aye, she was a bit stubborn at times as well.

"So where's Donald off to now?"

"He'll have run out of food again. It's the same every year."

Aye that would be it. Peter remembered one time a few years ago—it must have been just after the New Year—when Donald had run out of food. He'd had to drive to Oban where all the shops were shut of course. All he could find open was a Chinese restaurant, so he'd just had to drive home again hungry and ill-tempered. They'd felt a bit sorry for him. When he'd calmed down Donald had told them that according to the menu in the window they did Scottish food as well—fish and chips, stuff like that. But he hadn't liked to take the risk.

"We could easily have given him something—a tin of soup, maybe," said Peter as he turned away from the window.

"He'd never admit to being short. Anyway, he probably wouldn't eat it. Remember the box of chocolates?"

Peter laughed. They'd given Donald some chocolates a few years ago. Quite an unusual kind with marzipan in them. Jean thought she could remember Donald saying that he liked marzipan. After she'd bought them Jean had a feeling that it was actually coconut he'd mentioned. Something to do with the war, Peter said. Donald had been out east somewhere or wherever it was they had coconuts. Anyway, when the village had had the sale of work for that earthquake disaster, they'd noticed the same box of chocolates on one of the stalls. Maybe it was just a coincidence, but Jean*had* wondered.

She hadn't liked to spend too long examining it, though, in case they thought she was going to buy it. In the end, she'd asked Alice behind the stall, in a quiet moment, where she'd got those interesting chocolates. Alice said she'd need to ask Mrs Neil, but Jean said she didn't want to be nosy. So she'd left it at that. Later in the afternoon Jean thought that if she could maybe get Mrs Neil alone for a minute . . . But that was the trouble with ministers' wives. They were always talking to somebody.

"What did we give him this year?"

"Those socks. I showed you them."

"Oh, aye."

"With the tartan checks. Socks are always handy."

31 Scottish ways

ACROSS in Fairview, Miss Shuttleworth and her friend Miss McLachlan were conversing over breakfast.

"I must say, Marjory, this fish is very good. What did you say it was called?"

"It's a smokie."

"A smokie. Quite. But what kind of fish is it?"

"It's a bit hard to tell," mused Miss Shuttleworth peering at the headless specimen on her plate. "I don't really know much about fish. I think it's maybe cod. Or haddock, possibly."

"Oh, is that all? I mean—it's very good of course, but I thought it might be something Scottish—salmon, for instance."

"Smoked salmon is very expensive, Jennifer." And so were the smokies.

"Yes, of course, so it is. I'd forgotten. By the way, I was hearing about it on the radio last night."

At that point the telephone rang. And rang.

"Just ignore it," said Miss Shuttleworth when she'd finished her mouthful of smokie. "Whoever it is will go away in due course."

"But it might be important, Marjory."

"Very unlikely. And if it is they'll ring back later."

"But what if it's something urgent?"

"In Achanult?"

"But how do you know it's a local call?"

"Well most of my calls are. It'll be someone phoning to wish me a Happy New Year or something. You get a lot of it at this time of year. I find it best just to lie low till the fuss dies down."

"Quite. I must say I was a little apprehensive about a Scotch . . . what's that word again?"

"What word?"

"For New Year's eve."

"Oh. Hogmanay."

"That's it! What a funny word. It sounds a bit uncouth, doesn't it?"

"I can't say I . . . "

"You'll be used to it, of course. Anyway, what I was going to say was that I thought that things might be a bit noisy on Hoymanay. I remember my father saying something to that effect, about people singing in the streets, blowing bagpipes, drinking whisky."

"Not all at the same time, I hope."

"Well of course, I don't really know anything about it, Marjory. But I didn't notice any of that drunken behaviour here, I'm glad to say."

"I think people are a bit more discreet now."

Miss McLachlan finished her smokie.

"Excellent," she repeated. "In fact, I could eat another one," she admitted with a giggle. "I don't usually eat much fish at home."

"All this highland air has given you a healthy appetite, Jennifer."

"Yes, I suppose it has. In fact, I wouldn't mind taking some smokies home with me. They keep for a while, don't they?"

"Oh yes. That's why I bought them with the shops being shut for days . . . "

"Yes, of course. Mind you, I was amazed that your village shop opened on Christmas day."

"Oh, it always does. Only for two or three hours, though."

"They won't believe it at home. It does seem a bit . . . um . . . "

"Pagan?"

"Unnecessary, is what I was thinking of," said Miss McLachlan rising from the table to deposit the skeleton of her smokie in the dustbin. "Oh yes," she added, "I was going to tell you about that programme last night. Or did you hear it?"

Miss Shuttleworth paused. Jennifer had this habit of listening to the radio in her bedroom after she'd gone to bed. She had brought her own radio with her, a large black affair with a huge aerial. She did have a smaller one at home but had heard that you needed a very powerful radio to hear anything in Scotland—something to do with all those hills. Although she didn't play it loudly, Miss Shuttleworth had still found it disturbing late at night. If Jennifer should decide to come and live with her this was something which would have to be sorted out right at the beginning. She had thought of going through to have a word with her last night but after the reaction the last time she'd knocked on Miss McLachlan's door, she'd decided not to bother.

That was the time when she'd wanted to retrieve her map which she'd lent to Miss McLachlan earlier in the evening when they'd been discussing their proposed itinerary for the following day. She'd tapped quietly on Miss McLachlan's door. At once the radio was switched off. After a few seconds of silence, a hushed voice said,

"Who is it?"

"It's me of course, Jennifer. Who else would it be?"

"Yes, of course. What is it?"

"I just wanted to have another look at the map."

"Oh. Ah. Yes . . . umm . . . where is it?"

"I think you've got it."

"Have I? Just a moment then."

Miss Shuttleworth stood outside the bedroom door and waited. Nearly a minute passed before footsteps approached the door. A key was inserted and the lock turned. The door cautiously opened to reveal the flustered figure of Miss McLachlan protected by her heavy duty dressing gown buttoned to the neck. She thrust the map through the doorway with the words. "There you are, Marjory." and closed the door again before Miss Shuttleworth had a chance to reply.

Jennifer's behaviour really was very odd at times. Perhaps she'd thought there might be a clan raid with a bit of rape and pillage. Miss Shuttleworth couldn't remember ever having locked that bedroom door before—or any of the others—but presumably Miss McLachlan did so every night. How strange! So she hadn't done anything last night about Miss McLachlan's radio.

"No. I didn't hear it Jennifer. I was reading, actually."

"Oh, what a pity. You'd have enjoyed it."

"Oh?"

"Yes. It was a Gaelic programme."

"I see. What was it about?"

"Well, of course I couldn't understand much of it, Marjory. But some of it was about fish farming and grants from the EEC."

"How do you know?"

"I heard them saying it. Some words must be the same in Gaelic and English. Or nearly the same anyway. Is that right?"

"I wouldn't have thought so but I'll ask Mrs Nicholson."

"Well, I certainly thought a lot of the words were quite understandable. Is Gaelic a sort of highland dialect of English, then?"

"Not at all. It's quite different."

"Oh well. There was some singing too, and somebody playing a melodion, or something. It was pretty awful. They don't seem to sing in tune."

"Oh, I don't know, Jennifer. Some of the singers I've heard are very good," said Miss Shuttleworth, rising from the table. Jennifer really seemed to expect too much, sometimes. Miss Shuttleworth found herself irritated from time to time by her friend's quirks but tried hard not to show it, for the moment at least. Anyway she was leaving today, she'd hinted. Miss Shuttleworth hadn't liked to ask outright, which was rather unlike her. It was a bit of a strain, really. Once Miss McLachlan had decided to come and live with her, Miss Shuttleworth felt she could be a bit more outspoken. And if she decided not to come, ditto. Anyway, she should be off on the train later this afternoon.

"I think I'll stay another day and leave tomorrow, Marjory— if that's all right."

"Certainly. You know you can stay as long as you like."

"Yes, of course. I thought I'd like to have a walk round the village again."

The two of them walked out past the edge of the village. They made an incongruous pair—Miss Shuttleworth short and stocky with her stick which she didn't really need but always carried. Miss McLachlan tall and thin muffled up against the elements. She'd wanted to borrow one of Miss Shuttleworth's sticks as they were leaving the house.

"Whatever for?" asked Miss Shuttleworth. "You've never needed one before."

"I know. But if we're going to go out into the country, there might be some of those wild sheep."

"Oh for goodness sake, Jennifer. The sheep won't bother you."

"Well . . . "

"Anyway, a stick wouldn't suit you."

"Wouldn't it? Why not?"

Miss Shuttleworth thought quickly.

"You're too tall. My sticks would be far too short for you."

"I wasn't going to use it as a walking stick, Marjory. Just as a . . . well, whatever you use yours for. Why do you always carry a stick anyway?"

"Oh it's a tradition round here."

"Is it?" asked Miss McLachlan dubiously. "I can't say I . . . "

"I think we'd better get on our way, Jennifer. There's rain forecast for later in the afternoon. Just leave the sticks. I'll lend you mine if need be."

"Oh, all right. But I'll take my handbag."

And yet, mused Miss Shuttleworth as they set off, her friend had mellowed to some extent. When they'd been watching the news on television the other night there had been pictures of blizzards in Essex with cars stuck in snowdrifts.

"Aren't you glad you're up here, Jennifer?" she had asked her friend.

"Well, I must say it doesn't seem too bad at the moment. When does the snow usually come?"

"It usually doesn't. Our winters are quite mild, you know— as I think I've mentioned."

On the way back into the village they paused at the bridge. Miss McLachlan found herself pushed to keep up with Miss Shuttleworth who strode briskly on in all weathers. She did a lot of walking of course and quite right too. The views were splendid and the roads quiet. Miss McLachlan looked inland to the bungalows on the edge of the village.

"I must say it's nice to see those new houses there."

"Some people wouldn't agree with you, Jennifer."

"Oh? Why's that?"

"Well, a lot of the locals think they've altered the character of the place. And then there are the characters who live in them."

"Well I think they're a good thing. It shows the village isn't dying. New houses . . . new people . . . I'm sure it must be a good thing although I don't suppose the locals see it like that. What's that field over there for?"

"I think they used to play shinty on it. I don't know if they still do."

"Play what?"

"Shinty."

"What's that?"

"It's a game. A bit like hockey."

"I can't say I've ever heard of it."

"No, it's really only a highland sport, I think."

"Oh—do they wear kilts? Or is it women who play?"

"No, it's for men and they don't wear kilts as far as I know."

"What a pity! I thought you had to wear a kilt for these highland sports. Are those the goalposts?"

"Yes."

"They look a bit odd. They're the wrong shape, aren't they?"

"I doubt it. I imagine that's the way they're supposed to be, Jennifer."

"Well they don't look quite right. What are those sheep doing there."

"Looking for some grass to eat, I suppose. Not much of it about at this time of year."

"Why are they staring at us?"

"Oh, they're probably wondering whether to charge at us with their horns."

"What!"

Miss Shuttleworth couldn't restrain a smile.

"They're more frightened of you that you are of them you know, Jennifer."

"Oh?"

"Yes. Just run towards them waving your arms and they'll scatter in all directions."

Miss McLachlan considered this possibility.

"I couldn't possibly . . . anyway, somebody might be watching. But if you lend me your stick, I could walk slowly towards them and see what happens."

"Good for you, Jennifer."

"Umm . . . aren't you coming?"

"No, I'll just stay here. Somebody might have to phone for an ambulance."

"I don't think that's very funny, Marjory. On second thoughts I think we'd better make for home. I'm sure I can feel the rain coming."

As the two ladies headed briskly on their way, the small group of sheep slowly crossed the halfway line in the opposite direction.

32 Public approval

THE Rev Nicholson stared out of his study window. In the background he could hear his wife using the vacuum cleaner. He found the noise a bit disturbing in a strange way and couldn't really concentrate on what he was doing. At that particular moment it was a crossword puzzle. The vacuum cleaner was rather old and emitted a high pitched whine—G# according to Anna who understood about music.

But it altered its pitch every few seconds by a semitone, either up or down and it was this that he found particularly fatal to his concentration. It didn't seem to bother Anna. In fact she was more concerned that since they'd come to Achanult, the vacuum cleaner now whined in G natural, according to their piano, with the usual semitone variations. This meant of course, that either the vacuum cleaner had changed its tune, or else their piano was now a semitone flat. Probably something to do with the dampness of the west coast.

The Rev Nicholson sighed. He'd become accustomed to his wife's absence on Tuesday afternoons when the house was quiet and he could get on with things. Flicking idly through his crossword book—a Christmas present from Anna—he noted that he still had more than half of them to do. In this particular book the puzzles were arranged in order of difficulty, so he'd started at the beginning just to see what they were like. The first few weren't too bad but now, about a third of the way through, things were getting a bit harder. Of course the style of these crosswords was different from what he was used to. And the noise of the vacuum cleaner didn't help. He decided to have a break especially as his wife had now moved out into the hall. As he opened the door of the dining room—as they called his study—his wife caught sight of him and switched off the vacuum cleaner.

"I don't think this machine is working properly, David."

"Oh? Sounds all right to me. A bit flat maybe—or is it sharp? I can never remember."

"No, what I mean is that it doesn't seem to be sucking things up properly."

"Oh, I see. Probably something to do with the damp."

"What damp?"

"The general dampness in the air over here. I thought you said it affected things."

"Well yes, but I don't think that's the problem. D'you think you could have a look at it?"

"I don't really know much about these things, Anna. It's probably just too old. Anyway, I might make matters even worse. By the way, when are your Tuesday afternoon classes starting again?"

"In about a fortnight, I think." And then doubtfully, "If enough people turn up."

"Oh, I'm sure they will. I met Miss Shuttleworth a few days ago and she told me how much she enjoyed it and how keen she was to resume again."

"Oh! That was very nice of her."

"Yes. Mind you, she could hardly have said that it was the most boring time she'd ever spent and that she had no intention of repeating it. Anyway, I'll maybe mention it on Sunday, just to remind people."

"But you can't do that, David."

"Why not?"

"Well a church service is not really the place . . . "

"Oh, I'll just slip it in among the other intimations."

"If you really think it is a good idea . . . I'm not too sure."

"Well, we'll see."

"Can I just get into the dining room now that I've got the vacuum cleaner out—if I'm not disturbing you."

"If you must, I suppose."

"Were you working on something?"

"Oh . . . just one or two things. They can wait."

Mr Nicholson wandered through into the lounge, wondering how he could drum up support for his wife's afternoon class. Apart from the fact that it gave her an interest and an outlet for her talents, he had gradually come to realise that it was important that Achanult should have an opportunity to investigate all aspects of its cultural heritage. Things would have been a lot easier in the old days when ministers had great power in their communities. He'd have been able to order most of the village to attend the Gaelic class and they would have done so except for a few dissenters whom he would have had burnt at the stake for their impertinence! Well, maybe he wouldn't have had to be quite so strict—most of the villages would have spoken Gaelic already in those days.

But times had changed. Mind you, the church still had a lot of influence in the Highlands—or so he'd been told. In fact, he'd quite looked forward to being a figure of importance in the community. Especially after his years in Edinburgh when he'd felt unappreciated and neglected. Here in Achanult he was certainly a more prominent figure and still regarded with some respect, which he enjoyed. But things were undoubtedly changing and it was quite noticeable that a lot of incomers, such as Miss Shuttleworth, tended to treat him as an equal.

Of course, a lot of the incomers didn't go to church. Or if they did, it wasn't to his. Many of them went to the Episcopalian church in Forse.

Maybe it was just as well. A lot of these English seemed to be very keen, especially the women. A bit too much enthusiasm really. There was a lot of it about at the moment in fact—like that ecumenical business for a start. At Christmas there had been the non-denominational service in the village hall which the few members of the Episcopalian and Roman Catholic communities had attended. None of the Free Church members—who in any case were equally few in number—had come, which the Reverend Nicholson had found a bit disappointing. It was surely time to take a more liberal attitude in this day and age.

That at any rate was what he'd said to Father O'Brien and they'd both nodded sagely, comfortable in their temporary collusion. But as Anna had reminded him when he'd returned from the service, it was only an illusion. There was no real desire for closer cooperation. Mr Nicholson felt happy to agree with this and let his wife continue.

"After all," she added, "look at the Boyle family."

"Umm . . . "

"You know. I've told you about them."

"Ah yes."

"Sending their children to school in Oban."

"Well I suppose that must be the nearest Roman Catholic school."

"Yes I know, but . . . they're so young and it's such an early start . . . and a long day. Sometimes I see them coming home long after the other schoolchildren in the dark. I feel so sorry for them."

"I can see your point, Anna, but it's their decision."

"Hardly theirs. It's the parents. Or the father, anyway."

"Father O'Brien?"

"No, for goodness sake. Mr Boyle."

"Oh? In what way?"

"Well I've met Mrs Boyle once or twice. She's very nice really. I just got the impression she was a bit—I don't know— embarrassed or unhappy about it."

"I'm surprised she mentioned it to you."

"Oh, she knows who I am. That's maybe why she was a bit embarrassed. I certainly didn't say anything."

"Well, quite. It's none of our business."

"I know. But she insisted in telling me about it. She was waiting for the children to come off the late bus when I met her. I couldn't get away. She went on and on."

"Yes. Now you mention it, I remember you saying something. What exactly was the gist of her remarks again?"

"Oh, simply that *she'd* be quite happy for her children to attend school in Achanult but her husband insists on Oban."

"I see . . . Well . . . " The Rev Nicholson paused while he tried to remember the Boyle family. He'd thought he knew

195

most people in Achanult by now. Maybe they'd been at that ecumenical service. One or two strange faces there certainly . . . Oh well, he'd maybe see them again next Christmas if there was to be another joint service.

"It does seem a pity," continued Mrs Nicholson. "Mrs Boyle was saying that her children don't make friends easily with the other children in the village."

"Well, I can see her point of course but it's really her own decision—or her husband's. Mind you, I expect *he* tells everyone that it's his *wife's* idea and that he'd be quite happy with the local school."

"Oh probably. But whatever it is, it's the sort of situation that can lead to a degree of friction."

"Oh? I hadn't noticed anything greatly amiss."

"Well, you should hear Maggie Stewart. She doesn't like the Boyles at all."

"That hardly places them in a unique situation, Anna."

"I suppose not. But it's all so petty. I get a bit fed up with it sometimes. Don't you ever?"

"You shouldn't take these things so seriously, Anna."

"But surely that's part of what we're here for, isn't it?"

"Ah. Well, ye-es . . . but . . . "

"Of course Mrs Stewart says religion has nothing to do with it."

This was a common remark of Maggie's but no one was deceived. Like many other inhabitants of the village she had bided her time after the Rev Nicholson's arrival until she could be sure of what his attitude was on various matters of a religious and secular nature, the latter being by far the more important. She could then adapt her views accordingly.

Few of the villagers had found themselves able to be sure of the Rev Nicholson's attitude to many matters and were consequently reluctant to commit themselves too strongly on any issue. Maggie however, had discreetly sought to discover Mrs Nicholson's attitude to various matters on the assumption that her husband's would be broadly similar. This was a situation in which Maggie felt she had no equal and she had been delighted with her secret success.

"Well, Anna, I suppose we ought to be grateful that Mrs Stewart can affirm that religion has nothing to do with her dislike of them."

"Oh, I wouldn't take that remark too seriously. It's just for our benefit."

"I dare say you're right."

"Oh yes. She'd been asking me, more than once and not too subtly, what I thought of the idea of the ecumenical service. She even asked me if you and I always agreed on such matters."

"Did she? What did you say?"

"Really, David. What would you expect me to say?"

"Well you could have said that I had nothing against such things and left it at that."

"That's more or less what I did."

"Good, good. Mrs Stewart is a bit of a busybody, I sometimes think. Anyway, if it's not religion she's got against them, what is it?"

"Oh, well apparently they're from Garrynacreck."

"That name rings a bell. Where have I heard it before?"

"I don't know but anyway it's the name of a farm about ten or twelve miles away."

"And what's wrong with that?"

"Well it means that they're not local . . . don't belong to Achanult. It's actually only the wife who comes from Garrynacreck. Mr Boyle is apparently from Achanult, so Mrs

Stewart admitted to me but his parents were incomers from down Lochgilphead way."

"I see. It makes you wonder what the locals think of us."

His wife was right he reflected, about the pettiness of it all, of course. Yet another reason why he should not become involved with any one interest in the village. He'd be daft to go out of his way to seek disapproval.

33 Emigre

PETER went off to get some wood to light the fire. There wasn't much left but then there never was at this time of year. Wood didn't really last all that long. He reached into the shed and hauled out an old fish box that he'd got off the beach a few weeks ago. It should be dry by now. Peter liked to leave wood on top of the range in the kitchen to dry overnight but Jean thought it was a bit untidy, and what if somebody called in? So Peter would have to take it out again first thing in the morning. He seldom bothered with it nowadays.

Using the blunt end of his axe Peter smashed the fish box into small pieces. These boxes were quite good for starting the fire even if they did have "no unauthorised use" written on the side of them. He always found several each year. A bit sparky though—pine of some sort by the look of it. Jean wasn't too happy about sparky wood since the time when a hole was burnt in one of her slippers. Mind you, it was her own fault really—she'd been half asleep when the spark landed and although she'd soon been aware of a smell of burning, she hadn't been able to trace it immediately. Still, it gave her an excuse to buy a new pair of slippers.

Once the fire had been lit, Peter sat down beside it. You had to keep an eye on it for a while—nurse it almost—or it might go out. Patience, that was the great thing.

As the fire struggled reluctantly into life, Peter glanced at the book on the armchair. One of Jean's, of course. He wasn't really a great reader himself. *A Riever's Daughter* it was called. On the back cover Peter read "A thrilling saga of endeavour and passion in the wild borderlands of Scotland's turbulent fifteenth century." Aye, Jean read some funny stuff. Peter was just putting the book down again when Jean came in with two cups and a teapot on a tray.

"Oh, you've just reminded me," she said, lifting her book and putting Peter's cup and saucer down in its place. "I meant to tell you yesterday when I came in but getting rid of that deer must have put it out of my mind. Maggie Stewart was telling me that she's got a job in the library."

"Oh?"

"I think she's quite lucky, really. I wouldn't have minded a job like that—if I was younger."

"You?"

"Well, I've always liked the place—nice and warm. And quiet as well."

"Aye, well you should have applied for the job then."

"Don't be daft. I'm too old."

"Well, you should have applied when you were younger."

Jean said nothing. This was a new line of Peter's. Although he'd never said very much over the years, she'd had the distinct impression that going out to work was a man's job as far as he was concerned. Not that he'd ever stopped her. She'd never really considered it seriously herself. But as they grew older and with no children, well . . . Things were different in those days of course, and not the same opportunities.

Sitting down in the other armchair, Jean took a sip from her cup while Peter carefully placed some more pieces of fish box on the fire.

"Anyway," she said finally, "I'd never get a job like that. You maybe need some qualifications."

"Maggie's got the job has she? What exactly is it?"

"She says she's a librarian."

"Well, I'm sure she won't have any qualifications. She didn't stay on long at school, did she?"

"No, but you surely wouldn't need any qualifications anyway, just to stamp books and put them back on shelves."

Peter agreed, sipping his tea and losing interest in the conversation.

"Mind you," persisted Jean, "Maggie was saying that it's an important job and she's got a lot of responsibility."

Peter said nothing, which was one of his ways of ending a conversation. But Jean remembered something else.

"She was saying that Heather would be back soon for a visit."

Heather was Maggie and Jim's daughter who now lived in Canada.

"Oh? It doesn't seem that long since she was last here."

"One and a half years, Maggie said."

"Aye, it could be. Just a visit, then. She's not thinking of coming back to live in Achanult?"

"I don't know, I don't think so. Maggie didn't say."

Peter nodded. He quite liked Heather, who wasn't at all like her mother—a bit more of Jim in her really. A bit shy too, Peter remembered. Of course she was a bit younger then.

"She's still not married, then?"

"No—well, not that I know of."

"I think we'd all have heard if she was," said Peter, settling back in his chair now that the fire was going better. Maggie kept Achanult up to date with the minutiae of Heather's life in Canada—not that she regarded her daughter's status there as in any way minor. According to Maggie, Heather more or less ran Guelph and when she left her highly paid and important post to go on holiday, the town almost ground to a halt. So Maggie said anyway. Heather never said much herself, except to confirm that she was a secretary and quite enjoyed her work.

"It's funny how she's never married," mused Jean.

"Aye, how old would she be now?"

"Must be nearly thirty. Maggie keeps saying that her work's too important for her to get married, too well-paid just to stop. Heather's got everything she needs, Maggie says, she doesn't need a man to provide anything."

"That seems a daft reason for not getting married if she really wanted to."

"Och well, you can be sure of one thing. It'll be her own decision whatever it turns out to be."

Peter knew what his wife meant. Everyone in Achanult except Maggie knew that Heather had gone to Canada to escape from her mother's influence. So she'd stayed at first with some distant relatives until she found a flat of her own— a large, beautifully furnished apartment, Maggie said, adding that people on the up such as Heather, preferred to rent rather than buy. A lot of people in Achanult wondered what Heather's life in Canada was really like but it wasn't so easy to find out. Maggie accompanied her daughter everywhere on her visits home—this would be her third now—and any questions anyone asked Heather were likely to be answered expansively by Maggie.

"Aye," said Peter, "she'll be doing her own thing now, as they say."

"Not before time. And Maggie seems to have accepted the situation quite well now. Mind how huffy she was to start with?"

Peter smiled. Maggie hadn't wanted her daughter to leave. When she did, the village heard nothing about Heather for about a year. Now they heard as much as they wanted and more.

"She was saying that Heather often drives forty miles for a cup of coffee," added Jean, taking another sip from her cup.

"Oh?" quizzed Peter, who didn't like coffee much himself. He'd had some once somewhere . . . "Don't they have it where she is?—where is it again?"

"I can never remember. Something to do with golf, isn't it."

"Aye, that sounds right. It still seems an awful long way to go for a cup of coffee."

"Maggie says people out there are used to long distances— they think nothing of it seemingly."

"Bit of a waste of petrol, though."

"She goes in somebody else's car, Maggie says."

"Oh. Hasn't she got a car of her own yet? They're not that dear there, are they?"

"It's not the money, seemingly. Heather doesn't have a licence. Too much bother, Maggie said. Something about a complicated form to fill in. Heather took one look at it and threw it away. She just takes a taxi whenever she wants. It's much easier like that, Maggie says."

Peter looked doubtful. "Oh well," he said after a pause while he drank the last of his tea. "When is she coming?"

"In the spring sometime. Maggie didn't know the date yet."

So that would be something else for the village to look

forward to. Maggie, who was bad enough at the best of times, could be quite insufferable when her daughter was around. Even Jim made great efforts to be up and about more, shaving every day and dressing half decently. He would take Heather out for a drink most evenings to the noisiest places he could find, hoping to give the impression that this was his regular life style and would talk of taking her to a cabaret which everyone else knew as a singalong, accompanied sometimes quite successfully by Angus and his accordian. Angus, who was a real character, was reputed to be quite unable to play when he was sober, though this had never been confirmed.

Of course, Jim realised that there were more sophisticated entertainments available and would take Heather as far as Lochgilphead for an evening with the local Strathspey and Reel society. Everyone felt that Jim was overdoing things a bit and when Heather had gone back after her last visit he'd had to take to his bed for about a week just to recover. Mind you, folk said he was liable to do that anyway, visit or no visit, and maybe there was a grain of truth there.

"Why is it that Maggie doesn't go over there for a visit?" asked Peter as he passed his empty cup over to Jean.

"I've often wondered that. You'd think she'd want to see the place. Of course, she's never been a great one for the go'ʳ

"Maybe she can't afford the fare. Jim would have to go ... well."

"Oh, it's not that, Maggie says."

"Oh?"

"Heather could pay their fares with the money she earns. Maggie's told me that many a time."

"So why doesn't she go?"

"I don't know. She keeps saying she'll go one day."

34 Damp

LIFE could be difficult, thought Miss Shuttleworth to herself as she unlocked the front door. When Miss McLachlan had finally left she'd been glad to have the place to herself again. But after a few days she had forgotten most of her friend's annoying little eccentricities and rather missed her company.

She wondered how Jennifer felt. Difficult to tell, of course. Jennifer was so . . . well . . . so unforthcoming at times. Miss Shuttleworth had tried to pin her down a bit as she was leaving while at the same time not wanting to appear too enthusiastic herself. It had been bright and sunny with a cold touch to the air.

"Now I must make sure I haven't left anything," said Miss McLachlan, heading back into the house for the third time in five minutes. "I'll just check in the bedroom."

"Go ahead, Jennifer. There's no hurry."

As her friend disappeared, Miss Shuttleworth sighed and wondered whether she should start the engine. Miss McLachlan had actually checked everything last night, several times, but . . . .

"Well I think that's O K. I don't seem to have left anything. I'll just pull the door shut behind me, shall I?"

"Yes."

"I mean, you do have the key?"

"Yes."

"Right then, if that's everything . . . "

Miss McLachlan shut the front door of the house with a tremendous bang, which Miss Shuttleworth had been half expecting but which nevertheless set her teeth on edge. It was really her own fault of course. Not long after Jennifer's arrival,

Miss Shuttleworth had found it necessary to explain that most of the doors in the house needed a strong push or pull to shut them. If they weren't shut properly, warmth would escape into the unheated corridor. From time to time, Miss McLachlan forgot and the door of the living room would remain slightly ajar. Miss Shuttleworth found this most irritating, convinced that she could immediately feel the cold air even though she was sitting beside the fire. At such times Miss Shuttleworth reflected that things were a bit easier when you lived by yourself.

Once or twice she'd said, "could you just push that door shut, Jennifer?", but hadn't liked to do so too often. Strange really, mused Miss Shuttleworth, how restrained and constricted one felt on occasions, even in one's own house. Of course she didn't want to offend her guest. So a few times she'd just got up herself and not liking simply to shut the door and return to her seat, she'd gone into another room for a minute. She would then return with an unwanted book or paper and close the door firmly behind her. Once Miss McLachlan had said,

"I know you said that the doors were hard to shut because the wood had swollen, Marjory, but why don't you just get someone in to plane some of the wood off? Then they would close more easily."

Get someone in, thought Miss Shuttleworth. How typical of her friend! Jennifer was quite hopeless at small things like that and had been amazed when Miss Shuttleworth had replaced a fuse in the standing lamp plug. Living as she had done of course, there had been no need for Jennifer to bother with anything like that. But if she came to Achanult . . .

Miss Shuttleworth was quite proud of her own dexterity in such small matters. You had to do a lot yourself since no-one in Achanult rushed around to do it for you. When someone did eventually turn up to fix whatever it was, he—it was always a man—usually did the job fairly quickly and departed, generally refusing to take any money. When Miss Shuttleworth asked about a bill she would be told the job was just a wee thing and not worth bothering about. When she pointed out it must have taken nearly an hour, what with travelling etc., she'd be told "Och, I'll maybe see you later", as he disappeared down the path. Miss Shuttleworth was a little uneasy about this but eventually concluded that this seemed to be the way things were done in Achanult. Next time, though, she'd have to insist . . .

"Get someone in, Jennifer? I could easily do it myself. But if I do it now when it's swollen with this damp weather, it'll be far too loose when it dries out."

"Yes, I see. But isn't it damp and wet here most of the year?"

"Not quite, Jennifer. We do have a summer."

"Well yes, of course. But it's quite short, isn't it?"

"I wouldn't necessarily say so," intoned Miss Shuttleworth, reflecting that the year before last it had been almost non-existent.

"So the doors shut normally in the summer."

"Of course, and at other times of the year too. Everything just happens to be rather damp at the moment."

"Oh well, you're right to leave things as they are, Marjory. You wouldn't want to create wide gaps for the cold wind to whistle through in the summer."

So Miss McLachlan had eventually got the hang of the doors but had unfortunately extended her enthusiasm to the doors of Miss Shuttleworth's car. Settling herself in her seat, she crashed the door shut. The car shook and the glass rattled.

"Oh dear, I forgot. The car doors aren't stiff. Sorry about that."

"It's all right," lied Miss Shuttleworth, starting the engine.

"I wonder, Marjory, just before you go . . . do you think there'll be a toilet on the train?"

"I imagine so. I don't think they uncouple the toilets at the border."

"Well . . . "

"Hasn't there always been one before?"

"Yes, but . . . umm . . . well, you never know. Maybe—just to be on the safe side—have you got the front door key handy?"

Miss Shuttleworth turned off the engine and handed the latch key to Miss McLachlan.

"Trains have been known to leave on time here you know, Jennifer."

"Yes, right. I won't be a minute."

They drove quietly towards Oban. Miss Shuttleworth was a bit surprised by her friend's silence and wondered if she was perhaps a little sad at leaving Achanult. If so, that was surely a good sign that Miss McLachlan might already be missing the place. Miss Shuttleworth waited a further few moments, then said,

"You're very quiet, Jennifer."

"Oh! Am I?"

"Well, a bit, perhaps."

"I was just thinking, actually."

Miss Shuttleworth waited. After a few further seconds of silence she said lightly,

"So what were you actually thinking about?"

"Oh, nothing much. You'd probably think it a bit silly."

"Oh surely not," replied Miss Shuttleworth encouragingly, realising that this might be a good time to raise the issue again of her friend's feelings about living in Achanult.

"Well, I was just wondering why the house doors stick in this damp weather but the car doors don't. I think I've worked out why."

"Oh good!" said Miss Shuttleworth, somewhat deflated.

"It's because wood swells in the damp but metal doesn't. Now that I come to think of it, doesn't metal expand with heat?"

"I'm afraid I really don't know about these things, Jennifer."

"Yes you do," retorted Miss McLachlan. "That's why railway lines have gaps every so often, to allow for expansion. I'll show you when we get to the station. Actually, I'll be interested to see for myself. They may not need to bother up here."

"You sound as if you're quite at home here, Jennifer, showing *me* round Oban Station." Miss Shuttleworth hoped she sounded jocular.

"Oh well, railway lines are much the same anywhere, aren't they?"

They drove on in silence, past the uncomprehending sheep searching for grass on the tough rocky slopes. There was a timelessness about the landscape here which Miss Shuttleworth found very attractive at any time of the year. Man, you felt, had made little impression upon the place and the land was always the master. As they rounded a bend Miss McLachlan exclaimed,

"There's that stone again."

"Yes."

"It's quite impressive in a way. What did you say it was called?"

"*Clach mhòr.*"

"Ah yes. That's it, I'm not sure I can say it as well as you."

"I suppose I've had a bit more practice, Jennifer."

"That's true. If I saw it written down I could maybe make

a better try at it."

"It'll be on the Ordnance Survey map. Well, anyway, it's spelt c-l-a-c-h m-h-ò-r with a grave, I think, over the o."

"A grave? How exciting! Just like a foreign language."

"Quite." Jennifer really was a bit obtuse at times.

"I'll just write it down, Marjory," said Miss McLachlan taking a pen from her handbag."It's quite taken my fancy, you know. How do you spell it again?"

Miss Shuttleworth told her. Miss McLachlan looked at the words for a few seconds.

"Are you sure you're saying it right, Marjory?"

"Yes, quite sure."

"Doesn't sound right to me—not that I know anything about it. Where's the 'v' sound you're making?"

"That's the mh."

"What?"

"Mh sounds like a v."

"Goodness! How silly. Why don't they just write a v?"

"It's a bit complicated to explain at the moment, Jennifer. Perhaps when you come back . . . when will that be, roughly?"

"Well, I don't know, Marjory. As I've said, I'll have to give it a lot of thought. It's not the sort of thing one can rush into. It's very kind of you, of course, and I'll certainly be in touch soon."

So they'd left it at that. At the station, Miss Shuttleworth helped her friend on to the train with her luggage.

"Well, I think that's everything," she said feeling a bit awkward as she always did on such occasions.

"Yes, well thank you again, Marjory. Perhaps you should just go now. Goodness knows when the train will leave. And it'll be dark by the time you get home."

"Yes, it will. Anyway, I suppose the train will be off in a

minute or two."

"If the boat's arrived."

"Pardon?"

"I thought you said there were boat connections from somewhere."

"Oh, yes. Still, they don't always bother about things like that. That sounded like a whistle. I'd better go."

As the train rumbled slowly out of the station Miss Shuttleworth walked briskly to her car. As she looked out to sea in the approaching dusk a ferry boat from one of the islands slid quietly into the harbour. Probably bringing passengers for the train, thought Miss Shuttleworth as she opened the door and settled into the driving seat.

35 Good intentions

MRS NICHOLSON set out in good time. She liked to be early, especially on the first afternoon of the new session, although there wasn't much point really since it was very rare to find anyone turning up before two o'clock. She often felt that many of them regarded two o'clock as the time to set out for the class. However, here she was five minutes early and just as well, since only one of the radiators had been switched on. Mrs Nicholson switched on the other two and stood warming herself before the larger one. There was that damp smell she remembered from last year and the door was stiffer than ever.

She wondered if anybody new would turn up. Probably not. It was very hard to tell in a place like Achanult. She'd come to notice that most of the village, with one or two exceptions, had a reluctance to offend. They always expressed a polite interest in her Gaelic class, with a hint that they would be quite keen if only they had the time—and they must really try to make time later. Had Mrs Nicholson not known better, she would have expected to see half the village at the class. As it was, they'd be lucky to get into double figures as usual. She'd remarked on this curious fact to David.

"Oh, I think people are just like that," he'd said. "Especially here."

"It makes things a bit uncertain, though."

"Oh yes, absolutely. It reminds me of something I read in the paper the other day. You'd have been interested in it. Did I show you it?"

"I don't remember, David. Maybe if you told me what it was . . . "

"Something about Gaelic."

"Oh?"

"Yes. Wait till I think now. Yes, that's right. The sort of thing you're talking about. An opinion poll showed that—oh, I've forgotten exactly—but something like 90% of adults in this country would like to be able to speak Gaelic."

"That's very encouraging."

"Yes. But as someone else in the paper pointed out, it's really quite meaningless at the end of the day."

"Oh? Why?"

"Well, if you were to ask people if they wished they could speak, say, German or French, or Gaelic for that matter, most people would say yes. It's quite obvious. I wish I could speak lots of languages, just like I wish I could play the violin like that chap we were watching on the television yesterday."

"But you've never shown any interest in Gaelic, or any other . . . "

"Precisely. That's exactly the point."

"I don't think I follow you David."

"Well, according to the argument in the paper, of the 90% who would like to speak it, only about 10% are prepared to do anything about it."

"What about the others?"

"It's just wishful thinking. As soon as they realise what's involved—time, money, patience, enthusiasm, ability—all to be sustained over a period of years, they don't last long."

"That sounds awfully pessimistic."

"I suppose it is. I'm not trying to discourage you, Anna. I'm just telling you what this chap said in the paper. And I can see his point—or her point. It might have been a woman for all I remember."

The Rev Nicholson had recently been reading, with some alarm, about the increasing influence of the feminist movement in the Christian church. Not much evidence of it in Argyll certainly, but one had to be vigilant.

"Anyway," he continued, "the article ended by saying that of the original 90% who were interested, you'd be lucky to get 1 or 2% fluent in the language at the end of it all."

"Well, I think that's very depressing."

"Oh, I thought you'd be interested. I may have got some of the figures slightly wrong, but that's roughly the gist of the article. I was thinking that you might like to discuss it with your class."

Somewhat to Mrs Nicholson's surprise, almost all of last term's class had returned. The only absentee seemed to be Maggie Stewart. Even Donald Morrison was there, the last to appear. Mrs Nicholson greeted him.

"F*easgar math.*"

"Eh?"

"*Feasgar math.*"

Donald looked at her for a second or two then nodded and went over to his usual seat at the back. Mrs Nicholson sighed quietly to herself. If he couldn't even remember that . . .

"Well good afternoon, ladies and gentlemen—or as we say in Gaelic, *feasgar math*. You all remember that of course. We seem to be nearly all here." She picked up the register from last term. "In fact, as far as I can see, the only absentee seems to be Mrs Stewart."

"She's got that job now of course," said Mrs McKenzie with an air of importance. "In the library," she added.

"Oh yes, I think I did hear about that. Oh well, can't be helped."

"She did say to me," Mrs McKenzie went on, "that if the class was to meet in the evening she would be able to come."

"Out of the question," boomed Miss Shuttleworth.

"Well, yes . . . " faltered Mrs Nicholson

"Evenings are far too busy, what with one thing and another," continued Miss Shuttleworth. There was a general murmur of assent. "I think Tuesday afternoon is an ideal time, in fact. It doesn't clash with anything as far as I know."

"There's the carpet bowls," suggested Mrs McKenzie.

Miss Shuttleworth sniffed. "I don't really think that's relevant."

"Why not? Some of my friends go. They thoroughly enjoy it."

"No doubt," sniffed Miss Shuttleworth. "But I don't see how that affects us."

"Umm, I think," intervened Mrs Nicholson, "that if most of you are happy with Tuesday afternoons we might as well leave it at that, for the moment anyway."

"Quite right." said Miss Shuttleworth briskly.

Mrs Nicholson smiled wearily and went over to close the door. She had just returned to her desk when the door opened with a flourish and Maggie Stewart made an appearance which was marred slightly by the fact that the door stuck on the carpet when it was only half open and threw her off balance somewhat. Recovering, she closed the door firmly behind her and swept to her seat.

"I'm afraid the door's a little stiff," said Mrs Nicholson. "It's this damp weather I suppose. Anyway, it's nice to see you again, Mrs Stewart. We were just wondering if you would manage."

"Thank you. It's not easy to get away—did I tell you I was working at the library?"

"Umm, yes, I had heard."

"Of course, it's not easy to get away, quite a responsibility really but if I work a bit extra at dinner time I can slip away for a couple of hours."

"Oh good. I am glad. Now where shall we start?"

After some discussion it was agreed that they would start at the beginning again. This was a bit of a disappointment to Mrs Nicholson who would have liked to push on. But it soon became obvious that starting afresh was the wisest course since most of the class had forgotten just about everything. Strange really. Maybe she'd been going too fast. It wasn't very easy to tell since some of the class never gave an opinion, while both Miss Shuttleworth and Maggie Stewart were very reluctant to admit to having any difficulties. Still it had to be admitted that they hadn't actually done very much Gaelic last term.

At the end of last year Mrs Nicholson had tried to suggest that the first term had maybe been something of a broad introduction to Gaelic culture and that next term they really ought to get on with the language. Maggie Stewart had interrupted.

"I wouldn't have said there was anything cultural about Gaelic. Anyway, what we want is just ordinary everyday Gaelic—none of this cultural stuff."

"Of course," said Mrs Nicholson hastily, "but I was just using culture to mean the background, way of life—that sort of thing."

"Well . . . I suppose it could mean that," agreed Maggie, feeling that she was beginning to get out of her depth.

"Of course it can," asserted Miss Shuttleworth.

"Let me put it another way," persevered Maggie. "What we don't want, and I'm sure I speak for most of us—though it's entirely up to you of course, Mrs Nicholson—is any of that boring old-fashioned poetry and stuff like that. Nobody ever reads it anyway."

Miss Shuttleworth shrugged. She had been on the verge of pointing out that as far as she was aware, most Gaelic speakers couldn't read anything, but restrained herself, realising that she was in a minority of one on this issue. Before coming to Achanult she had not realised that illiteracy was something to be almost proud of.

So Mrs Nicholson reminded the class of their brief discussion at the end of last term. She'd been hoping that they would have remembered most of the vocabulary and would quickly learn some more so that she could then engage them in short conversations—which was what they claimed to want. There was still a problem with pronunciation though, and some of them such as Alec Cameron insisted that conversation was what he wanted but then refused to say anything. Maybe just as well really, in his case. Miss Shuttleworth seemed to be the only one happy to work from the book and with her background it was understandable that she found the oral side difficult. She'd once said to Mrs Nicholson,

"I just can't see how you get that particular sound out of that word. I think I must have aural dyslexia."

"I know someone who's dyslexic," said Maggie, eager to let everyone know that she was aware of the word, even if she was a bit vague as to what it actually meant.

"Is that wee Andrew?" asked Mrs McKenzie.

"That's right. You'll know him as well, of course."

"Yes, I've heard about him. I think he's a lot better now. He's been getting some special treatment seemingly. It's amazing what they can do nowadays. I remember when I was at school there was a girl in my class like that."

Mrs Nicholson dithered on the edge of her table. If she didn't intervene now, half the afternoon would be gone before they got started. But it was too late. Alec Cameron had been stirred to unfold a saga of somebody from the village school who hadn't been able to read and write but had gone on to be a ship's captain and had sailed all over the world.

"But surely he must have learnt to read and write to become captain of a ship," said Miss Shuttleworth eventually as Alec Cameron's tale wound to a close.

"That'sh exshactly the point," agreed Alec.

Miss Shuttleworth reflected that whatever the point was, it was lost on her. But as the other members of the class had nodded sagely, she said nothing. They all seemed to have heard the story before and knew the person concerned, which didn't surprise Miss Shuttleworth nowadays.

Eventually the conversation wound down. Resigned by now to the fact that they weren't going to get any serious work done on this first afternoon, Mrs Nicholson decided to seek the opinion of Mrs Abbott or, if Mrs Abbott didn't have an opinion, of her friend Mrs Grey.

"I wonder what you think, Mrs Abbott, about the class starting from the beginning again? That might actually help you since you missed a few classes last term."

This was a bit of an understatement. Mrs Abbott and her friend Mrs Grey lived near each other in the country a few miles from Achanult. The rest of the class—apart from Miss Shuttleworth—knew all about them of course, but they kept themselves to themselves apparently. Another fault of theirs was that they only came to the class together, so that if one was unable to come for any reason, the other stayed away also. Last term they'd turned up to enrol on the first day when Mrs Grey's only contribution to the afternoon was to ensure that her name was spelled correctly. After that they hadn't appeared until the second last week, citing illnesses and "other things" to explain their absence. Still, here they were again, silent as ever.

"Oh I don't really mind," ventured Mrs Abbott.

Mrs Nicholson sighed quietly as Mrs Abbott turned to Mrs Grey.

"What do you think, Aggie? Mrs Nicholson says we missed a few weeks."

Mrs Grey nodded.

"Things should be a bit easier this time," said Mrs Abbott turning to Mrs Nicholson. Then turning back to Mrs Grey she added,

"You were going to ask her about Betsy."

Mrs Grey shrank back a little.

"Oh it doesn't matter," she whispered.

"You can always ask," urged Mrs Abbott.

"Och no, it's all right."

"But I thought you said . . . "

"I know, but . . . I'll maybe see later."

The rest of the class watched this altercation with some surprise, widely mingled with curiosity. As the pair fell silent again Mrs Nicholson thought she'd better say something.

"Is there some sort of problem?"

"Oh, not really," replied Mrs Abbott. "It's just her dog."

"Dog?"

"That's right. She doesn't like to leave it. Well, it's getting old, you see. It misses her. She was actually wondering if she could bring it along."

"Oh no," protested Mrs Grey, shrinking even more.

"Yes you were," insisted Mrs Abbott. "She was," she added to Mrs Nicholson.

"Well," said Mrs Nicholson, "I don't know . . . I mean . . . I don't see why not . . . "

"What sort of a dog is it?" enquired Miss Shuttleworth cautiously.

"She's a sheepdog," said Mrs Grey after a nudge from her friend. "Of course she's retired now. She doesn't see too well."

"Her hearing's not so good either, is it Aggie?" added Mrs Abbott sympathetically.

"My dog's getting on a bit as well," said Mrs McKenzie as one dog lover to another. "It's a shame when they get to that stage. You don't know what to do for the best."

"Mind you," put in Maggie Stewart, "if its hearing has gone it won't get much benefit from being at the class."

Everyone except Miss Shuttleworth laughed.

"Seriously though," continued Maggie, "I've known a few Gaelic speaking dogs."

"Really?" enquired Miss Shuttleworth.

"I think Mrs Stewart means dogs that understand Gaelic," said Mrs Nicholson hastily. "We certainly always spoke to the dogs in Gaelic at home in Uist."

"That's right," said Maggie, recovering. "It's quite usual, isn't it."

"She thought of bringing it and leaving it in the car," persisted Mrs Abbott, "but it's been a bit cold."

"Well certainly, I don't mind," said Mrs Nicholson. "Does anyone else have any feelings on the matter?"

No-one did.

"You can always enrol it in the class," suggested Miss Shuttleworth. "We're a bit short on numbers, aren't we."

Mrs Nicholson smiled thinly. The afternoon was almost gone now and they still hadn't achieved much, for all her good intentions. Perhaps David had been right. It was really all so difficult. Yet, as far as she could see, the class seemed quite happy with the situation. Oh well, better look on the bright side. She glanced at her watch.

"Well, we still have a few minutes left. Can anyone remember the Gaelic for dog?"

36 Better things

LIMITED. That was the word. Limited. Mrs Maxwell had been trying to find the right word for most of the morning. There were plenty of other words of course, but they weren't really very polite. Come to think of it, maybe "limited" wasn't too polite either. Still, it was better than "philistine", which was better than "thick", both of which her husband had suggested.

Mrs Maxwell was a little on edge, a mixture of annoyance and resignation. The number of times she'd stayed in just in case someone telephoned! Her husband took a less serious view of the situation but then he never seemed to take anything seriously these days.

"You can't really expect anything else in Achanult," he'd said.

"Yes I know, but I'd hoped . . . we'd all hoped."

"Pointless. But we'll work something out. See what the others think. After all, there may be all sorts of reasons why no-one has expressed interest. And if we can identify these reasons—which seem pretty obvious to me—then we can change things a bit and maybe do better next time."

Mrs Maxwell stared at the fire and reshuffled the magazines on the coffee table. Bill kept saying that. Just to encourage her, she supposed. It wasn't so much encouragement she needed as a few concrete suggestions. She looked across at her husband.

"Well then, let's think of one reason."

"OK. People in Achanult are mainly interested in what goes on here in Achanult and can't really be bothered about anything or anywhere else."

"Right. Assuming that's true," said Mrs Maxwell quickly, "and I think it is to some extent, how can we change things a bit, as you put it, to interest them?"

"Make sure there's some sort of local connection with whatever you're doing."

"I see. But that really wouldn't be very easy, say, in my sphere." Mrs Maxwell had been a classics teacher before her marriage and had been hoping to introduce a classical element into the arts society.

"Oh I don't know. Supposing you wanted to speak about the Romans. You could entitle your talk *Achanult and the Roman Legions* or something like that."

Mrs Maxwell laughed.

"Honestly Bill, that's ridiculous."

"Why?"

"Well, there weren't any legions in Achanult for a start."

"How do you know? Wasn't there some legion that got lost somewhere north of Hadrian's Wall?"

"Well yes, the ninth . . . "

"Right. Tell them that it passed through Achanult."

"But there's no evidence!"

"Never mind that. All right, it passed near Achanult—or within a hundred miles of Achanult. Whatever you like. The point is, if people think there's going to be something about Achanult, they may turn up. And once they've been to one or two meetings of the society some of them may find, in spite of themselves, that it's all very interesting. But you've got to get them there first."

"I see. So it's Argyll and the Ancient Greeks then, is it?"

"Well I don't know about that one. Some people might feel that Argyll wasn't totally relevant to them. A bit wide ranging maybe."

Mrs Maxwell laughed again. Her husband's reluctance to take things too seriously had its advantages. She was beginning to feel a bit better about the whole thing.

Part of the problem was that she had been more involved than the others, at least at this initial stage. It had been her phone number that had appeared in the advert in the local paper two weeks ago. It had seemed quite a good idea at the time. The Rev Nicholson had suggested that there was no need to go to the expense of hiring the hall when all they wanted to do was to find out the extent of interest in an arts society in the village. Mrs Bates had also pointed out that they would look rather silly if only one or two people turned up. So it was agreed that they would put a notice in the paper, indicating their ideas and giving a phone number. Then they would have some idea of the interest locally. Now, two weeks later, there seemed to be no interest and no-one had telephoned.

The first to arrive were the Hastings within a few seconds of two o'clock. They always arrived on time for everything and always professed surprise to be first.

"One naturally expects the locals to be a little vague about the time," Mr Hastings had said on countless occasions, "but that's no reason for the rest of us to be late."

This was not an opinion shared by everyone—in fact only Mrs Hastings shared it. But even she, sensing their isolation, always added,

"Still, I suppose there's no real rush, especially at our age."

No-one disputed this, which only served to make the Hastings even more irritated. Mr Hastings would then give an airing to his favourite topic of declining standards in Achanult. The Hastings kept a watchful eye on their fellow incomers and were distressed to notice the extent to which people "let themselves go".

"We all start off with the best intentions, of course," Mr Hastings would say, "but I can't help noticing that gradually— over a period of years, I mean—some of us let the side down a bit. It's a pity really."

He would then inform his audience, some of whom might not have heard his views for weeks, of the regretful sights he had witnessed—gentlemen appearing in public without ties, shoes obviously not recently polished, and so on. The catalogue always ended with the distressing matter of men—Mr Hastings didn't like to say who—walking through the village without having previously shaved that morning.

"I agree that most of us have retired," he would say, "but nevertheless . . . I think Mrs Hastings has noted a similar decline also."

He always referred to his wife as Mrs Hastings. In fact few people in Achanult knew her first name (which was Audrey) and no-one ever addressed her by it. So this was the cue for Mrs Hastings to mention the time when she spotted someone from the village—she wouldn't say who, but it was naturally understood to be an incomer since she seldom noticed the locals—wearing shorts in the local shop. On this particular point she had found herself, although she didn't know it, in agreement with the locals, for whom trousers were for men and shorts were for boys.

Miss Shuttleworth turned up a few minutes after the Hastings and the others all appeared within the next five minutes. After the ritual remarks had been made and Mrs Maxwell had collected coats and hats—except for Mrs Hastings'—Mr Maxwell said,

"Well, I think you all know the situation." He shrugged his shoulders and looked at his wife who in turn looked at the fire. "Just to bring you all bang up to date, no-one seems to have expressed any interest in our arts society—or whatever we decide to call it."

There was a silence, broken eventually by Mr Hastings.

"Most unfortunate."

"I'm not really surprised," added Miss Shuttleworth.

"Maybe not," agreed Mr Maxwell, now looking out of the window, "but we'll have to decide what to do next, if indeed there is anything else we want to do."

"We certainly can't just give up," protested Miss Shuttleworth for whom the idea of an arts society had become a much needed antidote to the antics of Maggie Stewart and her friends at the community association.

"Well," replied Mr Maxwell hesitantly, "what does anyone

else think?"

In the silence the Rev Nicholson felt that he was probably expected to say something.

"Umm . . . I can see Mr Maxwell's point, of course. But, umm . . . surely we mustn't give up so easily? Life after all is a series of trials and tribulations . . . " He tailed off.

"Why can't we just go ahead anyway?" asked Mrs Nicholson. "I know there are only eight of us now but numbers may grow once we get established. And since we're a small group, we could meet in the manse—if you like."

"What a good idea!" enthused Miss Shuttleworth. The Rev Nicholson looked uncomfortable.

"Well if Mr Nicholson is agreeable . . . " began Mrs Maxwell. They all looked at him.

"Ah . . . umm, yes . . . certainly. Indeed." He hoped this wasn't the thin end of the wedge.

"You're welcome to my house too," said Miss Shuttleworth, "but you'll have to bring your own chairs." They all laughed, except the Hastings.

"We can meet here too, of course," added Mr Maxwell, coming away from the window.

"Splendid, splendid," intoned the Rev Nicholson. "Some sort of rotation can be worked out. Perhaps just as well. I can't always guarantee the manse, much as I'd like to—committee meetings, guild and so on."

He looked towards his wife. Mrs Nicholson decided that this was not the time to disagree. At that moment the telephone rang.

"I'll go," said Mr Maxwell. "It's maybe someone wanting to know about our group."

"Some hope," laughed his wife. Mrs Maxwell felt that things had got off to a good start. She'd been a little worried about it but now that everyone was being so positive about the situation, things were a lot better. Even Mrs Hastings thawed sufficiently to say a word or two of small talk to Mrs Bates. As usual, Mrs Bates herself had said very little, still feeling slightly nervous and uncomfortable. In fact she had no real enthusiasm for an arts society and had only come along to the first meeting because Mrs Nicholson had asked her if she'd like to go. Not liking to refuse outright, Mrs Bates had been unable to think of an excuse quickly enough. So here she was and she'd probably find herself on some committee or other if she wasn't careful. She tried to look attentive and nodded agreement with whatever it was that Mrs Hastings had just said. Silly woman, really. Why didn't she take that hat off?

"Wrong number," said Mr Maxwell, closing the door behind him.

"Again?"

"We seem to get a lot of wrong numbers these days," explained Mr Maxwell. "Does anyone else have that problem?"

No-one seemed to, though Miss Shuttleworth said,

"I suppose I might get some. It's a bit hard to tell."

The others looked at her. Mrs Bates nodded uncertainly. The Rev Nicholson cleared his throat.

"Quite. Well . . . umm . . . what is our next step?"

"I suppose that depends on whether we want to be official or not," said Mrs Maxwell.

"I don't think I follow you," objected Mr Hastings.

"Whether we want to be properly constituted, with a committee and so on, or . . . "

"Surely that can be left till later," interrupted Miss Shuttleworth. "Why don't we have one or two meetings first and see what happens?"

At that point the Rev Nicholson remembered what it was

he'd intended to say earlier. His wife had told him at the beginning of the week that she'd heard that there were plans afoot to re-establish a Gaelic choir in Achanult. He duly informed the rest of the group.

"So obviously there may be a conflict—a counter attraction, as it were," he ended.

"I don't see why," said Miss Shuttleworth. "I can't imagine that anyone interested in an arts society would want to be involved with a Gaelic choir."

"Oh, I don't know," mused Mrs Nicholson. "Actually, I'd have thought that you'd have been interested . . . as a learner."

"I see what you mean but I'm not too keen on all this massed singing. I've always found it a bit artificial."

"Oh? I think it can be quite good fun."

Most of the others nodded in agreement with Mrs Nicholson's last point. Sensing herself outnumbered, Miss Shuttleworth let the matter drop.

"What about you, Mrs Hastings?" asked the Rev Nicholson after a pause.

"Sorry?"

"You have one of the best voices in the village." He turned to the others. "Mrs Hastings trained as a singer, I believe."

There were murmurs of surprise and approval.

"So *that's* why Mr Hastings married you," said Miss Shuttleworth.

"Sorry?"

"Mr Hastings is very musical himself, I mean. I expect you met at music college or somewhere."

Mrs Hastings said nothing.

"So anyway," resumed Mr Nicholson, "you would be a great asset to a Gaelic choir."

One or two heads nodded in agreement.

"Oh, I couldn't possibly have anything to do with that sort of thing. It's a bit . . . how shall I put it . . . outside my field."

"Oh well," said Mr Nicholson after a moment or two of silence. "So . . . umm . . . where were we?"

"We'd agreed to go ahead and have our first evening meeting and see if we could attract some extra interest. I think that was your suggestion, Miss Shuttleworth," said Mr Maxwell, wanting to get on with it.

"Yes. So what will our first topic be? Any suggestions?"

The room filled with silence.

"That coal gives a good heat," whispered Mrs Nicholson to Mrs Maxwell, who nodded. Then Mrs Bates summoned up her courage.

"I seem to remember a suggestion last time that Mr Hastings could give a talk on . . . somebody . . . something about music," she added lamely.

The room now filled with unease. None of those present, with the exception of the Hastings themselves, could see Mr Hastings as a crowd puller. More like a deterrent. An introductory talk from him could well put off any prospective members for years. Mr Maxwell rubbed his hands.

"An excellent idea, Mrs Bates. Thank you for getting the ball rolling. Now, before we . . . umm . . . has anyone any other suggestions?"

Three or four people spoke at once. Their exact words were lost in the confusion but the general message was that *anything* else would be preferable

"Well, there seem to be quite a number of ideas there. We'd better decide which order to put them in."

"It obviously depends on where we are too," said Mrs Maxwell quickly. "We haven't got a piano, so Mr Hastings couldn't give his talk so well if the meeting was to be held here."

"That's right," agreed her husband. "There are lots of things to take into account. Perhaps we could come to some sort of agreement now."

And so the group settled down to an afternoon of difficult decisions.

37 Windy

JANUARY always seemed to be a windy month in Achanult. Peter stood at the window and looked out at the sea. There weren't any boats out there today and just as well. He could watch the sea for hours if it wasn't so cold over beside the window. A few draughts coming in maybe. You couldn't expect anything else, especially in this wind.

Jean had been on at him about this double glazing that everybody seemed to be getting nowadays. Peter couldn't see what she was making all the fuss about. She always sat by the fire anyway. So she wouldn't feel the draughts. And, as he'd always pointed out to her, it was only on windy days that the draughts were really noticeable—a day like today. He'd sealed off a lot of the draughts, but it was always cold by the window. Anyway, they could always draw the curtains. That made quite a difference.

Some of Jean's friends had got double glazing. That was where she got her ideas from. Daft, really. All that money for something you only needed in the winter. That's what Peter had said to one of those salesmen. There'd been quite a number of them in Achanult over the years but they never made much impression on Peter. They were just wasting their time. He remembered one eager young lad with his suit and briefcase.

"I can easily give you a quotation, Mr McQueen. There's no obligation."

"Och, it doesn't matter."

"I'll just work it out now. It's quite a big house, of course."

"Aye. If I ever do get round to it, it would only be the living room."

"Mmm . . . " The salesman had opened his briefcase and was working with his calculator. Peter watched him in silence.

"How does £200 sound?" he asked after a minute.

"Och, I couldn't afford anything like that. How much would it be just for the living room window?"

"That was what I meant. £200. They're quite big windows, you know. You're losing a lot of heat from them. To do the whole house would be—well, a bit more. But we can offer you a loan and you just pay so much each month. Couldn't be easier."

"Och, I don't think so."

"I can easily give you some figures, Mr McQueen."

Peter had got rid of him eventually. Persistent, they were. Since then he hadn't given any of them the slightest encouragement. Jean had to be kept away from them, of course. She'd be daft enough to be sold something.

Peter wandered back to the fire, taking his woolly hat off so that he'd feel the benefit of it when he went back to the window. Aye, maybe it was a bit chilly away from the fire but it was just this wind. A windy month, January. Not that the wind did much good at this time of year. For some reason, it never seemed to bring up much seaweed. The autumn was the time for that. High winds and heavy seas then would leave the beach covered in seaweed. It was the same every year. Peter had often wondered why. Once he'd asked Donald next door.

"It'll be like the trees," Donald said.

Peter hadn't seen the connection.

"They start to fall in the autumn,"Donald explained. "So the seaweed will likely just drop off about the same time."

Peter doubted this but didn't say so. You had to be careful with Donald. He had a way of telling you something. He'd heard it from his father or grandfather, that was it. He'd never come out and say it was his own opinion. For all that, you still didn't like to disagree.

So there wouldn't be much seaweed tomorrow. Mind you, it was surprising how things worked out. If there was a lot of seaweed now it wouldn't have time to rot down to be dug in. That took a couple of months at least. The stuff he'd got up in the autumn had rotted down nicely. Warmed up slightly, Peter walked over to the window. Aye, it was time the garden was dug. A bit windy today, though.

Through in the kitchen Jean was baking. She did a lot of that these days and had even started to make bread. Sometimes the bread you got in the village shop wasn't very fresh, she said. Of course Willie claimed to know nothing about it and blamed the delivery van. The bread came in a bag with a tag on it telling you when you should eat it by. A lot of the tags seemed to fall off in transit. Willie said it was these terrible roads and that anyway you could always toast it.

Peter wandered through to the kitchen. He liked the smell when Jean was baking.

"Well," asked Jean, rinsing her hands under the tap, "are you going this afternoon?"

Peter had forgotten again. She'd asked him last Tuesday if he was going to the Gaelic class this year and he'd said he'd need to think about it.

"I'll need to think about it."

"You've been thinking about it for about a year now. You might as well go, you know. It'll give you something to do, instead of wandering in and out of here."

"I just came in for a bit of heat. Anyway, I'd be too far behind the others."

"Not from what I hear."

"Then there's the cost—books and things."

"You wouldn't have to worry about that. Maggie Stewart says she can give you a book—quite a selection seemingly."

"Why? Has she stopped going? She'll need them herself."

"No, from the library. She works in the library. I told you."

"Oh aye."

Peter remembered. He'd never had much to do with the library but as it happened he'd been thinking about it lately. It was the local paper that did it, with that wee section about books just before Christmas. Suggestions for presents, that was it. They were all books on local issues—well, some of them were about Argyll in general but Peter had been quite interested. He did seem to have a lot of time now to read a book. Mind you, they were dear. One of them was £15, he remembered. An awful price just for a book. But they might have them in the library. He'd need to ask Jean. Now that Maggie was working there he'd maybe even go and have a look for himself. He'd never been too keen before, not really knowing anybody who worked there.

"I'll get the book out for you. Then you can have a look and see what you think."

Peter considered this. Things seemed to be moving a bit fast.

"Och, there's no hurry. What book is that, anyway?"

"The book they're using at the class."

"Oh, that. Aye. Mind you, Donald didn't seem to think it was a very good book."

"Donald's never been one for books."

This was true, Peter reflected. Donald didn't even get a daily paper, although he did go and read one every day in the library. Of course that was just so he wouldn't have to light a fire in the morning. Well, there was nothing wrong with that. A fine warm place the library was. He'd maybe need to have a look himself and have a word with Maggie.

Wandering back through to the living room Peter went slowly over to the window. It was really too cold and windy for a walk today. Watching the wind whip up the waves he wondered if the fact that this was a Tuesday had anything to do with the weather. He'd a feeling that he'd wondered about this before. He'd need to keep a record—it might be interesting. After all, there was old Mrs Muir along the road who kept records of the rainfall in Achanult, week after week. Of course, she'd nothing else to do but it was still a bit daft. All it told you was that some weeks it rained more than others which everybody knew anyway. The local paper always published her figures every week. He'd even seen it on the front page. So maybe he could keep a record of the weather on Tuesdays and see if it was always worse than any other day. It probably would be, on average anyway. Then maybe the paper would like to publish it, which would just show those sceptics—and there were quite a number of them—who doubted the rigidity of Peter's calendar. He wondered if you got paid if they put any of your stuff in the paper. Mrs Muir would know. Jean could maybe ask her.

Jean came through from the kitchen and stood by the fire.

"I'll just have a wee seat before I start the dishes. That dog was in here again. I wish you'd do something about it."

Peter rose from his chair.

"Oh, it's away now," said Jean. "I banged on the window but it just stood and looked at me. I'd to stop what I was doing and shoo it out. We should stop it coming in."

Peter nodded. The black mongrel from along the road belonged to Mrs Muir, the lady who kept the rainfall records. It had recently taken to coming into their garden and into all the neighbours' gardens. Peter quite liked dogs but Jean wasn't so keen.

"Och, it's harmless," he'd said to her the last time.

"Maybe it is but it eats the stuff I put out for the birds."

"It'll just be hungry."

"It's not hungry, just greedy. I'd rather watch the birds eating than that great brute."

So they'd closed the gate but the dog came in some other way. Once they'd spotted it coming over from Donald's garden. That was Donald's fault, of course. The dyke had been like that for years. Peter mentioned it every year and suggested that they do something about it. It wouldn't take much. The stones were already there somewhere, so all they needed was some cement. To his credit, Donald always agreed that they'd need to do something about it one of these days.

"You could have a word with Mrs Muir," suggested Jean.

"I don't know her."

Jean knew what was coming. Peter had this idea that women were more easily approached by other women.

"Well, I don't know her either," she said. "Anyway, I hear she's a bit daft about the animal, what with it being her only companion nowadays."

So they'd just left it at that. Jean went back to the kitchen to wash the dishes and Peter wondered whether to close the curtains. It would make the room a bit warmer but he'd have to switch on the light. He'd maybe just wait a bit yet.

38 In reverse

THE Rev Nicholson was having a bad morning. His wife had shouted up that there seemed to be no water, so he'd had to get up without his usual cup of tea in bed. Not that he was in any rush to get out of bed in this cold weather. He hadn't known it to be so cold since they'd moved to Achanult. That would be why the pipe was frozen. Anna seemed to think he should do something about it.

"What about the hot water tank?" he shouted down the stairs. His wife came back up.

"I can't hear you down there, David."

"Oh, I was just wondering if we could take some water from the hot water tank."

"I don't know if you're supposed to drink that. It could be boiled, of course. I was just going to have some fruit juice."

"Cold?"

"Well, we usually do. I can heat yours if you like."

"What kind is it?"

"Apple."

"Mmm. I'll probably just have it cold."

He hadn't been able to get anyone at the plumbers till about a quarter to eleven. In fact, he was about to ask Anna if she could take a walk round there to see if they could send someone when at last he got through. Mrs Duff seemed unsurprised by Mr Nicholson's news and was afraid that she couldn't say how soon her husband would be round. But he was round within half an hour and quickly had the water flowing again.

"Well that's quite impressive," said Mr Nicholson when the plumber had gone, muttering as he left about how it was the coldest he'd ever known and you just couldn't legislate for this sort of thing. "I sometimes wonder if the clergy still have some influence over here—not that I'd want to jump the queue of course."

"It could be that," replied his wife, "but it's just as likely to be a feeling of guilt."

"Guilt?"

"I remember hearing people saying at the time that he'd laid the new pipes too shallow. He made a habit of it, apparently."

"I see. Umm, what exactly does that mean?"

"Oh. The water pipe has to be laid at a certain depth where the frost can't get at it."

"Ah yes, of course. So why didn't he?"

"Laziness. It saves time, obviously."

"Oh well. I don't really know. One always tends to assume that these sort of people know what they're doing. I must admit I just let him get on with it."

"Yes. I suspect he was probably counting on your absence."

"Well, I did have a lot of other things on the go at the time." Mr Nicholson thought for a moment. "Umm, anyway, does that mean that this is going to happen regularly?"

"I hope not. I don't really think so. Apparently there hasn't been a frost like this for a long time."

So the Rev Nicholson was able to have his morning cup of coffee a bit later than usual but just in time for him to settle down to the crossword. This was becoming the most important part of the day for him and it was really the only bit of the paper he bothered with. He often wondered what percentage of the paper's readers attempted the crossword every day. There was never any correspondence about it nor any short articles in the paper, such as you got about chess and stamp collecting and similar things which the Rev Nicholson regarded as a great waste of time.

Mind you, crosswords did make the news sometimes. Only recently he'd heard a curious item on the radio about a crossword in America. There had apparently been a competition somewhere—he hadn't recognised the name of the town—with a prize of several hundred dollars for the first person to finish the crossword within the allotted time. The prize money was based on the figure of ten dollars for every correctly completed square—a typical American gimmick. It was quite obvious to the Rev Nicholson that Americans didn't take crosswords as seriously as he did, because, to give everyone a chance to win the prize you just had to be the first to complete the crossword, with every letter filled in. It didn't necessarily have to be all correct but in that case you lost ten dollars for every wrong square. So someone had simply filled in all the squares with the letter E—which took less than a minute and had demanded the prize with ten dollars deducted for each wrong letter. The organisers of the competition hadn't known how to react to this since none of the answers were correct. But as the contestant pointed out, there was nothing to say that they had to be. So in the end they worked out that he had twenty two Es in the correct places and were reluctantly about to present him with $220 when other competitors objected. The dispute ended with shots being fired and a couple of people being taken to hospital, which was apparently how they solved their crossword problems in

America!

The Rev Nicholson had thought that there might be some material in this story for a sermon and he'd said so to his wife.

"I'm not sure about that," she'd cautioned. "Don't you think you spend enough time on crosswords without drawing the attention of your congregation to them?"

Mr Nicholson thought this was a bit unfair but he'd left it at that for the moment.

He finished his cup of coffee and looked at his watch. So far so good. He'd just spent about a minute thinking about 7 across, a seven letter word of which he had the fifth and last letters. He couldn't immediately get the other letters, the relevant down clues still being unsolved. This was something that happened to him quite often and he found it a bit annoying. If he had the first three letters, then he could usually get the whole word even if it meant several minutes with the dictionary. But what could you do when you had the last letters? Then something stirred at the back of his mind. He had a vague recollection from his New Testament student days that there was some sort of reverse-index lexicon which gave you lists of all possible words ending in certain letters. Just what he needed!

It had been in Greek however, for people who found bits of stone with the first half of a word missing. He'd never had occasion to use it himself, though he recalled leafing through it out of curiosity. He was just wondering if such a work existed for the English language when his wife came into the room.

"That's Mr Gillespie on the phone."

With a sigh, Mr Nicholson rose from his chair and wandered through to the hall. In his absence his wife had a quick look at the crossword. Her eye caught the clue "Xmas and Easter". Hmm. He hadn't got that one. You'd have thought that would have been right up his street. But he'd only got two of the letters _ _ _ _ N _ S. Suddenly she realised the answer. At that point her husband returned.

"Anything important?" she asked.

"Not really. The boiler seems to have broken down again. Hardly worth telephoning about. Which reminds me, Anna, could you not perhaps deal yourself with messages such as that?"

"He asked to speak to you."

"He always does. Tell him I'm busy."

"He'll just phone again later. Anyway, I was busy too—busier than you by the look of things."

"What? Oh, the crossword. Well, I was just having a quick glance at it before moving on to something else."

"All right. Next time somebody phones I'll tell them you're busy with the crossword. By the way, I've solved one of your clues."

Mrs Nicholson wasn't much interested in crosswords which was just as well since her husband would have objected strongly to her attempting it. Occasionally, if he was really stuck, he would ask her advice but reluctantly and without any great enthusiasm.

"Oh? Well, I haven't had time . . . "

"It's 7 across."

Mr Nicholson glanced at the paper.

"Ah, yes. I hadn't quite got round to that one yet."

She knew better than to tell him the answer.

When his wife had gone the Rev Nicholson spent some time thinking about 7 across. "Xmas and Easter". Something to do with religion? Holidays? Festivals? Music? This interruption had obviously broken his concentration. He went back to thinking about the reverse-index lexicon. Perhaps he could compile one himself if one didn't already exist. Yes, that was a good idea. Sitting back in his chair he considered the matter. He'd always admired the way in which the clergy had engaged in academic pursuits, particularly in the last century—editing texts, compiling dictionaries and so on, not necessarily with any religious connections. He'd often felt that he'd have liked to have done something like that and now here was an opportunity. It would be a major undertaking, of course. No doubt Anna could help or even some of the more educated members of his congregation—there might be one or two there. Perhaps it would be more appropriate for him to assume the role of editor. Quite a challenge. He would look into the possibilities.

Returning to the crossword he tried some of the other clues but found that his interest had temporarily waned. This tended to happen when he'd been interrupted. Of course he really ought to insist on not being disturbed but . . . there were some things one just had to put up with.

"I'm sorry there are no peppers in this," said Mrs Nicholson as she put out the lunch. "I couldn't get any this morning."

"Oh, it doesn't matter. Are they supposed to be in risotto?"

"Yes. Well, I usually put them in—when I can get them."

"Why didn't you make something else—something that doesn't need peppers?"

"I wanted to do risotto. We haven't had it for a while. It's not very easy thinking of something every day. You never seem to have any suggestions."

The Rev Nicholson reflected to himself that this was true. He had little interest in planning menus and anyway he always had other things to deal with.

"And if I didn't cook something just because one of the ingredients wasn't available here, we'd have a pretty restricted diet."

Mr Nicholson, his mouth full of risotto, nodded. Living in Achanult had its drawbacks.

"Did you finish the crossword?"

"Umm, no. I didn't really have time. Did you say you'd got one of the clues?"

"Yes, the one about Xmas and Easter."

"Ah yes. I noticed that one. I didn't really have time to give it much thought."

"Do you want me to tell you then?"

"Well, if you like."

"Islands."

"Pardon?"

"Islands. They're both islands, aren't they? It fitted anyway."

"Ah, yes. Possibly. Very good."

Mr Nicholson took another mouthful of risotto. He'd never have thought of that. Now this was where a reverse-index lexicon would have come in handy. Right. He would see about it this afternoon. A couple of phone calls to Edinburgh should do it. With a feeling of urgency he took another mouthful of risotto.

39 In charge

MAGGIE Stewart quickened her step as the rain got heavier. She certainly didn't want to be late which was why she'd got out of bed a quarter of an hour earlier than usual. An awesome thing, responsibility. Maggie was delighted that she'd finally prevailed upon Mrs White even if her boss had seemed a bit reluctant. Climbing the stairs she unlocked the door to the library. To her disappointment, no-one was waiting by the door to witness her doing so. It was only five minutes to nine, of course. Maggie considered going downstairs again and returning in about four minutes—there might be a small queue then. The important thing of course, was not to be late, not even one minute. For then some busybody—one of the incomers, naturally—would be sure to notice and make some sort of complaint. In the end she decided to go inside and lock the door. She would then be able to open it with a flourish at nine o'clock precisely.

You'd have thought Mrs Reid would have been glad of a long lie in the morning, especially at her age. She must be near retiring now. Maggie wondered how easy it would be to get another cleaner, with those unsociable hours and the low pay. Her own pay was low enough but Mrs Reid's was worse, even allowing for the fact that she only worked part time. You really wondered sometimes why she did the job. She'd just got used to it probably. She was certainly set in her ways. She'd been telling Maggie only the other day when they'd been discussing pay—in a general way, of course—that she'd had a visit a few years ago from somebody who'd had something to do with a union.

"Wanted me to join a union," she'd told Maggie.

Maggie, who didn't like unions except when their views agreed with hers, gave a neutral reaction. She'd better wait to hear Mrs Reid's response.

"So I told him I didn't approve of these unions—always going on strike."

"You're quite right," said Maggie firmly. "We don't need any of that sort of thing here. You even have to pay to be in a union. I'm like you, I've no time for them."

"Oh, he said it wouldn't cost me much to join because my pay was below some level or other. I can't remember it all now. I think he was wanting to get my pay increased."

"And did he?"

"Oh no. Well, I wouldn't join his union, you see."

"That's typical of them. Selfish. Never think of anybody else."

"Anyway, I told him I was quite happy with things the way they were."

"You're right. Money isn't everything."

On the stroke of nine o'clock Maggie unlocked and opened the door of the library with a flourish. Unfortunately, no-one was waiting so she just had to go back in again. They wouldn't be long in coming though. Then there would be the post to see to—not that they got very much but Maggie liked it to be known that she had the responsibility of dealing with the mail. Then there were occasional telephone requests.

At first Maggie had taken it upon herself to deal with these when Mrs White was absent but since the fiasco over Mrs Munro's request, she'd been asked simply to make a note of the item. The Munros were a rather well-to-do family who'd recently moved to Achanult. Mrs Munro had asked Maggie for a book on composition. Apparently the English department at school was a little concerned about her daughter's progress. So Maggie had duly ordered a book on music which she'd then presented to an unamused Mrs Munro.

Nor was she able to do anything about the books, contrary to the impression she'd given to most of Achanult, apart from stamping them out and taking them back in again.

Yesterday Mrs McQueen had visited the library. As usual there was no sign of Peter, though he'd told Maggie the other day that he'd maybe look in.

"I've just come to see about these books, Mrs Stewart."

"Certainly, Mrs McQueen—which—?"

"The Gaelic ones. You were telling me about them last week."

"Oh yes."

Oh dear, thought Maggie, who'd since discovered that they had very little in the way of Gaelic books and they certainly didn't have the one Mrs Nicholson was using at the class.

"Most of them seem to be out, I'm afraid."

"Oh well, they'll be back soon, I suppose."

"Well, it depends. If it's a question of inter-library loans or a request outwith the region . . . " waffled Maggie, relieved that it was fairly easy to baffle Jean with technicalities. "If you'd like me to check . . . " she continued, knowing that she could rely on Jean's reluctance to bother people.

"Oh, I don't want to cause any bother."

Maggie smiled sweetly. "Well, if you're sure . . . what else can I do for you?"

"Well, you did say you might be able to order the book— the one you use at the class. I've forgotten what you said it was."

Maggie's smile vanished. It was true that she'd hinted to Jean that she could buy any book she wanted for the library but she had, in fact, been firmly told that any book buying was done by the librarian, not by the clerical assistant. In any case, the book fund allocation for the current year had already been used up.

"I can certainly try and get it for you, Mrs McQueen. It may take some time though, particularly if it's currently outwith the region. And I'm afraid there will have to be a charge."

"Oh, I wouldn't want you to go to all that bother."

"Are you sure?"

"Yes, I'll just leave it just now."

Maggie's smile returned. She'd handled that rather well, she thought. In the end Jean had gone happily off with her customary volume of romantic fiction.

The library gradually began to fill up. There were the regulars, elderly, mostly men, who came in to read the newspapers. They always sat in the same place, if possible. Donald Morrison would be in soon. He came in every morning. Maggie didn't like him very much. He would just give her an off-hand nod as he came in, although sometimes he ignored her completely. He was just like that at the Gaelic class. No wonder he wasn't married.

Her friend Alice might look in this morning. Maggie had mentioned to her that Mrs White would be away until the afternoon, so they could have a fine long chat. Alice knew that Maggie simply wanted as many people as possible to see her in charge—however temporarily—of the library, so she was a bit reluctant. But since she wanted to see Maggie about this business of a Gaelic choir, she turned up just before ten o'clock. Maggie was also interested in the choir but first she wanted to discuss whether her important role in the library would allow her time for the choir, which of course it would, but the ritual *had* to be enacted with a reluctant Alice, who only wanted to talk about the choir.

"Have you got a minute to spare?" began Alice. "I wanted to see you about this choir business."

"In a minute, Alice. I've got a lot on my hands this morning."

"I think it's quite a good idea."

"The amount of things I have to do! That's what happens when you're in charge, of course."

"There's certainly been a lot of interest even from people you might not have thought would be keen."

"So I told Mrs White there was no need to hurry back. Apparently young Janice . . . "

"They're living in Glasgow, I hear. Mind you, I suppose we'll all have to learn some Gaelic. I don't know how easy . . . "

"She'll be back in the afternoon. Away at a meeting again. I'm left in charge quite a lot."

"And it's been a long time since I did any real singing."

"It's not easy when you're on your own, what with the telephone . . . "

"It's men that'll be the problem. It always is. They just don't seem to want to get involved."

"I'm rushed off my feet sometimes. We're not too busy at the moment."

"I don't know what it is about men. They're too set in their ways, that's what it is."

"I had to open the place up this morning and I wouldn't be surprised if . . . "

"Mind you, I can think of a few men we *don't* want in the choir," said Alice, lowering her voice and looking surreptitiously around her.

"Of course, it means I've got to work that bit longer but that's what happens, isn't it?"

"That's right. What we need are younger men," insisted Alice, raising her voice for emphasis.

At this point Maggie became aware that the rest of the library had begun to take an interest in their conversation and was about to suggest to Alice that they retire to the office—or *her* office, as Maggie called it when Mrs White wasn't around—when a young woman came up with some books she had chosen.

After Alice had gone Maggie felt rather pleased with herself. She'd managed to hint at her importance in the library and

245

knew she'd given an impression of efficiency. It was a pity certainly, that the elderly gentleman who'd returned a book while Alice was there had wanted to extend the loan. Maggie hadn't known what to do about this and after much dithering had set the book to one side. Later that morning she recalled that Mrs White had covered such an eventuality in her instructions when Maggie had first started the job. But she couldn't remember what it was she'd been told to do.

From time to time during the morning the telephone rang. It was always Mrs White they wanted and Maggie's offers of assistance were politely declined, which annoyed her considerably. After all, it was probably just some routine query about books which Maggie felt she could deal with, no problem. Her irritation returned when she sat down to type up one of the letters Mrs White had left for her.

The headed notepaper contained the name of the main library in Oban and this branch in Achanult with four names including Mrs White's. There was no mention of Mrs M R Stewart, which annoyed her even though she realised that the notepaper had probably been lying around since last year. She then looked back to earlier correspondence to see if Janice's name had been on the heading. She was delighted to find out that it hadn't been but it was nevertheless a slight. She would have to raise the subject with Mrs White. After all, they were all working in the library together, even if some of them did have a lot of fancy letters after their names. Mrs. T. White, M.A., F.L.A.—whatever that meant. Maggie knew she could do the job just as well as them. Not only that. They got paid a lot more, whereas she did most of the work, some of it, it had to be said, outwith her own particular responsibilities. But she wouldn't have it any other way.

Maggie got on with typing the letter now that things were,

for the moment, a bit quieter in the library. Her typing skills were improving. Mrs White had been surprised at how slow she'd been to start with but a few weeks had made quite a difference. She typed mechanically just what was written, word for word. When she first started she'd had a critical look at things and even suggested improvements. She'd also altered on one occasion Mrs White's phrase "The Writer's Guild", which she knew couldn't be right, to "The Writers' Guild", which looked a lot better, she felt. Mrs White had told her not to do that again.

So Maggie had a wee huff for a while and now just typed whatever she was given. If her boss wanted to display her ignorance of grammar, Maggie wasn't going to stop her.

At one o'clock the library closed for an hour. Everyone knew this but Maggie nevertheless went round the room saying authoritatively to those who were left, "we close in five minutes." Donald Morrison got up and left before she got round to him. He would, of course. As the last elderly gentleman left, she switched off the lights, went out and locked the door. When she'd first started Maggie had turned off the lights for a few seconds at 12.55, just to remind people that they'd be closing in five minutes. Mrs White told her not to do that again, too. Too much like a pub, she said. You wouldn't have thought a lady like Mrs White would have known about pubs but perhaps there was more to her than Maggie thought. She'd make discreet enquiries.

40 Contact

IT WAS now a few weeks since Miss McLachlan had left Achanult and Miss Shuttleworth had heard not a word from her. This annoyed her rather more than she cared to admit but on the other hand, she did not encourage excessive familiarity—such as being telephoned for no good reason, or indeed for any reason. Jennifer was aware of this of course, but she could still have written.

But she hadn't and Miss Shuttleworth was growing impatient. There was no question of her taking the initiative herself since she did not wish to appear too eager. From time to time she wondered what Miss McLachlan's long silence could possibly mean. Had she turned her back on Achanult? Perhaps it wasn't quite what she'd expected. It couldn't be anything personal.

She'd wondered about finding some pretext for writing to Miss McLachlan but couldn't think of anything convincing. She'd even hunted through the house to see if her friend had left anything but to her surprise had found nothing. Nor had anything happened in the village that Miss McLachlan would have wanted to be told about. Miss Shuttleworth did consider writing to tell her about the proposed formation of a Gaelic choir—Jennifer having a fondness for music—but doubted that it was of sufficient interest or importance, particularly since it was only a suggestion and nothing was likely to happen for several decades.

So there was nothing for it but to wait. Miss Shuttleworth wasn't very good at waiting and found herself becoming annoyed with the postman. The amount of rubbish that found its way into her house! She always put it straight into the bin, though she was even more annoyed when the postman passed her by.

In the end she became so frustrated that she decided to telephone Miss McLachlan at her place of work. After hours of thought she eventually came up with what she hoped was a good reason. She would tell Jennifer that she would be going away for a bit—leave it vague—and so if there was no reply at Fairview to a letter or telephone call, that would be the reason and she'd get back to Jennifer as soon as she returned. None of this was true, of course but Miss Shuttleworth thought it sounded quite convincing. Miss McLachlan wouldn't know if she'd gone off or not and anyway, she could always say she'd had to change her plans at the last minute.

Leaving nothing to chance, Miss Shuttleworth carefully rehearsed what exactly she would say. After a lot of thought she eventually settled on what she hoped was a suitably authentic opening couple of sentences. That should be enough. Jennifer would be sure to butt in by then. She had an unfortunate habit of doing that. Then it would just be a question of reacting to whatever Miss McLachlan had to say.

Miss Shuttleworth paused. She'd better have a suitable answer to any question Jennifer might ask. Perhaps she'd better list the possibilities on a piece of paper and then consider and write down her own answers. That way she'd be half prepared for any tangent Jennifer might shoot off at.

Miss Shuttleworth rose from the sofa to find a sheet of paper. She then spent about a quarter of an hour writing down possible questions and her replies to them. It was all fairly straightforward but Miss Shuttleworth liked to be prepared. The only point which caused her any problem was the possibility that Miss McLachlan might want to know the reason for this sudden absence, in which case she could invoke an elderly and ailing relative. Something vague was best.

Now that she had prepared herself for the telephone call, Miss Shuttleworth's next problem was whether to phone now or wait till after six, which would of course be much cheaper. On the other hand, she recalled Jennifer saying that she could be reached more easily at work. But whether she was still at work was another matter. She was about to retire about now, though there seemed to be no urgency one way or the other. Jennifer was really impossibly vague at times. So she'd phone in the evening then, so that if her friend felt the need to talk at some length, which she usually did, it wouldn't be ruinously expensive.

Experiencing a feeling of relief and elation now that she'd finally come to a decision, Miss Shuttleworth walked out into her garden. It really was quite mild for this time of year, she thought as she looked down the road and noticed the post van.

She'd forgotten about that. Late again of course. He'd have been reading his paper in that layby as usual. Something really ought to be done about it. Surely that was the sort of thing that silly community association ought to be concerning itself with, instead of that hunt-the-thimble nonsense or whatever it was they got up to! Not that there was much chance of them doing anything remotely sensible while that dreadful Maggie Stewart had anything to do with it.

As the postman came near to her house Miss Shuttleworth slipped quietly back indoors again. She'd happened to meet him once or twice before but that had been enough! Rather too familiar he was. And she didn't like the way he looked at her letters, trying to see where they'd come from or who had sent them. While she waited behind the curtain Miss Shuttleworth reflected that there could well be a letter from Miss McLachlan.

That would be typical of Jennifer, waiting until the last minute, just as she was about to telephone her. Still, it would save a bit of bother. Miss Shuttleworth waited expectantly.

As she heard the post van approach her house then drive past without stopping, she reacted with suppressed fury. Three days running and no mail for her. Right! She would telephone Jennifer immediately and ask her what was the meaning of this. As she seized the receiver she remembered that the postman had once come back with a letter for her after he'd delivered mail a house or two further on. Even one of her neighbours had handed her a letter once which the postman had inadvertantly misdirected. She herself had also had to redirect some mail intended for the bungalow across the road. She'd simply put it back in the post box. You'd think the postman could read. Probably drunk. Opening her front door Miss Shuttleworth tiptoed cautiously out just in time to see the post van disappearing round a bend in the distance.

So there was nothing for it but to telephone. This farce had gone on long enough. Halfway through dialling the number Miss Shuttleworth realised she did not have her precious piece of paper containing her prepared remarks. Putting the receiver down again she went to get it but couldn't see it anywhere. After checking that she hadn't left it by the phone, it occurred to her she might have had it with her when she'd been out in the garden. In that case it could have been blown anywhere by now.

She rushed outside in a panic, her mind going back to the time when Maggie Stewart had claimed to have found a page from a letter to Mrs Maxwell in her garden after one of last year's gales. There certainly had been a lot of stuff blown around that night. And some people didn't help matters by putting their rubbish in those silly black bags. Dogs just tore them open and the mess was scattered all over the place. Now that was something else the community association should concern itself with, instead of all this nonsense about beetle drives. But of course it wouldn't. Tidiness wasn't one if its priorities. So this letter—or page—apparently asked whether the new minister was still as bad and agreed that something should be done about it. So Maggie said anyway, although she claimed to have disposed of the letter immediately, it being such a private matter. She was also a bit vague as to exactly how she knew it had been addressed to Mrs Maxwell. Naturally nobody in the village believed a word of any of this. It was just Maggie trying to stir up trouble again. Still, it made you think.

After about five minutes of increasingly frenetic searching Miss Shuttleworth eventually found her sheet of paper on the floor where it had fallen from the arm of the sofa. Surely she'd looked there? She must calm down. If Jennifer only knew the trouble she'd caused! She dialled again.

"Ah, good morning. May I speak to Miss McLachlan please?"

"Miss McNaughton? Which department? . . . "

"No, McLachlan. Jennifer McLachlan. Would you like me to spell it?"

"No, that's all right. I think I've got it. I'm fairly new here but I'll see if someone can get a hold of her for you."

Miss Shuttleworth fidgeted. She had known this would happen. She should have waited till the evening. Looking at the second hand of her watch, she decided she would wait one minute and no more. She could always phone back later in the evening. They should have found Jennifer by then.

After fifty seconds she heard footsteps approaching. Nervously she glanced at her sheet of paper.

"Hello? I'm sorry to have kept you waiting. I'm afraid Miss McLachlan's not here."

"Oh. Perhaps if I phone later? . . . "

"Well no-one seems to know when she'd be back. She's gone on holiday, it seems."

"Oh!" Miss Shuttleworth suddenly felt a bit faint. "Did she . . . umm . . . say where?"

"I don't know. No-one seemed to know. Would you like me to ask?"

"No, no. It doesn't matter."

"Can I take a message then?"

"No thank you. It's not important."

This, said Miss Shuttleworth out loud to herself after she'd replaced the receiver and given herself a few minutes to calm down, is just ridiculous!

41 Good material

"BUT I don't know anything about these things," protested Mrs Nicholson.

"Nonsense," said Alice. "You're just the right person for it. Who else would we want?"

The others nodded in agreement. Mrs Nicholson sighed. They were obviously taking it seriously. You could tell by the way Maggie Stewart had applied extra make-up, which she always did when she considered a situation important. Alice had her handbag and gloves with her—another sure sign.

"After all, it's really just an extension of the Gaelic class, isn't it?" asked Maggie.

"We-e-ll," began Mrs Nicholson.

"More of an addition really," put in Alice.

"It doesn't matter how you look at it," asserted Maggie. "You're the obvious person to be in charge."

"But I don't know anything about the musical side."

"Oh, it doesn't matter about that. We'll just play it by ear."

Mrs Nicholson smiled weakly. Of course one had to admire their enthusiasm but this was really a bit ambitious.

"Maybe we ought to see how people feel," she said vaguely.

"Oh we know how people feel," replied Maggie. "There's a lot of interest, you know."

"Oh?"

"Oh yes. And people were really pleased when I told them that you would be in charge of things."

"Oh."

"I said I'd have to see you first of course. So, . . . umm . . . here we are!" Maggie beamed. In the silence Mrs Baines coughed politely.

"It'll all be very informal," volunteered Alice.

"Well," said Mrs Nicholson eventually. "I don't want to give the wrong impression. I think it's a lovely idea. All I'm saying is that I don't have any experience and I really wouldn't know what I was doing."

"Oh you don't have to worry about that. There's bound to be someone who can read music. And then Mrs Baines can be at the piano, at least to start with."

Mrs Baines began her ritual denial of any musical ability but was cut short by Maggie.

"We might get somebody better—I mean somebody else who's got a bit more . . . umm . . . experience—later on. It's amazing how interest picks up once these things get started."

After they'd gone Mrs Nicholson lent back in her chair and closed her eyes, hoping the ladies would understand that she hadn't agreed to anything. They really would be better with someone who knew what they were doing. It was a fine enough idea, of course. She'd better have a quick word with David before things went too far. He'd be in his study. They'd been chatting together in the kitchen when the doorbell sounded.

Mr Nicholson liked his wife to answer the door whenever possible, as a first line of defence. When he'd heard Maggie Stewart's voice—and one or two others, for heaven's sake!—he'd made a dash for his study.

Safely ensconced in there, he'd turned his thoughts to his reverse-index project. He was rather at a loss what to do about it. His phone conversations with Edinburgh had not been very encouraging. He'd been told that there wasn't really much of a demand for that sort of thing and in any case a computer could do it in five minutes. The Rev Nicholson knew nothing about computers except that they seemed to be taking over from the human brain. Hmm. Perhaps there was a sermon in that. Yes, something along the lines of "where would we be if the Bible had been written by a computer and not by the human brain?" Yes, possibilities there! The Rev Nicholson, feeling pleased, made a quick note of it. Then he had second thoughts. There were sure to be a few people in this remote part of the country who still thought that the Bible had been written by God. One or two of them could be in his congregation, for all he knew. Might be safer just to leave it. Scoring out what he had just written he turned his thoughts to the reverse index again.

It must surely be worth doing*something*—anything that would indicate the potential of his idea to a sceptical world.

At that moment his wife tapped on the door and entered looking worried.

"I hope I'm not disturbing you," she said, noticing with

some surprise that her husband did not have a crossword in front of him.

"Not at all, not at all. I was reflecting on possibilities for a sermon but nothing seems to have come of it."

He paused. He really wanted to raise the matter of the reverse-index which he'd been about to mention before the arrival of Maggie Stewart and her friends. His wife however, got in first.

"You'll never guess what all that was about. They're hoping to start a Gaelic choir."

"Ah well, quite harmless I suppose," conceded her husband.

"And they want me to be in charge of it!"

"In charge?"

"Yes. You know—conductor, musical director, whatever you want to call it."

"I see. I'm sure it'll be very interesting for you," said Mr Nicholson vaguely, his mind still on the reverse-index.

"But that's not the point. I don't know anything about it."

The Rev Nicholson detected a note of anguish in his wife's voice and decided he'd better listen to what she was saying.

"Umm . . . I . . . what do you feel yourself, Anna?"

"Well, I've never conducted any choir before."

"Yes you have. In Edinburgh. The children at Christmas."

"Oh that. That doesn't count. I mean, it's not quite the same thing, is it?"

"I should have thought there were certain broad similarities. Anyway if it's a Gaelic choir, you'll have to be in charge of it. Who else speaks the language here?"

"Well of course, I don't know who the members of the choir would be . . . but . . . I can't think of anyone else locally who has Gaelic. But that's no . . . "

"You mean the choir will all be English speakers?"

"I suppose so, if you want to put it like that. But there are sure to be a few learners in the choir—like Mrs Stewart there."

"Oh so that's what she was here for!"

Mrs Nicholson sighed again. Sometimes she wondered if her husband ever really listened to her.

"Mind you," continued Mr Nicholson, "if most of them don't know any Gaelic, why don't they just sing in English?"

"Oh for goodness sake, David. What would be the point of that?"

"Well, I don't see what's wrong with it. After all, aren't operas sometimes sung in English?—Mozart, Verdi, that sort of thing . . . Gilbert and Sullivan. I'm only trying to be helpful. It must make things easier for them if they understand what they're supposed to be singing about."

"But I'll tell them what the words mean. That's what they want me for, I suppose."

"Well, there you are then. I think it's quite a good idea. You could at least give it a try."

When his wife had left, the Rev Nicholson reflected that their lives seemed to be busier than ever since their move to Achanult. Which was far from what he had intended. They'd both found new interests, which was no doubt a good thing, and Anna seemed to have quite a lot to keep her occupied. She did tend to worry about things, of course, but then she'd been doing that for as long as he'd known her. Fortunately he felt, all the things she worried about were really of no importance. On the other hand she didn't seem to care about the things which did matter.

Take the garden, for instance. The Rev Nicholson worried about the manse garden and now that spring was approaching he would have to come to some sort of decision—any decision at all so long as he wasn't expected to get involved in any way.

During the winter his garden had looked just about as good as anybody else's. Especially when it was covered in snow! But now that spring was on the way he'd have to talk to Anna about it. Hmm. Maybe he could let it lie fallow for a year. Yes, that was it. Plenty of biblical precedents too. Even better. He could mention that in his sermon on Sunday—something along the lines of a return to traditional values, respect for the land, all that sort of thing.

The Rev Nicholson lifted his pen. There was plenty of material here for a sermon. He jotted down a few ideas— continual exploitation of our natural resources; greed; gluttony . . . The possibilities were endless. Leaning back in his chair he felt a surge of satisfaction. That was next Sunday's sermon taken care of and with a bit of luck he could spin the theme out for two or three more Sundays. Of course Anna would go on about seaweed and compost but nobody would contradict him in the pulpit.

"Is this that decaffeinated stuff again?" asked Mr Nicholson as his wife entered with a cup of coffee for him.

"No. I told you, I couldn't find any in the shop last time. Maybe I should have ordered some."

"What's the point? It tastes just the same as the ordinary stuff to me."

"But that's the whole point, David. Isn't it?"

The Rev Nicholson sipped from his cup. Anna did get these odd ideas from time to time and of course, he could see her point. But it was just another instance of her worrying about the wrong things. The daft thing was, this decaffeinated stuff cost more than the ordinary kind. Not that you could get it in Achanult of course. There wasn't really much of a choice locally. Willie didn't drink coffee and as in many other cases, this tended to influence his attitude to his stock on the shelves. Still, you could get it in Oban. Sometimes.

"Well it's very nice anyway. I'm happy to drink anything really. And while you're here Anna, I'd like your opinion on a small project I have in mind."

Mr Nicholson then told his wife about his reverse-index ambitions. He had to tell her several times in fact, since she found the concept difficult to grasp. Eventually she seemed to understand.

"I think I've got the idea of it. What I'm not so sure about is what the point of it is."

The Rev Nicholson explained.

"Oh, I see. Crosswords and other things. What other things?"

Her husband admitted that he couldn't immediately envisage any other uses but it would certainly be useful for crosswords.

"Isn't it cheating a bit?"

"Cheating?" asked Mr Nicholson in genuine amazement.

"Well you're supposed to do these things with your brain, aren't you? That's the whole point of them. A mental exercise."

"How do you know?" he countered. "You never do them."

"Everybody knows that. Anyway, I did one of your clues the other day. I might actually be quite good at them."

"Well, why don't you do one occasionally?"

Mrs Nicholson who regarded crosswords as a silly waste of time replied,

"I don't seem to have much time these days. Anyway," she added, "you probably wouldn't like me filling in bits here and there."

The Rev Nicholson felt they were getting away from the point.

"We can easily get another copy of the paper occasionally if you really wanted. Well, maybe not all that easily. However the point about a reverse index is that if you're really stuck it can help you out."

"Yes, I can see that. But surely, if you can't do a crossword, it means it's too hard for you. You could try an easier one."

"But sometimes getting one word will be the key to solving the whole thing . . . "

"I know that. But I still think it's cheating. Were you allowed any sort of dictionary at that competition in Glasgow?"

"No, no. Of course not. But I thought it might be useful for beginners—as a help and encouragement. So I wondered if I might compile just a small sample, to give an idea of how useful the thing could be."

"Yes, I see."

"So, umm . . . have you any ideas?"

"Me?" asked his wife, astonished.

"Well sometimes the uncommitted observer can see things more clearly, you know. Anyway if you do think of anything, let me know."

As Mrs Nicholson returned to her coffee which she'd left in the kitchen, she reflected that her husband was getting himself involved in the most odd things. It must be this west highland air. So much for its reputed soporific qualities!

42 Tea break

"WELL, here we are again," said Mrs Nicholson brightly. "The numbers seem to be holding up quite well this term."

"So they should be," agreed Maggie Stewart. "It's a privilege for us. And it's nice and warm with a cup of tea into the bargain now."

This was a reference to Mrs Grey who, in return for being allowed to bring her dog Betsy to the class, produced a weekly abundance of biscuits and tea in two large flasks. Her friend Mrs Abbott brought enough mugs plus milk and sugar for everyone.

So all the class adjourned, as it were, at three o' clock for a cup of tea and a biscuit. Not quite all though, since Donald Morrison proved very reluctant to take anything, despite the persistent efforts of Mrs Grey.

"They're home-made, Mr Morrison."

Donald looked at the biscuits.

"I'm just after having my dinner."

"A cup of tea then?"

"Och no, I'm fine."

"Are you sure?"

"Aye. I'll maybe try one next week."

Everyone else helped themselves—even Alec Cameron who gave the impression that he hadn't eaten anything all day. So this was now their third week with a tea break. Mrs Nicholson had noticed that the break was gradually extending. She'd rather suspected that this would happen but the class didn't seem to mind. On the contrary.

"I think it's a very good idea to have a break like this," Maggie Stewart had said on the first occasion. "It makes the afternoon more pleasant—even more pleasant—to have a cup of tea and something to eat."

Various heads nodded vigorously, their mouths full.

"In fact, I might be able to persuade Alice to come now," mused Maggie aloud. "She likes a cup of tea."

"That would be fine," said Mrs McKenzie between mouthfuls. "The more the merrier I always think."

Miss Shuttleworth, who had mixed feelings about the tea break, felt it was time to inject a note of realism.

"But isn't she a beginner?" she asked pointedly.

"Who? . . . Oh Alice?" said Maggie. "She doesn't know a word as far as I'm aware."

"Then wouldn't she be a bit out of her depth?"

"Oh?"

"Well, we've been going for about a term and a half now. We may not have learnt everything but you wouldn't say we were beginners, would you?"

Mrs Nicholson agreed that they had all made considerable progress.

"Oh, you don't need to worry about that," sniffed Maggie. "Alice wouldn't really bother about the Gaelic. She'd just enjoy the chat and the cup of tea. You'd all get on fine with her. She's great company."

Miss Shuttleworth snorted.

"There are bound to be difficulties if new people turn up. I'm not saying we can't resolve them . . . "

"The only difficulty I can see is that we might not have enough cups," interrupted Maggie. As Mrs Nicholson attempted to steer the discussion in the direction of Gaelic, Mrs Abbott said,

"Don't worry about cups. I've got plenty more at home. I only bring enough for the class."

Mrs Nicholson had been told often enough by her husband that she should simply regard the class as a social service and that if she made things too difficult for them by expecting them to learn vocabulary and so on, they would soon disappear. She suspected that he was right but in any case, she seemed to have less and less say in the matter. Her husband had noticed himself in his long years in the ministry that the last thing his congregation wanted was to be compelled to exercise their brains on a Sunday morning. They came for assurance, he'd said.

This suited Mr Nicholson very well, just as it seemed to suit his audience. This was quite obvious from the reports he had got over the years after returning from his annual holiday. The relief minister preaching in his absence was always too "difficult" or "serious" or "questioning". They tended to be young men of course, sometimes not yet fully qualified. One of them had even quoted some Greek at the congregation. Mr Nicholson had been reminded of this recently when he'd heard of a proposal to have an occasional service in Gaelic somewhere in the area. He'd been rather taken aback at first by this news but later decided that there was no harm in it. In any case he was under no risk of being asked to make any sort of contribution.

When the class had finally finished their tea and biscuits Mrs Nicholson looked at her watch.

"Well, we've still got a little time. Would you like to have another look at the past tense . . . ? Or . . . is there anything else . . . ?"

"Can you tell me what the Gaelic is for Canada?" asked Maggie Stewart abruptly.

"It's just the same actually. I mean, there isn't any special word."

"Oh."

"America, of course is . . . Well there are actually two ways . . . "

"No, it was just Canada I wanted to know."

"I see. Well it's just the same word. But some of the names of countries are quite interesting. Maybe we . . . "

"It's because my daughter lives there," interrupted Maggie, deciding that Mrs Nicholson would never ask.

"Ah! Of course," said Mrs Nicholson. Most of the others had seen what Maggie was driving at long before. And most of them didn't want to hear any more about her daughter—at least not from Maggie.

"She's coming over for a visit soon—so I was wondering how to say, Welcome from Canada."

Mrs Nicholson thought for a moment.

"You know, I'm not sure we would say it like that in Gaelic. It's more, Welcome to, we would say. Like, Welcome to Scotland."

"Oh well," said Maggie happily moving on from Canada now that she had introduced the subject of her daughter. "How would you say, Welcome to Scotland?"

"Well," replied Mrs Nicholson, trying to involve the rest of the reluctant class, "does anyone know the Gaelic for Scotland?"

Miss Shuttleworth made an effort.

"That's right. Only it's not quite pronounced like that."

"Sorry. I've only ever seen it written."

"Oh? Where was that?" asked Maggie who had always thought that *Alba* was pronounced just as Miss Shuttleworth had sounded it but nevertheless now saw the chance of a triumph.

"On the banks in Oban."

"Oh yes, of course," said Mrs Nicholson. "That's all quite

new, you know. There were very few signs in Gaelic when I was young."

"The great mistake is to pronounce these words according to English rules," persisted Maggie. "You've told us that often enough, Mrs Nicholson. We've got to get rid of any English influence. How exactly do you pronounce it in Uist?"

Mrs Nicholson told her. "I think," she added, "that that's more or less the pronunciation everywhere."

"Yes, that's what I thought. I just wanted to be sure," said Maggie and then added quickly, "Heather would understand it, of course."

"Oh I see. She knows Gaelic then? Why is it . . . "

"I'm not saying she's fluent. But she understands a lot of it. Mind you, she may have forgotten some," Maggie added defensively, aware that Heather would be turning up in a few weeks. The rest of the class, most of whom had known Heather since her childhood, listened sceptically. But Mrs Nicholson hadn't known Maggie's daughter and added,

"Well, that's very nice. Maybe she'd like to come along to the class when she's here."

The prospect of both Maggie and her daughter together at the class prompted Alec Cameron to splutter,

"She never shpoke a word of Gaelic that I heard."

Amidst murmurings of assent Maggie retorted sharply.

"And how often did you talk to her? Of course she would talk in English to you."

Alec Cameron, having made his point, said nothing. As the conversation dried up, Mrs Nicholson remarked,

"Of course, Gaelic is still spoken in parts of Canada, isn't it? Maybe she'll have picked up some of that."

"Oh well, I don't know," replied Maggie. "It's more French they're into over there. She has to have a good grasp of that seemingly. A bit daft really. It's no problem to her of course, but there's no reason for all that French there. I mean, it's not France, is it? It should just be English for everybody—and Gaelic as well of course, for those that have it."

As Maggie paused, Miss Shuttleworth who had been waiting, like the rest, with increasing impatience broke in.

"These names of countries are very interesting, Mrs Nicholson. What other ones can you give us?"

"Yes, right. I'll just write a few on the board. You probably know most of them already. Scotland of course, as I've said is *Alba*."

"I heard it wash Caledonia."

"Pardon."

"Caledonia ish the Gaelic for Shcotland."

"Well, not really, Mr Cameron. It means Scotland of course but it's not Gaelic. I'm not sure what it is actually."

"I think you'll find it's Latin," volunteered Miss Shuttleworth.

"Is it not just English?" asked Maggie, feigning simplicity.

"Hardly," retorted Miss Shuttleworth. "The English for Scotland is Scotland, strangely enough."

"Well, Burns uses it, as everybody else here knows. And he didn't write in Latin—or did you think he did?"

"I thought he wrote in Scots actually."

While Maggie tried to think of a suitable retort to this, Mrs Nicholson quickly said,

"Maybe we could move on to another country. What about England?"

As she walked home Mrs Nicholson wondered, not for the first time, whether there was anything to be gained by continuing with the class. She had to admit that most of them duly turned up week after week and seemed quite happy with the situation.

What a strange bunch they were!

She found her husband in the living room watching television. Glancing at the screen she said,

"Isn't this a funny time of year to be playing cricket?"

"It's from Australia. It'll be off in a minute."

Mrs Nicholson sat down. Her husband had always had a vague interest in cricket but she hadn't noticed him paying any attention to it since they came to Achanult. There was no tradition of it here, of course. The weather saw to that.

As he rose to switch off the set Mr Nicholson asked how things had gone today.

"Oh, much the same as usual. I think I offended Mr Cameron."

"Oh him! Yes. How did you manage that?"

"Well, he was apparently convinced that Caledonia was the Gaelic for Scotland."

"Isn't it?"

"No."

"Is that all?"

"More or less. Mrs McKenzie had a word with me at the end. You know what Mr Cameron's like, of course. All these stories of life here in the old days. Well, he always likes to put in a mention of Caledonia, which he then explains as being tʰ Gaelic for Scotland."

"Which it isn't."

"That's right."

"Oh dear. Still, you've done him a good turn."

"I don't think he'll see it like that. It could be one less for the class."

"Well, never mind. By the way, I've just thought of something that might keep your class amused."

"I'm not sure the situation isn't hilarious enough already."

"Get them to translate all those cricket terms into Gaelic—you know, square leg and silly mid off, and so on. What's the Gaelic for that?"

Mrs Nicholson sank back in her chair and closed her eyes.

43 Neighbourly

PETER was having a busy morning. Last night's storm had brought up quite a pile of driftwood so he'd been down on the beach with his saw cutting some of it. As he wheeled some up the driveway Jean came down to ask him how much there was. It was fine to see him getting a bit of exercise, as long as he didn't overdo it. She often thought he didn't have enough to do these days but he would never take up any of her suggestions. He seemed to be quite happy just pottering about.

Mind you, all these old men were the same. Look at Donald next door. You sometimes wondered what he did with himself all the time. Well, she knew what he was doing at the moment—lying in bed with the flu.

Really bad, it was, so the nurse had told her. Jean had felt a bit embarrassed that she hadn't known anything about it. But then it was difficult with Donald. Sometimes you never saw him for days. He could be dead for all you knew. She really worried about it sometimes. When she'd seen the nurse's car in the driveway she'd kept an eye open and gone out to put something in the dustbin at the bottom of their own driveway, just as the nurse had left the house. Their dustbin used to be kept round the back of the house till Jean discovered this extra use for it. Very handy, it was. She could then be standing right next to Donald's gate as any visitor emerged.

The moving of the dustbin hadn't been a decision she'd taken lightly. The trouble was it didn't look quite right at the front of the house. A bit unsightly she felt. She'd given up asking Peter to make a wooden housing for it, just to hide it from view. Peter couldn't see the point. Nobody else had to cover their dustbin with a wooden box and anyway, why couldn't she keep it round the back like she used to? She told him it was to save him carrying it down the driveway. Well, you couldn't really expect him to understand.

So Jean had just happened to be putting the lid back on the dustbin as the nurse's car crawled towards the gate. (That was actually the second time she'd had to replace the lid since the nurse had spent a few moments writing something in her car before starting the engine.) Jean gave a wave and the window was wound down.

"Morning, Mrs McQueen."

"Morning, nurse. I see you've been visiting Donald . . . "

"A bad case of flu. Weak as a lamb, he is. I'll be in again later."

And she'd driven off. Jean wondered how she'd known about Donald. She must have noticed something. Donald didn't really like visitors of course, as everybody knew. That was why Jean hadn't raised the question of whether she should take some food round. Both of them knew that Donald wouldn't want it. It did occur to her that she might ask Peter to look in but she knew he'd be most reluctant. He'd tell you he didn't want to catch whatever it was that Donald had got. That was his usual excuse. Maybe he had a point. It was a nasty business, this flu.

"I was just talking to the nurse," said Jean as Peter wheeled some more wood up the driveway.

"Aye, I saw her car."

"She says Donald's got the flu."

"Oh well, we'd better keep clear."

"I was wondering if you'd like to go round and see if he's wanting anything."

"Och, he'll be O K. The nurse'll be seeing to him anyway."

Jean felt better for having tried. The nurse would be more useful to Donald anyway. She was a fine woman, Nurse Hendry, still keeping her strong Irish accent after all these years. Funny how so many nurses seemed to be foreigners these days.

There had been a lot of changes like that, thought Jean. Things that you'd got used to over the years were not quite the same. Progress was a great thing of course but Peter for one, remembered the old days with affection—when folk were a lot friendlier, in and out of each others' houses all the time. Peter had never actually been too keen on that. He felt you never had any privacy.

But all the older generation now would tell you what a grand thing it was that everyone's door was always open and folk in and out all the time. Maggie Stewart would tell you that things were still like that round her way. Peter said he doubted it. He couldn't think of too many people who'd be keen to have Maggie barging in on them. That was certainly one thing Peter wouldn't miss about the old days.

"Donald's not getting any younger, you know."

Peter hung his saw on the nail in the kitchen and took the cup of tea that Jean had poured.

"I mean, it's different for us," continued Jean. Peter, who was feeling his age after the morning's exertions, wondered what she meant.

"He's just there by himself," she explained.

"It's his own choice."

"I know. But if something happened . . . maybe we should go round and see him more."

"He doesn't want visitors. I'm surprised he let the nurse in."

"I don't think he had the strength to object. Mind you, if he's as bad as that and nobody to look after him, he'd be better off in hospital."

"You'd never get him in there. He'd be too frightened of not getting his dram."

"Goodness me! It would only be for a few days."

"Aye, but he likes a glass or two every night—maybe more, for all I know."

"I was just going to ask you how you knew."

"Oh, Willie mentioned it. He said that Donald goes to Oban as well to buy a bottle. He doesn't want everybody to know his business. He goes to the Co-op and Low's turn about. He takes his empty bottles back to Oban as well."

"Well, it's cheaper there and Donald's never been one to throw money away. Mind you, the empty whisky bottles you see lying about all over the place! Was that why the scouts were collecting them last year?"

"No, there's no money back on whisky bottles. They were just tidying the place up."

"So why does Donald take empty bottles to Oban?"

"It'll be because he doesn't want Willie to know. If he put the Oban bottles in his dustbin, folk would know where they came from. He buys the Co-op's own brand, it being a bit cheaper. I can't remember what Willie said he bought in Low's."

"Seems an awful fuss to me. Can he not just take the labels off the bottles?"

"Apparently he does that occasionally but it just makes folk suspicious."

"Aye, I suppose it would. You couldn't help being a bit curious. Of course, I don't know anything about whisky."

That was true, Peter reflected as Jean refilled his cup. She wouldn't know that you could often tell a brand of whisky from the shape of the bottle. But she was right. It was an awful lot of fuss on Donald's part.

She was right too that Donald didn't look after himself properly. She'd seen him with odd socks on and buttons missing from his shirt. No wonder he had the flu. Jean worried about these things. She'd asked Peter once whether he thought Donald had lost a sock. But of course Peter, being a man, wasn't interested in these things and couldn't really see that it mattered. Jean had the idea that a sock might have blown off Donald's clothes line in a gale. Well, the way Donald hung his washing out you wouldn't be surprised if one or two things blew off. She couldn't remember exactly when they'd last had a strong wind—more than a week ago anyway. But she couldn't remember whether Donald had had any washing out then either. And Peter of course, couldn't help. It would be just like Donald to leave his washing out in a gale. She'd often seen him leave it out in the pouring rain even though she knew it must have been dry before the rain started.

Once, years ago, she'd taken his washing in for him when the rain started and dried it in her kitchen. It was more or less dry anyway but Jean liked things to be just right. She'd returned his washing to Donald when he'd turned up a couple of hours later but he didn't seem very pleased. So she hadn't done it again although it frustrated her to see his dry washing still hanging there as the rain came on.

So she'd searched in the garden for a sock just in case, and had even had a quick look in Donald's garden when he was out. She'd even thought of asking Peter to keep his eyes open for a sock when he was down on the beach but his previous lack of enthusiasm put her off a bit. He often mentioned finding the odd shoe on the beach. But Donald hadn't lost any shoes as far as she could see.

44 Between the lines

MISS SHUTTLEWORTH had always prided herself on many things, one of which was her ability to read between the lines. She'd had plenty of practice in Achanult and could now understand what people meant, more or less.

Previously she'd assumed that all inhabitants north of the border spoke a kind of debased English, a rude and unsophisticated dialect. She'd now discovered that this was not the case in Argyll and there was surprisingly little wrong with their English. Something to do with the Gaelic background apparently. But she'd found it much harder to understand what people really meant. There was a reluctance to offend, a dislike of saying No, and a feeling that strangers should be told whatever it was they wanted to hear.

At first she hadn't really understood this but now she realised that phrases such as "I'll try to be there", or "I should manage to look in" meant that the speaker had no intention of going. She'd lost count of the number of people who'd said to her that the Gaelic class sounded really interesting and they'd need to make an effort to go. Not everyone was quite like this of course. Maggie Stewart for one, had a bluntness which Miss

Shuttleworth found rude, as did most of the village. But with the vast majority you had to read between the lines.

Miss Shuttleworth looked at the postcard again, wondering what Jennifer really meant. She read it for the umpteenth time.

Surprisingly warm here and no rain so farI've got a lovely big room (marked). Wide choice of food, all very good. Must be the French influence.Hope you're coping all right. I'll be in touch soon.

Jennifer

Well, of course it would be warmer. Jersey was several hundred miles to the south. If Jennifer was implying that Achanult was cold, why didn't she just say so? Come to think of it, she had said so. Several times, as Miss Shuttleworth recalled. And what exactly did she mean by saying "no rain so far"? It wasn't raining at the moment in Achanult either, as it happened. Miss Shuttleworth briefly considered telephoning Miss McLachlan in Jersey to tell her this but it was the peak rate at the moment.

And if Jennifer meant that her room was big compared with the bedroom she'd had at Fairview, then that was just too bad. Miss Shuttleworth herself had the largest bedroom—well, it was her house after all . . . Jennifer was too big, of course. She'd make any normal sized room seem too small.

Miss Shuttleworth set the postcard down on the kitchen table and wondered what she should make of the fact that her friend had gone to Jersey. She recalled a conversation they'd had one evening about the Hebrides. She herself was quite keen to go there. A bit expensive of course, but then if Jennifer were to share the cost . . .

"I'm not sure I'd be comfortable on an island," Miss

McLachlan had said.

"You're on one now," retorted Miss Shuttleworth.

"What? Oh—yes, but that doesn't count. You know what I mean."

"Do I? What is it that you wouldn't be comfortable about?"

"Oh . . . various things. I imagine they'd be a bit lacking in things . . . electricity, for instance. And what would the food be like? And the shops? They always look so remote and windswept." She lifted the book that Miss Shuttleworth had brought from the library to test her friend's reaction. "Of course, they're very picturesque," she added flicking through the pages.

"As far as I know they all have electricity although the amenities are not what you'd expect in a large town. I think it might be interesting to have a brief look at one or two of them."

"Mmm," said Miss McLachlan doubtfully. "I'd also be afraid of being cut off by bad weather."

"I don't think that happens in the summer, though I agree it can be a bit wild in the winter occasionally."

"Well, I don't know. I seem to keep hearing about gales round Rockall all the the time. That's somewhere out there, isn't it?"

"But nobody lives there, Jennifer. It's just a rock in the Atlantic."

"Oh I say, Marjory, you do seem to know rather a lot about the area. Do they all speak English, by the way?"

"Oh, I think so. Of course, I've no first hand knowledge. It's all from reading books—such as that one."

"Well, I suppose if one has an interest in these things . . . "

"Yes, it's surprising. It really is. Even the Inner Hebrides. I'd like to visit Iona, for instance."

"Iona?"

"You must have heard of it."

"Actually, I used to know someone called Iona. I didn't know it was the name of a place as well."

"It's a small island off Mull."

"Ah! Now I have heard of *that*. The Mull of Kintyre."

Miss Shuttleworth groaned silently. Jennifer really hadn't a clue. It was quite surprising that she'd managed to find her way to Achanult without first going on a misguided tour of Scotland. Still, she'd heard of Kintyre even if she didn't have the slightest idea where it was.

So here was Miss McLachlan visiting an island, quite a small island too. Miss Shuttleworth had never been to Jersey herself but she knew it wasn't very big. Jennifer must be trying to overcome her unease about islands. Perhaps her own enthusiasm had rubbed off on her friend.

Feeling quite encouraged, Miss Shuttleworth had another look at the postcard. She still wasn't sure what Jennifer was implying by "wide choice of food, all very good". If she meant that there wasn't a wide choice of food in Achanult, she was right. But there was always Oban and it was surprising how much one *could* get with a little careful planning. Quite what "all very good" was supposed to mean, Miss Shuttleworth was less sure. Presumably she was talking about the cooking. Well, about half the cooking in Achanult had been done by Miss McLachlan. She'd insisted—"my contribution"—and it was no better than Miss Shuttleworth's own cooking. In fact, Miss Shuttleworth thought it was rather worse and made a mental note of yet another aspect of her friend's lifestyle that would need correcting.

On the whole though, the cooking had been quite acceptable, apart from the fiasco with the haggis. Miss McLachlan had returned one day from a visit by herself to the shop.

"Guess what I've got, Marjory," she demanded, beaming.

"I think you'll have to give me a clue, Jennifer. Animal, vegetable or mineral?"

"Umm, I'm not really sure. Animal, I suppose."

"Well, I hope it's dead. I don't really want . . . "

"Of course it is. We'll be eating it."

"It's not a haggis by any chance?"

"Exactly right. That didn't take you long. How did you guess?"

"They're coming into season about now."

"Oh, I see. Like grouse, you mean?"

"Not quite, Jennifer. It's just that they tend to be eaten in droves about now. Something to do with the anniversary of the birth of Robert Burns. He was a Scottish poet."

"Oh. You know, I think I've heard of that—at home I mean. So how do we cook this haggis?"

"I don't actually know. I expect you have to boil it for two or three days."

"What? I thought we might have it for dinner tonight!"

"In that case, I'd better have a look in one of my cookery books."

Jennifer was so gullible. You could tell her anything, Miss Shuttleworth reflected as she went over to her bookshelf. You could probably sell her anything as well, so she'd better have a discreet glance at the sell-by date on the haggis. Willie might have had a herd of them left over from last year.

Once they'd found directions for cooking the haggis Miss McLachlan insisted on taking over. In retrospect, Miss Shuttleworth was quite glad about this, for when the haggis burst open halfway through its cooking, she was consoled by the knowledge it wasn't her fault.

"What do I do now?" moaned Miss McLachlan.

Miss Shuttleworth consulted her book.

"There doesn't seem to be anything in here about exploding haggis. I think we'll just have to treat it as mince."

"Oh dear. I'm not very fond of mince."

"Well, we'll just have to make the best of it."

So they'd eaten what they could of it. Miss Shuttleworth wasn't sure if it was properly cooked but didn't like to say so. Jennifer was suspicious enough already. Well, if either of them felt a bit queasy later, Miss Shuttleworth could always remind her whose idea it was.

"Well, what did you think of it?" she'd asked when she saw that Miss McLachlan had eaten as much as she was going to. Her friend considered for a moment.

"It's umm . . . well . . . different."

All in all, considered Miss Shuttleworth, it was rather impertinent of Jennifer to write "hope you are coping all right" from the safety of Jersey. She could cope a lot better without her friend's contributions to the cooking, for a start. Though she knew what Miss McLachlan meant. It was just another dig at the rigours of winter in Achanult, contrasted this time with the ease of life in the sunny south.

A few years ago she had held similar views herself but since coming to live in Achanult she had grown to see and like the attractions of the place, whereas Miss McLachlan could only see the negative side. She'd see to it that Jennifer changed her attitude once she came to live in the village. She certainly couldn't allow her to continue being so annoying.

Putting the postcard aside she picked up her newspaper and turned to the back page where there was a weather map of the UK. Without much enthusiasm she noted it was considerably warmer down in the Channel Islands, and dry too. Well at least it was dry here, she consoled herself, looking out of the window and noticing light drops of rain starting to speckle the glass.

45 Fossils and tartan

IN THE end the arts society had decided on fossils. It hadn't been an easy decision and there had been other suggestions to consider. But it was generally agreed that Mr Maxwell was a good speaker and his hobby was fossils. He had been a banker before he retired and so could also have given a talk on banking which was his only other main interest, or at least the only one he would admit to. He was actually well-known as a connoisseur of malt whisky but this was not felt to be an auspicious subject for the opening meeting of the society, especially as it was to be held in the manse. The Rev Nicholson was a little unsure of this last decision.

"Of course I can see your point but I just wonder if the manse is altogether suitable on this occasion."

Everyone waited for Miss Shuttleworth.

"I don't see why not," she obliged.

"Well, umm . . . it's not exactly . . . umm . . . central."

"Central?"

"Yes. What I mean is that it's not really ideally situated . . . umm . . . from that point of view . . . "

There was a puzzled silence.

"I don't see that that really matters too much," said Mrs Hastings. Her husband nodded. He hadn't said a word since the decision to postpone his talk on Bach.

"Perhaps not. Perhaps not. But as we all know, some people, particularly the elderly, are reluctant to walk too far in this sort of weather. We have to consider that, I think."

No one liked to disagree. Mrs Nicholson however, felt a little uneasy.

"None of our houses are particularly central," she admitted, "even if that mattered."

"That's just what I was thinking," agreed Mr Maxwell. "Still, we've got to find somewhere."

"Naturally, I'm quite happy that we should use the manse," said Mr Nicholson, abandoning his lost cause, "if you all think it's suitable."

So they'd agreed on the manse. They also agreed to put up a few notices throughout the village and in the local paper. There was some discussion as to exactly what form this advertisement should take.

"What do you think yourself, Mr Maxwell?" asked Mrs Nicholson.

"Well, what about something simple, to the effect that there will be a talk on fossils?"

"Ye-es . . . I suppose . . . "

"Some people might not know what fossils are," said the Rev Nicholson with a laugh.

"All the more reason for them to come and find out, surely," retorted his wife.

"Don't you think that the sort of person who doesn't know what fossils are is unlikely to derive much benefit from an arts society?" asked Miss Shuttleworth earnestly.

"Well, we all have to learn," said Mrs Maxwell tersely. Miss Shuttleworth really was a bit much at times. That sort of attitude might be all right in the Home Counties, but not here.

"I don't know that much about fossils myself," she added, "but coming back to the advert, I think it should say something about fossils in Argyll."

"Are there any?" enquired the Rev Nicholson.

"Of course. It's a good area," replied Mr Maxwell. "What my wife means is that we feel it's important to suggest some sort of local connection."

"Isn't that a bit parochial?" asked Miss Shuttleworth. Mr Maxwell explained while the others wished that Miss Shuttleworth would keep quiet and let them get on with the matters in hand.

"I know it's best to be prepared," said Mrs Nicholson, her worried look returning, "But I can't help feeling it would be tempting fate, it that's the right expression."

"Is that one of your island superstitions?" asked Mrs Hastings icily. She and her husband had no time for superstitions.

"Well, it's just that I find it very disappointing to go to a lot of trouble—getting in extra chairs, cups and saucers and so on, and then find that no-one turns up."

"We'll all turn up," said Miss Shuttleworth cheerfully.

"So I'd rather wait and see. I suppose you could say it was one of our island habits, right enough, tending to leave things to the last minute."

"Or later," added Mrs Hastings. "Still, that's one of the charms of the highlands and islands, isn't it?"

In the event, Mrs Nicholson was proved right. The only newcomer to attend was Mrs Grant, who everyone knew had been sent by Maggie Stewart. Still, she claimed to have enjoyed the evening though as someone remarked later, she could hardly have said it was the most boring talk she'd ever listened to. People in Achanult were much too polite for that. Even Maggie herself would only have spread her criticisms round the village once she'd got safely out of the manse. Mrs Grant was asked if she'd like to join the society and said she'd be quite interested but of course she had a lot of other things taking up her time. She'd let them know.

After she'd gone there was a short post mortem.

"Well, I suppose one new face is better than none," sighed Mrs Maxwell.

"Not in her case," said her husband. "Not only that, she'll tell everyone how boring it all was."

"Oh, but it wasn't," insisted Miss Shuttleworth. "I found it fascinating."

"Well, anyway," said Mr Maxwell, "I think in retrospect that Mr Nicholson may have had a point about the manse."

The Rev Nicholson roused himself.

"Well, yes . . . possibly . . . I umm . . . "

"What I mean is that some people find the idea of visiting a manse a bit off-putting."

"I see your point."

"Not that it is in the slightest, naturally. But . . . well . . . people who never go to church and even, I'm afraid to say, some of those who go to other . . . umm . . . denominations . . . "

"Quite."

"And another point to consider is whether it might not be a good idea to invite a more well-known speaker. There are quite a number of celebrities living in Argyll, you know. It shouldn't cost too much. It's always a question of getting these things off the ground, isn't it?"

So it was agreed to consider inviting a fairly well-known name to give a talk on any suitable subject. There was, as Mrs

Bates reminded them, a precedent. The community association had invited someone—she couldn't remember his name—to talk to them about tartan. He'd apparently given a talk on the radio about highland dress—though nobody in the village had actually heard it, and had published one or two articles on clan history.

"That was before you came to Achanult," said Mrs Bates to Mrs Nicholson.

"Yes, it must have been. It's quite a good idea."

"There hasn't been anything else similar though, has there?" asked her husband. "Not since we came here anyway."

Mrs Bates explained that although the village hall had been packed the evening had not been an unqualified success. The idea had originally come from Maggie Stewart who had recently bought a tartan skirt with various accessories which she wore to the lecture.

"Should women wear kilts?" interrupted Miss Shuttleworth.

"Umm . . . no, but it wasn't . . . "

"Yes I know. I just wondered. Did he say anything about that?"

"I'm not quite sure. It was a few years ago now."

Miss Shuttleworth nodded and subsided again into her armchair. Prompted by the others Mrs Bates went on to say that everyone had been very surprised when the speaker turned up in a suit, especially since several men in the audience had taken the trouble to wear highland dress. Many of the ladies were similarly festooned. It soon transpired however, that the tartans they were wearing had little or no authenticity. As the speaker discussed tartan after tartan and indicated the relatively modern origins of most of them, the audience grew restless. This was not what most of them had come to hear. Not only that, it seemed that there had been no such thing as a clan tartan in the great days of the clans.

"Isn't it ironic," asked the speaker, "that most of these tartans were invented in the late eighteenth and nineteenth centuries, when the clan system to which they refer had completely disappeared?"

Maggie Stewart, who was sitting in the front row as usual, didn't think that "ironic" was quite the word—"unlikely" would have been her choice. She'd brought along an old shortbread tin which once belonged to her grandmother in which Maggie kept buttons. On the front of the tin was a saccharine painting of Bonnie Prince Charlie, resplendent in his Royal Stewart tartan, identical to that of Maggie's skirt. So it had been a bit of a blow to her when what she regarded as early evidence was dismissed by the speaker, who showed them contemporary paintings of the Prince with not a thread of Royal Stewart tartan in sight. Maggie couldn't be expected to accept this.

"But what about those other paintings?" she demanded. "I've seen . . . we've all seen . . . " she added, sensing that the audience was behind her, "paintings of the Prince in a boat or with Flora MacDonald and always wearing the Royal Stewart tartan."

"Ah! You mean this sort of thing," said the speaker, selecting a slide and quickly showing it on the screen.

"Exactly!" lied Maggie, who'd never seen it before. The slide showed a painting of the prince, somewhat overdressed in Royal Stewart tartan, taking farewell of a small group of ragged crofters.

"Yes, well I was just coming to these. The point is of course, that they are all nineteenth century paintings and worthless as historical evidence."

Maggie fumed inwardly but said nothing. When the speaker

eventually finished his talk, the applause was a little on the brief side. He then asked if anyone had any questions. After a period of silence the Rev Neil thought he'd better ask something.

"All very interesting," he murmured vaguely. "I was wondering why tartan has such a prominent role today, in spite of its . . . umm . . . uncertain origins—which you have explained very well to us."

"Well, in brief," the guest speaker had answered, "it's a money spinner. Some people will buy anything if it's got tartan on it—especially Americans. And Japanese now, I believe. Bogus it may be, but it's best to keep quiet about that."

For once, Maggie agreed.

Miss Shuttleworth found Mrs Bates' story quite amusing. The others however, were a little more cautious and it was agreed that they would obviously have to be careful about choosing a guest speaker. Mr Hastings, who had been rising to leave for the last quarter of an hour, suggested that they could think about this in more detail on a later occasion. And so the first formal meeting of the arts society came to a close.

46 Not to be disturbed

THE Rev Nicholson put down his pen and leant back in his chair. He was finding it difficult to concentrate. From time to time he looked out of the window which reminded him of the problem of his garden. He'd tried to get his point across last Sunday and hoped he'd succeeded. After the service however, Mr Gillespie the beadle asked him what he was intending to do with his garden this year. Realising that he had not succeeded, the Rev Nicholson prepared to try again.

"Well, as I said in my sermon, there are times when nature needs a rest."

"Aye, I remember you saying that. That's really what reminded me to ask you what you were going to be planting this year."

The Rev Nicholson wondered how on earth Jesus had managed to get his message across in parables.

"What I mean is that the soil seems to have lost a lot of its strength and vitality."

"Lost its strength?"

"Umm . . . yes. So my wife was saying. She knows more than I do about these things."

"I'll come and have a look at it tomorrow."

"Well, I don't . . . "

"A bit of lime, maybe. There shouldn't be too much wrong with it. Mr Neil looked after it fine. If it needs anything else, we'll soon see to it."

So that was that. Mr Gillespie had turned up on Monday afternoon and pronounced the soil to be in good shape. So Anna had told him. Mr Nicholson himself had had to go to the library and one or two other little things. Later his wife had suggested that since Mr Gillespie was so interested in the garden, they should let him cultivate it for his own use. Mr Nicholson reflected that his wife had some very good ideas sometimes. It would mean having Mr Gillespie pottering about the place, of course. So he'd have to find some way of making it clear that he did not wish to be disturbed—unless possibly it concerned an urgent church matter and really, not even then.

He turned his attention back to the crossword. It was obviously a difficult one today, since he'd only managed three clues in the last twenty minutes. He decided to have a break and see if his wife had any more good ideas. Wandering through to the kitchen he found her polishing the kettle, which she did from time to time. He didn't really know why.

"Ah, there you are. I was wondering if you'd had any thoughts on that reverse-index idea we were talking about."

"Well funnily enough, something did occur to me last week at the class."

"I was intending to do it in English, Anna."

"Yes, yes. I know. But it gave me an idea."

"Oh?"

"We were discussing the word *pibroch*. It's a bit difficult to explain if you don't know any Gaelic but the point is that pibroch is a Gaelic word."

"But even I know the word!"

"That's because it's used in English as well. Anyway, what it means is piping."

"I see."

"So I was saying to the class that the root of *pibroch* is just the word, pipe. And then there's an ending put on, which is very common in Gaelic."

"The *-och* bit, you mean?"

"That's right—only that it's not spelt like that in Gaelic . . . "

Sensing that her husband was becoming a little confused, she added:

"The thing is, it's a very common suffix. And it occurred to me that you could do that with your index."

"Ah. Oh?"

"Any common suffix would do; I thought of -ION, but anything really would do."

"I . . . umm . . . could you give me an example?"

"Oh there must be millions. The first one in the dictionary—

I looked it up—is *abbreviation.*"

"Ah. Yes."

"That's the sort of thing you wanted, isn't it?"

"Yes. Possibly."

Back in his study Mr Nicholson resumed his contemplation of the garden. A few leaves whirled about in the strong wind. Surprising how windy it was in Achanult, persistent, biting . . . He still found it a bit uncomfortable after Edinburgh. Anna didn't seem to mind though. She'd be used to Uist of course, where they had gales all the time, even in summer. They wouldn't have any problems with leaves though. He'd been amazed when Anna had told him years ago, that there were no trees on her island.

The Rev Nicholson quite liked trees. They stood quietly at the back of his garden in their unobtrusive way and could be left to fend for themselves. It might have been better if they'd been evergreens, perhaps. Anna seemed to think that leaves were a good thing though, for compost or leaf mould or something. He'd noticed her raking them up a few weeks ago. She'd obviously missed a few or maybe they'd just been blown back off her compost heap.

That wasn't a bad idea of Anna's. If as she said, -ION was a common suffix, that was precisely the sort of thing that would prove useful in a reverse-index. He'd make a list of them in alphabetical order, starting now. The garden vanished from his thoughts.

That evening the Rev Nicholson should have been out paying a call on some of his elderly congregation. He'd been rather surprised to find how many of his flock were quite old and infirm. They rarely managed to come to church. Not very many young people came regularly but Mr Nicholson didn't feel that was his fault. It was the same everywhere. Back in

Edinburgh some of his colleagues had introduced elements aimed at the younger generation—folk music, guitar playing in church, that sort of thing. The Rev Nicholson, who had always been attracted by the *gravitas* of his calling, had been glad to find that there was none of that sort of thing in Achanult. There was the choir of course, but the organist dealt with that. At first Mr Nicholson had been consulted in detail about the psalms and hymns but he was soon happy to leave this to the organist, indicating that he was content to follow the same lines as his predecessor. It was always best not to disturb things too much.

The elderly and infirm who could not attend church expected to be visited at home from time to time. There'd been a bit of this in Edinburgh it was true, but nothing quite on this scale. It was becoming rather a problem and had been preying on his mind for some time.

As they sat by the fire after watching the news on television, Mrs Nicholson asked her husband,

"Aren't you going out tonight?"

"I don't think so. It's very windy, isn't it?"

Mrs Nicholson smiled to herself. In Uist this weather wouldn't have been considered exceptional.

"Look at those trees blown down on the news."

"That was in England, David."

"I know, but they never put anything on about the weather in Scotland during the national news. Haven't you noticed that?"

"Maybe it's not so windy here."

"Ah, but even if it was . . . Of course I'll be sorry to miss visiting . . . "

"Yes, that's what I was wondering about."

"So was I. So was I. In fact, I've been giving it a lot of

thought lately."

Mrs Nicholson concealed her surprise.

"As you know," continued her husband, "there are rather a lot of people in that position expecting . . . umm . . . requiring home visits. And of course, I'm not as young as I was."

"There do seem to be quite a few, certainly."

"So I was wondering if something could be done. It might be a good idea if people who enjoyed visiting others were encouraged a bit. This is the sort of thing you ladies are very good at, isn't it?"

"I'm beginning to think we have to be very good at most things. What exactly were you thinking of?"

"Just a suggestion of course, but if a group of ladies—or people, it wouldn't matter—could undertake pastoral visits it would take some of the pressure off me. It would need to be organised, naturally. Maybe you would like to do something about that?"

"Well . . . "

"But there's no rush, no rush. But if you could drum up some interest . . . "

His wife agreed. The Rev Nicholson leant back in his armchair feeling that, although he would not be able to venture out, the evening had not been wasted. As the wind rattled the windows he listened contentedly. It ought to quieten down later.

47 Multi-lingual

"I THOUGHT you might be interested in this," said Miss Shuttleworth as she handed a newspaper cutting to Mrs Nicholson. They were still waiting for one or two members of the class to arrive. Mrs Nicholson perused the cutting.

"That's very interesting. Where did you get it?"

"Oh, I get the weekly newspaper from home sent up. Don't know why, really. Anyway, I thought you might like to see it."

"Of course," said Mrs Nicholson glancing up as Mrs Abbott and Mrs Grey entered with the latter's dog Betsy following behind. Mrs Nicholson quite liked dogs and Betsy was no problem at the class. In fact, you often forgot she was there until she produced a lengthy yawn from time to time, a creaking, groaning sound rather like an old gate opening. Quite funny in a way.

"I think she must be bored," Mrs Nicholson had said once, as the rest of the class tried to suppress their smiles. Mrs Grey looked even more mortified than usual.

"It's just that she doesn't understand what you're talking about." explained Mrs Abbott. "It's her age as well. She sleeps a lot, doesn't she, Aggie?" Mrs Grey nodded silently.

From time to time Betsy roused herself and wandered vaguely round the room. Mrs Nicholson found this a bit disconcerting, especially if she happened to be in the middle of some explanation of the Gaelic language. But that wasn't very often these days.

Mrs Nicholson was just about to mention the newspaper cutting to the class when Maggie Stewart entered.

"Sorry I'm late. It's difficult to find time to get away." No-one said anything. As Maggie sat down Mrs Nicholson began.

"Maybe we could have a look at this before we start. Miss Shuttleworth has kindly brought in a cutting from her local newspaper about a Burns supper held there."

"Talking of Burns suppers, did you see that photo in the local paper?" interrupted Maggie Stewart. "Terrible!" she added to fill the silence.

"I'll pass it round so you can all have a look. It's the first dozen lines of *Tam o' Shanter* translated into Gaelic. Quite well done too."

"Who would have understood it?" asked Mrs McKenzie.

"Well, I don't suppose too many . . . anyway, you can read what the article says yourselves."

She passed the cutting to Donald Morrison and Alec Cameron who had recently taken to sitting at the front. Both looked at it briefly and then handed it over to Maggie Stewart who examined it for a few seconds.

"Are you sure this is a translation?" she asked Mrs Nicholson.

"Yes. It's not bad. Of course I know that a lot of the words will be unfamiliar to you. I just . . . "

"Oh no, it's not that. It's not poetry."

"What's not?"

"The Gaelic."

"No, that's right."

"But *Tam o' Shanter*'s a poem, isn't it?"

"Yes, but . . . "

"Well, how can this Gaelic here," insisted Maggie pointing for emphasis, "be a translation if it isn't poetry too?"

"Although it might not be perfect," said Miss Shuttleworth drily, "it's obviously a prose translation."

"We all know that," said Maggie scornfully, wondering what a prowess translation was. "But any English translations of Gaelic poetry, songs and so on, are always in verse, as far as I've noticed. Look at these Gaelic choir songs we were talking about the other day."

Mrs Nicholson thought she'd better head Maggie off before she spent an hour talking about the forthcoming Achanult Gaelic choir.

"Well of course, there's more than one way of doing things. There are a few misprints in the Gaelic, by the way."

"I thought I noticed something odd here and there," lied Maggie. "All in all, it's a bit . . . well, maybe it's all right for an English newspaper."

"I'm glad you mentioned spelling mistakes," said Miss Shuttleworth earnestly. "I couldn't find some of the words in my dictionary."

"Yes. Mind you, I've seen plenty of misspelt Gaelic in Scottish newspapers too," volunteered Mrs Nicholson who was beginning to admire Miss Shuttleworth's genuine interest in the language. "It's a common failing."

As the group finally settled down to consider for the umpteenth time the uses of the past tense, Mrs Nicholson reflected that a few more like Miss Shuttleworth in the class would be quite an asset. Although her pronunciation was still pretty awful—appalling really—she was undoubtedly improving. And she was always prepared to take an active and constructive part in any discussion.

As Mrs Nicholson stressed again the importance of aspiration she noticed from the corner of her eye that Betsy had decided to take an interest in her surroundings and was attempting to rise to her feet. This took some time and indeed had been known to fail on occasions, in which case the dog simply continued lying on the floor for another ten minutes or so. This time she made it and stood uncertainly on her feet. Past experience had shown Mrs Nicholson that there was no point in her continuing while the group's attention was diverted, so they all watched as Betsy padded silently off round the room. As the dog bumped into various table and chair legs Mrs Abbott explained again.

"She can't see a thing. Shame really. She can't hear either. In fact," she added as Betsy investigated Miss Shuttleworth's boots, "all she has is her sense of smell." Miss Shuttleworth looked down at the dog without great enthusiasm.

"I hope she's not bothering you," said Mrs Abbott.

"No, it's all right," replied Miss Shuttleworth. It was difficult to know what else to say. Mrs Nicholson had confided to her that the class couldn't really continue if they lost another couple of members, which would probably happen if Mrs Grey wasn't allowed to bring her dog. So she'd hoped that Miss Shuttleworth didn't mind the dog's presence. In fact Miss Shuttleworth didn't really mind at all, though she did wonder what would happen if Mrs Grey decided she had to bring an elderly sheep or cow.

"Mrs Butterworth says it's all right, Aggie," confided Mrs Abbott to Mrs Grey who kept an even lower profile than usual during Betsy's perambulations. Somewhat encouraged. Mrs Grey surfaced briefly,

"Just ignore her, Mrs Butterworth. She'll be back here in a minute."

"Shuttleworth!"

Mrs Grey smiled uncomprehendingly and nodded. Mrs Abbott intervened.

"Mrs Butterworth's telling us that her name's Shuttleworth, Aggie."

Looking puzzled, Mrs Grey shrank back a little.

"Sorry, Mrs Shuttleworth," continued Mrs Abbott. "That's her bad ear on this side. I never was very good at names."

"It's *Miss* Shuttleworth, actually," intoned Miss Shuttleworth, feeling that she might as well get it all sorted out there and then.

"Oh. Oh, I'm so sorry. I . . . umm . . . didn't . . . it's a nice name," ended Mrs Abbott lamely. Meanwhile Betsy, who had been the cause of this diversion, had now padded to the back of the room and was on the point of falling asleep beside the heater.

The group was now reluctant to return to the mysteries of the past tense. This was what generally happened after any kind of interruption when concentration had gone and everyone visibly relaxed. Mrs Nicholson had learnt to accept the inevitable—the only question was what topic would crop up this time.

The answer soon emerged as Alec Cameron was stirred to tell the class about Burns suppers he had known long ago. Although there was no tradition of such things in Uist Mrs Nicholson had encountered them in Edinburgh and knew what was involved. She wasn't really very enthusiastic but listened patiently as Alec Cameron continued his saga of drunken pipers and incoherent toasts.

"Well, I'm glad I don't have anything to do with that sort of business," said Miss Shuttleworth during a pause. Somebody ought to tell him to be quiet. Silly man. Why didn't Mrs Nicholson tell him that they were here to learn Gaelic?

"Of course we didn't have anything like that either in Uist," agreed Mrs Nicholson. "In fact, I still don't know much about Burns. I don't understand a lot of the words either."

"Oh I've never had any problem with that," asserted Maggie Stewart, "even though like you I've got a Gaelic background. Of course, if you haven't got an ear for languages . . . I always feel that we're very lucky having two, or you could even say three, languages in this country. I sometimes feel sorry for the English. They've only ever had the one language."

"What about Cornish?" asked Miss Shuttleworth quickly.

"Cornish? Oh, I've heard the way they speak there. It's just English."

"No, I don't mean that. I mean the Cornish language which was spoken till . . . oh . . . about two hundred years ago, I think. It was a language like Gaelic."

"Rubbish!"

"Well I admit I may not know much about it but you obviously know even less. Do *you* know what I'm talking about, Mrs Nicholson?"

As the class waited, a slow creaking yawn came from the back of the room.

"I think Cornish was certainly a Celtic language," replied Mrs Nicholson. Miss Shuttleworth nodded. "But I don't think it was like Gaelic. More like Welsh really."

"That's what I meant," said Maggie stiffly.

"It's the same thing surely," insisted Miss Shuttleworth.

"Well, yes and no," wavered Mrs Nicholson in desperation. The rest of the class had lost interest by now and were starting to talk among themselves. With a feeling of relief she caught Mrs Abbott's eye.

"Did you want to ask something, Mrs Abbott?"

"Well, not really . . . it's just she says . . . what was it again, Aggie?"

Mrs Grey declined to cooperate.

"She's a bit reluctant when she's not sure of something. Was it *eem*, Aggie?"

Mrs Grey nodded silently.

"She says she remembers hearing the word *eem* when she was a child," explained Mrs Abbott.

"*Im?* Oh. That means butter," said Mrs Nicholson.

Mrs Abbott smiled.

"There, Aggie. You were right," she enthused, and then added, "she used to go to Mull in the school holidays."

48 A bit funny

"THE nurse was saying that what he really needs is a holiday somewhere in the sun," said Jean as she stood over the sink washing the dishes. Peter never washed the dishes but he did dry them from time to time and he'd only started doing that within the last few years.

"Aye well, there's not much sun just now, though."

"I think she must have meant somewhere abroad—Spain and these sorts of places."

"Aye, maybe . . . "

"A lot of folk go there now."

"Well it's their own money, I suppose."

Peter took a dim view of foreign holidays. He knew that Scotland had the best scenery in the world, so what was the point of going abroad? And there was so much of Scotland. There was plenty of time for folk to think of going somewhere else when they'd seen their own country properly first. And that could take a long time. Peter himself had never got much beyond Argyll yet, except for trips to Glasgow which he didn't really enjoy. Maybe you'd get used to the crowds but it wasn't for him at all. So he and Jean generally stayed at home and maybe went for the odd drive now and again. Jean often thought that it would be nice to go somewhere different—

Spain maybe, and some of those other islands that folk talked about. Just to see what it was like. But she knew Peter wouldn't hear of it.

Maybe he was right. She had to admit she liked to get home to her own bed at night and you could hardly do that from Spain. They'd nearly gone to England once years ago, but Peter hadn't been feeling too well so they'd had to cancel. It was a pity that. Some parts of England were quite nice, she'd heard. And you wouldn't have to worry too much about the language. The food would probably have been all right too, even for Peter. Still, you could see a lot of these foreign places on the television now, so there was no need to go there. In fact, you were better off at home. So Peter said. It was a lot cheaper, for one thing. And a lot more convenient all round.

"She's wasting her time. I've never known Donald take a holiday, have you?"

"He has a holiday all the time these days."

"You know what I mean. He doesn't go anywhere."

Peter agreed. You'd never get Donald going abroad either. There was a canny side to him, right enough.

"The nurse was also saying that it's too cold in Donald's house and him being ill."

"Aye, well I suppose if he's in bed he'll not be getting up just to light the fire. A house like his needs a lot of heating though."

"It was his bedroom she was on about. Freezing, she said it was. And him with the flu."

"I don't suppose that would bother Donald."

"He's got an electric fire, hasn't he?"

"I don't know."

"I'm sure he does. I remember seeing it once. An old-fashioned kind of thing."

"Oh?"

"In the living room. I remember seeing it and thinking it could do with a dust. Anyway the nurse was saying she'd asked Donald if he had an electric fire and he'd said no."

"Maybe it was broken and he'd thrown it out."

"Donald would never throw anything out, even when it was broken. He's just like you."

Peter said nothing. He'd long since given up trying to convince Jean of the value of bits and pieces of old equipment. He'd a box in the garage full of bolts, screws, wires, springs, keys and things like that. He didn't use them very often but they were always there if you needed them.

"The nurse thought he was just being mean. If he'd told her where the fire was, she'd have switched it on in the bedroom."

"Well, she could always have had a look for it," suggested Peter who could see things from Donald's angle to some extent. Women could be a bit interfering at times. They meant well, of course . . .

"She probably wouldn't want to do that with Donald there. Anyway, he might have hidden it."

They both laughed.

"Mind you, she's a determined woman that nurse," mused Jean. "She'd have to be, dealing with the likes of Donald. So she borrowed an electric fire from somewhere and put it on in his bedroom."

"Oh, is that what she was carrying? I couldn't quite make it out."

"That would have been it. Mind you, she said it was a waste of time. The bedroom was just as cold next time she visited. She thinks he'd just switched it off as soon as she'd left. He would too."

"Aye. Of course electricity's an awful price."

"She was saying he could get some sort of allowance but he wasn't interested."

That was just like Donald, Peter thought. He'd want to do things his own way. He'd always been like that. Jean said he was getting worse but he'd always been a bit stubborn. In a way you could see why though, Peter felt. He'd sensed it himself, a feeling that in the changing Achanult you were being left behind or pushed aside. Nothing too tangible, mind you. Just this feeling that the place was changing and you weren't. Maybe that was just what happened when you got old.

Yet there was more to it than that. There were the incomers for a start, who were a part—and at the same time not a part—of the village. That was something fairly new. Donald had never accepted them really. Not that they would have noticed. Jean said it just gave him an excuse to retire further into his shell. Maybe it did but if all he wanted was a quiet life then you couldn't blame him.

That was another funny thing about the incomers. They all told you, whether you asked them or not, that they'd come to Achanult for the peace and quiet. Then as soon as they got here they started rushing around doing things—organising this and setting up that. Jean said that you had to admit they did some good sometimes. They'd often got something going again that had fallen off over the years. Aye, maybe. Look at the bus service, she'd said. They'd got that sorted out properly. Even Donald had complained to her when the company had cut the service right back but that only happened because people like him never used it. Well, why should he? He had a car. Mind you, even there he seldom used the village petrol station. All the incomers though, made a point of filling up there since it was permanently threatened with closure because it wasn't being used enough. One of them even wrote a letter to the local paper about it, Peter remembered. Probably Miss Shuttleworth, or if it wasn't her, it was the sort of letter she would write, telling people where to buy their petrol. Donald usually bought his in Oban although he never mentioned the fact. It was a bit cheaper there of course.

"So he's over the flu now, is he?"

"So she said. He's to take things easy for a bit. I don't suppose he'll pay any attention to that. He'll be up and about soon, off to the Gaelic class for one thing."

Peter nodded. It was funny how Donald had never missed a class—as far as they knew anyway. You wouldn't have thought he'd have stuck at it. Maybe it wasn't such a difficult language as folk made out. There was Maggie Stewart at it as well, though you could sort of understand that. She went to everything just in case something happened without her. But Donald?

He and Jean had often wondered. She thought it had something to do with Miss Shuttleworth. Like a lot of other people locally, Donald was quite proud of his Gaelic background, even though he himself had never spoken the language. He liked the way incomers and tourists found the placenames strange and foreign and you could tell that he was quite proud that they couldn't pronounce them properly.

"He probably thinks that there shouldn't be such a thing as a Gaelic class anyway," Jean had said one afternoon as they watched Donald drive off.

"He goes often enough."

"I think he'd rather the likes of Miss Shuttleworth were kept in ignorance. He probably feels it's none of her business."

"I don't see what difference it makes to him," said Peter with a frown.

"Well if you think about it, it might end up with her knowing more about Gaelic than him—and other local things like history as well."

"Oh well, maybe. So that'll be why he goes."

"I wouldn't be surprised. Didn't you tell me she'd been lecturing him about his house name and how to spell it properly? Well he wouldn't have liked that."

"No, I don't suppose so. Is that why Maggie Stewart goes as well?"

"It might have something to do with it. But she'd never admit as much."

"Och no."

Jean was probably right. Maggie had always been a great one for the Gaelic but when you asked her something she could never tell you. She wouldn't be very pleased either, if the likes of Miss Shuttleworth knew all the answers or even some of them.

Mind you, there was a fair bit of interest in Gaelic these days. It was becoming quite fashionable and not just in Achanult, from what he'd heard. He'd seen a road sign in Gaelic the last time he went to Oban. It looked like Gaelic anyway. He and Jean had wondered what it meant. And now they were talking about a Gaelic choir in the village. It must be about thirty years since the last one folded. Peter himself hadn't been involved with it, not being a great one for the singing. But quite a number of Jean's friends at the time had been members of the choir. There always seemed to be an awful lot of women in it, he recalled. Some of them used to come round to the house and sing one or two of the choir's songs—in an informal kind of way. A sort of ceilidh, really. He'd quite enjoyed it. Much more like a real ceilidh than the nonsense you heard nowadays. Of course that was before the days of television and record players, at least in Achanult.

Aye, some of their songs were fine tuneful things. Jean used to ask them what they were about but they were never very sure. They'd need to ask Mr Matheson.

Now he was a Gaelic speaker, Peter remembered. which was probably how he got the job of conductor, since he wasn't really much of a musician some folk said. Still, he did his best although there were a lot of people who grumbled about Mr Matheson's Lewis accent and thought he shouldn't be teaching people to sing like that. Well, you couldn't please everybody and they were lucky enough to get him, even if he was from Lewis. The funny thing was, the folk who complained the most—like Maggie Stewart's mother, now that he remembered—didn't speak Gaelic at all. She probably just thought that somebody local—like herself—should be in charge.

Jean had told him at the time that she'd heard that Mr Matheson had only agreed to take over the choir after he'd learnt that the vast majority of members didn't know Gaelic. That way they'd all sing as he told them, since they wouldn't know any other way. Aye, he was a canny man, Mr Matheson. It must be about fifteen years now since he died. He was buried in Lewis. Peter remembered the family coming over to take him back. A terrible day it was. Still, they'd be used to that in Lewis.

As Jean came back up the driveway Peter was standing by the door.

"He wasn't answering," she said.

Peter wasn't surprised. It had been her idea to go round.

"He'll have seen you coming."

"Well, he could still have answered. Maybe he didn't hear me."

"I could hear you from here."

"Och well, I didn't know if the bell was working."

"It hasn't been working for years." He'd told her that last New Year as they'd waited for Donald to open the door. She never listened of course. She got so worked up at the time of their annual visit to Donald that you could have told her that her house was on fire and she'd just have nodded. "He'll never fix it. It gives him a fine excuse the way it is."

"He might have been asleep. The nurse said he was a bit weak. I couldn't hear anything anyway."

"He'll have turned the sound down when he saw you coming. You should have had a look in the window."

"Oh, I couldn't do that," confided Jean. "Somebody might have seen me."

Very true, thought Peter. The whole street would have seen her. Most of them wouldn't have bothered with Donald though. You couldn't really blame them.

"The nurse said she'd maybe look in again tomorrow."

"Well, she gets paid for it."

"Och, he's not too bad. She was telling me that she's had to deal with a lot worse than him. One old woman wouldn't let her in because she's Irish, she said. That can't have been in Achanult though, surely."

Peter hadn't heard that one before but he could well believe it. Some folk went a bit funny as they got old. And there were a lot of elderly people in Achanult now. There just didn't seem to be the amount of younger families around like there used to be. Maybe it was all too quiet for them.

49 Somewhere suitable

SPRING was a pleasant time of the year in Achanult, reflected Miss Shuttleworth as she strolled, stick in hand past the houses at the edge of the village and into the countryside. If only it were a little warmer. That was the only drawback. That and the fact that there was just the one road through the village.

She still found this hard to adjust to. What it meant was that she had the choice of leaving the village on its north or south side. On the west was the sea, and on the east the hills. There were a few side roads in the village certainly, but they didn't go anywhere. Maggie Stewart lived down one of them, she believed. So that was another reason for avoiding them.

Sometimes Miss Shuttleworth took her car and drove out of the village for a few miles, but today she felt like walking. She'd had a letter from Miss McLachlan that morning, with only one spelling mistake and not a single misplaced apostrophe. Not too bad really. Possibly that talk they'd had last time Jennifer was up was partly responsible. More of a lecture than a discussion really but Miss Shuttleworth had been keen to get across her disapproval of current standards of literacy. Few people seemed to bother these days. Even at the Gaelic class it was the same. She seemed to be the only one, apart from Mrs Nicholson of course, who really cared. Maggie Stewart pretended that it didn't really matter how you spelt a word and the others, if they had an opinion at all, agreed with her. Terrible.

In her letter Miss McLachlan had indicated that she had returned from her holiday in Jersey to find that she was required to vacate her accommodation rather sooner than she'd expected. So she wondered if she might take up the kind offer of a room at Fairview for a short period till she found somewhere suitable. Although she was initially inclined to regard this last remark as somewhat offensive, the arrival of the letter had prompted Miss Shuttleworth to go for a walk to calm her excitement. She'd paced around the house for an hour or two, finding it difficult to concentrate on anything. In the end she'd decided on a good long walk before dinner. She'd have to be back by six though, since Jennifer had also said that she would telephone, if that was all right, to discuss matters in more detail. On the other hand Miss Shuttleworth was as ever, anxious not to appear too keen. So it might not be a bad idea if she was out the first time Miss McLachlan phoned, even if she was in.

In the event Miss Shuttleworth had been home by six but the telephone had remained silent. By nine o' clock her patience was wearing thin. This was typical of Jennifer, of course. You just couldn't rely on her. In fact she would probably get even worse if she came to live in Achanult, adopting some of the eccentricities of the locals. She'd already admitted to finding many aspects of Achanult life to be "charming". Or was it "amusing" she'd said? Miss Shuttleworth thought for a second.

It must have been "amusing" if Jennifer's behaviour in the village shop last time was any guide. The shop had been quite full, so they'd been standing waiting when a small child who must have been about three, toddled over and smacked Miss Shuttleworth vigorously on the leg. She decided to ignore him. After looking at her for a few seconds, the child smacked her on the leg again and announced, "You're a naughty boy!"

As Miss Shuttleworth tried to think of a suitable reply to this, she realised that everyone in the shop, including Miss McLachlan, was shaking with silent laughter. Miss Shuttleworth, who herself was far from amused, stared stonily ahead. As the smiles subsided, a woman whom Miss Shuttleworth didn't recognise but who seemed to be the child's mother, said to her,

"You were quite right not to let him see you laughing. It only encourages him."

Feeling increasingly uncomfortable Miss Shuttleworth had turned to Miss McLachlan.

"It's a bit crowded in here, Jennifer," she'd said. "Perhaps we ought to come back later?"

When they'd got outside the shop Miss McLachlan had said she wouldn't have minded staying.

"So I noticed, Jennifer."

"Well I mean, it makes a change from the supermarket at home."

"No doubt."

"Anyway, we wouldn't have had to wait long, would we?"

"Oh, about an hour."

"What? There were only three or four people in front of us."

"Quite."

Actually, Willie would probably have served them next. He'd done that before with Miss Shuttleworth when there'd been a queue. She knew of course, that he only did it so that the rest of the shop could talk about her once she'd left. That was why they were so keen to let her go first.

At half past nine the telephone rang. Although she'd been waiting for nothing else for about three hours, Miss Shuttleworth jumped slightly in her seat, spilling some of her cocoa on her dress. In her haste to rush to the telephone she spilt some more as she hurriedly set her mug on the mantelpiece. Reaching the phone she decided she'd better let it ring another couple of times to suggest an atmosphere of nonchalance. Picking up the receiver in mid ring, she said in what she hoped was a calm voice,

"Hello, Fairview."

"Hello, Miss Shuttleworth? Mrs Nicholson here."

"Oh."

"I'm sorry to trouble you. I just wanted to say that I've got the flu and so there won't be any class tomorrow."

"Oh."

"There's a lot of it going about seemingly. I hope you don't mind me disturbing you."

"No no. I wasn't . . . "

"I just thought I'd better let you know."

"Yes. Thankyou."

"So we'll meet a week tomorrow then."

"Fine. Goodbye."

Miss Shuttleworth replaced the receiver and trudged wearily back to her cocoa. She might as well go to bed.

By next evening the weather had returned to normal which didn't improve Miss Shuttleworth's mood. As she came out of the bathroom in her dressing gown she reflected once again that this unreliable side to Jennifer's nature was something which would have to be sorted out. Miss Shuttleworth didn't normally have a bath on a Tuesday evening but she decided to break with the habit of a lifetime on the theory that once she was settled in the bath, Miss McLachlan was very likely to phone. This time however, her friend had refused to cooperate.

In the end Miss McLachlan had telephoned the following afternoon. Miss Shuttleworth, when she'd recovered, voiced her surprise.

"I wasn't really expecting you to telephone in the afternoon, Jennifer."

"Oh, if it's not convenient . . . "

"No no, it's all right. What I meant was that it would be a lot cheaper in the evening."

"You're becoming very Scottish, Marjory."

"Really?" asked Miss Shuttleworth stiffly.

"Yes. Where's that place where no-one spends any money?"

"I really wouldn't . . . "

"Aberdeen. That's it. It's the Aberdeen influence."

"Aberdeen is at the other end of the country, Jennifer."

"I know that, but it's quite near you, isn't it?"

"I mean that it's at the other end of the country from me."

"Oh, is it? Well anyway, I'm actually phoning from the office so it won't cost me anything."

"That's very generous of them."

"Yes well, I suppose they're a bit embarrassed at having to evict me at such short notice. So they're allowing me to use the phone about alternative accommodation. Did you get my letter?"

"Yes."

"So, umm . . . what do you think?"

"Pardon?"

"Well you did offer . . . "

"Oh, I see. Of course. I'll be pleased to see you and we can no doubt work something out."

"Oh good. Right. It'll be next week some time. I'll probably just take a taxi from . . . umm . . . what do you call it? . . . Oban. I'll be able to take a taxi now that I know the way."

"I don't mind coming to collect you. It would be a lot cheaper."

"There you are again."

"Pardon?"

"Oh nothing. Maybe I'll ring you a bit nearer the time then, if that's all right?"

"Of course. I'll look forward to it."

As she put the phone down Miss Shuttleworth wondered if there was any substance to her friend's remark that she was becoming mean. Surely not. Careful perhaps. One had to be here. Of course, she was not ostentatious with money. She drove a small car which was a necessity not a luxury in Achanult. Anyway, lots of other people had cars and they didn't give the impression of having lots of money. And some of them hardly used their vehicles. She used hers fairly regularly, even more so when Miss McLachlan was visiting. Her friend, who had no car of her own, had been quick to see the advantage of a car in Achanult and had indicated to Miss Shuttleworth that she would like to learn to drive. Miss Shuttleworth was somewhat surprised.

"What! At your age?" she asked.

"I'm no older than you, Marjory."

"Yes, I know. But I learnt years ago. These things get harder as you get older. Still, by all means . . . "

"Perhaps you could give me a few lessons."

After a second or two to recover, Miss Shuttleworth said, "Out of the question, I'm afraid, Jennifer."

"Oh? Why?"

"Well, umm . . . I've probably picked up lots of faults that I would just pass on to you."

"Oh. I just meant a trial run, to see how I felt about it."

"I know, but . . . "

Miss Shuttleworth searched for a way to inform her friend that she would probably ruin the gearbox and various other expensive parts of the car.

"It's the insurance," she exclaimed finally. Jennifer wouldn't know anything about insurance. "But you could take lessons of course," she added.

"Oh well, I suppose so. Is it a man or a woman who does it?"

"I really have no idea. There's nobody in Achanult. You'll have to go to Oban. I think the instructors are usually men though."

"Oh. I don't know how I would feel about that."

Miss Shuttleworth restrained herself. Jennifer was really rather eccentric at times.

"Well, you could always take a few lessons at home, just to see how you felt about it."

"Yes, I suppose so. That might be better in a way. I'm not sure I would understand what the instructor was saying up here."

After Miss McLachlan's phone call Miss Shuttleworth began considering some of the arrangements that would have to be made. She'd need to get some food in, which would mean a trip to Oban. She could get a new lock for the bathroom door while she was there. It was really just a new key that was needed but she'd probably have to buy a new lock as well. It still worked after a fashion but Miss McLachlan, who insisted on barricading herself into the bathroom even if she only wanted to wash her hands, had complained about it more than once. And she wanted a stronger light bulb in the bedroom. Miss Shuttleworth sighed quietly. She'd better make a list.

50 Homecoming

THE great day had arrived and Maggie Stewart was up at five o' clock. This was a bit unnecessary but she hadn't been able to sleep much. Jim didn't have that problem, she reflected as she drew the curtains. Of course, the beer helped. Looking out she noticed the trees at the back of the house swaying in the wind. The forecast had said it would be a bit windy today.

Although there was nothing wrong with the weather in Achanult, and Maggie would briskly contradict anyone who suggested that there was, she had a secret aversion to the strong winds which were a feature of the winter—and the summer at times. So she was more than a little concerned at the prospect of the ferry trip. Although there was nothing wrong with the local ferry, and Maggie would immediately attack anyone who queried its shortcomings, she had to admit to herself that it would not be a pleasant crossing today. The boat was too small, really. So it bounced about a lot. It was too old as well and you had to stay in your car because there was nowhere else warm to sit. Still, it was a short crossing, usually. If the weather was bad however, it could take twice the time with the boat zigzagging its way across. Something to do with the currents, she'd been told. She herself had wondered if it had something to do with the drink. You heard all sorts of stories about some of these skippers.

If it was really rough they could go round by road. It would add some time to the journey but you could save a pound or so, with the ferry tickets being such a ridiculous price. A lot of people did that. All the incomers used the ferry though, just to let you know how well-off they were. Some of them still regarded going on a boat as a great adventure, which it maybe was if you'd spent your life in London or wherever it was they came from.

Maggie was blasé about the ferry, letting it be known that she enjoyed the crossing in all weathers. No-one believed a word of this since she'd been seen looking quite queasy more than once. Looking out of the window again she wondered if this might be a day for going round by road. If so, she'd better get Jim out of bed pretty soon.

As she went upstairs with a cup of tea for him, she thought she'd better find out what he wanted to do. Putting the cup down on the bedside table, she said,

"Here's a cup of tea."

As usual, there was no response. Maggie walked over to the window and watched the branches swaying in the early morning light. Other than trees, there wasn't much else to see from the back of the house. From the front they had a view of the cottages across the road. It was quite unusual in Achanult not to have a view of the sea or the hills but Maggie wasn't in the least bothered by that. So she said, anyway. Frequently. There was nothing wrong with the situation of her house and anybody who suggested that there was was soon put right.

She walked back over to the bed.

"Are you awake?"

No response. Maggie repeated the question. This time the bedclothes stirred and she seized her chance.

"I've brought your tea," she repeated more loudly. Her husband opened an eye.

"What time is it?"

"Oh, about six," said Maggie vaguely, glad that her husband was too lazy to look at his watch.

"Six!"

"Well . . . "

"For heaven's sake. What are you up so early for?"

"The forecast isn't very good. I just wondered what you thought."

"Eh?"

"About the ferry. Do you think we should go round by road."

"Don't be daft. Is that all you woke me up for?"

"I just wanted to know what your decision was, that's all."

Her husband turned over and closed his eyes again. So it would be the ferry then. Maggie took the cup of tea back downstairs.

They eventually left at about eleven o'clock, with Jim driving. Maggie never drove when the two of them were in the car together, unless her husband didn't feel able to for one reason or another—usually just the one. Even then, she could sense him criticising her driving.

When they got to the ferry the sea wasn't too bad. To Maggie's disappointment there was no-one she knew on the boat, so she'd just have to sit with Jim in the car. It was at times like these that she wished their car had a radio. She'd been on at Jim to get one fitted since Heather's last visit when she'd expressed surprise at the absence of music in the car. Everyone in Canada drove around listening to music all the time, apparently. Jim thought that was daft and Maggie felt he was right but she didn't like to say so since it conflicted with her assertion that her daughter's lifestyle was just perfect.

All Maggie's friends were constantly assailed by exaggerated stories of Heather's day to day existence. And although one or two of the stories were true, her friends and everybody else in Achanult gave little credence to them. Of course one of the reasons why Jim wouldn't get a car radio fitted—apart from the fact that it would cost too much, he said—was that Heather would play that loud pop music on it all the time. Jim liked Scottish music, not too loud. So did Maggie but then Heather was the one with the knowledge and the taste. Anyway, said Jim, it wouldn't stop at just a car radio. He'd have to buy another car, one twice as big, since Heather was constantly surprised by the smallness of everything in Achanult—from the sauce bottle on the table to the family car. Maggie was inwardly irritated by this but was keen to explain to everyone that her daughter had become used to greater things.

On the way home from the airport Maggie did most of the talking. This suited Heather fine, since she'd already told her mother all that had happened in her monthly letter home. Maggie was eager for more details naturally, but there wasn't much to add. Heather led a fairly quiet life, much as she had done in Achanult. It wasn't until they were back on the ferry again that Heather was able to get a few words in while Maggie's attention was directed to seeing if there was anyone she recognised on the boat.

"So have you been doing anything new?" Heather asked them both. Jim seemed a bit surprised at the question.

"What was that?" said Maggie, who thought she recognised a car a few places behind them. "Could you just move the mirror a bit?" she asked Heather. Jim always objected to her moving it but then he would be daft enough to turn round and stare if he thought he recognised somebody. It took Heather several attempts to get the mirror at the right angle for her mother, by which time Maggie had remembered why she'd felt she shouldn't have been getting into the back of the car at the airport. Eventually the mirror was just right and Maggie had a good look but it wasn't anybody she recognised. Same colour of car, though.

"So what was that you said?" she asked her daughter.

"I just wondered if you'd been doing anything new since the last time I was here."

"No, not really." Maggie seldom inflicted her flights of fancy upon her daughter.

"What about the Gaelic?" interjected Jim.

"Gaelic?" quizzed Heather.

"Oh that! Yes, there's a Gaelic class in the village. I go along occasionally."

"Every week," added Jim.

"I wouldn't have thought there would be much demand for that. Do many people go?"

"There's about seven, I think."

"Anybody I know?"

"Well, there's Alec Cameron and Donald Morrison . . . "

Heather's laughter caused a woman in an adjoining car to look over her newspaper at them.

"What's funny about that?" asked Maggie.

"Just the thought of those two learning Gaelic. Anybody else?"

"Mrs McKenzie."

"Oh yes."

"Miss Shuttleworth."

Heather laughed again.

"What's *she* doing there?"

"I often wonder myself."

"Doesn't she find it a bit difficult?"

"Oh yes. She's pretty hopeless. Her funny way of speaking is a great handicap, of course. Still, we all do our best for her."

"How do you get on yourself?"

"Fine. No problem."

"Don't you find it a bit hard?"

"No, of course not. I used to know a lot when I was young,"

said Maggie, who had by now convinced herself, if no-one else, that this was true.

"Did you? I didn't know that."

"Neither did I," added Jim.

"Well of course, I was very young at the time," said Maggie vaguely. "There's also going to be a Gaelic choir."

"Good lord," exclaimed Heather. "What's brought all this about?"

"It's Mrs Nicholson, the new minister's wife. She's from South Uist."

"You told me she was from North Uist," said Jim.

"No I didn't. It's South Uist. I should know. She's hardly Catholic, is she?"

"How do—oh, aye," finished Jim.

"Well, that makes it easier," suggested Heather. "If I remember my geography, the northern islands—Lewis and so on—are Protestant."

"That's right," agreed Jim. Maggie nodded.

"And by the time you get down to Barra they're Catholic. So if she's the minister's wife, she's more likely to be from North Uist."

"That's what I said," lied Maggie.

"No it isn't," asserted her husband and daughter together.

"Well, it's what I meant to say. Just a slip of the tongue."

The car fell silent for a few minutes. Heather wondered about the changes that had apparently taken place in Achanult since her last visit. You never thought that anything new would happen in the village and life seemed to go on in the same inexorable way while you lived there. But you only had to go away for a year to notice a difference when you returned.

By the time the car was driving off the ferry, Maggie had been silent long enough.

"There's quite a lot of Gaelic in Canada, isn't there?"

"I've no idea. Certainly not where I live. Mind you, I'm not sure if I'd recognise any if I heard it."

This was not what Maggie wanted to hear. Maybe she'd better keep her daughter away from the Gaelic class.

"I hear it's French more, where you are."

"Yes. We're supposed to learn it."

"How do you get on with it?"

"Oh, I don't bother. I did try but it's too difficult," admitted Heather. "Anyway, you only need it if you want to move up the ladder a bit. If you're at the bottom like me, English is all you need."

This was getting worse, thought Maggie. She'd need to have a discreet word with her daughter when Jim wasn't around.

"I'd forgotten about the weather," sighed Heather as they neared Achanult. "You can take it for granted that it'll be dry most of the time at home."

"At home?"

"What? Well, you know what I mean. Of course the winters are a bit colder. But they're not so damp."

"The weather was good enough for you when you lived here. Anyway, there's nothing wrong with a bit of rain. There are plenty of places in the world would be glad of some of the rain we get. Not that we get all that much anyway."

Heather said nothing. She'd noticed before that her mother was always a bit over excited for the first day or two. You were better just to go along with her for a while. After a few more seconds of silence she asked,

"Are you still enjoying your new job?"

"Oh, it's all right," said Maggie. "It's quite a responsibility of course. You'll need to come up and have a look round," she added, wondering if Mrs White would be away in the next few days.

"I don't know if I'd like to work in a library. Much too quiet. And I don't suppose you're allowed to smoke. That's what it's like in the library at home, anyway."

That phrase again! Maggie made a mental note to remind her daughter that Achanult was her home. As for the no-smoking, Heather was right. It was one of the great drawbacks of the job for Maggie who'd always been accustomed to having a cigarette whenever she wanted, which was fairly often. Mrs White didn't smoke which made matters worse. These non-smokers were so unreasonable sticking up notices all over the place. So Maggie was reduced to nipping out of the library from time to time into the solicitors' office with which they shared the same floor. Betty, whom Maggie had suddenly befriended, sat in there all day at her typewriter, smoking incessantly. They both agreed that smokers were very reasonable people and there was really no need for this no-smoking nonsense. Betty's boss didn't like her smoking but he was a man and just kept out of the way. Maggie would have been a lot happier with a man as her boss.

"Oh, the no-smoking doesn't bother me. I can take it or leave it, you know," insisted Maggie.

51 Decimal time

AFTER many hours of labour the Rev Nicholson had now completed his list of words ending in -ION. He'd decided to restrict himself to words beginning with the same letter, at least for the present, and after much hesitation had plumped for the letter A. He'd toyed with the idea of a less popular letter—say, Q—and therefore a shorter list, since there were one or two other things competing for his attention at the time . . . Easter was approaching and then there was that christening to see about. But he'd eventually decided that he could not compromise his high standards and so he now had a lengthy list in alphabetical order of all the words in his dictionary beginning with A and ending in -ION. All that remained now was to find an opportunity to put his list to the test.

A couple of days later Mr Nicholson was sitting by the window in his study engaged in the crossword. He liked to do this before he did anything else, on the grounds that the crossword would sharpen his mind and he would then be better prepared to consider other matters such as the church or the garden and what on earth he ought to do next in them. After successfully completing a few clues he came to 17 across: "Bête noire a backwardly mobile vehicle out east for this poet (5)".

He read it again. Sometimes when you read a clue you got the feeling that you'd soon solve it. At other times you could hardly understand the clue. This looked like being a tricky one. He decided to leave it for the moment. After he'd completed as many as he could of the rest of the clues he returned to 17 across and discovered that he now had the first letter, A and the last two, ON. With mounting excitement he wondered if the third last letter might be I: -ION, as he well knew by now being a common suffix. If so, there was only one more letter to get. Going quickly through the alphabet in his mind he soon arrived at the word ARION which he dimly recognised from his university days as the name of an early Greek poet who'd been rescued by a whale or something. No, that was Jonah. A dolphin, that's what it was.

With a feeling of triumph he wrote in the two missing letters and turned to his recently compiled list to check the word there. When he couldn't find it he was momentarily nonplussed and wondered if he'd overlooked it in the dictionary. When he couldn't find it in the dictionary either, a feeling of numbness crept over him. There was that other dictionary upstairs. He'd check in it. He was on his way back downstairs when it suddenly occurred to him. Arion was a person's name and most of these probably wouldn't be in a dictionary. Neither would most placenames and goodness knows what else.

Shattered by this discovery, Mr Nicholson returned slowly to his desk and stared out of the window for the next ten minutes, at the end of which he decided he might as well give the whole thing up. Fortunately, he hadn't wasted too much time on it. He stared out of the window for another five minutes, by which time he'd decided that the whole thing was a lot trickier than it seemed. While the list he had compiled was certainly not complete, it was nonetheless of considerable value and would be even better if the gaps were filled in. Was there not perhaps a dictionary of personal names or of famous people? A bit like *Who's Who* but more international—and historical of course. He'd look into it. What else? Placenames obviously. A world atlas should see to that. Maybe a bit selective but it should be sufficient for most cases.

Feeling considerably better, Mr Nicholson leant back in his chair. The situation could be retrieved. It was his own fault really. He hadn't thought the thing through properly at the beginning. There must have been other things on his mind at the time. Some church matters probably. Well they had to get some of his attention as well of course. So he'd continue his investigations later—maybe in the afternoon. Meanwhile he'd better get on and finish this crossword.

By the time his wife came through with some coffee, the Rev Nicholson was quite his normal self again.

"You're looking much better this morning," he remarked to her.

"Yes. I feel much better today. I thought I might go out for a short walk. It'll loosen me up a bit. I always feel so stiff after a few days in bed."

"Well don't overdo it. That was a nasty cold. I hope I don't get it."

"Oh, I don't suppose you will. You never seem to."

The Rev Nicholson hoped this was true. He'd spent the last three nights alone in the spare room as was his habit whenever his wife had a cold. It seemed to do the trick even though Anna had some theory about the infectious stage of a cold being much earlier than the obvious symptoms. They discussed it frequently.

"I'm not disagreeing with you," he'd told her again recently. "It's just that I find it difficult to sleep when you're making these coughing noises and snoring."

"Snoring?"

"Well it sounds like that. Of course I realise your breathing's affected. I suspect it may have something to so with being brought up on the west coast. Mind you, it's maybe better for you if I'm out of the way."

"Is it?"

"Probably. You don't have to worry about keeping me awake then." As his wife turned to leave the room, Mr Nicholson added, "You wouldn't be going anywhere near the library by any chance?"

"Oh, I don't think I'll go as far as that. Anyway, I don't feel like climbing those stairs just at the moment. Why?"

"Oh just a thought. One or two books I wanted to check on."

"You could always phone and ask, if it's important."

"Well, it's not desperately important. Anyway I might get Mrs Stewart and she's pretty hopeless, I have to say."

"She's only a typist, David. You can't expect too much. You could always ask to speak to Mrs White."

"I suppose so. She's away a lot, I'm told. Meetings and so on. Mind you, I've heard that even when Mrs White's there, Mrs Stewart likes to handle things herself."

Mrs Nicholson wasn't surprised to hear this.

"Oh well, you'll just have to go round yourself."

Her husband agreed that he might well do so, in due course.

Lunch was delayed a little since Mrs Nicholson had returned from her walk half an hour later than she'd anticipated. She should have known. It was very difficult to get away from people in Achanult. Things had been like that in Uist too, but all those years in Edinburgh had accustomed her to the fact that it was possible to walk down the street and pass dozens of people without saying a word. You couldn't do that in Achanult though. They'd think you were stand-offish. And of course, it was even worse being a minister's wife. You were expected to be interested in everything under the sun.

She decided it would be simpler if they just had some soup for lunch. Leaving it to boil for a couple of minutes she put some slices of bread on the table. Feeling quite hungry, her husband took a slice. The soup would be too hot to eat for a while. You could hear it boiling in the pan again.

After lunch he'd maybe go along to the library. That clue

had been a blessing in disguise, in a way. Arion must be the right answer. It seemed to be the only thing that would fit, though he couldn't quite work out why.

"Incidentally," he mused aloud as his wife put out the soup, "are dolphins black, do you know?"

"I don't think so." Mrs Nicholson had become accustomed to her husband's seemingly irrelevant remarks. It would be something to do with a crossword, probably."More greyish— or blue," she added.

"Ah. Hmm."

"There may be black ones. I don't know. If you're going to the library you could check there. Is it important?"

"No no, not really. Just a crossword clue that caught my attention." He didn't feel like going into details. On the other hand, his wife had previously revealed herself to be surprisingly talented with the odd clue. "I've solved it all right, I think. I'm just not sure of the reasoning behind it."

He sipped his soup. Still a bit too hot.

"I'll show you what I mean," he said and went off to his study. Returning with the paper he took another slice of bread. "It's seventeen across."

Mrs Nicholson considered seventeen across for a moment.

"Oh I see. Very good. Well, the word *noire* is just there to make the poet's name. I've never heard of him. I'll have to take your word for it."

"How do you mean, make the poet's name?"

"It's written backwards there. Isn't that what backwardly is meant to indicate?"

The Rev Nicholson had in fact failed to see this but nodded as he sipped his soup.

"Oh no. Wait a minute. There's an E there that isn't in the answer!" exclaimed his wife.

"Out east," said Mr Nicholson, realising for the first time the point of the phrase. He'd originally thought it had something to do with rickshaws.

"I don't think I get that," frowned Mrs Nicholson. Her husband explained.

"Oh that's very clever," she enthused. "You must be very good at these sort of things by now. Have you ever thought of compiling crosswords yourself?"

"I've never considered it. It's a question of time really. I do seem to be rather busy these days. Anyway, I'm not sure I'd be very good at it."

"You couldn't be much worse than—what's his name—the person who compiles that crossword in the local paper at Christmas."

The Rev Nicholson hadn't bothered with that crossword. His wife had completed it in less than ten minutes, although as she'd mentioned to him, one of the answers had to be misspelt in order to fit. As usual there was a prize for the first correct entry drawn from a box at the newspaper office a fortnight later, so there was always a large number of entries, quite a number of them completed correctly. Some people would do anything for a £5 book token. Maggie Stewart had won it once. Well, as folk said at the time, somebody had to win it but there was a suspicion that Maggie had put in several entries to increase her chances in the draw. Mind you, they said that every year, no matter who won it. It would have been easy to check these things simply by opening all the envelopes after the draw had been made but that would have embarrassed half the village. So nothing was ever done, by general agreement. The editor once thought of taking the drastic step of charging 10p per envelope submitted, which would have put an abrupt stop to the problem of multiple entries, as well as providing a modest sum—for charity, of course. But the fiction of a larger entry suited the editor, being consistent with his belief that everything in his paper was of interest to everybody.

On his way to the library the Rev Nicholson considered the idea of compiling crosswords. He would quite enjoy it, he thought—a challenge. No doubt one got paid for it as well if a newspaper could be found to carry it. Perhaps he might try one, just to see how easy it was. He could do one for the magazine. That would be very well received.

On his arrival in Achanult he'd discovered that the church produced a little magazine every quarter, with contributions of a spiritual nature from Mr Neil, items about the women's guild, the Sunday school, outings, and so on. The Rev Nicholson felt that this was all rather formal and encouraged his congregation to provide information on the notice board in the hall, as and when they liked, without the need to consult him beforehand. But the magazine was still in existence although it was really just a leaflet now.

So he would put a crossword in it for the children, based on biblical themes. A brilliant idea really. Puzzles for children were all the rage these days in church magazines although he'd heard that some of his more traditionally minded colleagues felt them to be scripturally unsound.

Feeling pleased with life Mr Nicholson climbed the stairs to the library, only to find the door closed. He looked at his watch. Exactly four minutes to two. He could always come back later. Examining a handwritten notice on the door, he discovered that the library was open in the afternoon from 14.00 hrs to 16.00 hrs. Not very long really. He decided to wait. After a minute or so, Maggie Stewart came up the stairs, smelling strongly of cigarette smoke. She seemed delighted to see him.

"Oh hello, Mr Nicholson. I hope I haven't kept you waiting long."

"No no. I was just noticing that you open at two o' clock." He pointed to the notice.

"Oh that. Yes, I just put it up this morning. Just to let folk know. I have to make all these sorts of decisions when Mrs White's not here," gushed Maggie as she switched on the library lights.

"Oh. She's away at the moment, is she?"

"She'll be back tomorrow. Afternoon probably. Is there anything I can help you with?"

"Umm . . . not really, thank you. I just want to have a look round. I haven't really time to get in very often."

As an elderly woman entered the library the Rev Nicholson returned her greeting, wondering who on earth she was. He moved over to the reference section to see if there was anything interesting there. If not, he'd have to wait until Mrs White came back. No point in asking Mrs Stewart, from what he'd heard. Anna was telling him just the other day that Mrs Stewart had had an argument with somebody at the class about the poet Burns and his use of Doric, as she called it. Someone—it might have been Miss Shuttleworth—had mentioned that Doric was actually a dialect of Greek, which Mrs Stewart had vehemently denied. Anna had remarked to him later how curious it was that those who knew so little were so keen to advertise the fact. Still, they both agreed that Mrs Stewart was now in the right place if she wanted to fill the gaps in her knowledge. Though neither of them thought it likely that she would.

There was some interesting stuff in the reference section but the shelf had a notice on it saying that these books were not to be removed from the library. He would have to see Mrs White about this. He could hardly be expected to spend long afternoons in the library, especially since some of his congregation might find it difficult to appreciate his interest in lexicography.

"I wasn't expecting you back quite so early," said Mrs Nicholson as her husband hung up his coat in the hall. "Did you find anything interesting?"

"Oh yes. Of course the library is very basic, to put it politely."

"I don't think Mrs Stewart would agree with you there," laughed Mrs Nicholson. "She's told me more than once that there's nothing wrong with the library."

"Oh well. Anyway, it's Mrs White I'll need to see. She wasn't there today. She may be there tomorrow afternoon, apparently. Which reminds me, when does the library close for the day?"

"At six, unless they've changed it. It's always been six, as far as I know."

"That's what I thought but Mrs Stewart had written up a notice saying it shut at four, or 16.00 hrs, as she put it. I didn't know Achanult had gone over to the twenty-four hour clock."

"Ah! I think I see what's happened. Mrs Stewart's probably got it wrong. She'll have thought that six o' clock was 16.00 hrs."

"Goodness me. Surely not. Why didn't she just write six o' clock?"

"She probably thinks it's more educated to use the decimal time system, as I've heard her refer to it."

Mr Nicholson smiled.

"She's a strange woman, isn't she? What's she like at your class these days?"

"Oh, much as usual. She doesn't really know any Gaelic and keeps arguing with all the others in the class. She has an unfortunate tendency to believe that she is always right. That 16.00 hrs business is a good example."

"Yes, I suppose it must be a mistake. Mrs White always advertises any early closing times well in advance, doesn't she? You don't suppose that Mrs Stewart could have taken it upon herself to close at four?"

Mrs Nicholson thought that with Maggie anything was possible.

52 Nothing'll come of it

PETER had the same problem every spring, wondering if he should try something different this year. But he never did. So this year as usual, he would plant potatoes, turnips and kale. Sometimes he planted brussels sprouts instead of kale but that wasn't always successful since the slugs tended to hide inside the buds and eat them. On the other hand the kale was attacked by caterpillars in the summer, so there were no easy answers.

From time to time he thought about using pesticides. Many people did, like Donald next door who sprayed stuff all over the place. He'd been doing that once when Miss Shuttleworth passed on one of her walks and she'd apparently told him off. He ought to be doing things the natural way, she'd said. Donald just waited till she'd gone away. That was his way of getting round these sort of people.

Peter was a bit like that himself too. You had to be really, with people like Miss Shuttleworth around. She'd trapped him more than once in his garden when he hadn't spotted her quickly enough. Last time she'd waved her stick at some kale.

"I'm glad to see that you don't use any of those dreadful pesticides."

Peter looked at the leaves half chewed by caterpillars.

"Well aye, but maybe I should."

"Oh no!" exclaimed Miss Shuttleworth earnestly. "You're quite right. I share your philosophy in these matters."

This reference to his motives was news to Peter, whose only objection to pesticides was that they were so expensive. He'd seen them in that garden shop in Oban. They had all sorts of things in there—beans of various kinds, peas, beetroot, radishes, and so on. Peter wondered who grew these things. Jean sometimes suggested that they could sow something different like radishes but Peter was a bit reluctant. He might not like them. You always knew where you were with potatoes, turnips and kale. And you had different varieties of them to choose from anyway.

As he stood surveying his garden he noticed Jean coming along the road, back from her shopping. It hadn't taken her very long but then she never bought very much. She just liked to keep up with the gossip, which she then passed on to Peter, who wasn't particularly interested but didn't like to hurt her feelings.

"Well, that was quite interesting," said Jean as she came up the driveway. "I bumped into Heather on the way home."

Peter, who knew that Jean had gone out mainly in the hope of meeting Heather, merely said,

"I'm surprised Maggie let you get home so quickly!"

"Oh, Maggie wasn't there. Heather was just by herself."

"Oh?"

"She and her mother aren't speaking."

"Eh?"

"They've fallen out over something. So Heather was telling me."

"For goodness sake. She's only been here a couple of days."

"I know. But the same thing happened last time, now that I come to think of it."

So it did, Peter reflected. Funny, really.

"What have they fallen out about?"

"Oh, Heather didn't say. I didn't like to ask."

"No. Well, I suppose it's none of our business."

"Anyway, I'll get the whole story from Maggie tomorrow."

Peter agreed. As Jean went to the house he tried to remember what it was Maggie and her daughter had fallen out about last time. Something to do with a present. Jean would know. He decided he'd done enough in the garden for the moment and wandered into the house, leaving his boots by the door. All this digging made you hungry.

"Was it something to do with a present that they fell out about last time?" he asked as he took his slippers from beside the range.

"A present?"

"Aye, Maggie didn't like the present Heather had brought from Canada—wasn't that it?"

"Oh, that might have something to do with it, right enough. But the main thing was the cigarettes."

"I don't remember that."

"You do. Heather forgot to get the duty free allowance of cigarettes for her mother. Mind? Maggie was in the huff for days."

331

"Oh aye, that's right. You did tell me."

"I had a job keeping a straight face when she was telling me about it. You know that voice she puts on when she thinks she's been insulted or whatever . . . "

Peter didn't know but to save time said,

"Oh aye, *that* voice."

"Well she told me, in that voice of hers, that it wasn't that she wanted the cigarettes for nothing. She would gladly have paid for them. And she'd written to Heather in her last letter to remind her to get them. They're a lot cheaper, apparently."

"Oh well. Maybe Heather forgot the cigarettes again this year."

"Maybe. I suppose we'll hear tomorrow."

Most folk in the village were quite glad to meet Heather by herself. You had a chance to talk to her then. When Maggie was with her, Heather never got the opportunity to say very much. She was much more open when her mother wasn't there and you sometimes wondered how well they really got on. Heather would hint from time to time that she got on fine with her mother now that the Atlantic was between them and you certainly couldn't blame her for wanting to get away. Folk still remembered how Maggie wouldn't let her daughter do anything by herself, interfering constantly, always waiting to see what time Heather came home at night and with whom. Of course, none of the local youths was good enough in Maggie's eyes. Aye, it wasn't surprising that she finally left. Maggie still tried to control affairs from long distance and still expected Heather to tell her everything that went on. But Maggie didn't know the half of it, which was maybe just as well.

"I was thinking," said Peter as he watched Jean peeling the potatoes, "Heather would be by herself now that Maggie's in the library."

"Oh! I'd forgotten all about that. Still, that's an idea. I'll maybe go along this afternoon."

"Are you sure she'll be there?"

"Oh, I think so. Mind you, I did hear her talking a while back about taking time off when Heather arrived. Anyway, I'll soon find out. Is that enough potatoes?"

"I don't know. Why?"

"You said last time that there was too much."

So there was. But he'd eaten them anyway. Peter didn't like to see food going to waste. But Jean was right. He didn't seem to need so much to eat nowadays.

Jean came back about four o' clock. Peter was watching horse racing on the television.

"What's that you're watching?" she asked, sticking her head round the living room door.

"Och, I just put it on to see what there was."

Jean watched for a few seconds.

"I never could see the interest in that. Why aren't they running? But look at the weather. Aren't they lucky. Where's that?"

"England. They never seem to get much rain. You left your library books," Peter added, pointing to them on the table as he went over to switch off the television.

"No no, I didn't mean to take them. I haven't finished them yet."

"So did you see Maggie?"

"Oh, she was there all right. Spent about half an hour telling me about her ungrateful daughter. I could hardly get away. I don't know what the other folk in the library must have been thinking."

"Och, they'd all be wanting to listen."

"Oh, some of them, I suppose. But I think there were one

or two who'd come for books. They had a bit of a wait."

"They'd be used to that with Maggie, though."

"Well, one man wasn't. I don't know who he was. I haven't seen him in there before. After he'd been standing at the front for a while he came round to where Maggie was talking to me and said he'd like to take this book out, if it wasn't too much trouble. So Maggie put on that voice of hers and told him that she was dealing with Mrs McQueen and that she'd be with him presently."

"That sounds just like her. She likes these big words."

"So she does. She's got a bit worse since she started in the library."

"Aye, she's a character all right. So what was she saying to you?"

"Oh, nothing much. She just wanted a grumble. The thing is, I've always quite liked Heather. So I found it hard to sympathise with Maggie."

"Aye, most folk would feel like that. You might as well shut the door. All the heat'll be going out."

Jean closed the door and came over to the fire.

"I'll need to be getting on with the tea. I found out why they're not speaking, though."

"Oh, was it the cigarettes then?"

"No, nothing to do with that. You know Heather's here for three weeks?"

Peter nodded.

"Well, Maggie had taken two weeks off, starting on Monday so that she wouldn't be at work while Heather was here."

"Oh aye, she wouldn't like Heather to be going about by herself."

"Anyway, Heather had said that she shouldn't have bothered."

"Did she? Maggie wouldn't have liked that."

"That's right. That's why they're not speaking. I think Maggie's over-reacting myself. Still, I suppose everything will be all right in a day or two. Now I'd better get on with the tea."

Peter decided to have a walk round the garden before his tea. It was one of these calm late afternoons that you sometimes get at this time of year, which made a change from that weather they'd had last month. He'd maybe do some more gardening tomorrow though the ground was still too wet really. The water didn't drain away very quickly. At one time he'd thought of arranging the soil in a series of lazy beds, like they did in the islands, so that the rain could run away between them. But Jean hadn't liked the idea. That sort of thing might be all right in Harris, she'd said, but this was Achanult and folk would just laugh. Jean was always worried about what folk would think.

Well, it was all right for her. She didn't have to dig the garden when the soil was wet, which it invariably was, no matter how late you put off working it. Of course, if Jean had her way, she probably wouldn't grow vegetables at all, Peter suspected. Most other folk didn't. Just flowers and silly wee shrubs. Except for the incomers. A lot of them grew vegetables, he'd noticed. Some queer looking vegetables as well, with glass frames and the like over them and things growing up poles. Peter didn't bother with any of that. Not because he didn't like the taste of them—though he knew he wouldn't— but because the soil and the climate weren't really suitable, which just showed you how daft a lot of these incomers were. Their names were in the paper every year at the time of the flower and vegetable show. Jean usually went to have a look.

Donald had just come into his garden as well, Peter noticed. He'd be wanting a chat about something. Peter hadn't had a chance to speak to him since he'd had the flu. He was all right now though, by the look of him.

"So what was Donald saying then?" asked Jean as Peter came into the kitchen.through the back door.

"He says he's thinking about getting a caravan."

Jean, who'd assumed that Donald wouldn't have said anything much, was surprised.

"What for?"

"For folk to stay in," explained Peter. What else did you get caravans for?

"Where?"

"Here—I mean in his garden."

"Eh? Who's going to stay in it?"

"Anybody who wants. He said he's heard it's going to be a good summer, so he was thinking of getting a caravan and tourists would pay to stay in it a week at a time. He seems to think there's a lot of money in it."

"I suppose he's maybe a bit short of money. But why doesn't he just put them up in the house? That would save him having to buy a caravan."

"Och he'd never do that. He'll hardly let *us* through the door. Mind you, we're not paying him. I don't suppose he's thought it out properly yet. It's just an idea he has. He gets these daft ideas from time to time. Mind when he tried to sell dried seaweed to the tourists?"

The whole village remembered that. Donald had discovered that you could get dried seaweed from that gardening shop in Oban, but it was a terrible price. So he'd got some from the beach and waited till it dried off a bit. He'd put quite a lot of work into it but he'd never sold any. It seemed that the tourists passing through didn't want to be bothered with bags of seaweed. Of course the smell wouldn't have helped.

"We could take in tourists, you know," said Jean when they'd finished laughing at Donald and his dried seaweed.

"Don't be daft. We're fine the way we are. What would we want with tourists in here?"

"It might be all right. A lot of folk do it, you know."

"You might get all sorts of funny folk. Foreigners and the like."

"Most of them would be English, from what I hear."

"Aye, them as well. Och no, I couldn't be bothered with any of that," declared Peter.

"They say you can make a lot of money from it."

"Oh, I dare say. Eh . . . how much would . . . ?"

"Och, I've no idea. You could ask Donald though."

Peter didn't think that would be a good idea. He didn't want Donald to think that Jean might be keen on the notion. He'd maybe just wait and see how Donald got on. If it was like most of Donald's other daft ideas, nothing would come of it.

53 Planning ahead

THE Gaelic class had only two more meetings before the term ended. Mrs Nicholson thought she'd better see them this week about what they wanted to do. Then they would have a week to think about it if necessary. It was a bit hard to tell what they would decide. They never seemed too keen, yet most of them turned up faithfully week after week.

Waiting as the group slowly assembled Mrs Nicholson knew from experience that she'd better get the essential matters out of the way first.

"Well, we seem to be all—oh no, someone still to come, I think."

"Yes, it's Mrs Stewart," volunteered Mrs McKenzie.

"Oh yes. Maybe she'll be in later. I know she's very busy."

There was a snort from Miss Shuttleworth that Mrs Nicholson pretended not to hear.

"So, first of all, I wonder, since we have only one meeting left after today, whether you want to continue or not?"

In the silence Mrs Nicholson looked round. She wouldn't really mind, to be honest, if they'd all had enough. Sometimes she felt that it was all a bit pointless.

"I'm certainly finding it very interesting," enthused Miss Shuttleworth. "I'd like to go on a bit further."

There were one or two nods of agreement.

"Of course it wouldn't be till the autumn," explained Mrs Nicholson.

There were a couple more nods.

"Well, most of you seem to want to continue. That's fine. I'm really only asking now because the education authority will probably be asking me at some stage in the summer. So I'll . . . "

She broke off as Maggie Stewart entered with her usual fulsome apology.

"Ah, we were just discussing next term. There seems to be a general agreement that we should carry on."

"Of course we should," insisted Maggie. "This sort of thing is very important to our culture and our . . . umm . . . "

"Yes. There's the question of numbers of course. We could really do with one or two more."

"Oh, don't worry about that," said Maggie airily. "I'll easily get one or two others for you, no bother."

This was a surprise to Mrs Nicholson. Several times over

the past months it had been hinted to her that there were a few other people who were quite interested in the class but who refused to come as long as Maggie was there. You could well understand. She wasn't at all popular in the village and the class would probably be a lot happier without her. But there wasn't a lot Mrs Nicholson could do about it. Well, she hadn't thought of anything so far. Maybe David would have some suggestion.

"Well, we'll just have to wait and see. Now the other thing I wanted to mention concerns this stuff I've been sent. I don't know if anybody will be interested. It's a two-week course in Stornoway . . . "

"Lewis," interrupted Maggie.

"That's right. Do you know it?"

"Well, sort of. I used to know somebody who came from there."

"Fascinating," drawled Miss Shuttleworth.

"Who was that?" asked Mrs McKenzie.

"Oh, nobody you would know," replied Maggie evasively. "It was a long time ago," she added, aware that Mrs McKenzie prided herself on knowing just about everybody in the highlands and islands. Mrs McKenzie looked a bit doubtful, clearly disappointed at being deprived of the chance to display her genealogical expertise.

"So anyway," continued Mrs Nicholson, "It's two weeks intensive language study—no English at all—and you can be boarded with Gaelic speaking families."

"That sounds quite interesting," said Miss Shuttleworth. "I suppose it's the best way."

"I'd certainly recommend it. So if anyone's interested . . . I'll just pass the leaflet round." She handed it to a surprised Mrs Abbott who looked at it for a few seconds.

"Very nice," said Mrs Abbott eventually, handing it to her friend Mrs Grey.

"What's this?"

"It's what Mrs Nicholson was talking about, Aggie. It's a Gaelic course."

"Oh. Where?"

As Mrs Abbott had another look at the leaflet, Mrs Nicholson explained.

"Oh Stornoway!" exclaimed Mrs Abbott. "I've been there. I had an uncle who lived there. Well, he was my father's uncle really. You'll not remember that, Aggie. Just before the war. Or maybe the war had started . . . that's right, I think it was 1940. I remember it fine. Everybody spoke Gaelic. I couldn't understand a word."

"Well, maybe you'd be interested in the course. It sounds just like what you experienced before," suggested Mrs Nicholson.

"Oh, I don't think so. I'm much too old to be learning Gaelic."

When the discussion of Stornoway had ended, Mrs Nicholson suggested that they might like to go over some of the vocabulary in the next lesson. This she'd noticed, was quite a popular exercise and it was surprising how many words they knew, or half knew. Much of this was due to placenames and indeed, house names in the locality, the majority of which were Gaelic or a mangled form of it. As a result, the class didn't find it too difficult to acquire a basic vocabulary but they found it hard to put the words into any coherent order.

None of this would have concerned Mrs Nicholson unduly, since she'd grown resigned to their ways and felt she had done her best, were it not for the fact that she'd been told that the education authority might send someone round to check the class progress. She hadn't mentioned this to them yet but she'd discussed it with her husband.

"I'm a bit concerned about it, David. They haven't really advanced very much, you know. It doesn't seem to bother them . . . "

"Oh, I wouldn't worry about that. Look on it as a sort of recreation class."

"That's all very well but the authority subsidises these classes. They'll expect to see some evidence of progress."

"The authority subsidises all sorts of things, Anna, and most of them are just a waste of time and money. Yours is no different!"

"Well, I had hoped they might have gained something. What am I to do if someone turns up to inspect things? I mean, there's Mrs Grey with her dog, Miss Shuttleworth and Mrs Stewart at each other's throats all the time, and then the two men who never say anything unless you don't want them to, in which case they'll go on for half an hour."

"Sounds fascinating. I'm sure he'll be impressed. Or she."

"But they haven't learnt any Gaelic to speak of."

"Oh, never mind that. Will the person who comes know any Gaelic?"

"I've no idea."

"Probably not. It'll just be some bureaucrat from Glasgow. In which case any Gaelic the class comes up with will do fine, if you give it your imprimatur."

"Really, David. I couldn't do anything like that."

"Oh well, you could always ask him if he'd like to take the class for a bit. That usually gets rid of them quickly—the inspectors, I mean."

"You're not being very helpful. I really am quite worried."

"Ye-es, of course. I can see your point," soothed Mr Nicholson, wishing again that his wife wouldn't worry about things that were of no importance. "Umm . . . when will all this take place?"

"I was told it would be towards the end of the course. We only have another two meetings left. I was wondering whether to mention it to the class. What do you think?"

The Rev Nicholson thought that on balance, it might be better not to. You could never tell what they might get up to.

As Mrs Nicholson slowly began reading out the vocabulary for the next lesson, Maggie Stewart interrupted.

"I was wondering if you'd mind if I taped this?"

"Taped what?"

"The vocabulary. Sometimes at home—of course I know how all the words are pronounced—but if I wanted to check, it would be nice to play back you reading them."

"Oh, I see. Well, if you want . . . "

"I haven't got my machine with me at the moment—I had to rush here straight from the library. But I'll bring it next week. It might even be helpful to record the whole two hours."

Mrs Nicholson's heart sank. The class was enough of a shambles without having it recorded for posterity. And it would only encourage Alec Cameron to waffle on at even greater length. Since he'd been on the radio that time, the sight of a tape recorder was all he needed.

"I'll probably be bringing it next week anyway—that's if we're going to have a ceilidh, like we did at the end of last term," added Maggie.

Mrs Nicholson had forgotten about that. Well, that settled the problem of whether to tell the class about next week's possible visitor. Things were bad enough without the inspector having to endure Maggie's musical selections and goodness knows what else.

"There's some quite interesting stuff at the library," persisted Maggie. "I'll be able to bring it along just for the afternoon."

Mrs Nicholson decided to nip this in the bud. To her surprise, most of the class were quite excited at the possibility of having a visitor. Maggie though, was unimpressed.

"Now that I think of it, I might not manage next week," she said huffily. "I'm taking the week off, with Heather being here, and we might be away somewhere for the day."

Mrs Nicholson nodded. The others, who knew that Maggie and her daughter weren't speaking, maintained a sceptical silence.

So the last half hour of the afternoon was unusually productive as Mrs Nicholson rehearsed with the group what they would do the following week. They all agreed to do a bit of revision at home.

"You know, fresh bread is the thing I think I miss most living in Achanult," said Mr Nicholson as he chewed a mouthful of the sliced white cotton wool sold as bread from Willie McLeod's shop. "Has there ever been a baker here?"

"I don't know. I doubt it. Even if there was, I suspect that most people would have bought this stuff."

"I can't imagine why."

"Well, it keeps longer, for one thing."

"Just as well. I don't suppose this was baked today, or yesterday."

"And it's probably cheaper."

"Yes, I imagine that settles it."

"Anyway, I'll do some baking tomorrow. I don't have so much time on a Tuesday."

"No no, of course not. Oh that reminds me. I was thinking about your class this afternoon. Wouldn't it be a lot easier if you changed it slightly?"

"In what way?"

"Instead of calling it a language class, or whatever it is, why don't you change it to a local history class, or highland culture—something like that? Then the inspector needn't be concerned with the fact that they've learned next to nothing of the language."

"It's a bit late in the day for that."

"Yes, but I was thinking of next term."

Mrs Nicholson looked doubtful. She wasn't sure whether there would even be a next term.

"I don't suppose it would matter what the class was called. I'd probably still get the same people and they'd probably still want to do things in their own way. But it's worth thinking about. It would be more honest, at least."

54 New beginnings

"YOU know, I'm beginning to recognise places," enthused Miss McLachlan. "That big stone's just round the next bend, isn't it? And the sheep are always here of course. Why are they never in the field?"

Miss Shuttleworth sounded the car's horn as a ewe meandered across the road. Sheep, she'd already decided, were deaf but one had to make some sort of gesture. Jennifer might regard them as picturesque but they did cause accidents.

"I suppose it's because there are gaps in the dykes. And

there's some fence posts down as well."

"Was it the wind that did that?" asked Miss McLachlan

"I doubt it. Probably rotted away or an animal could have leant on it."

"The wind is very strong up here though, isn't it?"

"Occasionally. You get used to it."

Miss McLachlan looked doubtful.

"I only ask because, knowing I was coming to stay here for a while, I've been listening to the weather forecasts for your area. It always seems to be raining and windy."

"Well it's neither today, is it?" asked Miss Shuttleworth pointedly.

"That's right. Still, I suppose it'll be back to normal tomorrow. The shipping forecast always has gales round here too. D'you know they're thinking of making electricity with it?"

"So I hear."

"Apparently there's somewhere here—I think it's the Outer Hebrides—or is it Shetland?—where there's a gale almost every day of the year."

"Well, it's not here," retorted Miss Shuttleworth stiffly.

Miss McLachlan fell silent. After about a mile and a half of peace Miss Shuttleworth wondered if she'd sounded rather harsh with her friend. She herself wasn't in the best of moods after her mishap that morning—although she hadn't mentioned it to Miss McLachlan. Knowing that her friend was coming, she'd decided to vacuum clean the car floor and seats. She'd have done it yesterday but that heavy rain had kept her indoors.

Not possessing an extension lead, the only way she could do the job was by driving her car up the side of the house and passing the vacuum cleaner out through the gable window.

The drive was really too narrow there and she'd scraped

the rear wing on the side of the house. So once she'd finished cleaning the inside of the car she'd gone round to the local petrol station where she'd had a bit of difficulty persuading the attendant to take the scratch seriously. That was typical of these people of course. All they cared about were engines and brakes and things like that. In the end, just to get rid of her, he'd suggested that she just spray on a little paint from an aerosol can. Unfortunately Miss Shuttleworth didn't have such a can. The garage had a few but none of them were the right colour. One of the colours was fairly close and the man suggested that that would do the job, even if it was only for the time being. He could then order the proper colour for her.

Miss Shuttleworth knew that he was simply trying to sell her a can of paint that he'd probably had for the last twenty years or so and which very likely wouldn't work properly. But she was concerned about rust damage if something wasn't done immediately. Deciding to go to Oban a bit earlier to see if she could get the proper colour there, she drove with one eye on the sky, hoping that no rain would fall on the scratch.

Things weren't much better in Oban. There was a larger selection of colours certainly but still not the correct one. Growing increasingly frustrated, Miss Shuttleworth decided this time to buy the shade closest to that of her car. She would then see about getting the proper colour later. After persuading a youth to spray it on for her she then wished she hadn't since traces of it landed on the tyre. These people really were hopeless. And they called themselves mechanics! She'd try and get it off when she got home.

The only good thing about the whole business was that the scrape wasn't on the passenger side—or the other side as Miss Shuttleworth called it—of the car, so Miss McLachlan could get in and out without seeing the mess.

And Jennifer still hadn't remarked on how clean the inside of the car was. Too busy talking about sheep. And the wind!

"I think I must have missed that stone, Marjory."

"It's about another half mile on now."

"Oh. I thought . . . oh well. A lot of the landscape is very similar round here. Quite good views though. You can see a good distance today. I don't suppose it's always so clear."

"Oh, it comes and goes. That reminds me, Jennifer. It might be better if you didn't make too many unfriendly remarks about the weather—in public at least. Of course, I don't mind and you're quite right sometimes. But some people will take it as a personal insult."

"Really? My goodness. Mmm. I suppose they've got used to it. Oh well . . . ah, there it is. How old did you say it was?"

"About four thousand years, I think."

"Amazing!"

Miss McLachlan lapsed into silence again. She'd have to come and have a proper look at the stone one day. On the other hand, there appeared to be some sheep in the field for once, some of them quite close to the stone. Still, you could see it well enough from the road. Maybe the sheep went somewhere else in the summer.

"I quite take your point about not offending the locals, Marjory. I mean, I didn't think they'd be offended about the weather."

"Some of them would be offended by almost anything you or I might say about Achanult, Jennifer."

"Goodness! How strange. Actually, seeing that stone there reminds me that I know one way to get on the right side of the locals."

"Oh?"

"Learn their language."

"What do you mean?"

"Gaelic—the stuff you said you were doing."

Miss Shuttleworth laughed.

"It's not really their language, Jennifer. Nobody speaks it here any more."

"Oh. How disappointing. So . . . umm . . . why are you learning it?"

"It's interesting."

"Is it? Well, I thought I might come along to that class you go to—just to show willing."

Miss Shuttleworth said nothing.

As they slowed down for the bridge before coming into Achanult, Miss McLachlan noticed that word again. She'd forgotten about it but now her curiosity was even greater. The thought that it might mean something rude made her hesitate. Or—wait a minute—maybe it was a Gaelic word. But hadn't Marjory just said that no-one in Achanult spoke Gaelic? In which case it would be silly to write something that no-one would understand—even in a place so odd as Achanult.

"Well, notice any difference?" asked Miss Shuttleworth as they entered the main street. Miss McLachlan turned her thoughts from CEARTAS and looked quizzically around.

"I . . . umm . . . not immediately . . . "

"I'm only joking, Jennifer. Nothing ever changes here—except the weather, which changes from bad to worse."

Miss McLachlan laughed.

"That's a local joke, Jennifer," added Miss Shuttleworth, "and only the locals are allowed to make it."

As they drank their tea Miss Shuttleworth reflected that everyone in the village would know by now of her friend's arrival. When she herself had first come to live here several years ago, she was a little surprised that everyone in the village knew her name and where she was from, even what her occupation had been. She herself knew nobody and was quite happy to leave things like that for a while. Some of the neighbours had called on her but she hadn't let them in, explaining that the house was still in a bit of an upheaval. It remained in a state of upheaval until the neighbours stopped pestering her. With a bit of luck she shouldn't have the same problem over Jennifer. She'd need to warn her though, not to accept any invitations from the neighbours. Or if she really had to, she could go by herself. But you couldn't visit just one without offending the others.

"I must say the days are noticeably longer here," said Miss McLachlan as they sat in the living room. "Only to be expected of course. But it's quite nice. At home I'd have had the curtains drawn well before now."

"I do try to leave that till as late as possible, Jennifer. I prefer natural light."

"Quite right. Talking of curtains, I notice that a lot of the houses here have those white lace type curtains shut all day. Is that another local tradition?"

"I think it must be."

"What's the point of it, do you know?"

"It's so that you can't see in."

"Oh. But I don't want to see in."

"You'd never persuade them of that, Jennifer. I mean, they're all looking in here."

"What?" Miss McLachlan went cautiously over to the window. "I can't see them."

"Oh, you won't see them. But they're there. Not all the time, of course. Sometimes they have something else to do."

"I see. Well, perhaps we ought to close our curtains. Just to annoy them."

"Come come, Jennifer. That's not very neighbourly of you. In any case, we'll annoy them even more by leaving them open."

"Really?"

"Yes. They'll see it as an offence against the natural order of things."

Miss McLachlan laughed.

"I think I'm going to find it quite amusing living here."

THE END